I0575573

Mafia Redeemer

The Mancinelli Brotherhood

Sabine Barclay

OLIVERHEBERBOOKS

All rights reserved.

No part of this publication may be sold, copied, distributed, reproduced or transmitted in any form or by any means, mechanical or digital, including photocopying and recording or by any information storage and retrieval system without the prior written permission of both the publisher, Oliver Heber Books and the author, Sabine Barclay, except in the case of brief quotations embodied in critical articles and reviews.

PUBLISHER'S NOTE: This is a work of fiction. Names, characters, places, and incidents either are the product of the author's imagination or are used fictitiously. Any resemblance to actual persons, living or dead, business establishments, events, or locales is entirely coincidental.

Copyright © 2023 by Sabine Barclay.

0 9 8 7 6 5 4 3 2 1

Published by Oliver Heber Books

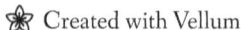 Created with Vellum

Those who least deserve love need it the most.

Find me writing Historical Romance as Celeste Barclay.

Happy reading,
Sabine

Subscribe to Sabine's Newsletter

Subscribe to Sabine's bimonthly newsletter to receive exclusive insider perks.

Have you read *The Syndicate Wars*? This FREE origin story novella is available to all new subscribers to Sabine's monthly newsletter. Subscribe on her website.
www.sabinebarclay.com

The Mancinelli Brotherhood

Mafia Heir

Mafia Sinner

Mafia Beauty

Mafia Angel

Mafia Redeemer

Mafia Star

Do you also enjoy steamy Historical Romance? Discover Sabine's books written as Celeste Barclay.

Chapter One

Lorenzo

"Maria, turn around. No, the other way."

"Why?"

"Shh. Can you not use an inside voice to save your life? Laura's over there."

I watch my sister do the opposite — of course — of what I ask. She cranes her neck to see the head of the Russian bratva's wife. She's standing with a friend and — oh, fuck us — one of her sisters-in-law.

"Put your damn hand down, Maria."

"They've already seen us. It would be rude not to say hello."

I keep from rolling my eyes, instead turning to Maria's husband, my brother Marco's best friend.

"Can't you control her just once?"

He practically snorts.

"Hi, Maria. Matteo, Lorenzo."

1

Laura's voice couldn't hold more disdain for my name and Matteo's if she tried. But she's warm to Maria. Who wouldn't be? Despite being a Mafia daughter — we hate the term Mafia princess — Maria is the kindest and sweetest person you'll ever meet. Unless you're one of her brothers. Fuck my life.

Maria ignores Laura turning her nose up at Matteo and me, greeting her warmly.

"Hi, Laura. Hi, Christina. You're Michelle, right? I remember meeting you at Laura and Maks's wedding reception."

The woman with the dark honey-brown hair darts her gaze from me to Matteo to Laura before settling on Maria before she nods. She remains quiet when Christina greets us.

"Are you here seeing the new release, too?"

She sounds friendly, but I know she's trying to determine the threat we present. I've already spotted their bodyguards. None of their husbands or cousins-in-law are here, but these guards are the most trusted men the bratva's Elite Group has. It surprises me that none of their immediate family is guarding them. It raises my hackles and makes me wonder if the men are in the midst of some dastardly plot against us. I am not paranoid. I swear.

"Yeah. It looks so good, and I gotta admit that man is hawt."

Maria grins over her shoulder at Matteo, who pretends to scowl. She nudges him with her shoulder. She's the sweetest and kindest person you'll ever meet, at least to everyone but her brothers *and* husband.

Her comment gets a smile from Michelle, but it drops the moment she realizes I'm watching her. I need to stop staring because now Laura and Christina are glaring at me. But this woman is way hotter than I realized when I saw her at Laura and Maksim's wedding reception — a parade of New York's

wealthiest and most influential, which included all the syndicate families. She was pretty from a distance. Up close, she's
making me wish my jeans were looser.

In a normal world, we might suggest sitting together even
though we pre-purchased our tickets and already picked out
our seats. I've known Maksim and Christina's husband,
Bogdan, since they moved to America nearly twenty years ago.
I went to school with them. I'm the same age as one of their
brothers, Nikolai, and one of their cousins, Pasha.

But we don't live in a normal world. We live in one where
kids who used to play on the same soccer team then took
physics together now carry guns to shoot each other if
provoked. Laura says something else, but I miss it. I'm too lost
in thought about how much I wish I were anyone else, so I
could talk to Michelle. They walk away, and Maria nudges me.

"We're getting popcorn."

There's no offer to see if I want any. I know my sister. She
doesn't share movie theater popcorn. You could lose a finger.

"You mean Matteo is getting you popcorn and sticking to
his Thin Mints. I'll get my own popcorn, thank you very much.
Yours has so much butter it's soggy in five minutes."

"I know."

She grins the same way she has since she was a toddler. You
can't not smile along with her. Even Mafiosos like Matteo and
me still find it infectious.

"Bambi, be nice to your brother, and maybe he'll let you
have a sip of his Icee."

Maria rolls her eyes and looks down her nose at me.

"Blue is gross. I only like cherry."

Bambi. Matteo used to call her that when we were all kids.
It's short for bambina. He stopped calling her that when she
beat him at the fifty-yard dash, and all the guys laughed at him.

3

Now that they're together, he calls her that all the time. It's sweet. As I watch Michelle glance back at us, I can't help but wonder what I would call her if I had the chance.

We follow the women and their guards into the theater. Of course, we all wind up sitting in the top row. That way we have a wall at our backs. But we're at opposite sides. None of us knew the other would be here. We naturally put space between us and anyone else. Now I understand why I couldn't buy out the row. Gauging from Christina's expression, she's thinking the same thing. We must have bought our tickets at the same time.

The previews are running, and I notice Michelle get up. She tries to signal a guard to stay, but the man just follows her. Maks would kill the man — literally — if he didn't stay with the woman. But it doesn't stop me.

"I'm going to run to the restroom really fast."

I lean over and whisper to Maria. It's no accident that she sits between Matteo and me. I close my recliner and hurry down the steps. I leave the theater on the opposite side from Michelle. She doesn't notice me as she heads to the restroom. I figure we still have about ten minutes before the movie starts. I nod to her guard, Mikhail. He narrows his eyes at me. Whatever. I beat the shit out of him a month ago when he tried to lift some product at a drop off that didn't involve the Russians. He wasn't as smooth as he thought, slipping in among some Canadians.

I duck into the restroom, and time it so I come out just as Michelle does. The way the restroom entrances face each, she can't help but see me. I smile at her, and she blinks one too many times before she returns the smile.

"Hi."

I keep the greeting soft, knowing Mikhail is trying to inch closer.

4

"Hi. You're Lorenzo, right?"

"Yeah."

She remembers me. Why does that please me so damn much?

"You're Carmine's cousin."

Fuck me.

"Yeah."

She just nods. Carmine was the black sheep of our family for years. I couldn't stand him. It never came to blows because our parents would have killed us, but I loathed him. Secrets I never imagined came out when he started dating his wife. Shit I didn't know about our shared grandfather and his paternal grandfather. It explained so, so much about why he acted the way he did. But before that, he did some fucked-up shit. He always put our family first, but it often made things way worse. And way worse included Laura and Christina's other sister-in-law, Anastasia.

"He helped Katerina's sister."

"He did."

Maybe she doesn't think Carmine is the devil, and I'm not entirely guilty by association. Maksim and Bogdan have another cousin, Misha, who married a Russian woman. When some men with a death wish kidnapped Maria, they took the sister of Misha's girlfriend as well. Carmine saw her when we freed Maria, and was relentless in helping Katerina's sister even after Maria was safe. It was the first time we realized his heart wasn't pitch black. It was just seriously bruised.

That family has as many tentacles as an octopus. Maksim, Aleksei, Nikolai, and Bogdan Kutsenko are all brothers. They have two cousins, Anton and Pasha Kutsenko, from one side of the family and Sergei and Misha Andreyev from the other side. I remember Anton danced with Michelle twice at the wedding. I remember thinking he was a lucky man. I remember wondering if they were going home together that night. But she left with Laura's sister.

I'm trying to come up with something to say since I approached her. I'm usually not at a loss for words. But I'm like a teenager who can't string a sentence together because he's too busy drooling over the hot girl in class.

"I know Gabriele's wife, Sinead, went to law school with Laura. Were you in the same class?"

I don't know why that came to mind. But I guess it's better than standing here with a blank expression.

"Yes. Sinead and I both pursued criminal law while Laura chose corporate law. But I had an opportunity to shift, so I took it."

"Shift?"

"Yes. I spent a year as an ADA. I hated it. Maybe if I lived somewhere other than New York, it would have been fine. I spent another year as a criminal defense attorney and didn't like it any more than that. I got a lot of guilty people off. My conscience couldn't take it."

Her eyes widen as she realizes what she said. She knows who I am just like she must know who Maks is. She's come to terms with her best friend being married to the head of one of the most powerful syndicates in the world. I don't know who she represented, but Maks's family and mine are exactly the type of people who are guilty as sin, but nothing sticks to us. Go figure.

"So you chose to go the corporate route?"

"Sort of. Philanthropic. I represent non-profits. Mostly charities."

"Charities get sued?"

She smiles, and it makes my dick twitch. It's like she's trying to hide it, not laugh at what I said. It makes a dimple appear in her left cheek. I have the strongest urge to kiss it and flick my tongue against it.

"Sometimes. I negotiate contracts, handle charitable solicitation regulation, and even employment disputes. I steer clear of tax law. I don't know enough, and I'm fine with that."

"Boring?"

"Complicated."

I grin.

"I'm an accountant. I know."

She blinks a few times just like she did earlier. Her gaze runs from the top of my hair, down my chest and over my muscular arms, to my crotch — which makes me wish yet again that my jeans weren't so fucking tight — down to my shoes. Then it comes back up again, pausing on my abs and pecs. My shirt is snug, but not so snug that you can see my six-pack. It makes me wonder if she's imagining it just the way I'm imagining her tits.

"Ms. Russo, the movie is starting. We should go back in."

Michelle twists, almost surprised to see Mikhail. Could she have actually forgotten he was there? She shoots me a sheepish smile.

"It was nice talking to you, Lorenzo."

"Enzo. And same."

"Chelle."

I watch her lead Mikhail back to their side of the theater before I hurry back to my seat. Maria leans away from Matteo and whispers to me.

"What took so long? I thought you fell in. Then I see Laura's friend coming in the same time as you. What did you do?"

"I talked to her."

"Talked?"

"Yes, talked."

"Mmm."

I glance down at my sister, and her expressions tempts me to pinch her just like I did when we were kids. I'm closest in age to her, and she was the bane of my existence for years. My next older brother, Marco, is best friends with Matteo. My oldest brother, Luca, was best friends with Matteo's brother, Emilio, but there's gnarly history there. If Carmine was the black sheep of the family, Emilio was the wolf that got exiled.

I never liked him, and after giving Luca the scar that runs from his cheek to below his collar, I don't care if I never see him again. But since Luca and Marco both had best friends, I often played with Maria and Carmine, who are the same age. I wanted to play with older kids not the babies of the family. But Maria was persistent, and Carmine egged her on.

My brow furrows as I scowl at my sister.

"What's that supposed to mean?"

"Shh. The movie's starting."

I sit back and try to pay attention, but my gaze keeps darting to Michelle, and I'm certain I see her looking at me a few times. But in the dark, it's likely entirely my imagination. Wishful thinking is more like it. I end up enjoying the movie, and I'm glad I came with Matteo and Maria, even if I was technically my sister's bodyguard. When we step out of the theater, I notice Michelle and the others coming out of the other door. Michelle's walking a step behind Laura and Christina, shoving a pen into her purse. She maneuvers to let a man pass her, and it puts her next to me as I walk past. I glance down as I feel something shoved into my hand.

I wrap my fingers around a napkin and glance down at her. She doesn't look up, instead laughing at Christina's joke that I didn't hear. I shove the napkin in my pocket until I get outside. I'm walking behind Maria with Matteo to her right. He has his arm around her shoulders, and she's whispering to him. I pull it out and glance down.

Michelle 212-555-6969

Dear God, the things her phone number makes me think.

Wish we'd had more time to talk about taxes. If you feel like crunching numbers some time, call me.

What the fuck am I supposed to make of that? Is she seriously suggesting we fuck? Does she get how that comes across? When I look up, I see her standing beside the driver's side of a car. The look on her face tells me she knows exactly how I interpreted her note.

I stop beside Matteo as Maria gets into his car.

"Are you good?"

My sister's brow furrows since they picked me up and they were going to give me a ride home. Matteo sounds just as confused as she looks.

"Aren't we taking you home?"

"No. I think I'll stop at Spotlight on the way home. I want to see if the new security cameras are capturing more of the front line."

That's not a lie. I just hadn't planned to do that tonight. I force myself not to look in Michelle's direction. Even if she isn't waiting by her car, I want to call her. She said call, not text. I'm down with that. I want to hear her voice, and I want to see if I can make her laugh. I don't know why that's so important to me since I can't see that little dimple, but I want to know I can make it appear.

Matteo nods as he closes Maria's door.

"All right. Are we set to go over the new build tomorrow? Carmine said he can meet at ten after he drops Serafina off in Harlem."

I'm an accountant, and Matteo is an architect. Carmine is our construction project manager because he's a structural engineer.

"Yeah. Tell him to bring the cookies and to not eat all of them this time. I know his wife's the baker, but he could fucking share."

Matteo grins as he suggests an alternative.

"I could have my mom bake a batch. They're just as good."

"They are. But I want Carmine to have to share. Little fucker."

Matteo laughs. His mom, Auntie Carlotta, was the best baker in the family before Carmine married Serafina, who owns two bakeries. Carmine brags and rightfully so, but it's annoying when he eats everything she sends before any of us can get so much as a bite.

"Good night, Enzo."

"Night."

I wait until Matteo's in the car, and the engine is on. I know I hold my breath, but that's my little sister along with my friend. There's always the risk. I breathe easier as they pull away. I turn around and notice Michelle's car is still in the same spot, but she's not standing next to it. I look around before I approach. She's sitting in it, but she gets out when I'm almost to the hood. She didn't want people to see her waiting. When she looks at me, her face flushes dark pink.

"I have never written a note like that in my life."

I cock an eyebrow and smile.

"You don't enjoy crunching numbers?"

Her face is scarlet now. It's adorable. That's not a word I use often. My niece is adorable, but she's six months old.

"Taxes are complicated."

"Only if you don't have a good teacher."

She notches up her chin, some bravery coming back to her.

"And are you teacher of the year?"

"Only if you're my star student."

We stare at each other. Where is this going? This isn't the type of flirting that usually happens outside a movie theater. As least, I didn't think it was. This usually happens over cocktails at a nightclub like the one I own. That makes me think about having her come to Spotlight and slipping onto the dance floor with her. Her body pressed against mine. Her pussy rubbing my thigh. My hand on her ass. My tongue in her mouth.

Holy fuck. Slow the fuck down.

But I can't. No one has had such an impact on me since — well, forever. I'm no monk, and I haven't been a virgin in more than a decade. But I can't remember ever wanting a woman so much. And yes, I absolutely want to fuck her, but I also want to talk to her. I want to make her laugh again. I want to see what she'll say next. But reality hits me when I look around.

First, I've been standing with my back to way too many people. Second, she's standing with me, and I can't see who's around us. I can't protect her. Third — wait. Protect her. The need to keep her safe — from me and the rest of the world — presses down on me. If I were a good man, I would walk away. I would have nothing to do with her. If she wants to be around New York's underworld, she can do it through Laura. I should back off. But I can't.

I seem to think that a lot.

"Are you usually such a flirt, Enzo?"

"No. Are you?"

"Definitely not. But somehow I'm not so sure about you."

"Why's that? *You* gave *me* the note."

11

"I have no idea what possessed me. You must be a bad influence."

I angle myself closer without taking a step in her direction.

"I think I could be a very good influence."

Her gaze sweeps over me again, but not as slowly as inside. Her eyes lock with mine, but I can't tell what she's thinking. She must have been a damn good trial attorney, even if she hated it.

"I know you're going to hate this question, but bear with me."

I nod. Should I dread this as much as she makes it sound like I should?

"I know this isn't a good comparison, but it's the only one I have. Are you like Maks and his family? I mean, like the not dating because of who you are? Or would I just be—"

"Chelle, you would not *just* be anything. I don't know what you know about Maks and his family, but we are a lot alike. That's all I will say about that. But I do not make a habit of flirting with women."

"You don't need to."

She blurts it out, then realizes what she said.

"I think the same about you."

She scoffs.

"Hardly. Somehow, I don't think our situations are at all the same."

"I think men find you very attractive and want more than just flirting."

There's that shade of scarlet again. This time I inch closer.

"I don't know about that, but I'm certain that's exactly how women and probably half the men you know think."

If half the men I know think that, it's a secret they'll take to the grave. Unfortunately, while my immediate family is forward thinking, not all the Mafia is.

"You flatter me, *piccolina*."

"What does that mean?"

Shit. Did I really just say it?

"It's a term of endearment."

"Oh."

She sounds disappointed.

"That I've never used before."

It's my turn to blurt my thought. I watch her pull out her phone and tap on the screen. Her eyebrows shoot up.

"Little girl. It means little girl."

"You don't waste time."

I didn't think she was translating it. I don't know what I thought she was doing. She looks speculatively at me before our gazes meet again.

"Is that the same as *malyshka*? I hear the Kutsenkos call their wives that. It means baby girl."

Now there's an insight I didn't have before. But it doesn't shock me in the least to think the Kutsenkos likely have the same proclivities as the men in my family. We like to be in control. We're bigger than the women in our lives. And I know I have the strongest urge to protect Michelle that I can't explain. It should be to protect her from me, but it's not. I can be honest about that. I want to protect her from the rest of the world, which will get fucking ugly if she's with me.

"Yes, *piccolina*. It is."

"Maks called Laura that the first night — the night your family attacked the Kutsenkos' nightclub."

Fucking Carmine. He organized that shit.

"Were you hurt that night?"

"No. Niko took Lanie and me to the office where Maks had already taken Laura."

"That's a relief."

It is.

"Enzo?"

"Yeah?"

"I haven't given a guy my number since college. That was a long time ago. I don't know what came over me, and I don't know what the hell I'm doing, all things considered, but I'd like to go out with you."

She looks terrified. Not when she was talking, but now that she's done. I take another step closer until I'm standing near enough for our shoes to touch.

"I haven't been on a date in ages. I don't remember the last one I went on that meant anything more than a way to kill an evening. I'd like to see you and not just to waste a night doing something other than work."

She flinches.

"Chelle, I own Spotlight and Constantine's. I'm an accountant, but I also own several businesses. I meant the nightclub and the restaurant."

"I'm sorry."

"Don't be. I don't know what you know, but it's enough to make your wary. Are you scared of me?"

"No."

Her answer is immediate. She elaborates, and it neither reassures me nor alarms me.

"I don't know what Maks's family is into. But I can guess. I keep those guesses to myself. I'm certain your families are more alike than terms of endearment. I'm not scared of you, but what your family does scares me. I've seen all the Kutsenkos with their wives. Those women figured out how to reconcile themselves to their husbands' — jobs — and none of them fear their husbands. If you're that much alike, which I think you are, then I know I have no reason to fear you. I hope I'm not wrong."

"One thing I can promise you is that I will protect you no

matter what, Chelle. But the one person you don't need protection from is me."

God, I hope that is true.

Chapter Two

Chellie

Body snatchers. That's the only way to explain what I just did. Body snatchers came and took control of me. But that can't fully explain what just happened. My brain was involved in writing that damn note. It was my brain that made me flirt with him. Zombies. That's it. Zombies ate my brain and left me with nothing.

Nothing but an aching pussy that would love nothing more than to find out if Enzo is as good at sex as he looks. I'm certain he's better. How could he not be? The man exudes sex appeal with every breath. It wouldn't surprise me if the labor and delivery nurses weren't slipping him their number the day he was born. I noticed him at Laura's wedding and thought he was the hottest man there. That's saying something considering Laura's in-laws could all be Armani models. There's not a dud in the bunch. I even thought about flirting with Anton, but — I don't know for sure — I think his interest lay in a completely different direction than me or any other woman. I would never, ever say that out loud since he's Russian. He's been nothing but kind to me, so I wouldn't endanger him.

But Lorenzo Mancinelli is another case entirely. I've never spoken to him before, and I've never been that close before. I just noticed him. I've seen him from a distance at a couple other events I've attended with Laura and Maks, but I told myself ogling him was pointless. Tonight, I'm pretty fucking sure he was ogling me first. If women had wet dreams, he'd be the reason for mine.

"Chelle?"

"I believe you. Enzo, I don't know why, but I know I'm safe from you."

"From me, not with me."

"I can't think of a more dangerous man than the ones in Maks's family or probably the ones in yours. But I don't fear you. What might happen if I'm within firing range is frightening, but I also know that if it's within your control — which I think you like to have a lot of — I'll be safe."

"I want to ask you out. Would you say yes?"

"I gave you my number and told you I'd like to do some number crunching. I'm pretty sure I was asking for something."

God. I have never blushed as much as I have tonight. Zombies. I'm blaming it on them.

"Do you regret saying that?"

I tilt my head as I study him. Is he trying to get out of this?

"Chelle, I don't regret coming over here. I don't regret flirting with you."

"Do you read everyone's mind, or am I just that obvious?"

"You're not obvious in the least. At least, not when you don't want to be. I think you're letting me know what you're thinking, even if you aren't saying it out loud. If you wanted to keep it to yourself, you would."

I watch him for a moment before I nod. The blushing I can't help. But I know I have the same inscrutable expression I used to wear in court and what I use now for contract negotiations. I may work for charities, but I give nothing away.

"I suspect you are just like that, too."

Now we stare at each other. Are we both trying to read each other's mind? Right now, I'm coming up blank. Can he tell what I'm thinking?

"I am. Would you like to get a cup of coffee?"

"At this hour?"

I laugh and shake my head before I answer my own question.

"I don't like coffee, but if I did, that much caffeine would keep me awake until tomorrow afternoon."

I see him retreat even if his expression doesn't change.

"But I would like a hot chai. Do you want an espresso?"

He grins, and it's like a choir of angels started singing.

"No. I don't like them. A spoon shouldn't be able to stand up in coffee. But a chai sounds nice. There's a place across the street."

He points to a little coffee shop I've driven past but never been inside. We're in Queens, near where Laura and Christina live with their husbands. I live in Manhattan. It's late, but not so late that driving thirty minutes home would be an inconvenience. I step away from the car, and he pushes the door shut. I lock it and drop my keys in my purse. I have the strongest urge to hold his hand. I don't. I slip them into my jacket pockets. I want — need — to know about him.

"How'd you get into accounting?"

He smiles again. He seems so easygoing. It's disconcerting to get to know these men. The ones in the mafia. You'd never guess one moment they're offing people, and the next, they're just regular guys who are dads and uncles and single, desirable men whose bones I want to jump.

"I studied Computer Science in undergrad. I like numbers and puzzles. Math always came easily to me, so accounting was in the stars since I was a kid. The computer science is just an interest of mine since I like video games. I don't play many anymore, but I did when I was younger."

I want to ask something, but I hold back. I'm worried I'd be prying.

"Chelle, what do you want to ask?"

"I'm not so sure I like how well you read me. It's disconcerting."

"Do you want me to stop?"

I look up at him, and after a moment, I shake my head.

"It's disconcerting, but it's — nice. You — understand me."

"I think so. I hope so. You want to know what I meant about accounting was in the stars. Something in your eyes changed when I said that. You want to know if my crime family ordered me to be an accountant."

I freeze. That's exactly what I wondered.

He slips his arm through mine and steers me toward the crosswalk. While we wait for the light to change, I turn to look at him.

"No one told me I had to become one. I like it. I know plenty of people think it must be boring, but I enjoy knowing that I help my family. Like I said, the numbers come easily to me. I can use my computer skills for forensic accounting when I'm valuating potential buyouts or mergers. I don't think tax law is all that fascinating, but I like the puzzle of figuring out how to maximize our earnings within the letter of the law."

I can only nod. It's out there that he belongs to a crime family. He said it, and he never tried to hide it. I've obviously known all along, and I'm standing next to him, so I must be okay with it. When Laura met Maks, his life scared the shit out of me for Laura's sake. I was terrified she'd get killed. She almost did. Until Maks, I'd never known a man could be so protective without being overbearing.

He never stops Laura from being Laura. Just the opposite. He encourages her and loves her just the way she is. But he's careful. He makes sure she and their twins are always guarded. He set what I think are reasonable limits, and Laura does too. I've watched them since they've been together over three years now. He's in the mafia, but he makes Laura happier than I've ever seen her. She's figured out how to live with what he does, so I don't judge.

We cross the street, and Lorenzo holds the door open for me. It's a cheery little place, and the guy behind the counter smiles at us. I smile back, but something passes between Lorenzo and this guy that I don't understand. Lorenzo rests his hand at my lower back, but he's not actually touching me. He's half standing behind me now, and it makes me feel — I don't know. He's gotta be almost a foot taller than me at five-feet-four. His shoulders are broad while his waist and hips are narrow. He's a perfect inverted triangle. With him standing behind me, I want to lean back. Let him wrap his arms around me and shield me from the entire world.

This makes no sense. If I did that, then it really would be body snatchers who possessed me. But it just feels so right. Intuition? Animal magnetism? Lust? All the above. I definitely feel lust. I'd like him to kiss me tonight, and I'd like to fuck before the week is out. But this is different. Which means I don't know how to explain it. Which means I'm not sure I like it. I like things that make sense. I enjoy having a reasonable and rational explanation for things. None of what I've done tonight is like the usual me. It's exciting but highly questionable.

"*Piccolina*, do you still want a chai?"

"Yes, please."

"What size would you like, miss?"

Zombies and body snatchers. I lean against Lorenzo and grin as I lock eyes with him.

"Large."

He knows I'm not just talking about a spicy tea. His arm wraps around my waist, and he leans down to whisper to me, ignoring the guy behind the counter.

"You might want a large, but I like things that come in small packages."

He straightens and orders a chai, too. He pays before I can even think to reach for my wallet. When I do, he shoots me a look that makes my toes curl. It's a warning, but it's so fucking hot. He doesn't let go of me when we walk to the back of the shop and find two armchairs. He pulls mine closer to his, so our legs are touching when we sit.

"What happened back there?"

"What do you mean?"

I know he knows what I mean. I wait. He watches me before he looks at the barista.

"It was very clear you are not my sister. He was checking you out right in front of me."

"We both have dark hair."

He leans forward, tucking hair behind my ear, before he whispers to me.

"There is no way he misunderstood your arm through mine as something brotherly. It's one thing to appreciate how beautiful you are. It's another to stare at your — figure — in front of someone who is clearly *with* you."

"He wasn't staring."

He shoots me a look that says don't be naïve. I mean, the guy looked at my chest for a moment longer than he probably should have. But I didn't think he meant any harm by it. He probably didn't, yet I can see Lorenzo's point. If a woman were behind the counter and stared at his dick for a moment too long, I'd be ready to claw her fucking eyes out. It's rude to check someone out who's clearly with a date or a partner. I get what he means.

"You think I'm beautiful?"

Why is that the question that comes out of my mouth? His eyes widen for a fraction of a second before he leans in again.

"*Piccolina*, you are the most beautiful woman I've ever seen."

Now there's an exaggeration if ever there's been one. His sister is gorgeous. Laura and Christina are beautiful, too.

"I dare you to disagree with me, Chelle."

Did his voice get huskier? More commanding? My toes curl all over again.

"Thank you."

We're staring at one another when the barista announces our drinks are ready. Lorenzo's out of his seat before I can uncross my legs. I watch him pick up the cups, but he puts them down. He gestures to the guy and says something I can't hear. The barista hands him a second cup, and I watch him slide one drink into it, making an extra layer. I wait for him to do the same for the other one, but he doesn't. He carries our chais over and offers me the one with the extra insulation.

"Isn't yours hot too?"

"It is."

I wait for him to elaborate, but I get nothing. I watch him take the lid off his after he puts it on the table in front of us. I can feel the heat coming through the two cups. When I put mine down, he reaches for it but catches himself. I reach forward, and he starts to pull back. I cover his hand with mine, and I guide them both back to my cup's lid. He pulls it off when I let go.

"Thank you for looking out for me."

My voice is hushed, and I feel — I don't even know. Tonight is intense.

"Always."

Just how long is always?

"I know Maria is your sister. Do you have any other siblings?"

I know there are as many Mancinellis as there are Kutsenkos, but I don't know how everyone is related. I haven't dared ask since they are not a welcome topic among Laura's family. She's going to kill me when she finds out that I had chai with a Mancinelli.

"Yes. Maria is younger than me. It's Luca, Marco, me, then Maria."

"And Carmine is your cousin. Who's the huge guy Maria danced with at Laura's wedding? He seemed like he's family, but he doesn't look like the rest of you."

"That's Gabriele. We're related like twenty generations ago. But his family has always been super close to mine. He's Carmine's best friend and has been since they were ten."

Sounds like trouble. And from what I've heard, it is.

"You and Maria's husband seem really close."

"We are. He's Marco's best friend. He's two hours younger than my brother. They've been inseparable since they were three. He may as well be Marco's fraternal twin and my third brother."

"So, there's you, Luca, Marco, Matteo, Carmine, Gabriele, and Maria? I feel for her."

"Don't."

He chuckles, so there's no harshness in his response.

"She gives better than she gets. Don't be fooled by how nice she is. She's ruthless."

I don't know how to take that. I don't know where to look. The women in Laura's family don't get involved in the men's business. Archaic, but they all appreciate it. For her sake, I do too.

"I don't mean she's like — she's competitive, Chelle. She's a tomboy through and through. Nothing about six men twice her weight impresses her. She's undefeated at playing chicken. She can take down Gabriele off Carmine's shoulders in the water. She has three pots of money when she plays Monopoly. The pile you see. The pile she hides but might draw from. And the pile she doesn't touch, and you didn't see her add to. She's so damn convincing that half the words she uses in Scrabble are probably made up, but none of us can prove it because she claims dictionaries are cheating. That's the ruthlessness I mean."

"She sounds perfect."

I grin and laugh. He narrows his eyes at me, but there's humor in his expression.

"Does she sound like you?"

"Maybe a little."

I put my index finger close to my thumb, and there's barely a hair's breadth between them.

"Are you competitive?"

"You should ask—"

Fuck. Well, he can't ask Laura.

"Laura? I got the impression she's the highly competitive one."

"We both are. Most people consider me the sweet one of the two of us. That's only because Laura makes it very clear where she stands along with everyone who comes near her. I'm more of a honey than vinegar. People assume I'm the sweet one,

25

so they underestimate me. It lowers people's guard and lets me learn about them before we face off, either in court or over a boardroom table."

He watches me as I speak, and I know my tone changed. It became the harder one I use as a lawyer. It doesn't seem to turn him off. Just the opposite. He picks up our drinks and takes a sip of his. Satisfied that it isn't still too hot, he hands me mine. I think some people might see this as — I don't know — babying me or something. Maybe controlling. I see it as him being considerate. I like that he cares enough to make sure I don't burn my mouth. I like that he's willing to risk burning his to protect me. That's not right. I don't want him to get hurt. I appreciate that he's willing to risk it to protect me. We sip our drinks in silence for a few moments. The companionable silence is nice while I savor the spicy taste. It's as close to coffee as I get.

"Did you grow up in the city or New Jersey like Laura?"

It shouldn't surprise me that he knows where Laura grew up, but it does. How much digging did they do when she entered Maks's life? I'm her best friend. Did I come up in their searches? Does he already know but is making small talk?

"Jersey. She and I met in elementary school and became inseparable. She went to Princeton for undergrad, and I went to Harvard. Like I said, we're both competitive. I might have been a bit smug when I got my Harvard acceptance, and she had to settle — I use air quotes — for Princeton. We went to law school together and were roommates for three years."

Does he already know that?

"*Piccolina*, I am not asking questions I already know the answer to. I know you're Laura's friend because I saw you at the wedding reception. I've seen you in passing at a few other events, but I genuinely want to get to know you. I'm not matching your answers against intelligence someone in my family gathered."

"Where'd you go to school?"

"Rutgers for computer science and MIT for accounting. I know most people think that's backwards."

"I think either way is impressive. My undergrad was in finance, so I have a little understanding of accounting. But computer science sounds way more challenging than understanding puts and options. Do you build your own computers?"

"I can."

He seems to hedge with that answer. I wait for more, but he's not forthcoming.

"Enzo, I won't take whatever you tell me and run straight to Laura and Maks."

"I know. And Maks has known me for years. Sergei and Anton love nothing more than to remind me that they both went to an Ivy League for computer science. I *only* went to Rutgers and MIT."

"There's nothing to sniff about either of them, and MIT speaks for itself."

"Yes, and when it does, it doesn't say, 'I'm an Ivy League.'"

I could see how rival families are intellectual snobs toward one another. Somehow, that makes complete sense. I know Maks and Aleks went into the — uh — family business straight out of high school and didn't get to go to college. But the others did, and they all went to Ivy or Top Tier schools. They all did it on their own merit, too. I get the feeling it's the same for Lorenzo's family.

"For what it's worth, I'm impressed."

"Thank you."

The moment lightens, and we move on to talk about other things from our childhood. I tell him about my older brothers. Sam, my oldest, died in combat six years ago. Right after I graduated from law school. Steven, the misunderstood middle child, is a stockbroker. He's what they made 1980s movies about. Young, hot, charismatic, and driven. My sister, Elizabeth, should have been the oldest for how organized and bossy she can be. She's an interior designer and loves everything just so. My parents are both practically corporate raiders. I could not do what they do. Look at stock prices and building prices all day. No, thank you. I learn Lorenzo's father is an attorney, and his mother works in finance and accounting too. I don't realize how late it is until the barista comes to stand next to me, ignoring Lorenzo, and says they're closing. He offers to take my empty cup and leans a little too close for even my comfort.

"Babe, hand me your cup. He can take yours, too."

I reach for Lorenzo's, and our fingers brush. I wink at him. I know I was rude by referring to the guy as "he" when he was standing right there, but now I get what Lorenzo meant earlier. I hand it over and barely mumble thanks. Lorenzo offers me his hand after he stands. He helps me up and pulls me against him. Fuck. He's hard — all over — and all I want to do is rub against him like a cat in heat. He can tell because his hand rests low on my waist.

"I could get used to hearing you call me that."

"I want to hear you call me *piccolina* again."

"So would I. Would you have dinner with me tomorrow?"

Would he have breakfast with me tomorrow?

"I'd like that. I have a late meeting at four-thirty, but I should be done by six."

"Where would you like to go?"

"Surprise me."

He grins and waggles his eyebrows.

"Anything you won't eat?"

"Why do I feel like you're going to find the spiciest food in the city?"

"I own Constantine's and Vita Bella. We can have the best table at either of them."

I press my chest against his as my hands rest on his waist.

"Somehow, I think you can always have the best table anywhere you go."

"True. But I rarely bother. For you, I'll make sure we do."

"Enzo, you don't have to impress me. I already want to see you again."

"Spoil not impress, *piccolina*."

That makes me shiver. We leave the coffee shop, neither looking at the barista as we walk past the counter. We head back to my car, and he still has his arm around my waist.

"Where'd you park?"

"I came with Maria and Matteo. I'll have a car pick me up from Donatelli's. It's just down the block and a family favorite. The owner is Uncle Salvatore's best friend."

"I can take you home."

Did I sound too eager?"

"I live in Manhattan."

"So do I. I have to head that way anyhow."

He hesitates, then nods. My brow furrows.

"If you drive me home, I don't think I can withstand the temptation to invite you up. When you say no — which you should — it might crush me."

"Why should I say no?"

"Because as much as I want you, I want you for more than a quick fuck, Chelle. I don't want you to wake up in the morning and regret anything."

"Why are you assuming I'd regret it?"

"Because your best friend is Laura Kutsenko. She will lose her ever-loving mind when she finds out you had chai with me. If you come home with me tonight, it'll put a rift between you which you'll regret."

He opens my door, but I turn toward him. I lean in and kiss him. Like really kiss. Like I want him to rip my clothes off in the parking lot and fuck me right now. Like I'd get down on my knees and deep throat him right now, and I don't even like giving blow jobs.

His hand goes to my throat and rests there for a moment, the pressure incredibly arousing. Then he slides it up my neck and fists my hair. He's in control now. I may have started the kiss, but he's taking the lead. He shifts me until I'm leaning against the rear passenger door. He inches his leg between my thighs and presses until my pussy rubs against him. Fucking hell. I want to come already.

"Little girl, I'm going to take you out to dinner tomorrow night. Then I'm going to take you out three more times. You decide where. Then, if after our fourth date, you still want this, I'm going to strip you bare in my bedroom. I'm going to lick every inch of you until you think you'll scream if you don't come. I'm going to suck your clit until I taste you coming. Only then will I fuck you until you're sore. Every step you take the next day will remind you that my cock was inside you, making you come all night. Every step you take will remind you how badly you need me to fuck you again. Every step you take will remind you that you're mine."

Oh, fuck. Oh, fuck. Oh, fuck. That is the hottest shit I've ever heard.

"I don't want to wait four dates."

"But we're going to. When we have sex, Michelle, it won't be some quickie. It won't be some casual fuck buddy arrangement. I'm serious. Once I'm inside you, I won't share."

"And if I already know I won't share, even though we haven't even fucked yet? And if I know a fuck buddy is not what I want from you? I may have started that kiss, but you definitely controlled it. I liked that. I didn't realize I would, but

I do. But you aren't deciding what we do and dictating to me, Lorenzo. I'm not a little girl. You are not the first man I've been with. I know what I want, and I don't need four dates to figure that out. I don't need four dates to be convinced I won't regret this. I sorta resent that you think I need that long to make up my mind. Don't you think I'm capable of making these types of decisions?"

"I didn't say that, and I'm sorry if that's how it came across. I want us to get to know each other for real. Once we have sex, there's no undoing that. I want whatever this is to be about more than just getting each other off. Once we have sex, I won't be the one to walk away."

"So, you assume I will be."

"I don't want either of us going anywhere. That's why I want it to be more than just physical."

I study him for a moment.

"When's the last time you had a serious relationship?"

"Senior year of college."

"That was — what — ten years ago?"

"Yes. I'm not a monk, Chelle. But I also don't do random hook ups or one-night stands. That has never been me. I've had fuck buddies and other arrangements, but I haven't had a girl-friend in a decade. You're the first woman in a decade that's made me want to open up. I don't want to fuck it up."

Arrangements? What the fuck does that — oh shit.

"By arrangements, do you mean subs?"

He freezes before he shakes his head.

"No. I am not a Dom, and I've never had a sub. But I go to BDSM clubs where I roleplay with certain partners more than once. Does that bother you?"

Does it?

I shake my head.

"No. I know nothing about that, but — the way you kissed

me. I've never been kissed like that before. I want more of that. I liked how it felt."

His hand had lowered to my waist, but it goes back to my hair and fists it.

"If there's something you want to try, tell me. I will do whatever I can to make it happen."

He kisses me again, and I sigh. I sag into him as he presses me against the car again. It feels beyond amazing to let him lead. It's not like I'm not participating. I am. I'm sucking his tongue as his cock thrusts against my pussy. His free hand grabs my ass and squeezes. It hurts, but I don't want him to stop. Other guys have gotten rougher than they realized and squeezed my ass or my tits too hard, and I didn't like it. With Lorenzo, I can't get enough.

"Tell me when to stop. If I hurt you, I'll be pissed, *piccolina*. I'm serious."

"It hurts, but you're not harming me. Don't stop. Harder."

And I mean it, and he obliges. It lifts me onto my toes, and I moan. But what he said a moment ago crashes over me, and I realize it does bother me. I pull back.

"You said you go and you roleplay as in the present tense. These arrangements — are you exclusive with these partners? Do they think you're only with them?"

"Chelle, there is nothing romantic about it. It's not a relationship. It's people who enjoy having sex in certain ways, and they've found partners who enjoy it too."

I nod.

"Chelle, I enjoy BDSM, but not enough to pick it or those women over you."

"But we barely know each other."

"And I haven't asked a woman on a date in ten years. It's not like I've lived in a monastery and haven't seen any women. I've chosen not to."

His hold on me has eased, and I nod. I don't know what just changed, but I suddenly feel sad. It's like the euphoria crashed and has left me on a low. He brushes back hair and pulls me against his chest, tucking my head against him. I wrap my arms around his waist and close my eyes.

"*Piccolina*, it can be as many or as few dates as you want. I just hope you'll want more than one."

Chapter Three

Lorenzo

I've done a lot of hard things in my life. I've killed. I've maimed. I've tortured. I've had to tell parents their child isn't coming home. I've told wives their husbands aren't coming home. I've been in an utter state of panic to rescue my sister from sex traffickers.

Only the last one was harder than saying goodnight to Michelle and closing her car door, then watching her drive out of the theater parking lot. I walked to Donatelli's, had two glasses of wine, then had Afonso drive me back to my place. I jerked off in the shower, picturing her sucking me off. I woke up in the middle of the night and jerked off, thinking about coming on her tits and belly. I woke up this morning so hard it hurt. I jerked off in the shower again, and this time I called out her name.

No woman has ever affected me this way. Not my first crush. Not my first girlfriend in high school. Not the last woman I dated in college who I really thought I might have a future with — until I realized she'd run straight to the feds if she found out who I really was. How did I know? We had the news on one night, and one of our guys was on trial for murder. She had very strong, very vocal opinions on syndicates and what should happen to people in the mob.

It took everything I had not to correct her. The mob are the fucking Irish. The Italians — the Sicilians — are the Mafia. Only we get a capital M. Anyone else being called mafia gets that name from fuckers who don't know. The Russians are the bratva, and the various Latin Americans are cartels. Since I couldn't explain that, I ended things the next week. I thought she'd get too suspicious if I dumped her and kicked her off my couch and out of my apartment when the news segment was over.

But I don't worry about that with Michelle. I don't think she's deceiving me to get something for Maks and his family. I approached her, not the other way around. And even if she thought about doing that while we watched the movie, she had to know Laura would never approve of her getting involved. So, she's come to some kind of resolution about having any kind of syndicate connection. More than that, she's willing to risk pissing off her best friend to be with me.

And knowing that is why I can't focus on my meeting with Carmine and Matteo. I'm looking at expense reports, and they may as well be in Greek. And not the Greek I know from statistics. I can't stop thinking about Michelle and how badly I want to see her. I texted this morning to see if she still wanted to have dinner with me. While Carmine and Matteo go back and forth about some type of plaster, I slip my phone out and look at my texts.

MICHELLE
You can pick me up at my office at 6:45.
Constantine's sounds nice. See you soon.

My *piccolina* knows what she wants, apparently. I like it. I've heard Luca, Carmine, and Gabriele call their wives that. It skeeves me out a bit to hear Matteo call my sister that. I think Maria and Matteo know we all feel a little uneasy hearing him since we all know what it means to the other married couples. None of us discuss it. That's why Matteo calls her Bambi when they're around other people. I don't think for a minute that any of the couples in my family are into Daddy Dom/Little Girl relationships. But I've heard Olivia, Luca's wife, and Serafina call their husbands Daddy when they thought no one could hear.

I didn't fully get it until now. I've called no other woman *piccolina*, and I can't imagine meeting anyone else I'd want to. The women calling their husbands Daddy has nothing to do with age play or incest. It's about knowing their husbands will take care of them now that they belong to a world that's frankly scary as fucking shit even to those of us born into it.

It's about them feeling safe and protected, knowing they can depend on their husbands. None of them need a father to tell them how to act or give them rules and time outs. That's not what the word means to them. Understanding this now makes me wonder if Michelle would ever call me that. Would she let me take care of her?

The real question is will she want to enter this world for real? If she does, then me protecting her and taking care of her is inevitable. There's danger associated with being with me. I don't underestimate that, and anything less would be negligent in a relationship.

"Are you going to keep staring at your phone? Or are you going to tell us how much fucking money we can spend?"

I shove my phone in my pocket as Matteo glares at me. I have no idea what he wants to spend money on. I glance at Carmine, and he looks just as annoyed. But I'm not sure if it's solely directed at me or if some of it is also for Matteo.

"Huh?"

Matteo snaps at me when he demands my attention.

"What the fuck is on your phone that's so damn interesting, Enzo? I have other shit to do today, and we're not making any progress. Can you pay attention, please?"

"Sorry. I have a few different projects on my mind right now."

Carmine snickers, and I stare at him.

"I talked to Maria this morning. Apparently, your newest project is Laura's friend. Maria says you couldn't stop staring at her. She said you looked at Michelle the way she looks at her popcorn. You wanted to gobble Michelle up."

Matteo glowers at me.

"That's why you can't concentrate? Did you actually go to your restaurants?"

"No. I wound up at Donatelli's, but I had tea with Michelle at the coffee shop across the street from the movies."

"What the fuck, Enzo? I'm surprised Maks isn't blowing shit up."

Matteo is being literal. Maks will lose his shit over this, and he's likely to take it out on some of our warehouses or cargo ships.

"Back off, Matteo."

My tone makes them both stare. I'm the easiest going in the family. I take after my mom. She laughs a lot and generally lets most things go without getting upset. But when she's pissed, you want to be as far away as you can get. Apparently, I'm the same. It takes a lot to get me riled, but when I am... My family says I leave a path of destruction worse than a typhoon. It's not like I throw shit or anything, but I make my point clear to any and everybody within earshot. According to my mom, I was such a mellow baby that I never learned how to self-soothe. That's why when I get worked up, it takes a while for me to calm down.

"You like her."

"Yes, Carmine. I do. What of it?"

"Relax. I'm not saying anything about it. I was just making sure I understand."

He puts his hands up before turning back to the expense report in front of him. He shoves it toward me.

"Can we get on with this? I told Fina I would go to a doctor's appointment with her. She burned her hand a week ago, and she's seeing a dermatologist today to make sure the skin's healing properly."

That makes me pull my head out of my ass.

"I saw the bandages at Sunday dinner. I didn't realize it was that serious. Is she okay?"

"Yeah. They just want to make sure the skin heals without reducing her range of motion for her fingers. It's been super painful for her, and I know this examination won't feel good. I want to get this over with, so I don't keep her waiting. I'll be royally pissed if I miss the appointment."

"You won't miss it. I'll focus."

I do as I say. We spend the next hour going over the expenses, real and projected, and Carmine leaves on time. Before I know it, it's already six. I shut down my computer and rub my eyes. After meeting with my cousin and friend, I ran payroll for our legit businesses that aren't individually owned. We have several casinos, trash collection companies, tow truck companies, and junkyards. Pretty much the stereotype of New

York Mafia. But they're useful, and the NYPD knows when to look away.

I slip my suit coat back on and head toward the door. We don't use the office suite in the Mancinelli Developers' building often. Matteo, Carmine, and I only came here because Carmine was meeting Serafina at her bakery that's close to Midtown. Matteo is picking Maria up from the hospital when she finishes her shift as a radiologist, and I agreed supposedly to make it convenient for them. It was really about being close to Michelle and not getting stuck in traffic. I'm almost to the door when Maks practically slams it against the wall.

"I'm surprised you weren't doing that to my condo door this morning, Maksim."

"Stay away."

"Please, do come in."

"Fuck off, Enzo. Stay away from Michelle."

"Did Laura send you?"

"Shut—"

"I'm not trying to be patronizing. I'm serious. Did Laura send you? Does she know, or did you find out from Mikhail?"

"She knows because Michelle told her this morning. I know because Mikhail nearly shit himself when Michelle showed up to talk to Laura, and he hadn't told me about you and Michelle before that."

"Did Laura send you?"

There's a moment's hesitation, and that tells me the truth no matter what he says next.

"No."

"Why not? Could it be because Laura can't stand my family but respects Michelle's choices? Just like Michelle respected Laura's choice to be with you."

"Something like that. But I wasn't manipulating Laura and using her against you."

"Fuck all the way off, Maks. You don't know shit about what I'm doing. Get the fuck out."

"You're not denying it."

"There's nothing to deny. If I wanted to fuck you over, I wouldn't do it through a woman."

"That'd be a first in your family."

I practically bare my teeth at him.

"I am not them."

I'm not Luca, Carmine, or Gabriele who all had a hand in Maks's sister-in-law Anastasia getting hurt and being abducted by a Russian rival.

"You may as well be."

"I get it. You're protecting your wife's friend to protect your wife from getting upset. Maybe you're even friends with Michelle and are doing it for her sake. But I am not using her to fuck you over. Believe it or not, you are not my main priority in life. The bratva isn't the center of my universe. Frankly, I don't give a flying fuck about you personally, Maks. I care about you staying out of the way of my family's businesses. I care about you not lying to get my family thrown in prison for life. I care about a lot of things, but you are not one of them. Since I don't give a shit about you, move. I have a commitment that I will not be late for."

"You mean your date."

I glower at him. We keep nothing in this office that matters. The desks are bare, and the drawers are empty. We use the conference room for convenience or when we need a respectable place to meet with clients or associates. I walk past him into the hallway.

"Lock up behind you."

I'm not worried about him staying behind and snooping. Let him. He won't find shit.

"Enzo, stay away from her."

"Why? So you can make your wife happy?"

"Among other things. Michelle is a nice girl."

"Laura is too, but not only did you marry her, you have twins together. It's a slice of the American dream. You're good enough to marry Laura, but I'm just some shit on the bottom of your shoes and not good enough for Michelle."

"Exactly."

He crosses his arms, and I want to knock the smug look off his face.

"Then let Michelle tell me that."

"She doesn't know—"

"And neither did Laura when you brought her into this world. But you let her decide. Michelle deserves the same respect. She can make her own choices. If I'm the one she chooses, then back off. If she doesn't want me, then I walk away and never bother her again."

I put my hands on my hips. I'm not as broad across the back and chest as Maks, but I'm just as strong. I know because I can carry Gabriele's two-sixty ass up and down stairs when he's dead weight. Maks can do the same for Sergei, who's the same size and build as Gabriele. The last time we had to do that was at the same fucking shoot-out with some low-level Colombian dickheads who tried to steal our coke to impress Enrique Diaz. Except they got confused and went after some bratva weapons shipments. That was a shitshow and a half.

"If you're just fucking around with her—"

"Enough, Maks. I get it. I don't have to explain myself to you, but for Laura's sake, I will. I like her."

He stands there and stares at me before he nods once. Now it's perfectly fucking awkward because we have to ride down in the same elevator. It's not like I'm going to ask him, "how do you like those Mets?" We don't look at each other until the doors open. Neither of us steps forward, then we both do. We jostle each other and manage to get out without slamming each other into a wall.

I go out to the town car waiting for me, and I pull out my phone.

ME

Do you want me to meet you in your office?
Or do you want to come out to the town car?

I wait for a response, and the minutes tick by as I get closer to her office. I wait for her to respond, but nothing comes through. Her meeting must still be going. I wait in the car, but when ten minutes go by, and I get no text from her, something doesn't feel right. She's not the type to stand me up. I'm certain of that, even if we don't know each other well yet. If her plans changed or she was running late, she would have texted me. Something's off.

I head into her building and look at the directory. I recognize the name of her firm and push the button for the twelfth floor. This feels like an even longer ride than going down eighteen stories with Maks. The doors open, and I look around. I spot the door to her office suite and head toward it. I open it, and everything sounds quiet. No one's around. I step inside, then I hear it.

I bolt toward the sound of a scuffle, then a woman's scream. It's coming from a corner office, so I try to open the door. It's locked. It's Michelle's office, and I'm certain that's her. I step back and kick the door hard enough that it splinters. I will never forget — but will always wish that I could — seeing Michelle pinned in a corner with a man with his hand halfway up her skirt. I'm across the space in three strides. I grab the back of his suit coat and yank him away from her. I'm at least fifteen years younger than him, even though he's tall and in decent shape. I shove him into the wall and put my forearm across his throat.

"I don't know who the fuck you are, but if you come near my girlfriend again, you will find out what it means to cross a Mancinelli."

I know he's a New Yorker. It's easy to tell just looking at him. If he's in business in this city and can afford the expensive suit he's wearing, then he knows my family name.

"She—"

"Say even one word that hints that she was asking for it, and I will break every bone in your feet, so you'll never walk again. Get the fuck out."

"But—"

"I swear by all that's holy, be glad I want to talk to my girl-friend more than I want to butcher you. Stay here another second, and I will change my mind. Go."

I threaten him, and I mean every word. But as much as I want to punch the shit out of him, I won't leave any marks. He won't be able to claim I attacked him without provocation. He's the type to assume Michelle would never speak against him. I don't want to put her in a position where she has to choose.

He hurries out of the door as I spin around. I'm back to Michelle before the douchebag is even out of her office suite. I'm careful as I wrap my arms around her, not sure if she wants a man as big and as strong as me holding her too tightly. She burrows against my chest, trying to get closer. She's fisting my shirt at my waist as she trembles.

"Please hug me, Enzo."

I am, but I realize she wants me to hold her closer. I tighten my embrace as I kiss her forehead.

"Shh, *piccolina*. He's gone. I'm here."

"Thank God. I was praying you'd wonder why I hadn't

come down to meet you. I was praying you'd come up to look for me."

"I was worried. I knew you wouldn't stand me up. I'm glad I got up here soon enough."

"Me too."

I don't press her to tell me what happened even though everything in me screams I should demand an explanation. I just hold her as she calms. She finally wraps her arms around my waist like she did last night. I rub her back, and she sighs. I guide her over to the desk, and I lean against it. She steps between my legs, and I tilt her chin up. I wipe away a single tear, and it's enough to make me want to find that guy and destroy every single thing that matters to him.

"Kiss?"

She whispers her request, and I lower my mouth to hers slowly. I'm worried about making any sudden moves. I don't want to spook her. Last night's kiss was about lust. About exerting control and relinquishing control. This one is about pure tenderness. It's slow and light at first. The intensity grows, but it's not an inferno. It's different. It's as though we're both saying how interested we are in something real without putting it into words.

"Enzo, I was so scared. I thought he was leaving with the other clients, but then he hung back to ask a question while I was packing my bag. I didn't hear or see him lock the door. He moved so fast. I pushed him as hard as I could and ran to the door. I tried not to let him back me into a corner, but he grabbed hold of my arm and forced me into one. He—"

She leans back and shows me her neck. I hadn't noticed the bruises forming.

"He strangled you?"

"Tried to. I knocked over that chair as I stumbled backwards. I was trying to get his hand off my throat, but he was stronger than me. He squeezed so hard I started seeing stars as soon as he did. I tried pulling back on his little finger. It did nothing. I tried kicking him in the groin, but he didn't even flinch when I nailed him. I shoved my thumbs into his eyes, and he tried to bite my arm. Nothing I did made a difference."

I'm fighting the urge to do more than just destroy his world. I'm fighting the urge to have him rounded up and sent to our garage in Queens. It's not some little attached two-car garage. It's an industrial one with enormous metal doors that we string people up from. It's our controlled environment where we handle people who need to disappear. But as strong as that desire is, being with Michelle while she needs me is way more important.

"Let's go, *cuore*. I'll take you home."

"What does that mean? And I don't want to go home."

"It means sweetheart. Where do you want to go?"

"On our date. I don't want you to drop me off. I'm upset, but I don't want this to ruin everything."

"Chellie, I'm taking you home. We'll order delivery and watch a movie. I'll stay with you until you fall asleep."

"No one calls me Chellie expect for Laura when she teases me."

"Oh. I—"

"I like it. It's sweet like you."

I chuckle. I don't think anyone but my mother has ever called me that.

"Let's get your stuff, and my driver will take us to your place."

"Enzo?"

I look at her.

"Will you stay until I wake up?"

Chapter Four

Chellie

I had an emergency appendectomy in China when I traveled there will Laura. She was my interpreter, and fortunately, she's fluent. But that didn't mean it thrilled me to have surgery in a country where I knew no one but my fellow foreign friend. I broke my leg skiing and had to wait for the emergency personnel to ski down and find me behind a tree I wiped out on. I got lost at an amusement park when I was five. I took my LSATs without studying at all.

I've done some scary shit. But never have I been as scared as I was tonight. I've made some shitty decisions walking home alone at night in New York. I admit that. But I should have been safe in my office. I should have been able to trust that my client wouldn't attack me. I seriously thought I was going to pass out, and he was going to assault me.

When Lorenzo burst through the door, I about pissed myself with relief. It was like everything was right again. He would deal with the fucker, and I would be safe. He would protect me, and I could breathe again. Literally — since the douche no longer had his hand around my throat — and figuratively.

"I'll stay as long as you need me to."

Forever?

"Thanks, Enzo."

I'm ready to take a step back, but he doesn't release me. I place my hand on his chest and offer him a reassuring smile. That's when I realize his heart is racing. He looks cool, calm, and collected. But under the surface, he clearly isn't. Is it from bursting in and rescuing a damsel in distress, or could it have been from our kiss?

"Stay for a minute."

His request is barely more than a whisper. I rest my head against him, and I feel his sigh. It's like the weight of the world was just lifted from his shoulders.

"Enzo?"

"Yeah. Let me just hold you."

I wrap my arms around him again, and my heart melts. He presses soft kisses to my forehead as I just enjoy another moment of peace. The rest of the world disappears as I inhale the hint of cologne that's spicy and musky. It's perfectly manly and perfect for him. When he loosens his hold, I nearly ask him to hold me again. But we need to leave. The evening custodial crew will be in soon, and I'd rather not have this closeness ruined with people watching us, waiting for us to get out of their way.

I gather my stuff, which he carries, and we head to the elevator. His hand slides into mine and entwines our fingers as though we've done it for years, and we walk out of the building. He points to a town car, and we head toward it. The driver appears and opens the rear door. I get in and slide over, not wanting Lorenzo to have to step into traffic.

He hands my work bag to the driver but gives me my purse. The driver pops the trunk, then I hear a soft thud. I guess my laptop and papers went in there. There's privacy glass that's up, so I don't know how the driver knows where to go. Maybe Lorenzo whispered it, and I didn't hear it. Maybe he planned to take me to my place all along. That would normally creep me out. But it doesn't.

"Come here, *piccolina*."

He opens his arms to me, and I inch closer. But that's not enough for him. I didn't have a chance to put my seat belt on, so he lifts me onto his lap. This goes against everything I learned in high school driver's ed, but as usual, I feel safe with Lorenzo.

"Will you tell what you and that bastard were talking about when the assault started?"

"Yeah. There's a gala coming up that one of my clients hosts annually. We'd just finished a meeting between my client and that man about his role in the event. He's a high dollar donor and is sponsoring almost all of it. My client left, and I thought he was right behind them. But he stayed behind to say how much he appreciated me explaining all the options for maximizing his donation. The door was still open when he started saying it, and I was looking down at my desk. I heard the lock turn, and that's when I looked up. He was blocking the door with his back to it. I told him he needed to leave and to unlock the door. I told him I had someone waiting for me. I tried to get around my desk so I could run to the door without him trapping me. But I knew either way I went, he could block me. I told you the rest, and you saw it."

"Do you blame yourself for any of it?"

"No."

"Good. I'll stay out of it, even though I don't want to. But you need to report him."

"I know. My boss is going to shit a brick. He has no tolerance for that. Someone assaulted his daughter in college. He's very conscious of making sure everyone in the office feels safe and that there is no tolerance for any sexual harassment. Not even a hint. But his boss — well, she's going to shit a brick too. But it won't be in my defense."

"The money's too important."

"Yes. That man's contributions help keep our client solvent. If the charity goes under, then they won't be paying us the big bucks they do. He figured that since most of the money he donates helps fund our client's legal fees, he owned me indirectly."

"Did he say that? Did he use that word?"

I get nervous. Anger now pulsates from Lorenzo, and I'm not sure if I should answer that question.

"*Piccolina*, do not make me ask you again. If you do, your ass will not enjoy the outcome. Did he use that word? Did he say he owned you?"

"Lorenzo, it's just a word. He was trying to intimidate me."

"So, he did. But you didn't answer my question. It was either yes or no."

He fists my hair and twists me onto my hip. His hand lands across my ass, and it smarts.

"Your thoughts are your own. I won't demand to know what you're thinking or what happens in conversations you have with other people *unless* it's about your safety and well-being. If I think there's a threat to you, you will answer my questions, or I will bare your ass and spank you until my hand is sore."

I stare up at him. There's so much in what he said that I'm not sure what part to think about first. The spanking part pushes through. Do I want him to spank me for real? Do I want him to have that kind of control over me? Do I want to accept punishments from him?

I'm an adult. No one has punished me for anything since I left home after graduating high school. He doesn't want to control anything but making sure I'm safe. He can't protect me if he doesn't know the truth about things that happen. Do I want him to protect me? I mean, who doesn't want to feel safe? But do I want him as my protector?

His hand slides up the back of my skirt until he can cup my ass. God, that feels good. Fuck. It feels even better as he squeezes. He's watching me. I know he's waiting for me to flinch or squirm or ask him to stop. But I love it. The tighter his hand, the more I want him to keep going. Between his hand on my ass and his hand in my hair, I can't go anywhere. I mean, I'm certain he'd release me the moment I told him to. I just know it. Nothing about this makes me feel trapped like I did with that piece of shit. Just the opposite. The more I think about it, the more in control I feel. The moment I want this to end, it will.

"You want to feel my hand across your ass because you want to know someone cares about what happens to you. That someone demands you're safe and taken care of. That I won't back down about this, even if you're the one keeping me from making sure you're okay."

"Yes."

I mouth the word more than say it.

He positions himself more in the middle of the seat before he rolls me onto my belly, over his lap. He pulls my skirt up, and I expect to feel the first spank, but it doesn't come. Instead, he glides his hand over my bare ass. Then he pushes his fingers beneath my thong and caresses between my ass cheeks. I want him to finger me so badly that I fight not to wiggle to get his fingers into me.

"*Piccolina*, I'm not looking for domestic discipline. I won't spank you for talking back to me. I won't spank you for arguing with me or having an opinion different from mine. I won't spank you for running late or not dressing a way that I want. I won't spank you for not picking out food I think you should eat. I won't spank you for being you. The only thing I expect is for you to be just the way you are. But I will spank you if something or someone threatens you, and you don't tell me. I will spank you if you put yourself in danger. I won't spank you if someone else does that to you. If you're with me, there are risks that come with it. I don't think I have to explain all of it since you know Laura and Maks. I suspect he has exactly the same rules for her."

"He does. She explained it to me almost word for word."

"If I'm punishing you — which I hope is next to never — then I normally wouldn't pleasure you after. But this is the first time we're doing anything like this. I don't want your memory of our first time being intimate to be one of pain with no pleasure. You haven't told me to stop, and you haven't tried to get up. Do you want this? Or are you accepting it because you feel like you have to?"

"I want it, Enzo. I didn't know I'd be into something like this. I don't think I would be with anyone else."

He sits me up, and I'm confused. His hand remains on my ass, but it's a soft hold that feels almost loving.

"I told you I belong to a BDSM club. You must know that means I've spanked other women."

Now I flinch.

"But — shh, *piccolina* — let me explain. That was role-playing for sexual gratification. Did it fulfill something in me I enjoy? Yes. But did I give a shit what happened to my partner when she was doing whatever she does in real life? Frankly, no. Do I care a great deal about what happens to you when we are and aren't together? More than I know how to handle. I have never spanked a woman because I care about her."

I cup his face and lean in, but I wait for him to nod before I start the kiss. When he takes over, I gladly let him lead. I tunnel my fingers into his hair with my right hand while my left thumb sweeps over his cheekbone. My emotions are an utter jumble, but the one thing I know for certain is I don't want to be anywhere but with him.

"I know you still want to wait the four dates, and I'm fine with that. But this is different. This is — intense — in a way no other guy has been with me. Ever. Not just at the beginning of a relationship, but the entire thing. If you want us to keep waiting to have sex, I won't disagree. I just want you to know that this has gone way past you being hot, and me being curious."

I tense. I just admitted a lot, and I feel super vulnerable.

"I feel the same. Roll over, little one. Let me spank you."

He offers me a lopsided smile that I can't help but return. It lightens what just got heavy, but it still reminds me we're moving in a direction I've never been before. I don't think he has either.

I position myself over his lap and take a deep breath. Just as I exhale, his hand lands across my ass.

"Ow!"

Holy fuck! That stings like a mother. Another one lands, and I freeze. His hand sooths some of the burn as he runs it over my quickly heating cheeks. The third one lands on my right ass cheek, immediately followed by the fourth one on my left cheek. He alternates sides until he lands three on my horizontal crack. I'm crying because of the pain, but I'm also crying because I feel guilty that I made him ask more than once when all he wanted was to help me. I pushed him away when what I really want is to hold him tight.

He inches my thong down my hips until it's around my knees.

"Pull your leg up."

I do what he says and bend my right one. I feel him slip my panties over that foot. Then I'm doing the same with the other side without him asking.

"I told you last night that once I'm in your pussy, I won't share. You will be mine, Michelle. I meant it. I'm going to finger you, then eat you out. If you want anyone else, then stop me."

"Anyone else? I can't think of anything or anyone besides what's happening right now. Please don't call me Michelle."

I didn't enjoy hearing him use my full name. I know he did it to make sure I know he's serious, but it doesn't feel right. He helps me up, and I sit on his lap again, my legs dangling over his while my ass rests between his thighs, so his trousers don't rub against it.

"Chellie, I won't use your full name if you don't want me to. I only want to hear you call me Enzo."

"Enzo."

"Hmm?"

"I just like saying it."

His fingers crawl up the inside of my thigh until his fingertips brush my pussy lips. He teases me by touching everything but inside me. I widen my legs and tilt my hips, my invitation clear. The heel of his hand presses against my clit, but that's the only relief I get.

"Do not wear panties again, Chellie. I will rip them off you every time you do."

He thrusts his fingers into me.

"I want what's mine, and I want nothing in the way of it."

Oh, God. This feels so good. He has large hands and broad fingers. They're not fat by any stretch. Two of them ease some of my need, but it's not enough. My legs fall completely open, so he thrusts a third one into me. Yes!

"I'm going to make you come this time, and you don't have

to ask. But your orgasms belong to me just as much as your pussy does. I want to watch you every time you find pleasure. I want to be the only one who gives it to you."

"Enzo, you're ruining me for anyone else."

His expression hardens, but he says nothing. Instead, his thumb works my clit until I whimper with the need to come. He's relentless. I fist the material over his calf since it's all I can reach. I press my left foot into the seat and my right one against the floor. My pussy begs without words as I drip from how wet I am. He said I can come when I want, but he's tormenting me by bringing me to the edge then backing off.

"Enzo, please. I need you."

"I'm giving you what you want."

"But not what I need. I want you to finger me, but I need you to make me come. *Please.*"

He thrusts hard as his thumb moves in circles until I scream. I have a brief fear the driver can hear me, then I don't care. I don't know how he does it because I'm in a haze, but he turns us, so I'm on my back, and his shoulders are between my thighs.

"I will always give you what you need, *piccolina*. I will try to give you what you want, too."

He latches onto my clit as his fingers continue to work my pussy. He hums as he tastes me. I'm glad he likes it. He's flicking me with his tongue as his left hand presses on my belly to keep me in place.

"Put your hands over your head and hold on to the seat."

I do what he says without hesitation. Can we have those four dates all in a row? Can we have sex by this weekend? I feel like I'm going to explode without it.

"I'm coming, Enzo... Yes... Fuck... Yes."

I feel wrung dry, but he doesn't stop. My clit is sensitive after coming twice, so my third orgasm slams into me, and I forget to hold on to the seat. My hands fist his hair and press his face to me. He grazes his teeth over my clit as he grasps my wrists. His grip is tight, but not enough to hurt me as he pries my hands from him. He gathers them in one hand, pushing them away. He leans back and slaps my pussy, not once, but three times.

I jerk off the seat when his mouth immediately returns, and he sucks on me until I come. He licks me until I'm certain I won't leave a sticky mess anywhere. Then he sits and lifts me to straddle his lap. He tucks my head against his chest. I can feel his dick pressing against me, and it's making me horny all over again. I try to reach between us, but he stops me.

"If you take my cock out, I will fuck you. Our first time will not be in the backseat of a car."

"But I want to return the favor."

He presses my shoulders until I sit back.

"You never have to pleasure me in return for what I do for you. You don't have to give me a blow job or let me fuck you to make amends after a punishment. What I give, I give freely. When a spanking is over, it's over. All is right again when you let me hold you."

How is he so perfect?

How the fuck did we get from running into each other last night outside a movie to me sitting on his lap after he just spanked me, fingered me, and went down on me? Why doesn't any of this seem shocking? It feels absolutely normal.

Since I don't know what to say, and he doesn't seem in a rush to carry the conversation further, we sit in companionable silence. I'm still on his lap with my head on his shoulder. He's still got his arms draped around me. There's still some rush hour traffic, so it takes a while to get to my place. When the car stops, I realize I'd dozed off for a few minutes. God, I hope I didn't drool. I climb off Lorenzo's lap and straighten my clothes.

I look for my thong, but he grins and pats his suit coat pocket. He's keeping it.

Just like on the way to the car, he holds my hand after the driver passes him my work bag. He holds the elevator door open with his free hand at my lower back. We're not the only ones on the elevator, so he shifts to stand behind me. His arm slides around my waist, and I love it. It feels like we've been a couple for years not two people who haven't even had their first actual date.

As we step off on the fifth floor, I think about the view outside my living room window. It looks directly at the building across the street from me. I bet Lorenzo has a penthouse with views all the way to Jersey or even Connecticut. I bet my place is a shoebox compared to his. I'm not embarrassed, but it's a stark reminder that we come from very different worlds.

I slip my key into the lock and open the door. He's still carrying my bag, so he puts it down on the entryway table where I point. I hang up my purse on the hook above it. He slips off his suit coat and hangs it beside my purse. It feels so domestic.

"Would you like me to make you dinner?"

I think about the pasta I have that would be easy and quick. Wonderful. Marinara out of a jar. I'm certain his mother makes it from scratch with a recipe twenty generations old. What else do I have that I can make? I didn't get any meat out to defrost since I didn't think I'd be having dinner here. Turkey sandwiches, anyone?

"Let's order whatever you want. Or we can still go out. I assumed you'd want to go home. I didn't ask, *piccolina*."

"I don't mind going out."

He puts his hands on my hips and gazes down at me.

"Don't do what you think I want. What you want matters

just as much. Are you tired and wanting to stay in? Or do you want a distraction and to go out?"

"You're a distraction no matter where we are."

That just tumbled out of my mouth, but it makes him smile. He's handsome to begin with, but when he smiles, he'd soak my panties if I still had any on.

I think for a moment before making a suggestion.

"Can we do Thai?"

"Of course. Do you like it spicy?"

"A little less than medium. You?"

"The hotter the better usually."

He must have an iron stomach. He pulls out his phone and taps on a food delivery app. It only takes a moment for us to order. I open a bottle of wine, cringing that it probably isn't anywhere near what he's used to. But he sips it with a smile.

"I'm going to take my suit off. I'll be right back."

I head into my bedroom, and I'm tempted to leave the door open. As clear an invitation as any. But not yet. Let's get through this date. I pull on jeans and a nice shirt before heading back to the living room.

"You look beautiful no matter what you wear, *piccolina*."

He leans forward and kisses just behind my ear. Last night, I wore a dress with cowboy boots. Earlier, I had on a suit with two-inch heels. Now I have jeans and pull-on shirt with bare feet. He was in a suit last night and one tonight. Does he own casual clothes? Then again, Matteo had on one too. I guess they're just very formal. They're definitely suave.

He follows me to the sofa, and I pick up the remote.

"Would you like to watch a movie?"

"Sure. We saw an action movie last night. Is that what you like?"

"Yeah. I suggested it to Laura, and it didn't take much to

convince Christina. We all like them. But I could go for a comedy or suspense."

I don't like Rom Coms, so there's no chance I'm recommending one. And it would feel too calculated or too obvious to do that. We sit and scroll the listings on three streaming platforms before we go back to the first one and settle on psychological thriller. I pointed it out, and he agreed. I wonder if this is the sort of thing he's into or if he's indulging me. When the opening scene starts with a guy beating the shit out of another one in an abandoned warehouse, I regret my choice. Is this what he has to do? Does this remind him of work?

"Relax, *piccolina*. It's a good movie. It's just a made-up story."

How does he always know what I'm thinking? It's cool and disconcerting at the same time. We get thirty minutes into it when my doorbell rings. I pause it, and he goes to the door. I consider getting plates and setting the table. We could both see the TV from the table, but it feels more natural to just sit on the couch together.

When he puts the bags on the coffee table, I open them and pass him his food. I can smell the rich aromas, but I know he didn't order it as spicy as he could. I'm happy with my regular pad thai with no spice. I still think it's a delicious dish.

We start the movie again, and before I realize it, we're sharing our food, feeding each other. It doesn't really dawn on me until after the movie's done. When we finish eating, he clears everything and puts the empty containers back in the bags. He drapes his arm around my shoulder, and I curl up beside him. We watch most of the movie with my head on his chest and his head resting on top of mine. This is the most perfect date I've ever been on. I still want him to stay, but I won't insist. When it finishes, he picks me up, so I straddle his lap like I did in the car.

"It's easier to see you like this. You're tired."

I am, but I don't want the evening to end.

"What's your day like tomorrow? You know I go to an office. What's your typical day?"

I'll come up with anything to keep him here a little longer.

"Tomorrow, I have to go to Jersey to some casinos we own. I'm doing a quarterly audit."

"Fun."

I grin at him, and he taps my backside.

"Tons. In the afternoon, I'm stopping by one of my restaurants. There are some new menu items my chef would like me to try. What time do you finish tomorrow? Would you like to come with me?"

"I'd love to, but I won't be done until five. I don't want to hold up your afternoon."

"I'll take care of something else. We can have dinner at Constantine's and try out the new dishes. I can pick you up."

"Isn't it a couple blocks from my office?"

"Yes. Just on the other side of the Flat Iron Building in Chelsea."

That's more like five blocks, but that isn't too far. The weather's been pleasant, so it should be a nice walk.

"I've never been to Constantine's. What type of food is it?"

"It's an Italian-Mexican fusion. I never would have imagined it would work, but my chef is a childhood friend who went to an amazing culinary school and was a sous chef in a Michelin star restaurant. He wanted to cook what he likes, and I wanted a restaurant that makes money. It's a perfect partnership."

"Sounds like it. I'll meet you there at five-thirty."

He hesitates, then nods.

"I told you I'd stay with you until you fall asleep. Do you want me to?"

"You don't have to."

"Don't deflect. Tell me what you want."

"Yes."

I'm not used to being so frank so early in a relationship. It's both refreshing and intimidating. I stand up and head into the bathroom to brush my teeth and take off my makeup. I don't wear much, so I'm not scared for him to see me without it. I change into pajama shorts and a tank top with a shelf bra in it. I open the bedroom door, and he walks over from the sofa.

I'm not quite sure what to do, so I shuffle over to the bed and climb under the covers. He walks around to the far side, and I feel it dip as he sits. He kicks off his shoes before he rolls toward me. He slips his arm over my waist as he spoons me.

"I'll lock the door behind me, Chellie. Sleep. I'll stay as long as you need me."

I want to say all night, but I stifle a yawn. My eyes drift closed, and I know I'm asleep within minutes. I wish I'd basked in the feel of him cocooning me, but I was too at peace to stay awake. Would every night be like this if he slept beside me?

Chapter Five

Lorenzo

"I want everything you can find on Simon Shapiro. He's the head of a venture capitalist company."

I stand in front of Carmine as he works in his home office. He barely looks up at me, and I want to snatch the computer out from under his nose. I know he's reviewing plans Matteo sent over, and I know they're time sensitive. But I'm not feeling patient right now.

"Why?"

"Because I want it."

That makes him look up.

"Why?"

I stare at him, unwavering and fighting the urge to cross my arms.

"You never ask for personal favors. Not even when we were kids, and your padding broke before the varsity homecoming game. You went out with a busted sternum plate and had the wind knocked out of you rather than ask a favor from me."

"Things change. Can you find out about him or not?"

"You know I can. Why are you being so testy? What did this guy do to you?"

"I just need to know."

Carmine sits back and studies me. He says nothing when he leans over his computer again. I think he's ignoring me, but a moment later I could hug him.

"Simon Shapiro, age fifty-six, principal at Shapiro and Grimes, graduated with a BA in Communications from Buffalo thirty-three years ago. He got into venture capitalism because his father was the original Shapiro in the company name. He's done well for himself with some very dubious connections with international investors. He lives in the Upper East Side with a house in the Hamptons. Flashy car, flashy third wife, flashy clothes. All the stereotypes wrapped up in one disgusting package. Looks like he's been sued three times by women who've worked for him. They've all accused him of inappropriate touching and intimidation."

None of that shocks me except for the SUNY Buffalo part. I'm not knocking the school. I assumed his family would have bought him a better degree than that. Finding out that he's harassed other women only confirms what I'd guessed. He's a predator and believes his money will always get him off. It probably has until now.

"Did he settle?"

"Yeah. Hang on."

I watch him as he clicks on a few things.

"They were big payouts. Hundred-twenty for the first one. Seventy-five for the second. And hundred-forty for the third."

Three hundred thirty-five thousand is no small thing. He did a shit ton more than inappropriate touching and intimidation. He assaulted those women. I'm sure of it. I'm sure he would have done that to Michelle if I hadn't arrived when I did.

I have never felt such an overwhelming fear mixed with rage as I did when I saw her cowering with his hands on her. If she hadn't been there, I would have killed him. The only reason he's still alive is because his disappearance would cause too much attention and make her ask too many questions.

"Who is this guy, Enzo? Are you thinking about doing business with him?"

"Definitely not. Not before you told me, and absolutely not now."

"Then why ask about him?"

"He approached someone I know."

Carmine tilts his head as he watches me.

"Michelle."

He drops her name and waits for the bomb to explode. But I won't give him that satisfaction. He grins when I don't respond. Fuck. That confirmed it as much as blowing up at him. He grows serious a moment later.

"Are you going to tell Maks that this guy went near Michelle?"

"No. She's Laura's friend, but I'm not telling him anything unless she asks me to."

"You sound — acquainted."

"No, I am not fucking her."

Yet.

"I didn't say you were. Just the opposite, actually. I think you like her, and you plan to hold off having sex with her until you've properly courted her."

"Courted? When the fuck do you think we live? Eighteen sixty-five?"

"Don't deflect. If she were someone you wanted to fuck and be done with, you would have. Or you'd set something up at your club. Everything about you right now tells me she means something to you. So, knowing you, you'll take your time."

"Knowing me. When's the last time I dated someone?"

"College, and I remember how much you liked her until you realized she hated everything we are."

"You weren't even here. You were in California. How the fuck would you know?"

"I wasn't in Massachusetts either, but our family talks. I might have been exiled to Stanford, but there were still some people in our family who didn't disown me."

"Maria."

Carmine grins.

"You know she and I have always been close. Until Gabriele moved here, she was my only friend for years. I might have fucked up, and Uncle Salvatore might have sent me to Palo Alto rather than throttle his baby sister's only child, but Maria never ignored me."

He could sound resentful, but he's matter-of-fact. Everything he said is true. He caused a lot the trouble that made our uncle send him away for four years, but he'd had good intentions. He'd just been too hurt and spiteful to explain any of them.

"You figured it out. I like her. We had a date last night, and I was supposed to meet her at her office. When she didn't come downstairs and didn't answer her phone, I got worried. Her office was completely empty since it was after six-thirty. I heard a noise in her office that sounded like something falling off her desk. I kicked the door in to find that fuck face with his hands on her."

I won't say that he had his hand under the hem of her skirt. Hearing that out loud will push me around the bend. I'm already clenching my fists so much they hurt.

"And he lived?"

"What do you think? I couldn't whack him in front of her."

He rolls his eyes. There are enough cliches about us to fill a tome. We may as well reclaim some of them.

"Did you at least threaten him?"

"Of course. I didn't threaten to kill him or anything else that would be grounds for him to sue me. But I told him I would break every bone in his feet, so he could never walk again. I don't trust that this will be the only time he goes after Michelle. I think he'll keep trying until he gets what he wants and knowing I'm in the picture will only make him want her more. He's the type who wants to take from a family like ours, so he can brag about it."

I pull out my phone and tap the screen as Carmine watches me. He sighs and turns back to his computer while my call rings.

"Luca, I need you to adjust the schedule. I want Afonso and Luigi."

Luca is our underboss or Uncle Salvatore's second-in-command. One of his many duties is to set the schedule for the men who guard the women in our family. It might sound trivial to some, but that's the most important responsibility any of us could have. Not a single woman in our family is helpless. Of course, my sister is the best shot in the family followed closely by our mom.

They all carry weapons and know how to use them. But that doesn't change the fact that the men who'd attack them will always be larger and stronger than them. Most likely faster despite their size. They go nowhere without guards. Usually, it's a family member. But for routine things like going to work or the gym or the grocery store, one or two of our men accompany them.

Afonso and Luigi are two of our most trusted men who rotate among the women in our family. Afonso's twin, Alonzo, is our strongest guy besides Gabriele. While I'd like him to guard Michelle, he's already assigned to Luca's wife and infant daughter. I'll have to think about who I want assigned to her. Even if this shit hadn't happened, I'd want her to have a security detail.

Luca doesn't agree automatically.

"Why?"

I'm sick of hearing that word today, but it's a reasonable question.

"I need them to follow someone and make sure the guy knows he has two extra shadows. They don't have to do anything to him. Just be present."

"Who is it?"

"The guy's name is Simon Shapiro."

"I don't recognize it. Have we done business with him?"

"No. This is personal."

There's a long pause. I'm certain he's thinking the same thing Carmine did. I don't ask for personal favors.

"Did a deal go bad?"

He's trying not to flat out ask, but he knows I know what he's doing.

"Luca, I just need the guys to do this for me. I'll explain later. Can you spare them?"

"Of course. I'll make it happen. Do you have an address or something? Do you want to give them instructions?"

"Sure. Have Luigi call me. Thanks."

We hang up, and I look back at Carmine. He's still working, acting as though I'm not even in his office. But there's a hint of shit-eating grin on his face.

"I know, I know. You're not going to say I told you so. You're just going to let me know you're thinking it."

"If you say so, Enzo. You should have asked Luca about setting up a rotation for Michelle."

"You know why I didn't."

"Yeah. You didn't want to explain to your big brother what you had to explain to me. But the problem with your pride is you've left Michelle unprotected. Get over yourself, Enzo. Between this fucker and being involved with you, she needs guards."

He's right. Fuck. I pull my phone back out and call my brother back. I give him an abbreviated version of what's going on with Michelle, including my connection to her. Of course, Luca asks the same thing Carmine did: am I going to tell Maks? By the end of the call, Carmine's as smug as ever, and I feel like my big brother is bossing me around again. Fucking middle child life.

"Enzo?"

Hearing Michelle's voice is like a choir of angels singing on high.

"*Piccolina*, I'm downstairs. Do you want me to come up?"

Today felt like it lasted for forever. Afonso and Luigi got on a call with me, and I explained to two of our Made Men what I wanted. Their families have been *Cosa Nostra* for five generations at least. I didn't have to spell it out. I've been trying to stay occupied between meeting with Carmine, talking to Luca, then talking to the guys. But there were a few hours with nothing for me to do but wait for it to be time to pick up Michelle. Well, that's not true. I had plenty of work to do. But I couldn't concentrate on any of it.

"I'm coming down. I was going to walk over and meet you there."

"I know. We can still walk."

"Okay. I'm getting on the elevator now, so I'll lose you. Be there in a moment."

I wait in the lobby, and I feel like my chest eases enough for me to breathe again when she steps off the elevator. Her smile brightens everything about my day. She stops next to me, and I lean to kiss her cheek, but she turns her head in time to snag my lips.

This isn't a kiss for other people to watch, and it definitely isn't one that two people who still haven't had a proper date should share. We pull away at the same time, aware we're in public. But I would have happily kept going. I open the door for her, and we head toward my restaurant.

"Were you worried about me, Enzo?"

How do I answer that? No, I wasn't worried because Afonso and Luigi are already tailing Shapiro. I can't tell her that.

"Of course, *piccolina*. Yesterday still has me rattled."

That's one hundred percent the truth. It's why two of our most highly positioned Made Men are taking care of this. Carmine, Gabriele, Marco, Matteo, and I are all *capos*. It's like lieutenants if Luca were a colonel and Uncle Salvatore were a general. Matteo's father is still a *capo*, but he doesn't get involved in the dirty work like he did when we were younger. Carmine's father technically got promoted to one when Uncle Salvatore became don, but it was more a courtesy. He keeps his hands clean, and that's exactly what we need. He keeps us looking legitimate when we commit insurance fraud all the time.

Below our positions are Made Men. They're of Italian descent, usually Sicilian in our branch. It's not automatically hereditary, but it pretty much is. Half a step down are associates. They're our non-Italian men. They serve us just like Made Men and are loyal to our family, but they can't be born into the *Cosa Nostra*. They are few and far between. Beneath even that are the *soldati* or soldiers. They haven't risen through the ranks to Made Man. They run our low-level street hustles, rough people up, and steal. Enforcers are practically at the bottom of the ladder, but for years, Gabriele existed in limbo.

He wasn't a *capo* because of his ties to Carmine, but he was far more respected and trusted than a regular enforcer. The man can have the patience of a saint. He scares the shit out of people just from his size and his demeanor. But anyone who knows him knows he's actually the least inclined to violence of all of us. He sets bugs free and would take every wounded animal to a vet if he could.

Carmine didn't officially earn the title of *capo* until he came clean about what happened to him when he was a kid. He'd served as one, but Uncle Salvatore refused to acknowledge it. That was the same time when Uncle Salvatore promoted Gabriele, too.

Marco, Matteo, and I earned our positions by our actions and commitment to our family, but we basically stepped into the roles and title when we were old enough. We didn't have to prove ourselves the way Carmine and Gabriele did.

Chellie brings me back to the present.

"I told my boss, Enzo. Anderson took care of it. Simon knows he's not welcome in our office again, and he's to stay away from me. Susan wasn't thrilled when Anderson told her, but my boss had a hunch and did some digging through public records. Apparently, Simon's been sued before. Three women accused him of inappropriate touching and intimidation. I don't know what happened to them, but Simon settled them all."

She's not telling me anything I didn't already know. Before I left, I asked Carmine to dig a bit more. This kind of man not only makes dubious business deals, he makes dubious friends. I want to know about everyone in his life from his barber to the doctor who examines his prostate.

"Are you going to have to deal with him through your client?"

She hesitates, and I stop. She turns to look up at me.

"Yeah. That's unavoidable because he's such an important donor. But I don't have to meet with him. I don't even have to talk to him. I can do everything through email."

"Did Anderson or Susan tell your client what happened?"

She shifts from one foot to the other. Finally, she shakes her head as she looks down.

"Why can't you look at me? Did you tell them not to mention it? Or are you frustrated because they wouldn't?"

"I told them not to. I'm not ashamed of it. I did nothing wrong. But I don't want our client picking sides and not choosing us. They bring us a shit ton of billable hours, and they're well connected. If they fire us, then other charities will follow them. I don't want one asshole to ruin my job. Anderson wouldn't fire me, but Susan would."

If Susan were a man, I'd deal with her the same way I am Simon.

"What happens when your client wonders why you won't hold meetings with Simon anymore?"

"I don't know. I'll cross that bridge when we come to it."

I don't press the issue even though I want to. I don't want to ruin our night. We walk into Constantine's, and Manny, my manager — yes, he's been teased plenty about that — seats us. It's not like I can't pick out the best table in the place. But it does make it feel a bit more like a date when he pulls out Michelle's chair and offers her the wine menu. I watch Enrico wipe his hands as he leaves the kitchen.

"Hey, boss."

He slaps me on the back as he comes to stand beside me, looking at Michelle. If the man weren't gay as the day is long, I might take offense to how appreciative his gaze is.

"Michelle, this is Enrico. We've known each other since we were toddlers. He used to serve me mud pies."

"Which you ate."

"I did not."

I grin. My mother says I did, and his mother said I didn't. Who can remember the truth? Not us since we were three. We became friends for real in elementary school. I'm a Mancinelli, and he's a Martinez. Our names were close enough that we always ended up next to each other in lines. I'm fully Italian as in both my parents', my siblings', and my cousin's, and my first language was Italian, followed by Sicilian, then English. Enrico's mother is of Italian descent three or four generations back, and his father moved with his family to New York from Mexico when he was fifteen. That's why it's an Italian-Mexican fusion restaurant.

Michelle laughs, and I grin. Enrico looks at me like I sprouted a second head. He shifts his gaze to Michelle then back to me. I don't like that knowing expression. He sees way too much. Fortunately, he starts explaining the new dishes before I get too uncomfortable.

"I have an avocado y palmito salad that combines avocado with palm hearts, along with mixed greens in a light vinaigrette. I can also offer you pasta con mole, so fettucine with mole sauce. I'm refining a pollo con hongos y crema pasta which is grilled chicken with mushrooms in a cream sauce over pasta. And finally, polpette en tamales. It's Italian meatballs wrapped in a corn-based dough steamed in banana leaves."

I watch Michelle, and she looks interested in all of them. Thank God because they'll all be delicious. I'll make a pig of myself if I ask for them, and she isn't interested in eating half.

"Bring us a sampling of each, Rico. Thanks."

He nods and turns on his heels before calling out orders as he enters the kitchen. The staff all speak English, but half speak Italian and half speak Spanish too. The commands come in English, Spanglish, and Itanglese. Somehow, they all know what he's saying. Michelle laughs and shakes her head.

"I can't wait to see what happens with those dishes."

"A food coma."

I reach across the table and take her hand. She turns them, so we can entwine our fingers. Her thumb rubs the outside of mine as she speaks.

"How was your day?"

I don't want to tell her it was fucking frustrating.

"Productive. I had a meeting with Carmine about a project's budget. I talked to Luca about some assignments for guys who work for us. I got some regular accounting work done. Not exciting, but good. How about you, *piccolina?*"

"Other than dealing with my boss's boss, it went well. We brought on a new client about two months ago, so I've been reviewing contracts for them with the various vendors they want to use. A few of the contracts are not in the client's favor, so I'm redlining them and getting ready to go over them. The client's new to the nonprofit world, so I want to make sure no one takes advantage of them. Another client is a publicly traded entity that wishes to start a nonprofit and is trying to figure out where to incorporate."

"Delaware, Arizona, Nevada, Wisconsin, and Texas, in that order."

That's an easy answer for an accountant. Delaware is often the preferred choice, but other states have unique benefits for organizations. I know because we have at least a dozen nonprofits that are shells for our less than legal enterprises.

She shifts uncomfortably.

"I recommended Nevada since it's a tax haven. This client is — uh — they'd prefer to keep their connections to the IRS limited."

I lift my chin, and my jaw sets.

"The Kutsenkos."

"Enzo, this has been in the works for a while. Laura handles their corporate stuff, but this isn't her area of expertise. It's mine."

"And they thought dragging you into business with them is okay."

"They didn't drag me anywhere."

"Your name will be forever linked to that charity. That means your name is forever linked to theirs. A little IRS probe will easily connect you to any and all of their shady shit."

She releases my hand and sits back. She crosses her arms, and I could kick myself. I still stand by what I said, but I just ruined our date by picking an argument and insulting her friend. She watches me for a moment, then leans forward and keeps her voice down.

"Are you pissed because you're actually worried? Or are you pissed because it's them, and you don't want me favoring them?"

"Both."

It's my turn to sit back and cross my arms. She shifts into the chair beside me instead of across from me. Her hand goes to my thigh as she brings her lips close to my ear. It slides closer to my cock as she speaks.

"I know you don't like them, and I can guess at probably a dozen reasons."

Her hand cups my cock, and I'm ready to jump out of my skin.

"I'm doing this as a favor to Laura not for Maks or any of his relatives. Even if they weren't all married, I wouldn't be interested. Not when all I want is to taste you."

She sits back and pulls her hand away, but I'm faster. Mine dives under the tablecloth and presses hers back to my dick.

"If you aren't careful, I won't wait until we're at your place before I give you what you want."

Her eyes dart to the bathroom. No.

"Come with me, little girl."

We stand, and I lead her to the office. I glance over her head at Manny and shoot him a warning look. I have never taken a woman into any office before, so his shock is understandable. I use my key to let us in and lock the door behind us.

When I turn, Michelle is already kneeling with her hands on her thighs. Her head is down, and her gaze is on the floor. Perfectly submissive. At my club, that would be perfect. I'm not so sure I'm crazy about it now. I want her to submit to me, but I don't want her submissive.

I don't know how to explain the difference in my mind. I want her to let me lead and be in control, but I don't want to do things *to* her. I want to do things *with* her.

I wrap my hand around her upper arm, nudging her to stand, but she refuses. I pull on her arm gently to make sure she understands she doesn't have to kneel. She shakes her head.

"Enzo, I want this. Please, let me."

"Is kneeling for me arousing?"

"Very."

"Do you enjoy being submissive?"

"Not usually. But I've never really had a chance to find out."

I shift, so I'm standing directly in front of her. I unfasten my belt, then my pants, before unzipping them.

"May I?"

"Of course, *cuore.*"

She pushes my trousers low on my hips and pulls down my boxer briefs. She eyes my cock, and I leak. Fuck. I want to be inside her cunt, but I'll take her mouth. Fuck. I'll take her hand if that's all she offers. Anything to have her touching me.

She starts at the base of my cock and licks up to the tip. She does it a second time before swirling her tongue over the head. She flicks the small opening, and I leak some more. She puts her hands at the small of her back before leaning forward to take me inch by inch.

She takes an inch then draws back. She does it over and over until I hit the back of her throat. If she were my sub, I'd push her head down, forcing her to take all of me. She shifts her weight so she can take more of me. Her eyes are closed as she concentrates, but her face looks relaxed.

As she starts to bob, her hands come to the front of my thighs. She glides them, her thumb running along the inside, until she gets to the top. She wraps them around the back of my thighs and presses me forward, telling me to go deeper. I flex my hips and feel my cock easing down her throat. She grasps my ass and works my cock.

Holy fuck. This is the best blowjob I've ever had. My knees feel weak, and I put my hands behind me to brace myself against the door. Nothing has looked more sensual than the way she's sucking me off. She's not in a rush. She looks like she's savoring every movement. I'm going to come embarrassingly fast.

"If you don't want to swallow, let go. I'm too close."

Her eyes drift open, and she looks up at me. Our gazes meet as she continues. I can't stop, and I don't want to. My cock twitches as my cum shoots down her throat. Her right hand wraps around my dick as she strokes and sucks me while the left hand massages my balls.

I tilt my head back and groan. Her tongue sweeps over me, cleaning every last drop before she licks her lips. I want to pounce and give her as good as she gave me. But I feel too depleted. I'm not even sure I can stay standing. I help her to her feet and move us to the desk chair. When I sit, I position her to straddle me. She happily climbs onto my lap, but she catches my hand as I prepare to work her clit.

"Enzo, you took care of me last night. You asked for nothing in return. I want this to only be about you."

"But—"

"Shh."

She places a finger to my lips as she kisses my cheek.

"Touch me later. Right now, I just want to hold you like you held me."

She wraps her arms around me, and I rest my head against her chest. It's like the softest pillow. I sigh, but my line of sight is directly pointed at her other breast. I use one hand and unbutton her blouse. I pull aside her bra and latch on. Fucking pure heaven. My hand cups it and brings it more fully into my mouth while my other hand slides under her skirt and caresses her ass.

"No panties. Good girl."

"I want to be the very best for you, Da — darling."

Darling was not what she was going to say. She scrambled to come up with an alternative. I've been around my brother, cousin, and friends long enough now to know what she didn't say. I won't push her right now, but it becomes my new mission. I want to hear her say it. I continue to suck her tit as I knead her ass cheek. I'm getting hard again, and she can feel it because she wriggles against me.

"I'm not fucking you for the first time on a desk chair in an office in a restaurant with a dozen employees buzzing around."

"But you could."

I bring my hand down on her bare ass, pushing her hips forward, so her pussy rubs against my still bare cock. I do it two, three, four times until she's moaning. They aren't hard spanks, just enough to move her.

"We are going to eat dinner, then I'm bringing you home.

I'm going to spend all night worshiping your pretty little pussy, but I will not fuck you."

"Are you trying to torture me?"

If only she knew what I was capable of. She wouldn't use that term so loosely.

"No, little girl. I plan to pleasure you until you can't keep your eyes open."

Chapter Six

Chellie

When he said bringing me home, I didn't realize he meant to his place. Dinner was amazing. And I don't just mean giving him the blowjob of my life. The food Enrico brought out was the best I've had in ages. Everything was superb, but I couldn't stop thinking about what was going to happen after the meal was over.

We've just walked into his penthouse, which has views all the way to Jersey just like I suspected. He has four bedrooms, which surprises me for a bachelor. But he explained one is his, one is his office, one is his home gym, and one is for any family member who wants to crash. Apparently, that happened a lot more often when most of them were single.

"Strip for me."

I turn around as he enters the bedroom behind me. I walk backwards toward the bed as I unbutton my blouse and let it slide down my arms to the floor. I turn away from him and point to the zipper at the back of my skirt. He steps close, and I feel his heat, then his cock as an arm wraps around my waist.

"I told you to strip, little girl. I didn't say let me undress you."

His hand grabs my ass over my skirt and squeezes until I go up on my toes. Then I feel the material loosen around my waist. He steps back, and I shimmy it over my hips. I shake my ass for good measure, since he seems to like it. I'm still facing away from him when I unfasten my bra, but I twist so he can see my tits as the bra drops on top of my blouse and skirt.

He's back against me as his hand presses on my belly. It's perfectly possessive, and I love it. His other hand cups my breast, and I lean my head back onto his shoulder. He rolls his finger over my nipple, and my eyes drift closed. He kisses my neck as his hand skims down my belly to just above my pussy.

Please touch me. Please.

"You said you don't have experience with BDSM. I want to tie you to my bed and make you come. Is that something you're willing to try?"

"Yes."

My answer is a puff of air.

"You need a safe word. One that you won't accidentally say when you actually want to keep going. One that I'll know immediately means stop. No questions asked. No demands. It ends when you say so."

Nothing's coming to mind because all I can think about is him touching me and doing things that might push me to my limit.

"Um, prunes."

I have no idea why I blurted that out. He chuckles, and it's a dark, delicious sound. When I laugh, it sounds like a nervous cackle.

"Prunes it is, *piccolina.*"

Both of his hands go to my hips and hold me in place.

"I'm going to tie you to my bed, then I'm going to enjoy what's mine, Chellie. All of you. There isn't a part of you I won't touch, a part of you that isn't here for me to pleasure. Climb on the bed on your belly."

I step away from him and walk around to the side that has his alarm clock. When I lie down, I smell a hint of his cologne and shampoo on his pillow. My eyes close as I inhale. It calms any nervousness I have. I hear him open the bedside table drawer, then the wrapping on something crackles and tears. I open my eyes to see he has a brand-new bottle of massage oil. It's jasmine, just like the perfume I wear. It's my favorite scent.

When I shift my gaze up to him, I know he picked it for that reason. My eyes drift closed again, and I sigh. I wait for him to move my arms or tell me where to put them. The instructions never come. Instead, the cap snaps open, and I feel liquid drizzle down my spine. The sensation alone is arousing. He brushes my hair out of the way before feathering his fingertips through the oil.

He slowly eases the tension from my back and shoulders. All the knots from work, from my fear last night, my anticipation for right now. He works out all of them until I feel like a melted puddle of gooey sugar.

"Roll over, little girl."

I follow his instructions, but I'm a million miles away, floating in blissful relaxation.

"Arms over your head."

I do as he says, watching him remove his tie, then wrapping it around my wrists before leashing me to the headboard. He rests a hand on my belly again, and I love it. I might insist he keeps one there permanently. It's reassuring. His other hand squeezes oil onto my chest. He runs his hands over my tits and between them, spreading the oil until his palm glides over me.

The hand on my belly skims over the opposite ribs from the hand that was on my chest. Then it's back on my belly and sliding down between my legs.

"Open for me."

"Mmm."

I do as he says, and his hand slides down my pussy. It moves up and down, and I wait for his fingers to finally enter me. But they don't. The heel of his hand rubs just below my clit, teasing me with no relief. His fingers run along the outside of my pussy lips and almost to my ass. He does it over and over, and all I can concentrate on is that hand and what it is and isn't doing to me. Eventually, his fingers move closer and in between my pussy lips, but they never dip into where I need them. My hips undulate as I try to get him to touch me where I need it.

"What's wrong, *piccolina*? Don't you like this?"

"You know I do. You know what I need."

He leans forward and kisses my neck just above where it meets my shoulder.

"I know exactly what you need, *cuore*. I'm giving it to you."

Does that mean we'll have sex before the four dates? Please, yes.

His fingers move to my left inner thigh, the back of them trailing up my leg, to the joint with my hip, and over my mound to cup it. He does the same thing with other leg, alternating and teasing me three more times on each side. Then he's rubbing that spot again just below my clit. The ache is turning into a burn. He knows it and presses more soft kisses to my neck and shoulder.

"Shh, *piccolina*. Not yet. Soon."

"Enzo."

I moan this name, and that rewards me with the tip of his ring finger pressing into me. But only the fleshy part of his finger, no more. I tilt my hips, inviting him to take more. His free hand has been caressing my belly up to my throat throughout this. He turns his head and licks my right nipple. I arch my back, pressing my hips into the mattress. That only pulls me away from that single, torturous finger. When I lower my back to lift my hips, that pulls my nipple from his mouth. He knows exactly what he's doing to me. Driving me insensate with need.

"Enzo, please. It's almost too much."

"Use your safe word."

I shake my head. I don't want it to stop. I want way more. I want all of it. I want to risk defying him and reach for his shirt. I want him not to stop me when I unbutton it. Even if I could, I know he wouldn't strop his ministrations to take it off. I long to trail my hand over his chest to his abs, but the tie restraining me prevents that.

"Do you wish your hands were free to touch me like I'm touching you?"

"Yes. No. I don't know. Both."

I want to feel him, but I also love that I can't. What's wrong with me?

He alternates sucking one nipple then the other. His tongue flicks them before suckling. I can't concentrate on that as he continues to massage my pussy, but it adds to the bevy of sensations and emotions ricocheting through me. He lifts my left breast and sucks hard as his fingers finally enter me. He strokes the inside of my pussy, continuing the massage. He doesn't thrust and withdraw. He caresses until he finds my g spot.

Holy fuck me.

"Do you need me to take care of you, *piccolina*?"

"Yes."

"Do you need me to make you come?"

"Yes."

"Do you need—"

"I need it all. Please, Enzo."

My voice trembles, and I fear I'm close to tears.

"Shh, little one. I'm here. You know I'll take care of everything you need."

"I do. And I need you so much right now."

He kisses up my neck, along my jaw and to my mouth. I open for him and pour every ounce of longing into my kiss. When he pulls away, I yank on my restraint. My instinct is to wrap my arms around him and not let him go. When his hand leaves my pussy, I wail. But he soon climbs onto the bed between my thighs. I watch as he lowers himself and positions my legs over his shoulders.

"Whose pussy is this?"

"Yours."

"What do I get to do with it, baby?"

"Whatever you like."

He hums before swiping his tongue along me, dipping it inside before flicking my clit. His fingers slide back into me, and my thighs quiver. The thumb of his free hand rubs my clit as his tongue continues to lick me. The fingers not buried in me are long and thick. They press from the outside against the spot inside me that he's working. It drives me wild, and my hips buck. I watch him, his eyes closed as though he savors what he's doing.

I need so much more. I need to feel full like I'm certain only his cock can make me feel. As though he reads my mind, all four fingers are inside me. He's drilling deeper into me, twisting his hand as he does. Oh, God. Could he be...?

I feel the thumb to that hand slide from just before my clit to my opening. He is.

"Enzo, yes. All of it."

Then he's giving me what I need. His fist is inside me. It's almost painful how full I am. But this... I'll never beg him to stop. Now he's thrusting but never pulling his hand all the way out.

"I need to come."

"Ask, *mia piccolina*. I told you I'd take care of you, but my little girl asks because her pussy is mine."

My little girl. He says it in English and Italian. God, how I want to be. I don't want to be a little. That's not me. I want to remain a thirty-one-year-old, but this man says he'll take care of me. And he is. Sexually, but I don't doubt he will no matter where we are or what we're doing. It unleashes something in me. A calm before the clawing need returns.

"Please, Daddy. Let me come."

"Come for Daddy."

I do. I explode and tremble as the most powerful orgasm I've ever had rocks my world. He's agile and faster than I expect. He pushes up and lunges until his forearm is by my head. His lips are beside my ear as his body presses onto my left leg and side. He doesn't give me all his weight, but it's enough when his cock rests on my hip.

"You are *mia piccolina*, my little girl. Your pussy, your ass, your mouth, your hands, every part of you is mine to worship. But I will have more. I will have all of you."

I turn my head and gaze into his chocolate eyes that have flecks of gold. He wants my heart and my soul. He's right that he already has my body. He's on the way to earning my heart, but I think he's possessed my soul. Maybe that's why I said what I did. I don't want to take it back, and he seems glad to hear it. It just shocked the shit out of me.

I'm unprepared for the second orgasm that slams into me. It's not a gentle growing crest. It's a tidal wave that drags me under, twists me like a washing machine spin cycle, and pushes me back up to the surface. It's too much. I'm trembling and can't catch my breath. He withdraws his hand carefully, then rears back onto his knees, tugging the tie off my wrists. Before I know what's happening, he scoops me into his arms and rolls onto his back. I'm stretched across him, his hand cupping my ass as his other holds my nape as we kiss. I want to stay like this forever.

"Chellie, talk to me."

I hear the nervousness in his voice, but I don't want to talk. I lift my head, my right hand cupping his face. I pour all my wordless feelings into my kiss. It goes on and on, tender and dare I say — loving. My right leg presses between his, making his thigh rub against my already sensitive clit. The hand on my ass tightens, guiding me to rock on him. I pull my hand from his cheek and reach for his belt, but he stops me.

"If you take me out, I will be inside you. If I'm inside you, no level of determination will keep me from spilling. I don't want to get off tonight. I need to, but I don't want to. I only want you to."

"Why? Why do you think four dates is the magical number?"

"Because I want to prove to you that this isn't all we have."

Not prove to me this is all he wants. That's implied. What we have. What is that exactly? It's nothing I've experienced before. I'm pretty sure he hasn't either. It's not just his words. It's the way he says them.

"Enzo, do you think I'm a little?"

"No. Nothing so far makes me think that, but are you?"

"I enjoy reading DDLG romances among other types, but I don't relate to any of those characters. I don't think I am. I called you that because — I guess — hearing you call me *mia piccolina*, my little girl, baby — I don't think you want a little or are a Daddy Dom. But it made me feel as taken care of as you promise. I guess it just made sense."

"And I don't call you *piccolina* in either language because I think of you as an actual little girl. You're smaller than me, for starters. I'm almost a foot taller than you and weigh a lot more. You are little compared to me. And you are a girl." He grins. "If you're with me, you do need protecting. But even if I wasn't who I am, I'd still want to share the weight of your world with you. I'd still want you to feel taken care of and adored."

"You adore me?"

"Very much."

"I adore you."

It's as close to I love you as you can get, but neither of us is ready for that. At least, I'm not. I could be sooner than I imagined, but not yet.

"Chellie, I haven't wanted to be in a relationship ever since I realized just what my life means. You're the only woman I've wanted to let into my life since I was a teenager. I dated some women in college, but it always ended before it could get serious. The first hint that they wanted to know more, to become more involved emotionally, I shut down and shut them out. I don't want to do either of those things with you."

"Good. I don't want you to. Just the opposite. What you said about wanting all of me? I won't settle for less from you."

He eases me off him until he can roll onto his side and look at me. Then he sits up and hurriedly strips off his shirt.

"Put this on. Seeing you naked is way too tempting and distracting. All I want is to suck your tits and make you come on my cock. We need to have a serious talk, and I can't do that while you're like this."

I grin but take the shirt. I slide it on and am about to lie down.

"Button it."

"Yes, Daddy."

Sabine Barclay

I cock an eyebrow, and he pounces. He pushes me onto my back.

"You are two seconds from me fucking you until you're so sore you can't think about anything but me inside you for the next week. You're two seconds from me coming inside you, and once I do — condom or not, birth control or not — you will be mine in a way no woman ever has been. I won't trap you and refuse to let you go. But I won't be the one to walk away. The only way to end this once I come inside you is for you to break up with me."

"Then do that. Four dates is arbitrary and frankly stupid. That's not what I want. I don't need four dates, and you clearly don't need them either. I don't want anyone else. I don't want to walk away. I only want to get closer and not just physically. I know enough about Laura's life to know about what I'm getting myself into. I haven't run from you, Enzo. I'm not going to. You say you won't let me go, but all you're doing is holding me away from you. We've just been pretty fucking intimate, and you know I mean more than just you fisting me — which dear Lord above was — fuck — so good. I want more. I need more before I can give you more."

"If that's what you want, then we definitely need to talk before we go further."

He sits up, and dread replaces the bliss I felt. When he turns, so he can see me as I sit up, I know whatever is coming is far more serious than I expected.

"Chellie, I don't know how much of Laura's life you really know. But I can promise you it's a fraction of reality. There are things about her marrying into the bratva that you can't and never will know. If we get more serious, there's only one reason in my mind. I want us to be us permanently. I know that alone is a lot to digest. If that happens, there are things about my family and our life that no one can ever know. You and Laura can't bond over similarities. You can't share them. You can't tell anyone, which means you'll keep secrets from your family and friends. It means there are secrets I can't risk telling you. There are lies I'll tell you — either by word or omission — because knowing them endangers you, my family, the people who depend on me."

"And you."

Shit. This is a lot like what Laura told me right after she got married. I didn't think she was exaggerating, and I don't think Enzo is either. But it's a lot to know I'm taking this on. Not I might. I am.

"Yes. I won't lie about us, but I will have to lie about work."

I know what work means. At least, I have a pretty fucking good idea what it is. Drugs, guns, stealing, bribery, extortion, killing. How the fuck am I okay with this? When I think about the actual things he must do, I should be appalled. I should run. I should call the cops or the feds. I can reconcile myself to it. Is it because bad guys deal with bad guys? Bad guys — am I five? But what else do I call them? Sociopaths? Psychopaths? I can't see Enzo as those, and I don't want to try. Who he is with me is someone different. Who he is with me makes me feel better than I ever have with anyone. Romantic or not.

"Chellie?"

I hear the nervousness. I take his hands in mine.

"Enzo, I won't ask you to confirm or deny what you do. But you know I must have a good idea. If not from meeting the Kutsenkos, then from watching movies and remembering things from the news. The latter might be exaggerated, but it had to be based on some reality. I don't want to know the truth about that. I'd rather it be something there that I can accept but am not in the know. I can keep the two parts of you separate even if one overlaps and sometimes has to overshadow the other. I believe to my very core that you will never purposely endanger me. I don't think you would ever agree to let me get involved in any of it. Just the opposite. It scares me you'd probably die to protect me. I trust you."

He stares at me for a moment before bringing my hands to his lips. He brushes the softest kisses over my knuckles before kissing my palms. He laces our fingers as our hands rest between us.

"That's all true. But I need you to understand more. I can never leave this. Not only would it make us targets immediately and leave us undefended, it would make the rest of my family vulnerable. I was born into this and that might mean my children are too. We've talked as a family now that Luca has a baby, and none of us — not my parents' generation or mine — want her or any of our future children involved. But we just don't know."

"So, our children."

That's a pretty big thing to say.

"If you want the same future as I do, then yes, ours. I'm a shitty Catholic, but I still am one. I won't have kids without being married, and I won't get divorced. Carmine's parents live separate lives, and we're all happier for it. But they will never divorce."

"I'm lapsed Lutheran. We're about as close as you can get to Catholics without being Episcopalians. We accept divorce, but I don't want one. I won't have children without being married either. I'm not opposed to it or disapprove of it. I just don't want that for me. I need to think about whether I can live with knowing our kids could become what you are. I want to say I can, but I need to think about that."

"That's fair. Until I met you, I never imagined this would be a conversation I needed to have. Even with my brother, cousin, and friends getting married, I still didn't think about whether I would be in this position one day. I told you I will lie. Sometimes I will tell you I'm some place I'm not or with someone I'm not or doing something I'm not. Sometimes I just won't tell you what's happening, and you'll hopefully never be any the wiser. You need to know and accept that there are very few things I won't, can't, or haven't already done. I draw the line at women and children. They aren't part of this business, and we should never drag them into it. Archaic, and just how I want it because of you and my sister and the other women in my family. I also draw the line at infidelity. I will never stray, Chellie. If I commit to you, it's because you're the only woman I will ever want. I won't seduce anyone to get them to do what I won't. I won't sleep with someone to get what I want. I will walk away before I have to do that. I won't betray you."

The fidelity part is the most adamant he's been since he started talking. I don't know his family, but somehow I think that's a value they uphold. I think he knows that as desperately as that would hurt me, it's something his family wouldn't forgive, either. I widen my legs to stretch them beside his and scoot forward. He does the same and lifts mine over his.

"What happens if something happens to you? Like right now while we're dating or later when we're..."

"Married, *piccolina*. That's where I want this to go. If you don't want that, then we end things whenever you want."

"You've told me that more than once. I understand why that's important to you. I don't want out, Enzo. I wouldn't have said yes to a single date, and I wouldn't have had chai with you if I didn't see something in you. This isn't about being able to say I dated a mobster."

"I'm not Irish."

"Huh?"

My brow furrows. That came out of nowhere.

"That's something else for you to understand. The mob are

the Irish. The O'Rourkes. Did you hear about them from Laura?"

"I know the Kutsenkos don't get along with them, and that something happened to Laura and Anastasia because of them. I know — I know your family did something to Anastasia too."

"We did. Carmine, Gabriele, and Luca thought to send a warning. It went horribly wrong and way beyond their control. It nearly cost Anastasia her life. The O'Rourkes are one of three principal rivals for us. The Diaz family is the other. Did you hear about them?"

I look down and nod.

"What do you know?"

"Laura grew up beside Pablo and Juan. She was so close to their family that Enrique Diaz, the *jefe*, has her initial and her sister's on his arm. They're at two points of a cross with a P and J on the other two. She will not talk about them at all. I know better than to bring them up. I know Juan is dead, and I can guess why. He didn't really want her until Maksim did. I've known that family as long as I've known Laura. I used to play with Juan and Pablo. I've been to parties at their parents' home. I know their mom, Margherita, is sick right now. Cancer. I know their dad, Luis, travels to Colombia way more than he should. I know there are some other cousins, but I don't know them well at all. Only in passing. Laura never knew them that well, either."

"All of that is true. Three of the other cousins are brothers. They go by *Tres J's*. Javier, Joaquin, and Jorge. Stay away from them, Chellie. Pablo and *Tres J's* have another cousin, Alejandro. We've been getting along with the O'Rourkes and Diazes more than we ever have, but it's a time bomb waiting to detonate. Latin American syndicates are cartels. *The* Cartel are the Colombians. We're the Mafia will a capital M. These days people throw that around as indiscriminately as their do mob.

But we are Sicilians. Some Mafia syndicates are from other parts of Italy like Serafina's family. They're from Venice."

"Wait. Who's Serafina?"

"Carmine's wife. Her mother is Sicilian, and her father is Venetian."

"So, she's Mafia on both sides of her family?"

"Yes."

Wow. I know Lorenzo's sister, mom, and aunts were probably all born into the Mafia, but it feels even more intense to have different Mafias for each side of the family.

"That's a secret, right?"

"Yes, and no. It wouldn't take much for people to figure out if they know her maiden name and where to look. But it isn't something we broadcast any more than acknowledging we're the Mafia in the tri-state area. If you want to be truly accurate, we're *Cosa Nostra*. It's Italian for 'our thing.' My family are *the* Italians. Just like the Kutsenkos are *the* Russians, the O'Rourkes are *the* Irish, and the Diazes are *the* Colombians. If you hear those countries, then you know which families we're talking about."

"I know Maks's family won't target me. But would the O'Rourkes and Diazes?"

"I want to say no, but it's not impossible. You asked what to do if something happens to me. You go to my family immediately. Do not go to your place. Do *not* go to Laura and Maks. I'm serious about that, Chellie. Aunt Sylvia has a policy that Laura adopted too. All women can have sanctuary at any of our homes until their family can get to them. I know Maks will keep you safe, but I can't promise he wouldn't use you to get to me or my family. The only reason to ever go to them if there's a problem is if you're certain you'll die if you don't."

My eyes just keep getting wider and wider. I figured I could go to Laura since she's my best friend, but it makes sense why I shouldn't now that I'm involved with Enzo. It also means that there are times we're going to be — what — enemies?

"I know what you're thinking, *piccolina*. This doesn't have to pit you against Laura. I pray there's never a time where you need to get to my family because of an emergency. But if I'm hurt or get arrested, you leave me and you get to my family. Promise me, Michelle. You will not stick around if I tell you to go. I won't stop protecting you. You know what that means."

I do. I scoot as close as I can get and wrap my arms around him. I kiss his bare chest and shoulder. He hugs me, but I'm not ready to let go when he loosens his hold. He lifts me until I'm fully straddling his hips.

"Little one, I'm scaring you, and I'm sorry. I hope we only have this conversation once and then never have it again. I wish we didn't have to have it at all. But you need to know what you're agreeing to. I need you to agree by your own free will."

"You said it's your aunt's policy. Why does she have it?"

I feel him sigh, and I can already feel the sadness that's coming.

"Aunt Sylvia didn't come to America until a few weeks before she married Uncle Salvatore. They didn't know each other and didn't meet until she arrived. Never have two people been a better match. My uncle is hardly the soft and sweet kind. At least, not until he met Aunt Sylvia. Who he is with her and their daughters is a man I never imagined. But people would be fools to underestimate her. She grew up in Sicily, and her father heads their branch. A few years after moving here, members of a rival family chased her younger sister, Sophia, after they killed her guards. Those men assaulted her and killed her, too. She was pregnant, and they knew it. She passed three different homes while she ran, but she knew no one would help her. Aunt Sylvia refuses to allow that to happen to another woman. So, any syndicate woman may seek shelter with us until their family can safely reach them. It changes nothing between the men except for peace long enough to get their woman and go home."

"Their woman?"

"Lady? I mean, it could be a wife, a daughter, a mother, a sister, an aunt, a cousin, a granddaughter. Is female better?"

"What about girlfriend?"

"In this world, we know what girlfriend means. It's a wife waiting to happen. None of us in any of the families have had serious girlfriends after college except for Bogdan and Niko. Niko stopped within a year or so of graduating college. Bogdan lasted the longest before he abandoned trying until he met Christina. I'm certain none of them knew who or what he was. At least, not without guessing. It's too dangerous to bring just anyone into our lives, into our families."

The story about Sylvia's sister is heartbreaking and terrifying at the same time. Could that happen to me? Not only would I die, but so would our child. Not mine. Our. With Enzo and only Enzo. That's easier to wrap my head around than it should be.

"Maks has to be away for business a lot. Do you?"

He hesitates before he nods.

"Sometimes he's gone for travel, Chellie. Just like me. But sometimes he's still in New York, just like I will be. Each family has a place where we can control the environment and everything that happens there."

I suck in a breath so deep that I feel my chest expand. I doubt he means an office where they negotiate big deals.

"I know you can guess what I mean. Never look for it, Michelle. Swear to me. Never."

"I swear. That's the second time you've used my full name. I don't like it. I know how serious you're being."

"I just want to make sure—"

"You're not a Daddy Dom, and I'm not a little. I don't need a stern talk from a parent. I'm thirty-one and able to understand the gravity of this, *Lorenzo*. It feels distant when what I need right now is to feel closer to you than I ever have. This is scary as fuck shit. I don't want to feel like you're pushing me away when I already feel adrift. Don't do that."

"Shh, *piccolina*."

He pulls me as close as he can. He cups my cheeks and kisses me, and I melt against him. I shift restlessly, wishing I could be closer to him. When I pull back, we stare at each other for a moment before he reaches between us and unfastens his belt. I unfasten his pants and pull down his zipper.

"Condom?"

He asks, and I shake my head.

"I know I'm clean, and you must be if you go to a club. I'm on the pill."

I push down his boxer briefs before I guide his cock into me.

"Daddy."

"*Piccolina*."

We speak at the same time. This isn't about sex. About getting off. This is about being as close together as we can be. I pull his shirt over my head, and we press our bodies together, skin-to-skin.

"I didn't mean to push you away, Chellie. Just the opposite. I never want to let you go."

"I know that. That's why you're telling me everything. But it just feels so wrong when you call me Michelle. At least it does when we're like this. I don't think you liked it when I called you Lorenzo, but I think I also made my point."

"I've thrown a massive amount of shit at you, and you haven't run. You aren't calling the feds. We're physically as close as we can get."

"It's still a lot to take in and digest. I don't know how I'm going to feel about this in the morning or the days to come. Regardless, I'm not going anywhere. Enzo, I have no idea what the hell that movie in the theatre was about. My mind was on you the entire two hours. I compared you to Maks and the other men in his family. I compared myself to Laura. I thought about how our situations could be alike. I thought about the man I suspected you are. The man you could be with me, and the man you have to be when you aren't. I guessed some of the stuff you told me. A lot was news to me. I knew before I walked out of that theater that I wanted you for more than a good fuck. Something about you is a magnet to me. You're the hottest man I've ever seen, but you're way more than your looks. Those will change over time just like mine will. That's not why I'm here."

"I am considered the pretty one in the family."

I grin.

"So, I've heard. But that's Pasha in the Kutsenko family."

I wrap my legs around his hips, letting my ankles rest on the bed behind him.

"Daddy, where do we go from here since I'm all in?"

Chapter Seven

Lorenzo

I'm truly all in as we sit with our bodies connected. My need to get off or get her off is nothing compared to the peace I feel just being inside Michelle. It's like coming home after a long work trip and feeling like I can relax. Like I can breathe again. Don't get me wrong. I want to fuck her until she screams my name in ecstasy. But for right now, I'm happy exactly as we are. We're having an intensely personal conversation, and it feels right to be like this as we do.

"I don't know exactly where we go from here. I've thrown a lot at you, and there's still more for me to explain."

"Then what do you want, Enzo?"

"I want us together. I want to move forward, assuming our futures are the same. I know you thought about this during the movie, and I'm certain you've thought about it since then. But this is a huge decision for you. It is for me too, but it's not the same. You're entering a world you don't know, which means you'll rely on me and people you don't know very well. You'll give up a lot for it while I give up next to nothing. That won't seem fair because it isn't. I don't want you to regret that or resent it. I started carrying a knife with me at all times when I was twelve. Not that long after, I got into a fight where I needed it. More often than not, I carry a gun. I haven't when I'm with you because I didn't want to freak you out. But now that you know more, I'll go back to wearing one. I've used it more than once, Chellie. I'll use it again. I've survived not because of it, but because I can assess situations fast and make life-altering decisions without hesitation. I rarely have the luxury of time. That's how I know what I want with you."

She shifts, and I groan. Fuck. She feels good, and she wants to get even closer. I want it to, but short of sharing one body, we can't get physically closer. But I think she wants emotional closeness just as much, and she wants more of it. I do, too.

"My guess is intuition keeps you alive, Enzo. I trust mine too. Laura and I traveled to China during summer breaks, and I visited her while she studied in Russia. She doesn't know it, but something happened while I was in Russia. I was followed. My intuition told me something was off before I ever saw anyone. It was intuition that told me not to trust a group of women approaching me. When I darted into a store, they followed me and tried to corner me. A group of men came in too. It was intuition that told me to duck into the back of the shop, and an older man hid me. I didn't know he was there. I didn't know if I was protecting myself or handing myself over to them. When I saw the shop owner, I just knew to trust him. I trust my instincts. I think you have too much honor to deceive me about us. I get why you'll lie, but I don't think you'll lie about us. You said you wouldn't, and I choose to believe that. What you've told me is enough to implicate you in enough crimes to lock your entire family away for life. I don't take that kind of trust lightly, and I don't believe you do either. Don't underestimate my ability to assess situations fast and make life-changing decisions without hesitation."

"Obviously, the four date rule is shit now. And you were right about that."

I grip her hips and grind her against me as I twitch inside her. She moans as she rocks, flexing the muscles that hold my cock deep in her pussy. I groan in response. I lift her hips so she can ride me. She pulls her legs back, so she kneels. I control our speed. I control how deep I go. I control her pleasure, and she surrenders to it.

"Daddy, I want to make you come. You said that will really make me yours. I want it."

I move us, so she's on her back. We both hate the few moments I pull out, so I can finish stripping. Then I'm back where I belong.

"You are going to take all my cum, *piccolina*. I'm going to fill your pretty little pussy, and you're going to keep it there until morning. When you wake up, you're going to feel it on your thighs and remember that you belong to me now."

I come from a big family. Between my siblings, cousins, and friends, I've had very few things that are entirely mine. I've always been fine with that. The life of a middle child. But the possessiveness I feel toward Chellie is startling. I'll never keep her locked away or insist that I be her entire world. But I'm not exaggerating by much when I say she belongs to me.

"And you belong to me, Enzo. Your cock is mine. You want to own my orgasms. Fine. But I own yours. Only I get your cum. Don't fucking jerk off when I'm not around. If you want to get off, then it's with me."

She grins when she finishes speaking, and I know she's teasing me. But I know that humor masks the fact that she really means what she says. I nuzzle her neck as I rock my hips, giving her only shallow thrusts.

"I'm hard the moment I think about you, and I've been thinking about you a lot. You're going to be getting me off often if that's the case."

"I will."

Our mouths fuse as I thrust hard. She arches beneath me as her hands grip my ass. She presses me into her, and I give her what she wants. I surge into her over and over as we continue to kiss. She digs her heels into the mattress to meet each thrust. Fuck. I'm getting too close too fast. But when I try to slow my pace, her nails dig into my ass.

"Harder."

She pants the one word, and it almost pushes me over the edge.

"Put your hands on the headboard, little girl. Do not let go, or I will pull out, spank you, and come on your ass. You will not come."

Her hands fly above her head, and I watch her hold on so tightly that the tips of her fingers turn red. I grunt as I slam into her. I support myself on my left forearm as I tweak her nipple. She cries out as I pinch harder and harder until she gasps. I release it before I lick, then suck her tit.

I'm going to spend a lifetime worshipping these. I could happily suckle like a newborn baby and fall asleep with her in my mouth. She doesn't have big breasts or small ones. My guess is a C or D cup, and they're perfect. I want to feast on them, and I plan to whenever I want. I never thought I was a tits or ass guy. I've always liked them equally, and I want to fuck her ass into next week. But her tits are divine.

"Daddy, harder."

"I'll hurt you."

She shakes her head and pushes her hips up higher.

"Please, Enzo. Daddy."

Hearing her call me that tempts me to lose all control. She

couldn't scream her trust any louder than when she says that one word. It means the world to me that she wants me to take care of her. Love her. I'm certain I'm on my way to falling madly and passionately in love with her. The idea of her acting younger than me does nothing. It doesn't stir my arousal or my tender feelings. That's not why I call her *piccolina* either. It's the trust that comes with the word. The knowledge that she believes I can and will protect her. That I will look after her like I promised. That's everything to me.

I return to kissing her as I move faster, trying to get even deeper than I know is physically possible.

"I want to make you come. Tell me what to do, Enzo."

"Keep doing what you are. I'm barely holding on. I'm not coming until you do."

"Then harder."

"I'll hurt you."

She cups my cheeks and stops moving. I do too, my brow furrowing in confusion.

"Enzo, I haven't had kinky BDSM sex before. But I've had rough sex. I know what I want with you. I know you're scared you'll harm me because you're bigger and stronger than me. I want to feel you lose control because you make me lose all of mine. But I *know* that even when you lose control with me, you'll still hold on to enough to never harm me. You wouldn't forgive yourself if you did. That's why I trust you for this and for whatever BDSM you're willing to teach me. I know I'm safe with you."

God. I think I love her already.

Our kiss is tender again, but it only lasts for a moment. Then I kneel, raising her hips off the bed. I know I'll leave fingerprints, and I love it. I pound into her, and it only takes four thrusts before she's begging to come. It almost kills me, but I stop moving. She wails her frustration. I start moving again.

Five thrusts, and she's begging. I stop again. When I know she's on the cusp of true frustration, I let her.

"Come for me, Chellie. Come on my cock."

"Daddy!"

Her head tilts back, and the cords in her neck strain. Her eyes are screwed shut, and her nipples are tight little nubs, begging to be suckled. I lower her hips and keep thrusting, but I'm back to sucking her tits.

"I need to come again. Please may I?"

"Yes."

I barely let go of her nipple long enough to mumble the word. I feel her entire body tighten again as she strains to keep her orgasm going. I can't wait any longer. For all my talk, I should pull out. I shouldn't risk trapping her since no birth control short of abstinence is a hundred percent. She still has her hands over her head, so she isn't pushing my ass to get me deeper. I could pull out. But I won't. Instead, I lean forward to whisper to her.

"I'm going to fucking explode if I don't come inside you. I told you the moment I was inside you, you became mine. We are going to make a life together, Chellie. And one day, when you're ready, I'm going to come inside you, and our lives will be bound forever."

"I want that. I want a life with you. I want *all* of it."

"Do you? Do you want me to get you pregnant with my cum?"

"One day. Until then, I want to practice every moment we can."

Is this just dirty talk?

"Tell me exactly what you want, *piccolina*."

She looks at me for a moment, trying to tell the same thing I am — it's not just dirty talk. I nod, and her gaze turns seductive in a way I'm not sure she even realizes. She turns her head to whisper to me.

"I want your cum right now. One day, you'll breed me because you can. You better tie me to the bed and fuck a baby into me when you do. There won't be anything I can do because I belong to you."

Dear God above. I've never come so hard as I am right now. I can barely hold myself up on my forearms. I'm shaking, and I'm worried my arms are going to give out. I go to a BDSM club. Dirty talk isn't something new to me. I've said way dirtier shit than she just did, but it's because my Michelle said it that made it so fucking hot.

She pulls me closer, and I settle most, but not all, of my weight on her. She wraps her arms and legs around me, and I don't even notice that I didn't tell her she could let go. If she were really my sub, I would punish her for that. But all I want is to hold her and be held by her. Our kisses are back to being tender again.

"I'm going to squash you."

I roll us, keeping her top leg over my hip as we lie on our sides. I'm no more ready to pull out than I was a minute ago. I keep a tight hold on her ass, knowing once again that I'm likely to leave marks. As I stare down at her, I know our dirty talk will never include me calling her a slut or a whore. I've used those words before, but I can't with Chellie. When I look at her, I can only imagine praise kink between us. She means too much to me for those words. They just don't seem right for her.

"What are you thinking about?"

She sounds nervous. That's not how I want her to feel after the first time we have sex. I never want her to feel that way any time we have sex.

"I was thinking I love our dirty talk, but there are some things I will never call you."

"You mean like slut or cum dumpster or whore or—"

"Go back a moment. What did you just say? Did someone call you that?"

"Shh. Enzo, calm down. You know you're not the first man I've slept with, but I hope you're the last."

She hesitates, and I make sure she understands exactly what's happening between us now. I fist her hair, and I feel her sigh. The rougher I am, the more relaxed she becomes.

"I better be the last, Chellie. I just told you we're going to have a family together. That sure as fuck means I won't share you, and I know I made it clear a family means marriage, and marriage means forever."

"So, you meant what you said."

"I meant it as much as you meant what you said."

Her smile is beautiful. Absolutely exquisite. She steals my breath away. I let go of her hair and stroke her cheek.

"Daddy, I could take or leave talking dirty during sex. Whether I was the one talking or listening. I've been called things I would never tolerate outside sex. In real life, I don't want to be bred like a horse. But the idea of you tying me up and putting me at your mercy excites me. The idea of getting pregnant from that — I don't know why that excites me too. It feels like it should be wrong."

"No. It's not wrong as long as you agree to it. What we do together is our private business. Whatever fantasies we want to explore are perfectly fine because I know neither of us would force the other. If there's something you don't like, then we don't do it. If there is something you do like, we can do it as often as you want."

"I hope you know the same is true for you. If you don't want something, I hope you don't do it just for my sake."

"I think you already know I will always need to be the

dominant one when we're intimate, but I still believe we can be equal partners in our entire relationship."

She hesitates. When I start to pull back, she puts her hand on my chest.

"Wait. I know you need to be in control, and I believe it's because there's a lot of shit in your life you can't control. I think not having control would make you anxious and unable to enjoy being with me. I get it. I prefer to submit because all I have to think about is what's happening in the moment. I never get to do that. I'm always thinking about work or what I still need to do or what's coming up or whatever. I never live in the moment unless I'm with you. I like the anticipation of trying to guess what you might do, but I love not having to plan it. I appreciate not having to be in charge for once. We give each other what we need. I don't think this will be a bad thing, but there's no way we can be equal partners. Not when there is stuff you have to hide from me. But I'm okay with that because, at the end of the day, I want to be the woman you turn to. I want to be the one you know you can rely on to let yourself escape for a few hours. I want to be the arms you walk into."

"How are you so wonderful?"

"Ha. I don't know that everyone would agree with that."

"I don't care about everyone. You're perfectly wonderful to me."

She kisses me, and I relax. She strokes hair back from my forehead, and I feel that escape she just mentioned. We both fight the need to yawn as our bodies release the tension that built up again as we talked. My body no longer agrees with my mind, and I pull out. I press her onto her back and latch onto her breast as my hand drifts down to her pussy. I resume the massage I gave her much earlier. My fingers move slowly, lulling her rather than arousing her. I switch tits back and forth as I fight to stay awake.

"Daddy, I'm going to come."

She tells me in drowsy whisper as she does.

"Shh, *piccolina*. Sleep."

I doze off moments later, still sucking her tits. A man in bliss.

What the fuck time is it? Where is my phone?

I glance up at Chellie and realize I really fell asleep sucking her breast. It's the best sleep I've had in ages, but now I need to find my pants before my phone wakes her. I know the pattern. Ring three times. Stop. Ring three times. Stop. Ring three times. The pattern will continue until I answer. It's work. It's someone in my family, but there won't be any good news. I glance at the screen.

"Marco?"

"Yeah. You need to come in."

I look at Chellie, and she hasn't stirred. I slip out of bed and go into the bathroom. Partly because I don't want to disturb her, but also partly because I don't want her to overhear.

"*Perché?*" Why?

"Is someone there?"

"*Sì.*" Yes.

"You never bring anyone home."

It's a statement, so I don't respond.

"Enzo, we need you at the garage. We finally have a lead on who took Aunt Sylvia months ago."

That was before Maria and Matteo got married. Someone broke into Aunt Sylvia and Uncle Salvatore's home while their daughters were sleeping upstairs. Uncle Salvatore had been at a meeting and came home unable to find Aunt Sylvia. Turns out, men came in through a bootleggers' secret entrance into the basement and took her at gunpoint. She knew she'd wake Pia and Natalia if she screamed for the guards. She didn't want to risk them getting in the middle and getting shot.

She's elegant and sophisticated, and far too often underestimated because of it. She killed at least two and injured the others long enough to escape. We thought it was related to problems Maria was having with a guy she was involved with before she and Matteo started dating. We discovered the issues were unrelated, but never learned who was behind the attempt to abduct my aunt.

It's my turn to ask.

"*C'è qualcuno lì?*" Do you have someone there?

"Yeah. One of the guys who lived. He's contract."

That means he doesn't belong to a syndicate. Basically, he's a mercenary. We need to find out who hired him.

"*E hai bisogno di me?*" And do you need me?

"We got his computer, but we can't get into it. It's more than just some standard lock screen."

I run my hand through my hair and look over my shoulder as though I can see Chellie through the door. I want to ask if this can wait until morning, but this is about Aunt Sylvia as much as it is about business. No one would call me in the middle of the night if someone else could get into the computer.

"*Va bene. Dammi un'ora.*" Fine. Give me an hour.

"An hour? Enzo—"

"*Mi ci vorranno almeno trenta minuti per arrivare al garage. Devo fare una doccia e salutarla.*" It'll take me at least thirty minutes to get to the garage. I need to shower and say goodbye.

"Who—"

"I'll see you soon."

I hang up. I don't need to explain myself to my brother, and I really don't want to. I need to think about how I introduce Chellie into my family before they even meet her. I put my phone on the counter and jump in the shower. As I wash myself, I think about how she told me I better not jerk off. I might have a slightly rebellious side which tempts me. But I really don't want to give myself a hand job when I have a gorgeous girlfriend in my bed. I'd rather slip back into bed and back inside her, but I can't. Duty calls.

I towel off and brush my teeth before I run a comb through my hair. When I step into the bedroom, Chellie sits up, pushing hair out of her face.

"Enzo?"

"I have to go in to work, little one. I'm sorry I woke you."

"It's all right."

She pushes back the covers and turns away.

"Stay, Chellie. It's the middle of the night. Go back to sleep. I don't know when I'll be done, so I may not make it home before you need to leave for work. I'll have a car take you to your place then to the office."

She stands up and walks to me. The light shines around me from the bathroom, illuminating the siren as she approaches. I slide my arms around her and pull her tight.

"You know I'd rather be here with you."

She reaches between us and cups my hard on.

"I'd rather you stayed too."

My hands grip her backside and lift her until her legs wrap around my waist. I carry her to my dresser and place her on the cool surface.

"Hold on to the edge. Daddy needs a little snack to tide him over."

I kiss along her collarbone, down between her breasts, and over her belly, until I get to her pussy. She opens her legs as I lick her clit. She's wet for me, and I know some of that is still my cum. I thrust three fingers into her, and she moans.

"Daddy, are you making sure your cum stays in me?"

"Yes."

I growl my answer as I finger fuck her and keep sucking her clit. When she tries to press my head closer to her, I grab her wrist and push her hand away.

"I'm fucking you, little girl. I decide what you get. If I want to make you beg, I will. If I want to make you scream, I will. If I want to edge you for being impatient, I will leave your little cunt hungry and empty. I'll make you ache until my cock fucks you tonight. Is that what you want? To ache all day for me? I'll know if you get yourself off."

"No, Daddy. I only want you. I need you. Please."

Fuck me. I stop with just eating her out. I pull her off the dresser and walk to the bedroom door. I pin her against it, and her arms cross over her head. I thrust into her, and her legs tighten around my back. I press my body against hers, making it impossible for her to move unless I do it for her.

"Is this what you want? You want me so fucking hard I can't see straight? You want more of my cum?"

"I want all of it. It's mine."

I love the possessiveness in her voice. It matches mine.

"I'm going to fuck you the way I want, and you're going to take it, aren't you?"

"Yes."

The way she says that word. The breathy moan. It always makes my cock twitch.

"You can't get away, can you?"

"I can't."

"I can do whatever I want with you, can't I?"

"Absolutely anything."

"And why's that?"

"Because I belong to you."

"That's right."

"I need to come."

"Ask, *piccolina*."

"Please, may I come?"

"No. Try again."

"Please may I come, Enzo?"

"No."

I snap my answer. I know she's not teasing me, but I want her to know what I expect to hear.

"Please may I come, Daddy?"

"Yes. Come because I'm making you. Come because you need my cock inside you. Come because I fucking told you to."

Her hands grip my shoulders as she tenses around me. Her cunt is so fucking tight that I can't stop. My kiss is brutal and demanding. I'm still hard, so I'm not done with her yet. I keep thrusting until she pulls back.

"Enzo!"

"That's right, little one. Scream my name every time."

She collapses against me, and I carry her to the bed. I sit with her clinging to me like a koala. Her head rests against my shoulder as she pants. I can barely catch my breath, too.

"Chellie, I have to go. I don't want to. I think I'll be home by tonight, so we can have dinner. If I'm going to be later than that, I'll make sure someone lets you know."

She sits back.

"Someone?"

"When I have this kind of work, it means you can't reach me by phone. I won't have it on."

"So, you can't be found."

I nod.

"If you ever need me, you can call my sister or mom. They'll make sure someone gets in touch with me."

"But only if it's an emergency, right?"

"I'd rather you not ask what I had to eat or what I'm wearing. But if it's important — even if it isn't an emergency — call or text. They'll get the message to me."

I ease her off me until she's standing.

"I need my phone, then."

She goes for hers while I get dressed. She cocks an eyebrow when I pull on a nice t-shirt and a pair of jeans. Neither are favorites, which is good because I'll never wear them again.

"What?"

"That shirt is the equivalent of me walking down 5th Avenue in just a bra and panties. It leaves nothing to the imagination."

I grin.

"I promise where I'm going, I'm not getting anyone aroused."

That makes the smile drop from her face. She nods and ducks her head as she unlocks her phone. I walk over to her after slipping on a pair of loafers. Her hair hangs down, hiding her face. I kiss her forehead as I take the phone from her.

"Yes, that is where I'm going. But I didn't mean to make you think about that. I meant this is work, not a night out with the guys."

"Are you really going to be safe?"

This will be the first test of many for her. Maybe it's just as well that it's happening so soon. If she doesn't like this uncertainty, better we find out now.

"Yes, *mia piccolina*. I promise."

"But what if—"

I pull her in for a hug.

"We control this place. It's why we go there. It's not on any city records or in any files. It's a *Cosa Nostra* neighborhood. People know to turn the other way."

"But what if—"

"If something happens that's beyond our control, I will

make sure someone gets you and takes you to my parents. Wait there until I come for you."

"What if you can't tell people something went wrong? I'll never know what happened to you."

"Chellie, you're my girlfriend. I'll make sure my family knows who you are. Once they do, I won't have to tell them to remember you. They'll know to get you."

She nods and steps back. I program my mom's and sister's numbers into her phone.

"Be careful, Enzo."

"I will. I'll see you soon."

Chapter Eight

Chellie

It's been nine days. I didn't hear from Enzo for the first three. His oldest brother, Luca, called me. I guess Enzo gave him my number. I'm glad he let me know Enzo wouldn't be home for dinner. But then I had to wait thirty-six hours to hear from anyone again. The next thing I knew, Enzo was calling me from the airport, and I could hear engines in the background. He said he had to travel for a few days. I didn't ask where, and he didn't volunteer.

It's been a long and lonely week. Nine days shouldn't have felt like nine hundred years when we just started dating. But it didn't feel like we'd only gone out a couple times. Not with the way things stood between us when he left. It felt like we'd always been together. It felt like I was on my way to happily ever after. But now I'm not so sure. I haven't spoken to him since he was at the airport. I don't know if he'll feel the same way when he gets back. I know I do. I know with even more certainty that I want exactly what we talked about.

I talked to my sister, Elizabeth, about the guy I was dating. I was evasive, and she pointed it out. I said I didn't want to jinx it. But I needed to tell someone how much I'm into Enzo and how much I miss him. For the first time in a long time, I didn't feel like I could share what's going on with Laura. I know she'd get it, but it sucks that I can't talk to the one person who'd understand better than anyone. But my sister is an awesome listener who doesn't try to fix things unless I ask. She lets me talk to work things out.

I've been lost in my daydreams for hours upon hours this week. I'm *way* behind on my work. Like if my boss finds out, I'll never have a weekend or vacation day again. But I can't concentrate. Part of it is worry that he's changed his mind. Part of it is fantasizing about a future with him. I'm practically ready to doodle *Mrs. Michelle Mancinelli* or, if I really wanted to go old-fashioned, *Mrs. Lorenzo Mancinelli.* I rather like that one. With so many Mr. Mancinellis in the family, it must make it confusing when someone says mister or missus. I like the idea of people knowing that not only would I be a Mancinelli wife, I would be Enzo's.

The hardest thing has been keeping this from Laura. I've been cagey when I've seen her. I went to the park with her and Christina and their three kids. Laura has twins, Konstantin and Mila, and Christina has a son, Lev. They're the cutest kids and all inherited their fathers' ice-blue eyes. As toddlers, it's already clear to see Konstantin will be the spitting image of Maks, and Lev will be a mirror of Bogdan. Mila looks a lot like Laura except for the eyes. The girl is an old soul. In the past, I've thought about how nice it would be to have a family like my friends do.

But this was the first time I looked at their kids and thought about what mine would look like with a specific man. What they would look like if they were fifty percent mine and fifty percent Enzo's. I liked what I saw. It made my heart hurt as much as it excited me. Would my children and Laura's grow up to hate one another? Would they grow up knowing they're mortal enemies? Would kids be what finishes my most cherished friendship?

My daydreaming made Laura ask questions. Thank goodness I'm a lawyer too, or I would have felt like I was being cross-examined. As is, I felt like I was practically giving a deposition as she kept asking me about last week. What I did. Where I went. Who I saw. Who I'm going to the gala with.

The gala. I hoped Enzo would take me, but it's tonight. I'm trying to get these fucking fake eyelashes on without smearing the black glue all over my eyelid and fingertips. I know I'm supposed to use the little plastic tweezers, but I feel like I have even less control with them.

There. Both fuckers are on. I finish applying my makeup. I've already coaxed my hair into what is supposed to look like beachy waves. I'm not the greatest at styling my hair, but I think it'll hold. Lord knows I volumized it as much as my fine hair can handle. I've pulled the sides up, so they won't fall in my eyes. It shows off the earrings my parents gave me for my eighteenth birthday. I slide an amethyst ring onto my right ring finger before clasping a matching bracelet and necklace.

I look at my left hand, and my daydreams come back. The way Enzo and I talked, it might not be long before I have an engagement ring. Then again, it could have all been ridiculous dirty talk, and I'm living in fantasy land.

I look in the mirror one more time as I run my hands over my floor length champagne-colored evening gown. I attend a lot of these functions since they're all fundraisers for my clients. I have a collection of gorgeous gowns and cocktail dresses that cost more than the condo I live in. I wish I could write them off as a business uniform expense.

I've tried the rental websites, but it's almost guaranteed I'll need something altered. Sometimes it's having the hem length shortened. Sometimes it's having the straps shortened. Sometimes it's having the waist taken in. I never buy a dress that I'm unwilling to wear at least five times before I consider it an investment paid off. It's not like I go to an event every week, but in spring and summer, I often have three or four in a week. The guest lists often overlap.

All right. I'm as ready as I'll ever be. I grab my wrap and purse. I call for an Uber and head downstairs. When I step outside because it says my ride is almost here, I find a black town car parked out front.

"Ms. Russo?"

"Yes."

"I'm Afonso. Mr. Mancinelli sent me."

I look between him and the car. I don't know him, and I'm scared to get in. Just as I'm about to say no, and the Uber shows up, my phone pings.

"Hold on, please."

LORENZO

The car is for you. You're safe with Afonso. I wish I were in the car waiting for you.

I can't help but smile.

ME

Thanks.

"I just need to cancel the Uber."

I walk over to the car and lean forward. The driver already looks pissed. I can't blame him.

"I'm sorry. I didn't know a car service was coming. Can you record it as though I actually got in?"

"No."

Ok. Sorry, dude. No need to be that rude. He's looking at me like the saleswoman in *Pretty Woman* who thought Julia Roberts was a hooker. I mean she was. But I'm not. I open my purse and pull out a twenty-dollar bill and hand it to him.

"Hope that helps."

I don't wait for him to say anything else. I walk back to the car, where Afonso is standing with the door open. I slide in and notice the privacy glass is up. He closes the door before I can tell him where to take me, so he obviously already knows. I sit back and watch the blocks whip past.

I didn't fall back to sleep after Enzo left in the middle of the night. I showered and got dressed. Then I headed home. I didn't fall back to sleep there either. Both beds felt empty without him, and he's never even been in mine. Now I wish he was in it every night.

We get to the hotel quickly, but it takes forever for our turn to pull up. Someone from the hotel opens my door, but I find the button to drop the privacy glass.

"Thank you, Afonso. I appreciate it."

"My pleasure, Ms. Russo."

I leave the glass down and accept the hand offered to me. I adjust my wrap as I head toward the door. Normally, I love to look around and see who I recognize. I'm nosey enough to wonder who certain people's dates are or whether couples who can't stand one another can play nice. But tonight, I just want to get inside. I don't want to think about other people who have a date.

"Good evening, Ms. Russo."

A shiver runs down my spine at the slimy voice. Fuck my life. He would be the first person I encounter. I turn around.

"Mr. Shapiro."

"You look lovely this evening."

"Thank—"

"My girlfriend always looks lovely."

I startle as an arm slips around my waist. I look up at Enzo. Holy fuck. He's the hottest man I've ever seen. Hottest man on the planet. I lean into him, so glad to have him near me to begin with, but even more so as Simon Shithead Shapiro gawks at us.

"You're really with..."

Simon trails off as Lorenzo kisses the top of my head, then glares at him.

"Yes, Mr. Shapiro. Lorenzo is my boyfriend."

"Boy—"

"Soon-to-be fiancé."

I try to hide my surprise as his fingers press tighter into my waist. I look up at him again, and I see nothing but sincerity in his gaze. I loop my arm around his waist and forget about Simon as Enzo offers me a chaste kiss. He whispers to me.

"I missed you, *mia piccolina*."

"I missed you, too, D."

That's the closest I can come in public. Enzo shifts his gaze back to Simon, and the man realizes we've caught him sneering at us.

"I told you to stay away from Ms. Russo. Maybe you didn't understand me because you were so scared you were going to die that night. Let me make it clear to you now. You speak to my girlfriend as your lawyer and nothing else. You make sure every communication is professional. You don't chat. You don't get her alone. You don't approach her. You don't do a damn thing that might make a possessive and protective boyfriend like me decide he wants to chat with you. Back off."

"Or what, Mancinelli? You going to threaten me in a room with a hundred people?"

"I don't threaten, Shapiro. I promise. So hear me very well right now. I promise you will not like what happens if Ms. Russo even blinks when she hears your name. Who here is going to stop me? I know who you are now. I know who you owe money to, which happens to include my family. If I don't deal with you, the Kutsenkos, Diazes, or O'Rourkes will. I wouldn't mind having any of those three families indebted to me, so I might just turn you over to them. Unless you want us to collect what you owe tonight while you're here, stay away."

"He owes people money?"

Enzo glances down at me before he smirks at Simon.

"Shapiro, I happen to be many things. But one of them is a forensic accountant. Imagine what I discovered while on a long flight with nothing to do but examine every financial statement ever issued to you or through you. You have a funny way of managing money. It makes it look like you have more money in one bank than you do, while another bank is supposed to have next to nothing but really holds it all. My brother could be in the Caymans before morning."

I watch Shapiro's eyes nearly fall out of his head. What the fuck is Enzo talking about?

"*Cuore*, on Monday morning, you need to call your company's accountants and have them audit all the Once A Warrior Foundation's books."

Rage pulses through me. I take a step closer, but Enzo tries to stop me. I shake him off.

"You've been embezzling money from a foundation for service members?"

He doesn't answer.

"I have been with that organization since the day it started. My brother's name is on the plaque beneath the foundation's name when you step off the elevator. You're stealing from families like mine whose husband, brother, father, son didn't come home the way he left. Ones whose wife, sister, mother, daughter didn't come home the way she left. You piece of shit." My voice drops. "I see how you fear Lorenzo because he's a

Mancinelli. Fear me far more, Simon. I will take everything you have ever had. I will take your family. I will take your home. I will take your cars and boats and beach houses. I will take your money and your assets. I will take your reputation. And I will take every last shred of your dignity. Only then will I hand you over to Lorenzo to do whatever he wants. I promise you, you picked the wrong lawyer to fuck with. Leave before I start making calls right now."

He shifts his gaze to Enzo then back to me before he tucks tail and scurries away. It feels better than heaven when my boyfriend wraps his arms around me. I melt against him.

"You look stunning, little one. And what you just said — I'm ready to drag you into a dark corner and have my way with you. That was hot."

"I'm so glad you're here, Daddy."

I'm whispering, but right now, I don't care who hears me. Enzo is here, and he's holding me.

"I told you I'd come with you. I wasn't about to let you come with someone else or by yourself. If it wasn't Shapiro, I figured it would be some other douchebag since I knew you'd be gorgeous."

"You look very debonair in your tux."

"Thank you. I missed you, Chellie."

"I missed you, too. I didn't think you'd make it. I wasn't really looking forward to it, but now I can enjoy it."

"I'm sorry I had to be away so long."

I just nod. I don't know what to say. His hand slides dangerously close to my ass for a moment before he lets go of me.

"I had to go to Belgium and the Netherlands."

It surprises me he's telling me that. Does that mean it was legit business?

"Diamonds. Antwerp is the world's diamond capital, and the Netherlands has been known for them for like six hundred years. I had to meet with several buyers and influential people who help set pricing."

I force myself not to look at my left hand. But when Enzo brushes his thumb over my left ring finger, I can only stare at him. He kisses my cheek before we look for our seats. I'm just about to sit when I notice a couple walking through the door.

"Oh, fuck."

I mutter under my breath, and Enzo follows my gaze.

"Pasha and Sumiko?"

"Yeah. I haven't told Laura anything. I don't know them well, but we know each other. They'll tell Laura before the first course. I need to call her before either of them text her. Shit."

I look around and see the doors to the terrace are open. I tilt my head toward them, and we head outside. I pull out my phone and grit my teeth.

"Hey, boo."

She sounds much happier than she's going to be.

"Hey. I can only chat for a moment, but I need to tell you something."

"That you're dating Enzo? Yeah. I know."

My stomach knots.

"Are you mad at me?"

"Of course not. I wish you'd liked Bogdan when you met him or Aleks or Niko. But those wouldn't have been good matches, even if I wished it made you my sister for real. If you have to be with one of the Mancinellis, Enzo's the only one worth anything."

"Laura!"

"What? I'm certain he's right there with you. Maks said he got back from wherever he went about an hour ago. I figured he'd go straight to the event to see you. I'm also guessing Pasha and Sumiko just walked in if you're calling me from there."

"I—"

"I wish you'd told me sooner, but no one understands better than I do why you hesitated. I may have issues with Lorenzo's family, but none are personally directed at him. Sergei says he's very protective of you."

"Sergei? How the hell does—"

"*Piccolina*, the moment Laura figured it out — which was undoubtedly before any of the men in her family — she told Sergei to watch out for you. Carmine says Sergei or Anton have followed you all week."

I stare at Enzo while I wait for Laura to say something. She remains quiet.

"Did you hear what Enzo said? Is it true that Sergei and Anton have been following me?"

"Of course. Never mind that you've been seen in public with Lorenzo. The moment I heard he was traveling, I asked them to watch out for you."

"Laura?"

"Yes, Enzo."

"Did you assume I wouldn't have someone guarding her? Or do you assume my men aren't good enough?"

"Short of the men in my family, no one is good enough for my best friend. You'll do."

"Laura!"

I gasp at that last comment. She's dead serious, but she didn't have to say it. At least, not when Enzo could hear.

"Good. I'm glad we're on the same page. You can have whoever you want follow Chellie. But they stay out of it."

"Until they're needed. Your pride means nothing to me."

I listen to them go back and forth as though I'm not the one holding the phone.

"Are you both finished? Laura, this was a courtesy call."

"No. It was a 'I better tell on myself before someone else

does.' You've done that since we were kids. I was the 'say nothing unless they can prove it' kid."

"Yeah, well, between the two of us, we did all kinds of shit and barely ever got in trouble. I trusted Maks, and now I need you to trust Lorenzo."

"When's the wedding?"

"Laura! Stop."

I seem to exclaim her name a lot tonight.

"Whatever. We wouldn't be having this conversation if you weren't already practically living together."

"You seem to know so much. He's been gone for more than a week."

"And you barely went out the week after running into each other at the movies. I've watched eight other syndicate marriages happen since mine. I know how this goes. As long as you're safe and happy, I won't get in the way. Even if he is a Mancinelli. I might hold that against him, but I won't hold it against you. Lorenzo, the moment she's in danger or you make her unhappy, it won't be my husband, brothers, or cousins coming after you. It'll be me."

From Enzo's smile, I'd say he believes her, but he also respects her even more.

"Just don't send Ana. You know she terrifies Uncle Sal."

"I've already talked to Maks, Chellie. He's not thrilled, but he accepts this. He knows better than to even think about this affecting our friendship. He sure as shit won't say a word about it. Lorenzo, I know she'll pick you. Don't be a douche and make her."

"Laura, I'm glad she's friends with you. And not just because it meant Chellie and I met properly. There are details you will never share from your family. But Chellie has you, and you know what this is like. The women in my family will welcome Chellie, but you're already as close as sisters. I hope you can help make this easier for her."

"Chellie, I want to talk to you alone for a moment, please."

Enzo nods, but I know he wouldn't stop me even if he didn't like it. I take a few steps away and lower the volume on my phone.

"Yeah?"

"You definitely scored the hottest one in the family. You got yourself a Maks."

"Doesn't everyone say Pasha is the pretty one?"

"He is. Maks is the hottest."

"Are you seriously not mad that I didn't tell you?"

"Lanie will be. But you know I understand. I'm certain he's told you what to do if something goes wrong. Go to his family first. Always. But if you can't get to him, nothing's changed. Come to mine. Everyone knows how close we are. We'll always protect you no matter who you marry."

"You make it sound like that's a foregone conclusion."

"With these men, it is. The moment he decided on a first date, you might as well have signed a marriage license. They don't play around. If you're not absolutely certain already, then you better get certain fast. If you don't think you can do this, end it. Because when he falls in love with you, there's nothing he won't do for you. You'll break his heart if you don't feel the same. Nothing will ever be more important to these men than their families. You can understand why. To him, you're already as good as part of his."

I'm watching Enzo as I talk to my best friend, the wife of the head of the Russian ma — bratva.

"I don't think I'm in love yet, but I'm sure I'm three-quarters of the way there. I understood what Maks meant to you from the start. But now that I feel the same thing for Enzo that you must have felt about Maks, I feel shitty that I wasn't more supportive. I wasn't as onboard with you and Maks as you are about Enzo and me."

"I've been in this life for three years now. I'm in a different place. I can be happy and scared for you at the same time. Just promise me one more thing."

"Sure."

"Listen to Lorenzo and trust him. You might not like it. You might not understand it. You might not agree with it. But he will put you first even when he thinks he can't. When he tells you to do or not to do something, it's for a reason. Don't ask questions. Just do it."

"I will. I gotta go. The dinner's about to start."

"Have fun, Chellie Belly."

I giggle.

"Bye, Laura Snora."

When we were nine, she and her little sister had to sleep over at my house because her parents went out of town. She shared my room and had a sinus infection. She sounded like a chainsaw. I teased her mercilessly for a week, and the nickname stuck. She calls me Chellie Belly because of a trick I could do as a kid where I could basically make my tummy roll up and down but also side to side. I can't do it anymore, but the nickname stuck.

"Everything all right?"

"Yeah, Daddy. Don't frown. It'll give you wrinkles."

I stretch and kiss his cheek.

"Laura's cool with everything?"

"Yes. She gave me some good advice. I wish I'd been more understanding when she and Maks got together."

"You knew nothing about this world then. You were rightfully scared for your friend. It's different for you."

"I know. I thought I got how she felt about Maks when they

started dating, but I realize now that I didn't. Not until you strode into my life and made me fall for you."

"I made you, huh?"

He pulls my chair out for me before I sit. I lean over to him.

"Yeah. You do this thing with your tongue and with your fingers. And the things you do with your cock. How could I not?"

"So, you only like me for my body?"

"It is a temple."

"Will you worship it tonight?"

"Tonight, and all the others to come."

"I'll hold you to that, *piccolina*."

I slide my hand up his thigh now that he's seated next to me. The tablecloth hides me when I cup his dick.

"I'll do the same, D."

I let go of him, but he presses my hand against his thigh before releasing it. We're forced to make small talk throughout the dinner, but once the dancing starts, I realize he's skilled.

"My mom thought we should all learn to ballroom dance. For some reason, she was certain we'd need the skills later in life."

"Apparently, you do."

He grins and nods. I narrow my eyes.

"What aren't you saying?"

He glances toward where I saw Pasha and his wife dancing. He looked just as graceful as Lorenzo.

"My mom and aunts knew it would make us agile and light on our feet. Ballroom dancing was more acceptable than ballet, so that's where they stuck us. None of us understood until we were older. We realized at first when we became high school athletes. Then it dawned on all of us they want us agile for more than just sports."

"Oh."

What do I say to that? The moms wanted to be sure their sons could dodge knives and bullets. He watches me as he tells me this insight into his family. Is he testing me? Is he nervous I'll run away?

"Well, your dance instructor did a good job. You could compete."

He grins and shakes his head before he juts his chin toward Pasha Kutsenko.

"You know, they all had to learn too back when they still lived in Russia."

I already knew. Pasha is Maks, Aleks, Niko, and Bogdan's cousin. Anton is his older brother. Their other cousin, Sergei, has a younger brother named Misha. The men are like a defensive line when they stand together. You'd never imagine they once took ballroom dancing, but it's a joke among the wives. It has nothing to do with their moves on a dance floor.

"I'd heard. Did your sister have to take lessons too?"

"Yes. And she hated it the most."

"Why?"

"Because when we had to practice at home, she was the only one any of us the guys could or would partner with. It meant her practices were like four times as long as each of ours, and I don't know how her toes survived. Trust me. She's paid us back in spades."

I bite my bottom lip before I smile.

"*Piccolina*, you'll meet her, and you'll get along like long-lost friends. I know your loyalty is to Laura. But I think you'll like my sister and the others."

"I don't doubt that."

"You're worried they won't like you."

"I have an Italian last name, but that's about as far as it goes. And to top it off, my best friend is the *pakhan's* wife."

I know little Russian, but I know that's what they call their leader. It's the equivalent of don, which I know is Enzo's uncle's position.

"It's not just Italian, it's Sicilian and southern Italian. Do you know when your dad's family came to America?"

"Yeah. 1906. I read once that more than a hundred-thousand Sicilians came to America that year."

"Do you know what part they came from?"

"Trapani. They went to New Orleans and settled there for a few years before coming to New York. It was my grandparents who moved to Jersey. They sent my grandfather to Vietnam as an engineer. He got injured and met my grandmother while she was a nurse. When they both came home, they got married and moved close to her family. He did well for himself, so it meant my dad went to private school and a good university for undergrad and grad school. It meant we got to live in the same neighborhood as Laura, and Juan and Pablo Diaz."

"How well did you know Juan?"

"He was Laura's oldest friend. They'd lived next door to each other since they were toddlers. Laura and I became friends in elementary school. Sometimes I wasn't sure if I was following them, or Juan was following us. During high school, we added our friend Lanie, and Juan hung out with the guys more. But the Doyles and Diazes always had Sunday dinner together. I went plenty of times. I — um — had a crush on Pablo in high school."

"You did?"

"You can wipe that shit-eating grin off your face."

"And why's that?"

I look around, spotting Pasha and Sumiko again. I know Sumiko went out with Pablo for a few months, but had no idea what he was or what it meant. I've always known his family was into something with a Cartel. It just wasn't until college that I realized Pablo's dad, Luis, was a big deal and that Pablo would become a big deal one day. But I never learned any specifics.

"Because Pablo was the first guy I had sex with."

"What?"

He stops, and a couple bumps into us. He looks around before picking up the beat.

"It was the summer between my junior and senior year of high school."

"Were you seventeen?"

"Yeah."

"That motherfucker is a predator. That was statutory."

"He was nineteen. The age of consent in New Jersey is sixteen. It wasn't a crime."

He shoots me a look. It's easy to understand.

"*I* got *him* drunk."

"He knew what the hell was going on. Being drunk only meant he was lucky he got it up."

"That was a long time ago, Daddy. It only happened a few times, and it's been over—"

"Just how many is a few, Chellie?"

I look over his shoulder.

"The entire summer. But that was more than ten years ago. I haven't exchanged more than ten words with him in the three years Laura's been married. Even before that, it was only when I happened to be at Laura's parents' house, and they hosted Sunday dinner. I talked to him at their wedding reception."

"You danced with him."

"You remember that?"

"Believe me, I noticed everything about you that night."

"If you weren't Italian, I would have tried to hook up with you. Let you take the drunk bridesmaid home and all. Daddy, he and I are not friends anymore. We're on friendly terms in public, but it's not like I call him or text him. The Doyles never do Sunday dinner with the Diazes anymore. There has been nothing between us in a decade. And frankly, after the other night, none of my past partners are worth remembering."

"You liked it?"

"You know I did."

"Once we can leave, we are. Do you want to go to your place or mine? Think about where you want to spend the next week or so. If it's my place, we stop by yours and get everything you need. If it's your place, we stop by mine, and I get a week's worth of clothes."

"I don't care where we go. I just don't want to sleep alone again, Enzo."

"Neither do I. Your place then."

"Yours is way bigger and nicer."

"Yours feels like a home. Mine feels like a condo."

"I like your place, but mine is a bit more — inviting."

"Haha. Mine feels sterile in comparison. I'm not as much of a homebody as I would like. I'm out a lot of nights, Chellie. I own a nightclub and a few restaurants. I work security at other clubs my family owns. I've never given it much thought beyond a comfortable bed and a desk big enough to spread out reports."

"Other clubs?"

I think I know what he means, and I already hate it. He kisses my temple, and I lean against him. But we're aware we're at a work event for me, so we keep it appropriate.

"Yes. You know I mean strip clubs. Carmine never enjoyed going to them, but he owned them because we do other kinds of business there. He was glad to hand them over to Matteo when he and Serafina got together. Then Matteo married my sister, and Marco wound up responsible for them. I still work security some nights, and I have meetings there. Chellie, I'm not into strippers. I don't watch them. I don't pay them. I don't date them or fuck them."

I can only nod. I don't consider myself an insecure person, but neither do I think I'm hot. It's unnerving to know my boyfriend spends his nights around naked women.

"I know you're trying to keep your expression neutral, but I can tell how you feel, *piccolina*. Marco and I are the only ones left who aren't married. My family already knows about you. My brother won't dare argue when I tell him I'm no longer working at them. I can't change who we meet there or why we do. It's where the nice men of society do business with the unsavory ones like us. It's where they want to measure dicks and always come up short. It's a mostly cash business which has other benefits. The strip clubs aren't going away, but eventually, none of us will actually work at them. When Marco marries, they'll probably come to me just because I'm an accountant. I won't have to go to the office there, but I will oversee their management."

All I can do is nod. He must have hated hearing about my past with Pablo because I sure as fuck hate hearing that he's near naked women. There is no way they don't hit on him. He's sex in a suit. I shrug one shoulder.

"I don't mind them. I've been to a few. It can be hot."

"Do you want me to take you to one?"

"We could, if you want."

"Little girl, we can go to all of them, so the women know I'm with you."

"Am I that transparent?"

"No. I just know I'd be losing my ever-loving shit right now if you told me you worked at a male strip club."

"Oh, I've been to the Hanger Club several times."

That stops him dead again. He leads me off the dance floor, and I have to practically trot to keep up. He slows down as we cross the ballroom and head back out to the terrace. He looks around and draws me into the shadows. He fists my hair and grabs my ass mercilessly.

"You sounded awfully flippant about going to see men walk around with their dicks in your face."

"You know men's clubs aren't fully nude."

"No, but the height of the stage puts their junk right in your face. I know they walk around and offer lap dances the same as at female clubs. I know they try to offer more than just a dance to women as hot as you."

He isn't wrong. More than one has tried to slide his hand up my skirt, and it's been tempting to let a few. But I never have.

"I know you don't go with Laura or the women in her family, so who? When was the last time?"

"I went with Laura before she got married. I have friends other than her. I've been for some birthdays and bachelorette parties. The last time was about a month ago."

His hold on me tightens as he presses his leg between mine. There isn't a lot of give to my dress, but there's a slit in the back that he tugs up.

"No panties. Good girl."

He slides his fingers down my ass crack until he can slip three into me. I'm already soaked. He groans when he feels it.

"Is this from thinking about those strippers?"

"You know it's not. You know I've been like this since the moment I heard your voice. From the moment you touched me, I haven't wanted anything more than for you to fuck me. Daddy, you know damned well it's different. Me going every once in a while versus you working there regularly. Those women make money selling the idea of sex. How am I supposed to know that my drop-dead gorgeous boyfriend is around naked women all night and not react? I trust you. I don't trust them."

"That's completely fair. It doesn't mean I like knowing you've gotten wet for other men. First, you tell me you used to sleep with Pablo. Now, I know you enjoy seeing other men mostly naked."

"Enzo, you would get hired somewhere like that just from a manager seeing you stand outside the door. You'd make more money than any other guy there. Your body is like a fucking Armani model. Going there or not is entirely my choice, and I have no reason to check out men in banana hammocks when I can be in bed with you."

"In bed. On a dresser. On a table. On a counter. Against a wall. Against a door. In a tub. In a shower. I will fuck you everywhere in my place and yours. You won't be able to walk into either place without knowing I fucked you there, and you're mine."

His fingers work my pussy, and I ache. I can't help rocking against his thigh, desperately needing release.

"I want to go home. I don't care if the speeches aren't all done. I don't want to stay. Please, can we go?"

"Do you need to come?"

"Yes. But I really just want to be alone with you."

My hands grip his upper arms, and a wave of emotion sideswipes me. I don't know where the urge to cry comes from. It makes no sense.

"Chellie?"

"I missed you too much. I don't want to share you anymore. I want to be alone with you."

"Too much? Is that as in you don't want to do this again?"

"No. Too much as in I'm embarrassed now. I feel clingy and stupid, and I just want to go."

He turns us, so we're completely in the shadows. If we

137

remain quiet, no one will know we're here. He pulls my dress up, and I bunch it around my waist. He leans to whisper in my ear.

"I'm going to make it better, *cuore*. Then I'll take you home, and we'll run a bath. I'm going to make love to you all night because I missed you too much too. We're out here because I was being clingy and stupid. I need you, but all I want is to make you sigh my name. Come for me."

His fingers work me as his thumb rubs my clit. I grip his arms as I try to balance in my ridiculous heels when I feel like my legs will give out. His mouth meets mine, and his swallows my moans. I suck his tongue, letting him know just what I want to do to his cock. I can feel my orgasm building as I squeeze my eyes shut.

"Mmm-uh."

I come, and tears burn the back of my eyelids. Why do we have to have such intensely personal conversations? Why do I have to be falling in love with him already? He pulls his fingers from me and pulls out a handkerchief from his trouser pocket. Who knew men still carried those? He licks the fingers that were just inside me before wiping them. He offers it to me, and I feel my face flush. I take it and try to turn around, but he snatches it back.

"There's no point in turning around when I've already buried my face between your thighs. I said I would take care of you, and I will."

He's gentle as he wipes the stickiness from my pussy and thighs. He folds the handkerchief several times before shoving it in his pocket.

"Let's get your wrap and go."

"I don't want to talk if anyone stops us. I want to get in the car and suck you off."

He pauses and stares at me. I can barely see his face, but I can guess he looks surprised. He takes my hand and practically drags me back into the hotel just like he did off the dance floor. We rush back to our table and are about to beat a hasty retreat.

"Ms. Russo."

Fuckity, fuck, fuck, fuck.

"Hello, Ms. Martinez. It's nice to see you again."

"Same. That's a lovely gown. How have you been?"

She's talking to me, but she's looking at Enzo. Is there something between them? She's sizing him up, and I'm pretty sure her eyes just lingered on his groin.

"I'm well. Let me introduce you to my boyfriend, Lorenzo Mancinelli."

"Boyfriend? It's a pleasure to meet you, Lorenzo."

"The same, Ms. Martinez."

Neither sounds that familiar with each other after all. Enzo definitely doesn't like the informality.

"Your Salvatore's nephew, right?"

"One of them."

The ice in his voice could chill a polar bear.

"My company is awaiting a bid from your developers for a new office complex in the Bronx."

"Thank you for considering us."

Enzo smiles and drapes my wrap around my shoulders. There couldn't be a clearer sign that we're about to leave.

"Michelle, did you know the foundation is looking to expand and will occupy some floors in that new building?"

"I didn't. What a small world."

"It is. I can't wait to see your boyfriend's proposal."

"Ms. Martinez, that proposal will come from either my brother or my cousin. They handle our construction department. I'll be sure to tell them you said hello. Now we must say goodnight. We have another commitment."

He presses his hand against the small of my back, and I turn to lead the way.

"Michelle, I'll stop by your office tomorrow. I'm sure we can update the contracts for this project and slip in Mancinelli Developers where the named party goes."

Bitch.

"I have several meetings tomorrow. Email me when you decide for certain who'll do the build. I'll finish the contracts and courier them to you. Goodnight, Barbara."

Get me the fuck out of here.

Chapter Nine

Lorenzo

Luigi is waiting for us when we step outside. I gave Afonso the rest of the night off once I got here. I knew I was only a few minutes behind him and Michelle. Otherwise, I would have insisted his brother, Alonzo, go with him. One to drive and one to guard. I caught a glimpse of her as we pulled up.

I knew I wouldn't make it to her place in time since I was changing into my tux in the car. I came straight from the airport, and Luigi had the monkey suit in the trunk. It's a damn good thing my parents forced me to go to these stupid shindigs since I was a teenager. I can tie a bowtie in my sleep.

I wait while Michelle slides into the car and whisper to Luigi, telling him we're stopping by my place, then going to hers. Once the door is closed, I lift my girlfriend onto my lap. My hand slides under her dress and up her thigh, back toward the promised land.

"Enzo, I want to taste you."

"Later. Pull your dress up."

I help her, and she gathers it around her waist like she did on the terrace. I move her to straddle me, then I hurry to unfasten my pants. Then I'm inside her, where I belong.

"Fuck, Chellie."

"I know. I missed you so much."

Nine days away from her was the worst torture I've ever endured. We made some progress, learning more about the men who took Aunt Sylvia, but we still don't know everything. The trip to Europe came out of nowhere, but I was the one most available to deal with a transaction crisis. No one knew why I was pissed about going, but I made my displeasure known. Buying and selling diamonds shouldn't have been that difficult.

She swoops in for a kiss, and I love every second of her forcefulness. Her need for me. It matches mine for her. She rides me as she holds onto the headrest. Her silky hair hangs down her back, and I love the waves. It's different from how I've seen it before, but I don't think they're natural. It's something special for tonight, and I'm glad I didn't miss it. She was like an angel, and somehow I've redeemed myself enough for God to let me into heaven to see her.

Our kiss builds until I'm yanking at her zipper, tugging down her dress, and tossing her strapless bra against the far door. She's pulled my bowtie off and is close to popping the buttons off my dress shirt. Then we're skin to skin again. My hands run up and down her back, over her arms, and around her waist. They skim along the outside of her thighs and down to her ankles. I want to touch every inch of her, and I wish her gown didn't cover any of her.

"Please may I come, Daddy?"

"Fuck yes, little one."

She nips at my lip and fists a handful of my hair as her cunt squeezes my dick like she plans to get every drop of cum wrung out of it. I wrap my left arm around her and flip us, so she's lying down. I move her hands to hold the end of the seat. Then I lose it. I thought I'd only had threads of self-control left that night at my place, but I held back more than I thought. Now I thrust over and over, and her moans are a mix of pleasure and pain. She watches me, and I pant out my question.

"What's your safe word?"

"Prunes."

"Use it if you need to."

"I know. I need more, Enzo. I won't break."

I lean forward, lacing the fingers on my left hand with hers where they still hold on to the seat. The other hand braces against the door as I pound into her. I feel like a savage. An animal that's paced in its cage for too long and demands to be set free. This isn't like the rough sex I've had before at my club.

This isn't about dominance and submission. This isn't about who's in control. This is about me pouring everything I have into making Michelle know how much I need her. This is about making her as addicted to me as I am to her. This is about giving every single bit of me to her. And that is fucking terrifying.

"Fuck... Yes... More, Enzo... More."

"No. More and I will have no control. I will hurt you, Chellie."

"No, you won't. I know you can't."

"I won't risk it."

"Trust me, Daddy. I'll stop us if it's too much. Please. Just let go."

I hit my breaking point. I can't deny her, and I don't want to deny myself. Sweat drips down my back and from my forehead. Her skin glistens from her own perspiration, and her pupils are fully dilated. I see the trust in her gaze, and it melts me. There is no reservation there. It's just pure openness. I want this woman for forever.

I bite her shoulder, not hard enough to leave any lasting marks. I release her hand and pinch her nipple as hard as I dare. She screams and bucks underneath me, but I don't relent. She whimpers, and I think I've gone too far. It's like a bucket of cold water, but before it splashes across me, she whispers in my ear.

"Don't you dare fucking stop. I want to be so sore that I can't think about anything but you for the next week. I want you to fill me with your cum until it drips out around your cock. Show me how much you need my pussy. Show me that the only woman you're ever going to fuck is me."

"Your pussy and your body are mine to do whatever the fuck I want, *piccolina*. If I want to fuck you hard or fuck you slow, I decide. Don't tell me what to do, or you won't like how I edge you. I'll come all over your tits and face. I'll make you wear my cum for the rest of the night."

"I'll tell you exactly what I want, Enzo. Tell me you'll edge me, but we both know how much you want to come inside me. You aren't pulling out until you have no more cum to jiz. It feels too good to stop, and you are way too possessive not to take what I give you and show me just how much control you have."

"You know me so well already. Not only will you be sore in the morning, you're going to bed with my handprints across your ass."

I pull out and yank her upward. I maneuver her onto her hands and knees before slamming back into her. We can see ourselves in the window's reflection. I rest my hand between her shoulder blades as the other grips her hip. I trail my fingers down each side of her spine before my palm lands on her ass over and over between thrusts.

"Argh! Yes!"

"Fucking take my cock."

"Yes, Daddy."

It's her turn to press her hand against the door to brace herself. My hand leaves her hip and grabs her hair. I tug her head back and lean over her. I kiss her neck, her jaw, her cheek, and the shell of her ear.

"Chellie, what are you doing to me?"

It's a ragged whisper as I fight not to come.

"I don't know. I've never felt like this. It's scary and exciting and..."

I wrap my arm around her waist and thrust one more time. She trembles and cries out. Then I'm coming. I struggle to catch my breath, and as I float down to Earth again, I notice how red her ass is. Fuck. I was way rougher than I realized. Shit. She won't be able to sit for days without being in pain. What the fuck did I do?

I pull out of her and ease her into my arms. I cradle her on my lap and stroke her hair, kissing her forehead.

"I'm so, so sorry, Chellie. I'm sorry."

"What? Why?"

She pushes against my chest and twists to look at me. Her eyes widen with panic.

"Enzo?"

I shake my head as my hand hovers near her ass. Her dress is twisted and knotted around her waist, and I'm worried the outside fabric will chafe her skin.

"Enzo, what's wrong? What happened? Are you hurt?"

"Me? No. It's you. I lost control, and now you really are going to be in pain for days."

"No, I'm not."

She shakes her head. I press my hand to her ass, and she yelps.

"See. I did that to you. I was too rough. I spanked you too

hard and too many times. I fucked you in a car on a seat with next to no padding or give. I probably slammed your head into the door, too. Fucking hell. Why didn't you stop me? Why didn't you safe word?"

"Because I didn't want to. Enzo, stop. Don't ruin this with misplaced guilt. I'm in my thirties. If I didn't want this, I would have said prunes. I'm not a little girl for real. I'm a consenting adult who just had the most mind-blowing sex of my life."

"It was?"

"Yes. I have never felt more desired, more sexy, more anything than just now. I don't know. It was like — like the most feminine I've ever felt. To know you want me that much is exciting, empowering. To be the one you finally let your guard down with makes me feel — special."

"That's how I want you to feel. But I'm still scared I hurt you, Chellie. You just don't realize it yet."

She looks around and realizes we've been outside my building for a while. Luigi won't dare open the door until I rap on the window. He's likely leaning against the trunk, rolling his eyes. I'm absolutely positive we aren't the first couple to have sex in this car. It's why they get washed so fucking often. Half of us were probably conceived in the back of cars, since our parents are no better than any of us, even though they might pretend like they are.

Next time, we're taking a limo and not a fucking town car. She holds up her dress and once again straddles me. She kisses my cheek before pressing a soft kiss to my lips. She eases my head against her chest and holds me for a moment. Then she lifts to rest her weight on her knees. She offers me her right breast, and I suck. Why the fuck is this so calming? Do I have some kind of Oedipus Complex? Was I breastfed too long? Not long enough?

The longer I worship her breast, the calmer I feel. She's

stroking my head and my back, and it's the most soothing thing I can remember since I was a kid.

"I know we need to get out, but let me take care of you for a moment, Daddy."

That's what it is. It's feeling taken care of. I never imagined I needed this, and I don't know that I did before I discovered I could have this tenderness with Michelle. I turn my head and kiss her sternum before kissing up between her collar bones.

"My sweet *piccolina*. Thank you."

"Enzo, look at me for a moment. We both like it when you're in control. I think we just proved that. Nothing has ever made me feel more special than knowing you want to take care of me and be with me. I cherish it. I feel cherished. But this goes both ways. I want you to know that you're safe with me. That you can be a tough ass to everyone else. But if you just want a breather now and then, all you have to do is let me hold you. I'll shield you from the world. *No one* will get past me. I can promise you that. I definitely don't think I'm a Mommy Domme, and you sure as fuck are *not* a little. I can't even picture that. Like it does not compute. But when I see you upset like that, feeling guilty over something you didn't do, something inside me just wants to hold you against me. I want to — I don't know — have you suck on my tits. It's calming to me, too. It doesn't exactly feel maternal, but it sorta feels like it might solve the world's problems for a few minutes."

"I definitely don't see myself ever letting you spank me. I have no interest in stuffed animals or fuzzy jammies unless it's for Uncle Sal and Aunt Sylvia's little girls or my niece. I admit I enjoy coloring with them, but I don't want to do that on my own. I cannot imagine you trying to tell me to wear a coat and threatening to put me to bed without dinner if I don't. But there is something incredibly comforting about the way you hug me, about — what do I even call it? Breast sucking? I'm not curious about what your breast milk will taste like. It's not like that."

Will taste like.

I almost flinch when what I said dawns on me.

"Yes, will, Enzo. We talked about kids in a general sense the other night, and I know it was in the middle of sex. But if we're in this for good, then that's our future. I don't see me rocking you to sleep or anything like that. But if it makes you relax and feel as cherished as you make me feel, then I'm definitely not going to stop you."

It also makes me feel fucking vulnerable, but I don't want to run from that. It's an emotion I've tried to avoid whenever it even hints at creeping up. But I feel completely exposed right now, and I don't want to change anything. She wants me to trust her. I do.

"Daddy, you owe me a soak in the tub."

"Let's go, *piccolina*."

We put our clothes back on, and I tap on the window. Luigi nods as I get out and conveniently looks away as Michelle stands. He'll wait for us to come back down. My phone buzzes as she puts her purse and wrap on the entryway table. What the hell?

"Maks, it's rather late—"

"We have a problem. Where's Michelle?"

"With me. Why?"

"Take her to your uncle's. Call me when you get there. Go now."

He hangs up, and I'm left staring at my phone then Michelle.

"What's wrong? What happened to Laura?"

"Nothing. At least I don't think it's her. He wants me to take you to Uncle Salvatore's."

"Is it me?"

I won't lie.

"Probably. Or it could be something that affects my entire family or all our families. That means you too now. Come on."

She looks down at her gown. I know she'd rather be in something more comfortable, but there isn't time to go to her place. I know Aunt Sylvia would offer her something, but they aren't the same size. Chellie is somewhere between Serafina and Maria. I tap Carmine's contact as I open the door and usher Chellie out.

"Are you at Uncle Sal's yet?"

"Hey. We're about to leave."

"Can Sera grab some jeans and a shirt or something like that, please?"

"Why?"

"Michelle and I are coming from her gala. I have clothes there, but she's still in her gown."

Chellie is shaking her head, mortified at what I'm asking. She's never met my family for real. I kiss her temple as we get on the elevator.

"Sure. I'll ask her right now. Fina!"

I hear muffled voices in the background as we ride down to the lobby. Carmine tells me his wife grabbed something, and I tell Luigi the change in plans. I'm on edge, but I don't think Chellie notices. At least, I didn't until she takes my hand, and hers is freezing. I let go and wrap my arm around her, my free hand reaching across my lap to take hers again.

"Should I call Laura?"

"No. I don't know what Maks has or will tell her. Right now, we let Uncle Sal and Maks do the talking until we know what's going on."

"But—"

"No, Chellie. Knowing them, Maks will tell her everything he can. But I don't know what's happening. Don't put her in a position where she has to lie to you to protect her family. And don't freak her out if Maks hasn't spoken to her yet."

She looks down at our joined hands and nods.

"I didn't mean to snap at you. I'm anxious too."

"Do you think something's happened to your family?"

"I have no idea. But I don't like that I've sucked you into this. *Us* just got really real."

"What does that mean? Do you not want to be with me now?"

"No. It means I'm fucking selfish as shit because all I want is to be with you. It means that I'm ready to climb out of my skin not knowing if you're in danger because of me. It means I'm not letting you out of my fucking sight until we're at my uncle and aunt's with fifteen armed guards patrolling the property."

"Look at me."

I turn my head, and her fingertips rest on my jaw.

"I do not freak out until there is a reason to. I'm scared, but I'm not going anywhere you don't tell me to. I'm going to listen to what you and your family say, and I'm going to follow the instructions. You are going to do whatever it is you have to do. Then we are going to climb into bed, and you're going to hold me until we both fall asleep. Whether that's tonight, tomorrow night, or in nine days. If this has anything to do with me, then tell me what you can. If it doesn't, then I won't ask questions. But if this is about me, don't fucking push me away. You will discover very early in this relationship just how stubborn I truly am. Then you'll have no choice but to call Laura because you won't know what the fuck just hit you."

I love her.

The look in her eyes is one I recognize. Every Mafia daughter grows into it. I've seen hints of it in Olivia and Sinead, but Maria and Serafina have had it for far too long. My mother and aunts have it, just like my grandmothers did. It's a resolve that is utterly unwavering. It's a mind that can compartmental-ize. And it's a heart that can weather whatever hurricane is about to blow through and still love anyway. I am marrying this woman.

The hand that was on her shoulder fists her hair as the other comes to rest heavily on her throat. We stare into each other's eyes, and something passes between us. I think it's an understanding that it's us against the world. That we're about to be tested, and we will pass together. I glance down at her lips, and she opens them.

"When we climb into that bed, it won't be to sleep."

"Promise, Daddy?"

"My sweet *piccolina*, you can take that to the bank."

"When this is over, will you take me to your club?"

I didn't expect that.

"Um — Are you sure that's—"

"I won't know until I go. Are you uncomfortable because I'm likely to see who you've fucked?"

"Yes."

"Good."

"What?"

"I won."

She grins, and my hand tightens around her throat. It's not tight. I don't want to scare her.

"Competitive?"

"And fucking possessive. I don't give a shit who you fucked in the past. I don't love the idea of you being around naked women who want to fuck you. But let the women from before see just who took you off the market. Let them know that you're training me to be exactly what you want."

"I'm not training you, Chellie. You're not my sub. We

explore what we like together. I never want our sex to be something I do *to* you. I never want you to just take it."

"That's not what I meant. I guess that was a little sex talk tossed in there. But I'm serious that I can live with meeting those women. I know I'll be jealous, but I can handle that because I know you aren't going back to them. If you didn't want me for keeps, I wouldn't be in this car with you."

No truer words have been spoken. She wouldn't have been at my place if I wasn't serious, and if she had been, I would have sent her home with Luigi and driven myself to this meeting.

"Is there anything specific that intrigues you, *piccolina*?"

She thinks about that for a moment.

"You know I like being restrained. Or rather, unable to move on my own. Like I can only go where you decide. I like it when you press me against the wall. You crowd me, and all I can focus on is you. All I can feel is you. I'd like to be spread eagle for you."

"You like the idea that I'll do whatever I want to you, and you can't stop me."

"Yes."

"Why?"

"Because I trust you to make me vulnerable. The idea makes me feel more desirable than I ever have. You want me so much that you're unwilling to let me go anywhere. You want me so much, and there's nothing I can do to stop you. It feels powerful in its own way."

"It is. When you submit, you're the one who really has control. You say your safe word, and it ends immediately. I don't decide that. You do. When I command you to do things or I do them to you, it's because I want you, and you let me have you. *Piccolina*, I've never wanted any woman the way I want you. You have more power over me than I think you'll ever know."

It's true. And I'm the one feeling vulnerable by admitting that.

"This fucking dress."

She mutters it as she pulls it up her thighs and straddles my lap. Her hands slip under my tux jacket, and two fingers slide between the buttons over the center of my chest.

"Enzo, I don't know all the things we can explore. I don't know if we'll like the same things, though I think we will. I want the pleasure it can bring both of us because you fuck like a porn star." She waggles her eyebrows at me. "But I crave the closeness I think it'll bring us. Do you believe in—"

She shakes her head, embarrassed by what she was going to ask.

"Yes, I believe in soulmates. And yes, you are mine."

She leans forward, nestling against my chest. Her fingers slide farther under my shirt, and I feel her sigh. I rest my cheek on the top of her head. She's not completely relaxed, though.

"What's the matter, *cuore?*"

"Does being soulmates mean we're truly compatible? Like to live to together and have a family?"

"If the other couples in my family are any guide, then it means we're compatible beyond measure. It's not like none of the couples argue. They do. But in the end, they want the same thing. It's just a question of how to get there."

"Lanie is going to shit a brick."

That throws me.

"Huh?"

"Laura, Lanie, and I were the Three Musketeers in high school. We went our separate ways for college, but all wound up here in the city afterwards. When Laura started dating Maks, Lanie and I were terrified for her. But I got over it. Lanie took a fuck ton longer. She refused to go to Laura's wedding. I know she regrets it. They've reconciled, but it's not the same. Not just because Laura is a wife and mom. But because she chose Maks over us. Lanie's going to think me being with you is the ultimate betrayal. It'll be worse than with Laura."

"Because you know how much it bothered her, and now you're going to do the same thing."

"Yes. I feel badly that she's really going to be pushed out. There are things Laura and I will understand about each other she never will. Laura and I will never discuss these things most likely, but we'll just know. Lanie won't."

"Marco's single."

She laughs and sits back, so we can look at each other.

"Marco isn't her type. He's a guy."

"Hmm. My sister's married and not into girls, and the only other females are in elementary school. I've got no one to offer her."

"She wouldn't even if you did. She knows as much about Juan as I do, which is not everything. She knows he fucked Laura over and nearly got her killed. But she sided with him and thought he was the wronged party. She doesn't hold it against Laura, but she holds it against Maks and his entire family. She believes that because Juan was a cop, it automatically made him a better person."

"Juan Diaz was as dirty as the day is long."

"We know. Not only that, we've known since high school that his family was into shady shit. Laura knew more, but Lanie and I understood it had something to do with what we called the mafia. Now I know to call it the Cartel. The reason I brought her up is that I've been friends with her for fifteen years. She knows more about me than anyone but Laura. I feel guilty because I would walk away from her without looking back if I was walking toward you. And this isn't the impetuousness of a new relationship. Even if we stopped dating, I would turn to you. I don't know how to explain why. It's something I just know unequivocally."

"And your family?"

"You'd never ask me to choose, and they won't either. They've asked me questions about Maks and his family. I just give them the same look I give people who ask me questions about clients. They know what it means. She's like another daughter to them. They just want her happy. They'll want the same for me."

"You can't believe it'll be that easy. Laura isn't really their daughter. You are. Once they know my family and I are anything like Maks and his, they won't be so eager."

"My mom is a venture capitalist, and my dad is a hedge fund manager. If anyone can turn a blind eye, it's both of my parents."

"Maybe. But their clients aren't their daughter."

"I know. But they don't assume people are inherently bad when it comes to the things they do for family."

I don't want to argue about it, and I know she's trying to placate me. She's not so naïve as to think this will be easy, but she doesn't want me to walk away out of guilt. I appreciate it, but she's right. I would never ask her to choose between her family and me. If they can't accept me, then I will walk away. Regardless of what she might say, I can't make her give up her family when I can't give up mine.

"Actually, speaking of my parents. They'd like to meet you."

That shocks me even more than her suddenly bringing up Lanie. They know about me?

"Oh?"

"Relax, Daddy. Your thighs are already like steel. I didn't know they could get harder, but they did."

I try to relax, surprised that she noticed I tensed. I thought it was just my gut sucking in.

"What have you told them about me?"

"I told them I met a new guy I'm really into. I told them things are moving really fast, but I'm not swept away in a current. I've really been giving this thought rather than just going with the flow."

"Did you tell them my name? If they work in finance, they must know my family. Shit. What if we've snagged deals away from their clients?"

"I didn't tell them your name, but I asked them that when I brought the conversation back to Laura and Maks. The Mancinellis have, but they both know that even if it were personal between your family and their client, it wasn't personal against them."

"They're very objective."

"Yes. They've both been in the business for nearly forty years."

"Are any of the other families clients? Will it put them in the middle?"

"I don't think so. The Kutsenkos are venture capitalists too, and they handle a lot of their own stuff. That's Laura's job now that she's their in-house council. Do the Diazes have a family member who's a lawyer other than Enrique?"

"If you haven't guessed, Enrique is Uncle Salvatore and Papa combined. Javier is basically his fifth year associate. Pablo is equivalent to Luca. Jorge is equivalent to me as their CPA. Joaquin has always been a nosy fucker, so he's like Sergei and Carmine. Though I'm the one with the computer science degree like Sergei and Anton. Alejandro is — who knows? He seems to do whatever the fuck he wants and travels a lot."

I know exactly what Alejandro does, and it would give her nightmares for the rest of her life.

"What about the O'Rourkes? Who's their lawyer?"

"Those fuckers are always in trouble. Dillan, Seamus, and Cormac are all lawyers. Now that Dillan runs things, he's rarely practicing, but always strategizing. He's like a fucking Soviet chess wizard. Seamus handles everything corporate, and Cormac handles everything criminal."

"Aren't they brothers?"

"Yes. Sean and Shane are the twins, but Seamus and Cormac may as well be. They're barely ten months apart. Because of how their birthdays fall, they were in the same grade. Seamus did his undergrad at Columbia, and Cormac went to John Jay, but he's no slouch."

John Jay College of Criminal Justice is one of the few schools of its kind. It specializes in criminal justice, forensic science, and forensic psychology. It's not as prestigious as Colombia, but it's served Cormac well. His record for wins is as good as Sinead's. It's pretty much undefeated except where the evidence is so rock solid it would be impossible to get an innocent verdict. He doesn't have the same success with pleading down as Sinead does because of his clients and his own family name. He uses plea deals judiciously, so no one claims he's strong arming the DA's office.

"Did he study forensic psychology?"

"How'd you guess?"

She gives me a wry grin.

"Forensic psych is as much about understanding why criminals commit crimes as it is about understanding how people perceive those crimes. It's useful for deducing prosecutorial strategies and jury selection. Laura took a bunch of those classes as electives in college."

"That explains so fucking much."

Now she really grins as she nods.

"Where'd they go to law school?"

"NYU."

They're both smart, even if they look like fucking mouth breathers. They cultivated the look for when they aren't in court or at a conference table. They're both almost as big as Gabriele, so they're underestimated just as much. It's the same with Sergei and Anton. People see them and assume they're meatheads or knuckle draggers. It means all five of them get to observe situations without people realizing just how much information they're taking in. But just like Gabe, Sergei, and Anton, put them in their designer suits, and they're imposing as fuck.

"And Shane?"

"He's in construction management."

"Like Christina."

"Yeah, and Carmine. Very similar, but he definitely didn't start out working for the city."

"Does he head their construction division like Christina heads the Kutsenkos?"

"Yes. His business administration degree helps him oversee their imports, exports, and jointly owned shipping business. They have a collective construction company, and he's the head of that."

"Sounds like he has a lot of responsibilities."

"He does, but he likes it. He's the quietest of the family and comes across as the most mild-mannered, but he's actually the stubborn one. He's the best negotiator out of the bunch because he digs his heels in and won't budge. It suits him for import/exports, running a shipping company, and dealing with construction issues."

"They're Irish, and he's the stubborn one. Fuck everyone in his path."

"Pretty much."

"Who's equivalent to you?"

"Finn. He's a CPA with training in forensic accounting, just like Pasha, Sumiko, and me."

We're pulling into Uncle Salvatore's driveway, and Chellie peers into the dark. She sees the guard shack as we pass through the gate. We already entered the gated community, and now we're entering a gated property. One of at least a dozen fucked-up things in our world is that all the Kutsenkos live in the neighborhood. They all moved to Manhattan like my generation, and all of them have moved back to Queens now that they're married.

What's even more fucked-up is that Luca and Olivia, along with Carmine and Serafina, bought houses here, too. Theirs are new constructions at the far end of what has been a pretty old money community. I think Gabe and Sinead will buy here too once they start a family. Carmine and Serafina are talking about it, and Luca and Olivia already have their daughter. It wouldn't surprise me if Maria and Matteo don't start looking around, too. It's just like when we were kids and lived close enough to go to the same schools.

I don't wait for Luigi to open the door for us. I help Chellie out, and I can tell nerves hit her as she sees the men patrolling the grounds. There are solar powered lamps along the brick pathways that shine more light than you'd expect. They're in all black, carrying rifles, and wearing night vision glasses. They want to see into the trees and over the top of the walls. She's taking in the house's enormity before glancing down at her gown.

"I guess this fits since I'm walking into a castle."

"*Piccolina*, they're going to love you." *Just like I do.*

"I hope so. I know all the names, but I don't know who's who other than Gabe's the largest, and Luca has a scar."

I nod. I don't think about my brother's scar since he's had it since he was fifteen. A present from Matteo's older brother after a fight that ended their friendship. They'd been almost as inseparable as Matteo and Marco, but they got in a fight, and Emilio sliced his face. It was Emilio's mom who stitched it shut after Emilio dumped him in the living room with a sobbing Carmine, who was only eleven.

Emilio'd passed out in his bedroom while Luca nearly bled to death. Uncle Salvatore put up with Emilio until he was eighteen for Uncle Domenico and Auntie Carlotta's sake, but he washed his hands of him once he left for college. He's essentially been banished. He comes on missions only when it's absolutely necessary. That reminds me.

"Chellie, when you meet Matteo, Auntie Carlotta, and Uncle Domenico, don't mention their older son Emilio. He's made some shit choices over the years, and he's the reason for Luca's scar. You might hear him mentioned in passing, but we don't see him often."

Technically, he's still invited to the holidays and all big family functions, but he chooses to only come to Christmas. It's the only one that we truly can't fault him for being at. The rest, like Thanksgiving and Easter, he goes to his girlfriend's family.

"Okay."

"I'll explain another day. For now, let's go inside, and I'll introduce everyone."

I don't bother knocking before opening the door. We can hear voices in the living room, and it sounds like everyone is here. I lead Chellie inside.

"Enzo?"

"Yes, Mama. We're here."

I slide my hand into Chellie's and give it a squeeze before we enter the lion's den. Everyone looks in our direction as Maria steps forward. I know she takes Chellie by surprise, but she gives my girlfriend a hug. For all her mischief making,

Maria is the sweetest person you'll meet. You'd never guess she's been raised with hardened criminals.

"Hi, Michelle."

"Hi."

I barely hear my sister as she whispers.

"There's a lot of us, and we're noisy. But no one is as scary as they appear."

She links arms with Chellie and practically pulls her away as she starts the introductions. I open my mouth, but she shoots me a look over the top of Chellie's head. Having her introduce everyone makes it more lighthearted than me introducing Chellie as my girlfriend to a bunch of men so deep in the Mafia world she can only imagine half of what they do.

"Michelle, these are my parents, Massimo and Nicoletta. You know Matteo. These are his parents, Domenico and Carlotta. Yes, Nicoletta and Carlotta. Lettie and Lotta. They were destined to be best friends."

Chellie smiles warmly at my parents, but I can tell she's not sure if there's something she should say besides hello as she shakes their hands. Fortunately, Maria continues.

"This is my cousin Carmine and his wife, Serafina."

"Hi. I have some things you can borrow in a bag on the stairs. Though that gown is absolutely stunning on you."

Sera gushes, but it's entirely sincere, and I can tell that between Maria and Sera, Chellie is feeling a little less nervous.

"The two with the baby are my oldest brother, Luca, and his wife, Olivia, and their daughter, Petra."

I watch her eyes light up when Luca turns his daughter, so Chellie can see the little cherubic face. She's sleeping and blowing bubbles, and it makes me think about what children with Chellie would look like. But Maria interrupts my daydream by continuing the introductions.

"I think you already know Sinead, but this is Gabriele. And the last man standing is Marco."

She shoots my next older brother a smug smile, and the teasing in her voice makes my lips twitch. Marco is the one who swears he'll be a bachelor until his last breath. He's seen the rest of us pair off, and our parents are blissfully happy to the point of nauseating. But he refuses to consider bringing someone into our world. There's no one from any of the families beneath us who interests him. We'll see.

"And last but not least, are Uncle Salvatore and Aunt Sylvia, and Uncle Cesare and Auntie Paola."

Chellie's shaken hands with everyone, but now that she's meeting Uncle Salvatore, I can tell her apprehension skyrockets. She still looks as friendly as she did a moment ago, but she's leaned imperceptibly closer to me. I can tell because her elbow brushes my arm as she extends hers to shake my uncle's. I know she must have seen all of us from a distance at Laura and Maks's reception, but Uncle Salvatore is the quintessential silver fox except his hair isn't entirely gray.

He has some strands woven in amongst his deep mahogany-colored hair. We all share that same shade of hair. But he's suave without being a Guido, and his aura shows maturity and self-confidence. He owns who he is without being arrogant. His code name is *Pantera* — Panther. He gained the name when he was younger for being sleek, stealthy, and deadly. Nothing has changed.

He and Aunt Sylvia make the perfect-looking couple. My mother is a beautiful woman, but Aunt Sylvia looks like she just stepped off the runway. Where my mom embodies the in-shape, stylish, approachable middle-aged mom, Aunt Sylvia is the most innately elegant woman I have ever seen. It's like a Sicilian Martha Stewart met Princess Diana, and Aunt Sylvia was the result. She's also much younger than the others, barely in her mid-forties while the others are in their fifties. Uncle Salvatore married late, and he always espouses good things come to those who wait.

"Miss Russo, welcome to our home."

"Thank you, Mr. Mancinelli."

"Salvatore, please."

"Michelle."

"Did you have dinner before you left the event?"

Short of saying "didja eat," it's about the most Italian mom thing Aunt Sylvia could have said.

"Yes, thank you, Mrs. Mancinelli."

"Sylvia. If you say Mrs. Mancinelli, you'll get Nicoletta, Carlotta, Olivia, Serafina, Sinead, Maria, and me answering."

Aunt Sylvia smiles, and I sense more than see Chellie relax. At least, until she looks back at Uncle Salvatore, who's looking at me. Niceties are over, and now it's time for business.

"Michelle, I hate for us to be rude, but Lorenzo and the rest of the men need to meet."

"I understand."

I wrap my arm around her as she turns to me. When our gazes meet, we simply look at each other. Neither wants to give anything away to the others. I don't raise my eyebrows, but she can tell I'm wondering if she'll be all right. She doesn't smile or nod, but I can tell she's saying yes. I kiss her forehead before I let go. I follow the other men toward Uncle Salvatore's office and look back as I go. I see Serafina step forward and point to the stairs. I have to trust things out there will be fine because I doubt they will be in Uncle Salvatore's office.

Once the door's closed, he taps his cell phone. He puts the call on speaker, and Maks answers on the first ring.

"Enzo, someone's put a hit on Michelle."

Chapter Ten

Chellie

It's a lot to fucking take in. So many faces staring at you, assessing you. I just met — let's see — Salvatore, Sylvia, Carlotta, Domenico, Nicoletta, and Massimo — yeah, my brand-new boyfriend's parents during some type of crisis that no one seems scared about besides me — Luca, Olivia, Carmine, Serafina, Gabriele, and Marco. I see Sinead — who I haven't been around since we graduated law school — and Matteo and Maria again.

That's twelve new people, and three people I don't know very well. Sinead and I didn't run in the same circle, and there's like two hundred people in each year at Yale. We had some classes together, but we weren't study buddies. She faced off with Laura in moot court, and I was around her a bit through law review. But that was mostly digital work sharing for the school journal.

"Would you like to get changed? Lorenzo has a room

upstairs, and I brought you some different things to try. I wasn't sure what you'd want or what would fit."

Serafina's accent is as thick as Sylvia's, so it's obvious they both grew up in Italy. When Gabriele said hello, it was a diluted version of theirs. Like he grew up there but maybe came here as a kid.

"Would you like me to show you upstairs?"

"Thank you."

I almost say she can point me in the right direction, but she's trying to be friendly. I follow her, and she scoops up the bag. When we reach the top of the stairs, I realize just how huge this castle is. It's like a hotel hallway. There are doors lining both sides.

"Down there are *Zio* Salvatore and *Zia* Sylvia's room. Their daughters Pia and Natalia each have their own. Uncle Dom and Auntie Carlotta have a room, and so do Uncle Massi and Auntie Nicoletta. Mama—Paola—has one too. Down this way is everyone else's."

She points to them as we pass each. Cesare's is at the very end of the hallway. He and Paola really do live separate lives.

"Why do you call Salvatore *zio* and Sylvia *zia* when the others are uncle and auntie?"

"My mom is *Zia* Sylvia's older sister, so even before I moved to America, they were family. Everyone has called the others uncle and auntie since they were children, so those of us who've married into the family do too. The others call *Zia* Sylvia, Aunt Sylvia because they were adults when she married into the family."

"And you call Paola Mama?"

"Yes. She feels like a second mom, which is really nice because my parents still live in Venice."

"Venice?"

Serafina hesitates as she lays things out on the bed.

"My father is the head of the *Mala del Brenta.*"

She watches me, and I can tell she's deciding how to proceed from how I react.

"Is that Venetian *Cosa Nostra?*"

"Sorta. It's Venetian Mafia. My mother grew up *Cosa Nostra* in Sicily. I was born and raised in Venice, but I spent my summers in Sicily. My mother's family is very close with Gabe's. His father works for my grandfather and uncles."

I nod, uncertain what to say. Then something strikes me.

"Sylvia named off all the women with the Mancinelli last name. She named all of you. How is Maria still a Mancinelli? That means Carlotta and Domenico are Mancinellis, too."

"They are. Uncle Domenico was adopted as an infant. He's *Zio* Salvatore, Uncle Massimo, and Mama's second cousin. There's no blood relation, but Uncle Massimo and Uncle Domenico are best friends who married best friends who had sons who are best friends."

I remember what Enzo told me about not saying anything about Emilio. Serafina must mean Matteo and Marco.

"Matteo is two hours younger than Marco. Both were born on their due dates."

She cocks an eyebrow and grins.

"What does Maria call Domenico and Carlotta? And what does Matteo call Massimo and Nicoletta?"

"The same things they always have, uncle and auntie. But you'll notice I call Paola Mama and Cesare Papa. Olivia calls Auntie Nicoletta Mama and Uncle Massimo Papa. Sinead is still getting used to it, but all the wives who married into the family call the others uncle and auntie too. It's rather nice."

I'm sure it is. Except I'm not so certain how my mom would feel hearing me call another woman Mama. It almost makes me feel like I should call mine Mommy again since Mom sounds sterile in comparison. Fucking-a. I'm getting miles ahead of myself. I know Enzo and I are talking about a future, but we aren't there yet.

Serafina puts her hand on my upper arm and gives it a squeeze.

"It's a gigantic family, but it's a loving one. Most people would assume they wouldn't like outsiders. But that's not the case. We've already accepted you because you're important to Enzo. That's all we need to know."

"You and Maria grew up with this stuff. What about Olivia?"

"No. Her family tree is about as complicated as mine, so it'll be easier for her to explain. Sinead's family has ties to the Irish, but not close ones."

That surprises me. I never would have guessed because I know Sinead's mom and sister died a long time ago, and I think her dad's sick. But I guess I should have figured there was some connection with a name as purely Irish as Sinead O'Malley.

I pull my attention back to the conversation when Serafina speaks again.

"Do you think anything here will work?"

"All of them. Are jeans and that green top all right? They aren't too informal together?"

"They're great. You saw everyone downstairs. The men always have suits on since it—"

She snaps her mouth shut.

"Since it?"

"Gives off a certain impression."

I don't believe for a moment that's what she meant. It makes me think of something Enzo said.

"It's to hide their guns, isn't it?"

She says nothing, and I realize I'm going to get a lot of that, and not just from Enzo.

"Enzo said something about normally wearing one, but

hadn't been because he didn't want to scare me. A suit coat would hide shoulder or lower back holsters. I don't think any of them would ever wear hip holsters."

Her expression doesn't change, but neither does she deny it. Silence is consent.

"The women are all casually dressed, and don't worry about being barefoot."

She looks down at my strappy high heel sandals. I didn't think to change them since we never made it to my place.

"Thank you so much for this. It's very kind of you."

"I know you're very close to Laura Kutsenko. I don't know how much you know about her in-laws, but if our families weren't rivals, they'd probably be friends. We aren't that different."

I can only nod to that. Serafina's husband is probably the most hated man alive to the Kutsenkos. At least he was. They seem to have tempered their loathing to just disdain. Except for Niko. I doubt he'll ever get past what Carmine, Luca, and Gabriele did and how close he came to losing his wife, Anastasia. Apparently, Carmine was the mastermind. I only know because I overheard a conversation I shouldn't have.

"I see you know about Carmine."

Shit.

"I hope you can give him the chance to prove he's not that man anymore. He owns the shit he's done, and he will always feel guilty about it. More than anyone can know. Even me. But there's a lot more than meets the eye. Stuff you'll learn now that you never would have if you were only friends with Laura. Things only *our* family knows."

The way she says that word — family — makes me think she's reminding me I'm now one of them. If it wasn't in the context of not being a rat, it would be very inclusive. It doesn't feel like a threat so much as a warning.

"I admit I'm biased, but between each side is the truth. I'm willing to keep an open mind to find that middle."

"Thank you. I couldn't stand Carmine when we were kids. I broke his nose when we were twelve because he pushed me into a wave that knocked me over, flipped me around, and caused me to skin my knees and elbows. I loathed him at eighteen because of something that happened at *Zia* Sylvia and *Zio* Salvatore's wedding. I thought I would always despise him. I love him more than life now."

She offers me another smile before stepping out of the room. I could have gone into the en suite bathroom, but she's offering me real privacy. I pick up the jeans and top and put them aside before folding everything else. I put the extra clothes in the bag and perch on the end of the bed. What the fuck have I gotten myself into?

My phone buzzes in the clutch I put on the bed when I came in the room. I wince.

"Hey."

"Are you at Salvatore's yet?"

"Yeah. We got here about fifteen minutes ago."

"Thank God."

"What's happening, Laura?"

"I don't know. Maks won't tell me anything, but he's on the phone with the Mancinellis. He and the others are in his office. I just wanted to hear your voice for myself."

"Are you pissed?"

"That you fell in love with Lorenzo? I'm still not thrilled, but I can hardly blame you. What do you think of the others? I'm sure they're all there, too."

"They are. Laura, they're nice people. Nothing about them seems insincere. Serafina just said that if the families weren't rivals, they'd probably be friends."

"Some of them."

"I met Carmine, Luca, and Gabriele. Serafina said that he's different now than when everything happened."

"He is, and we've all seen it. But it's still all too fresh for anyone to trust that this new version is here to stay. Gabe's just Carmine's minion. He does whatever Carmine tells him to."

Nothing about the man I met downstairs gives me that impression. It makes me wonder if some of Carmine's and Gabriele's behavior are personas like what Enzo said about Cormac and Seamus. Do Carmine and Gabriele want to be underestimated? I know Sinead's reputation as a lawyer. Nothing makes me think she'd go for a guy who's a pushover or someone's bitch. But I'm not going to argue with Laura.

"Laura, what's going to happen when shit happens between the Mancinellis and the Kutsenkos?"

"You mean what's going to happen between us. You're my best friend and have been since we were kids. You supported me even when you were scared for me. I can return the favor. I don't think we'll ever double date, but Maks won't ask or tell me to stop being friends with you. Would Lorenzo?"

"Absolutely not. He'd probably break up with me before making me choose."

I remember Maks saying he wouldn't stop seeing Laura just because Lanie and I disapproved. He told us not to make her choose because it would only hurt her. It's not that I think Lorenzo wouldn't fight for me or for us. But I think he's the type who would sacrifice what he wants for what he believes is best for me.

"Do you think you can separate what our husbands will do from our friendship? I think I can, and I believe you can too, Chellie Belly."

I laugh, and it eases things.

"I believe I can too. There's already shit you can't tell me, and I try not to pry. You get how that goes, so I won't have to explain. I won't hold that against you."

"Like Lanie did."

I close my eyes as I ask the obvious.

"We're going to lose her, aren't we?"

"Yes."

Laura hasn't sugar coated a damn thing in her life other than cookies.

"After your wedding, she claimed you and I were closer, and that left her out. But now she thinks I'm closer to her than I am to you because you can't go out as often as we did."

"That's not Maks's fault, but she refuses to believe that. I was breastfeeding twins for eighteen months. That didn't give me much freedom or energy to go out."

"And I told her that. But she's going to think I betrayed her, and she's going to blame you as much as she will Lorenzo."

"Maks once asked if I thought Lanie was into me because of how jealous and possessive she was. I told him I never got that vibe. I told him she never had an issue with Juan, even when I thought I loved him once upon a time, and later when he thought he loved me. She didn't seem to care even though Juan and I were fuck buddies for years."

"Because she knew you'd never end up with him. He wasn't a threat. She's had three girlfriends cheat on her, and her mom never hides that she likes her sister and brother better because she had them with her quote-unquote good husband. Lanie's baggage is that people are always picking someone else over her."

"I know, and it didn't help that I got pregnant so soon. I never really had a chance to hang out with her between getting married, then morning sickness, then being so big that I could barely move for four months and needed a nap every two hours. I slept more than the twins did as newborns."

"It's been the three of us for nearly two decades. The only time we've been apart is when we all went off to different colleges. Even then, we still talked all the time. She didn't begrudge us going to law school together because we came home practically every long weekend, or she came to see us. There's no way she won't feel left out now."

"Chellie, you and I are good. No matter what happens between the men, you and I are solid. Hopefully, that'll make her see we can still all be close."

Laura believes that no more than I do, but we can try. Sharing this mutual problem is making it easier to deal with tonight. If she was blowing sunshine and rainbows up my ass to distract me, I'd still be thinking about what's happening downstairs with Lorenzo.

"I gotta go. I'm being rude staying up here so long. I'm in Enzo's room. Serafina brought me some clothes because we came from the gala."

"Go and be with your new family."

"They're not—"

"Bullshit."

"But—"

"Bullshit, bullshit, bullsheee-it."

She sing-songs the last one.

"Fine. But nothing is official, even if we're headed down that road. I get why things happened as fast as they did with Maks. There's something about these men."

"But only with the right woman."

"True. Love ya, Laura Snora."

"Love ya."

"Bye."

"Bye."

I hurry to get changed and head back downstairs. All the women are in the living room chatting, and Olivia is nursing

Petra. It makes me think about Laura mentioning nursing her twins. I want that. I want kids and always have. But now that I'm with Enzo, I'm actually thinking about it as more than a hypothetical or distant possibility. The thought passed through my head a few times with other guys, but it never took root. It was always gone as fast as it came.

"Sorry that took a while. I got a call. Serafina, I put the clothes back in the bag and left them on the bottom stair. Thanks so much."

"You're welcome. Anytime."

When Maria pats the spot between her and Olivia, I sit on the sofa with them. I'm just about to ask Maria about her day when we hear voices raised. I recognize Enzo's immediately.

"The fuck we are."

Then a door slams. I look at Maria, then Nicoletta. Their expressions match, and it's as though they're bracing for something. Maria leans forward and whispers.

"I guarantee he won't take it out on you, but he's pissed. Like super, super pissed. Enzo never gets upset. He's the mellow one like Mama. But when he does, if the shit ain't fastened to the wall, Typhoon Lorenzo will blow it across the room."

She hurries to lean back as the footsteps get closer. It's not just one set, so either someone came out of the office with him, or they followed and closed the door more quietly.

"Chellie."

I'm already watching him approach. When he sticks out his hand, I stand and hurry around the sofa. He takes it and pulls me close. The rage is pulsating off him, but he's gentle.

"I'm going to talk to my girlfriend. Alone."

We head upstairs to the room Serafina showed me. He goes to stand by the window and pushes open the curtains. I don't know what to do as I watch him stand with his hands in his pockets, gazing into the dark. Is this the eye of the storm? The time when it fools you into thinking it's over. He exhales and turns toward me. He looks me over, and I don't know what to make of it.

"Come sit with me, *piccolina*."

He walks to the bed and kicks off his shoes. He climbs on and opens his arms to me. I follow him and lean against his chest.

"What happened, Daddy? Maria said you don't get upset."

"I usually don't. I take most things in stride, but when I get angry, it's zero to a hundred."

"She called it Typhoon Lorenzo."

"That joke's getting old. But it isn't far off. Mama said I was such an easygoing baby and kid that I never learned how to self-sooth, so it takes me a while to calm down. I think I don't get angry unless there's a good fucking reason, so when I am, it's justified that I'm pissed."

"What did you find out from Maks? And before you start, I talked to Laura. She called to make sure I'm okay because Maks wouldn't tell her anything."

"Did she upset you?"

I lean back. It wasn't an accusatory tone at all. It sounds like he's scared I'm going to bolt.

"No. We talked about Lanie. She knew if she tried to be cheery and distract me with stupid shit, I would tune her out and worry. She knows giving me another problem to solve will keep my mind off whatever's right in front of me."

"I'd like to know what you decided, but right now there's something more urgent. There's no easy way to say this, but this is about you. Someone's targeting you to get to the Kutsenkos. Maks doesn't know who for sure, but we have an idea. We don't know why beyond the feeling that whoever this is knows they can't get directly at any of the Kutsenkos, so they think going after you is the next best thing."

"But why me? I mean, why not an extended family member? I hate saying that, but why a friend who has no real ties to the bratva?"

"I think it's because all the Kutsenko women's families aren't what they seem. They have connections besides the men their daughters married. Whoever this is can't target any of them without bringing in way more trouble than they're willing to accept. None of the other women have friendships as close as the one you and Laura have. Plus, Heather's dad is a retired cop, and Anastasia's dad and Katerina's dad have ties to the bratva in Russia."

"And Laura's previous clients are an interesting collection of who's who in the underworld."

Enzo stills, and I realize I may have just given away something I shouldn't have.

"You mean the Triad."

Okay, maybe I didn't.

"Yeah. Because she was the only one at her firm who spoke Russian or Chinese, she attracted clients from those countries, as well as older Eastern European clients who spoke Russian."

"Did you know about those connections?"

"I guessed, but said nothing. Neither of us ever got into the specifics. But the rich foreign clients who almost never wanted to speak English in their meetings made me think twice about whether those terra-cotta pots were solely made of clay or if it was only vodka in those bottles. She asked no questions, so no one told her any lies."

"The wives wouldn't be any better targets than the men. It means their families aren't either. Whoever this is believes you're unprotected, therefore, an easy mark. I think whoever is doing this believes Maks won't tell you what's happening because it would mean admitting too much about him and his family. I'm certain they know Maks will assign you security, even if he never tells you. But they'd have to keep their distance, which means this piece of shit thinks there's time and space to get to you."

"Did they say they're going to kill me?"

"Yes."

That's as blunt as Laura was. Fuck. I burrow against Enzo's chest, and he lifts me onto his lap. I curl up, tucking my arms between us.

"*Piccolina*, whoever this is doesn't know about us yet. If they did, they would have sent the threat to me, too. Or they'd know there's no way anyone is getting close enough to you to do anything. Maks will make his detail discreet, but mine will be right next to you. It'll also include a member of my family."

"Maks will..."

Will what? Have someone killed on my behalf? Make sure I go nowhere alone ever again?

"There's no way he'll agree to letting my family take care of this alone. And frankly, I'm not insulted. The more men guarding you, the better I'll feel."

"And what do you mean, a member of your family?"

"Unless it's going to work or something else uneventful, one of the men in my family always accompanies the women. They all have bodyguards, but no one will ever be more dedicated to protecting the women we love than us."

He tilts my chin up and drops a soft kiss to my lips. Neither of us makes any pledges because it's too soon for those feelings to have fully developed. But we both know we're on a short track to them.

"Chellie, no one who isn't related to me will ever be good enough to protect you when I can't be there. I'll never trust anyone with your life the way I do my brothers, cousins, uncles, and dad. As far as I'm concerned, Gabriele's like a cousin. He's been a part of this family since he moved to America when he was ten. He and Carmine became best friends the moment they met. His dad had a similar role as Uncle Domenico, Marco, Matteo, Carmine, Gabe, and me."

"But you all have other things you do."

"And none of them take precedence over family."

"But you all work for your family."

"You know what I mean, Chellie."

He watches me in silence as he considers what to say next. I hope he lets me in rather than shuts me out. I want to understand what's happening. I want to know he and his family can accept me. If he shuts me out, then I don't know that I can do this. It's obvious family is everything to Enzo. If he can only consider me his and not part of the bigger picture, then I don't want to live in fear every day because I know nothing and have no one to go to.

"My dad and uncles don't really guard anyone anymore, but they all can. They've all been *capos* like we are. Uncle Sal was an underboss like Luca is now. They both spent some time as *capos* before assuming that role. My dad is our *consigliere*, but he was a *capo* first."

I only know what these positions are because of the movies. But how accurate is Hollywood? Nothing about Salvatore makes me think of Don Corleone. Nothing about the other men makes me think of Ray Liotta's character in *Goodfellas*.

"Chellie, maybe the old-school families were like the movies, but we aren't. The men don't cheat, and we don't shoot people because they look the wrong way at us. We aren't sitting around some table smoking Stogies and counting our money."

He says it with humor in his voice, but I wince anyway.

"Since the words aren't knew to you, and maybe you have some understanding of them, I may as well explain. *Capo* is short for *caporegime*, which is like a lieutenant if you want to give it rank. *Capo dei capi* or *capo di tutti capi* are bosses of bosses, or the senior most capos. Everyone but Luca and my dad are those. Since Marco is the next oldest after Luca, who's our underboss or heir, Marco technically carries either of those titles alone. But no one inside or outside our family sees it that way. Marco, Matteo, Carmine, Gabriele, and I are equals."

I can't believe I went from fearing he would tell me nothing to being terrified that I now know too much.

"Do the other women know this? I mean, I guess Maria and Serafina must. But what about Olivia and Sinead?"

"Olivia probably does because she's married to our second-in-command, but I don't know about Sinead. Probably because Gabriele would want her to understand the risks of being with him. I don't know when he told her, but I'm pretty sure he has."

"These risks. Are they why you're telling me?"

"Partly. I want you to know I have the authority to deal with this threat, but I also want you to know that I have the ability to."

That, I'm not asking any follow-up questions about.

"You said your dad is the *consigliere,* and that Domenico is or was a *capo.* Why isn't he the underboss or *capo di capo*?"

"*Capo dei capi*, and Uncle Domenico was until Marco was old enough to take on the job."

"You didn't name Cesare."

"Uncle Cesare married into the family because Auntie Paola got pregnant at nineteen. They were having fun but never intended to get serious. Both of their fathers insisted they marry. My grandfather and Uncle Cesare's father were rivals. My family ousted Uncle Cesare's, so my grandfather never welcomed Uncle Cesare. Basically, my grandfather forced them to marry to punish Uncle Cesare for touching Auntie Paola and to punish her for not staying a virgin. *Nonno* was nothing like Uncle Salvatore, Auntie Paola, and Papa. He was a hard man to be around let alone love. I did because he was family, but I didn't like him. He never did anything to me, but he scared the shit out of me. He was cruel to Carmine, as though the mess with his parents was his fault. *Nonno* refused to allow Uncle Cesare anywhere near the family business. Papa and Uncle Salvatore offered him positions once Uncle Salvatore became don. But he's always declined, and Uncle Salvatore hasn't forced him. It's actually just as well. Without our last name, he's able to do a lot of shit no one thinks twice about. He's in insurance and has been very helpful."

Another thing I'm not asking any follow-up questions about. I don't want to know anything about their insurance fraud. Unless I marry Enzo, I won't have spousal privilege not to testify against him. I know that's why he chose the wording he did. This is a shit ton of family history to absorb.

"I said my dad is our *consigliere*. That makes him Uncle Sal's top advisor because they trust each other, and because my dad is also a lawyer. They may argue like only brothers can, but it's always because they both put our family and the people who depend upon us first. They never do it outside Uncle Salvatore's office. If we're in there, don't come near it, Chellie. Call me or text me, even if you're in the kitchen or living room."

I nod.

"I need to hear you, *piccolina*."

"I won't, Daddy."

I'm noticing I call him that when I'm scared and need reassuring. He gets it because he holds me tighter.

"Can you tell me why you're so angry? I heard what you said as you came out of the office."

"I wish you hadn't. And I'm not angry anymore. Being in here alone with you helped."

"Because you aren't around your family?"

"Because I'm holding you."

I tilt my head up and pucker my lips. It starts softly, but when I curl my fingers into his hair, he mauls me. He rolls us until he's on top. He's been hard the entire time I've been on his lap, but neither of us did anything about it. Now he thrusts against me.

"I want to lose myself inside you, *piccolina*. I want to fuck you until you scream Daddy. I want to come in you and know that one day we're going to have a family of our own. I want to know that I made that child as much as you did."

"So that you can possess me in every way?"

He pauses his thrusts as he shakes his head.

"No. I won't trap you. I want it because I see what my brother has, and for the first time in my life, I want that too. Am I saying it now because I wish we were having sex? Yes. Have I meant it every moment of every day since I met you? Yes. I was arguing with my family because they suggested letting Maks's family decide how to move forward."

"If this person sent the threat to them because of my connection to Laura, then why not let them? Is it because you want your family to have more power than his?"

"I couldn't give two shits — I couldn't even give one shit — who's in power. No one is coming near you, Chellie. I don't care what security Maks offers or sets up behind my back. No one decides how you're going to be protected but me. I am going to be possessive and controlling about this. I will not relent. You are my woman, and I know how barbaric and archaic that sounds, but it's the truth. I trust my family with my life and yours, but no one is as motivated and determined to do *any and everything* to protect you. So Maks can fuck all the way off if he thinks he's in charge, and my family can join him."

He kisses me again, and he reaches between us to unfasten my jeans. My hips are moving on their own as I shift to give him the room to slide his fingers down the front of them and into me.

"You are mine, *piccolina*. All of you. I won't settle for anything less. I'm going to make you come, so the only thing on your mind is me because you are the only thing on mine."

I look around, and my eyes land on the wall beside the window.

"Daddy, pin me against that wall and fuck me as hard as you can."

"What?"

"I need you inside me, but if we do it on the bed, people will hear us. Do it against the outside wall, and no one will hear you as you fuck your cum into me."

"Strip, *piccolina*."

Chapter Eleven

Lorenzo

I can't get my clothes off fast enough. I walk back to the door as I unbutton my shirt and flick the lock. Then I'm tossing it onto the bed, followed by my socks, pants, and boxer briefs. My tux coat and bowtie are still in Uncle Salvatore's office.

I wrap my arm around her and pull her against me, so she lands hard. My free hand wraps around the base of her throat, but I don't squeeze. She's never done anything BDSM, so we *are not* jumping straight to breath play. But it holds her in place.

"Why do I get to decide? Why do I own your orgasms, *cuore?*"

"Because I belong to you, Daddy."

"That's right. I will give you everything I can, Chellie. All of me that I have to give. I won't settle for less from you."

"You will have everything, all of me. I wish we had lube."

She mumbles the second sentence. I raise an eyebrow, and

she blushes. She looks so damn beautiful. I wish I could capture this moment forever.

"I've sucked you off, and you've fucked my pussy. I want you to fuck me in the ass. I want you to claim every part of my body. I want your cum in and on me, Enzo. I want to look down and see it. I want to feel it. I can be just as possessive and controlling. I want to know that no woman has what I have."

"And what's that?"

"You. I have the man who will do anything for me, and I believe him when he tells me that. I have the man who's brave enough to follow through with any threat he makes to anyone who might endanger me. I have the man who can be so fucking tender with me it makes my heart swell and feel like it could explode. I have the man who makes me feel like the most beautiful woman in the world. I have the best man there is. He's mine, and I'll be damned if I ever share that with anyone else."

I back her against the wall, and my mouth devours hers. I can't get enough. Everything she just said. All of it. I know she meant it, and it makes me feel like Superman. Her hands grip my ass and pull me closer. I press more of my weight against her, but it's not all of it. I don't want to crush her.

"Daddy, stop holding back. You won't hurt me. You know I love this. Please."

I take a half step forward and press almost all my weight on her. I don't care what she says. I will not risk hurting her. She whispers to me, and I almost can't hear her.

"You keep telling me you won't trap me, but please don't leave me."

I lean back enough to look her in the eye, and I finally see fear. It wasn't there when I told her what's happening. It wasn't there when I explained I will be controlling. But the thought of me walking away from her scares her. And I hate seeing even a hint of fear in her eyes.

"Chellie, I'm not going to. I'm selfish as fuck for bringing you into this world. But I can't let go even when I know I should. I don't want to live without you. I don't know that I could now that I know you. I'm not going anywhere."

"Then stop telling me you won't trap me. Stop offering me ways out. I don't want to go anywhere. Every time you do, it makes me think you're leaving yourself a way out, too."

"That's not it at all. I don't want you to regret picking me."

"My only regret will be if you shut me out. I don't want to fall even more for you and not have you feel the same."

I hoist her, and she wraps her legs around my waist. I thrust into her, and we both sigh. Then we're moving together, and I'm fucking her as hard as I dare. No. That's not right. This isn't gentle or slow, but it's not fucking. This isn't about getting her off then getting myself off. This isn't about her giving herself to me, and me taking. This is entirely different. I've never felt this way during sex before. All I want is the intimacy we're sharing. All I want is to feel us being one with nothing getting between us, nothing separating us. So, yes. I'm thrusting as hard as I dare. Yes, I'm kissing her as though she's my last meal. But this isn't fucking.

"Daddy, are we making love?"

"Yes, little one."

Our gazes meet, and they don't waver as we move together. She's gripping my shoulders until she suddenly cups my face and dives in for a kiss. I swallow her moan as she comes.

"I want to make you come, Daddy. I need to make you come."

"Not until I give you at least one more orgasm."

"I might die before that happens. Please, Enzo. I need to know you feel the way I do. I need to give you that."

This isn't the possessiveness we shared earlier, which — by the way — I fucking loved hearing. I want to know that she'll fight for us because this life won't be easy. She's desperate to show me she loves me as much as I love her. She wants to give me pleasure because there aren't words for what's happening right now. I grip her hips and rock mine as I come.

"I'm not ready to put you down yet, *mia cuore.*" My sweetheart.

I walk us to the bench at the foot of the bed, and she remains wrapped around me as we kiss. They're not the feverish kind, but we fill them with the same emotion as a moment ago.

"Daddy, can I tell you a story?"

"Sure."

"In the days of the Greek gods, man and woman were joined at their backs. They had four arms, four legs, and one head with two faces. They were one. They did everything together and were perfectly in tune with one another. Because of this, Zeus grew angry, fearing they might have more power than him. To punish them, he split them in two, making man and making woman. He gave them vices that kept them apart, but in their hearts, they always longed for their mate. Their souls weren't at peace while they missed their other half. It was only when they found each other that they felt whole. Daddy, I feel whole finally."

"So do I, *piccolina.* Aristophanes was right. Or rather Plato's *Symposium* was right. I know that story too, Chellie. Aristophanes said something like, when the right two people meet, something wonderful happens. Plato didn't believe this in truth, so he wrote it as a satire. But he was right. It is real." I lean forward, so our foreheads touch. "It has to be because I'm sitting in here with you with our bodies joined. Four arms, four legs, one head with two faces, and the parts of a man and woman that fit together to make them one."

We move so we can rest our heads on each other's shoulder,

and I have a sense of peace I haven't felt since before I was twelve and started carrying a knife. Before I became a Mafioso. We run our hands over each other's back as my left one cups her ass. We're perfectly at peace, even though I'm not hard anymore and can't stay inside her. She unwraps her legs, and I think she's about to shatter that peace. I tighten my hold on her ass.

"Shh."

She kneels as she soothes me, allowing her to bring her tits to my face. She offers me one, and I gladly suck. There has to be something wrong with me. I have no interest in role play. Not her being younger and definitely not me being younger. But there is something calming about this. A shrink would say I either wasn't breastfed long enough or was breastfed too long. That I have some sort of mommy issues. I don't give a shit. It's what I share with the woman who's my soulmate.

"Enzo, you know I don't feel like a mommy when I do this, right?"

Once again, she whispers so softly I strain to hear her. I nod.

"It's not maternal feelings. But they are tender. I don't have the right words, so I want to offer me to you in a way that's not sex. I want to take care of you, and this feels like the only thing I can do because I don't know your world. And I can't protect you from it even if I did."

"I get it, my sweet *piccolina*. I need to receive that tenderness as much as you need to give it. It's all that I have."

"Oh, Enzo. No, it isn't. You have all of me. Mind, body, heart, and soul."

"Some of me — a lot more of me than I want — will always belong to the *Costa Nostra*. It can't be any other way. It just is. But everything else I can give... I give it all to you."

"I can live with that."

God, I hope so. She has no idea just how hard life can be.

"Enzo, what happens now? How do I explain a Mancinelli man outside my office?"

"Someone will be in the lobby. They will park as close as they can. Your floor is quiet, so the only time anyone might notice is when they're going to the restroom. The complication would be any of your clients who recognize someone in my family."

"You want someone outside my office door? You think the threat is that credible?"

"Yes. Maks wouldn't have called if it were a simple matter they can handle with no one being the wiser."

"Does that mean he and his family accept that we're together? Will they try to cut me off from Laura?"

I practically snort at that.

"God help any of them if they try that. Laura hasn't walked away from you, so no one is dumb enough to tell her she should. Besides, all of them care about you. You're Christina's friend now too. Konstantin and Mila adore their Auntie Chellie, and I bet Lev does too. They want you safe and happy, even if that means me."

"Won't the men get tired of babysitting me?"

"First of all, it isn't babysitting. We're all trained to be body-guards. It's part of our job. It isn't babysitting when someone is guarding Mama or Maria or Auntie Carlotta, Auntie Paola, or Aunt Sylvia. Second of all, they know that being trusted with the women we care about most is a sign of respect. That level or kind of trust doesn't go to many people. So no, it isn't babysitting, and they won't get tired of it."

"What about the men in the car and lobby? You can't assign three members of your family to me. Then there wouldn't be enough for the other women."

"Until there isn't a threat anymore, you'll have a member of my family. Once things are safe again, you'll have a rotation of two of our most trusted men. All the women go about their daily lives when they go to work or run errands. When it's a routine we know, then we allow top Made Men to guard the women. But a family member goes with the women any time they're going beyond that. There's no dictating where and when they go places. They do what they want just like women who don't need guards."

"What if there's a conflict in people's schedule, and the men in your family aren't available?"

"Someone is made available."

That comes out harsher than I intend, and she retreats. She nods and says nothing else.

"Chellie, I didn't mean to snap at you. Your concerns are valid, and I didn't mean to make it sound like they aren't. My brothers and cousins trust me with the women they love, and I take that privilege seriously. They'll do the same for us."

She smiles shyly at me. I know what I've implied, and we just agreed we're soulmates. But it still feels like it's too early to actually say I love you. We haven't even made it to the fourth date yet. Nothing about this life is slow paced. Everything happens like it's on roids. It's bigger, faster, heavier than it would be for regular people.

"I'm going with you tomorrow. I want to really study your building, so I can plan for the guards. Luca is in charge of assigning men to jobs. He'll add you into the rotation. We know we can't be up our wives' and girlfriends' asses. It wouldn't be — You know what I mean, Chellie."

The moment I say up her ass, she smirks. I give her a playful spank. She rises on her knees and sticks her ass out. I give her three more that are much heavier than the first. She gives me a peck on my nose, then settles back onto my lap to listen. Who are we?

"It wouldn't be good for any of the relationships for that to happen. There are a few rules, though. I need you to take them seriously."

"I will."

"Let me tell you the ones I can think of right now. Then you can decide whether you agree."

"If there are rules, it's because you want to protect me. They're ones the other women already agree to, so if they can live with them, so can I."

"Don't go anywhere without telling your guards. If they say no, then you listen. They'll only tell you no if they think it's dangerous. Whether they want to do whatever it is, is completely irrelevant. No one gives a shit about their opinion. But you will listen to their guidance. Don't tell anyone your schedule for the day if they aren't a part of what's happening. Tell them you have other stuff and stay vague. If you want to drive yourself places, that's fine. But you let your guard inspect your car if it's been anywhere where one of our men hasn't been watching it. They will follow you. You do not let them get more than two cars behind you. You accept rides from no one, Chellie. Not Laura. Not Christina. Not your sister or your brother. I don't believe anyone in your family or the Kutsenkos would hurt you, but you make the others targets. Tell them you'll meet them wherever it is, or you need your car right after you're done. I need to take your car to one of our shops. I need to make some aftermarket changes. I'm putting a tracker on it. Go wherever you want, and I won't question you. But if something happens, I need to be able to find you. I'm going to put a sensor near your engine. If you open the door, and the dome light doesn't come on, you run. You do nothing but drop your shit and run as fast as you can."

"Are you telling me someone might try to blow me up in my car?"

"Yes. Ask Heather and Aleks. Ask Sinead and Gabe. It happens, and you need to know what to do."

She clings to me and trembles. I reach behind me and grab my shirt, which I drape over her shoulders.

"I'm not cold. I'm scared for you. If you and your family have to do these things, it's because there have been threats in the past, and there will be threats in the future. I hate knowing you aren't safe."

"Shh, *piccolina*. We take the precautions we have to. Can you live with these rules?

"Yes."

"I don't want domestic discipline, and we've already agreed to no age play because neither of us wants it. But I will punish you if you break these rules, Chellie. They're there for your safety. I will spank you, and neither of us will enjoy it. If you don't take them seriously, we're done."

"What?"

She jerks back, and her head slams into the underside of my chin, whipping my head back and making me bite my tongue.

"Oh, shit. Enzo, I'm so sorry. I—"

"It was an accident, and I know that. But I am serious. It won't just be your life you risk. I can't do that to our men, and I won't be able to live with knowing I'm putting you in danger when you could be safe."

"I'm entering your world, not the other way around. I knew that from the very beginning. I expected there to be way more limitations than you've described. It actually shocks the shit out of me how much freedom I'll have. If these things let you sleep at night beside me and make it so your family won't tell you to leave me, then I can live with them."

"My family won't tell me that. They know that conversation wouldn't end well for anyone."

"You've explained your expectations and given me your rationale. I won't break the rules intentionally."

"I'll punish you even if it's an accident. I won't go any lighter on you. If you do it by accident, then it means you don't understand the full gravity of the situation or you didn't put enough thought into it."

"Yes, Daddy."

"There's something else I didn't explain to you that I should have. If I come home and tell you I need you to leave me alone or to go in another room, I'm not angry at you or trying to hide something. I either need to get cleaned up, or I need time to calm down. It means something went wrong, and I don't want you to see me like that. Don't offer to help. Don't try to do anything to help. Just give me space, and I will come to you as soon as I can."

I'm stroking her cheek as I tell her this because I hate the idea of ever telling her I don't want to see her for any reason. But shit does happen, and I do come home bloody sometimes. I do come home ready to rage against the world. I never want her to be around that. I never want her to see the man I really am.

"You said come home, and I made it sound like you'd be sleeping beside me every night."

"I know. This is happening faster than I wanted because I wanted you have time to take all this in. I wanted you to be able to take your time coming to a decision about us. I know you said you had nine days to think about us, but that's not long in your world. It's a lifetime in mine. But when we say home, I want it to mean the place we live together. I don't care if it's the one I have now or the one you have now. We can get a place together. When you're ready, that's what I want."

"I've never lived with a guy before."

"I've never lived with a woman before, either."

"I want to get to that, but I'm not sure I'm actually there yet."

"We can have a lifetime to get to each stage. It doesn't have to happen all in a month."

"It pretty much did for Laura."

"Maks was the first of our generation to get married. Women and children were always off-limits in the past. My generation has fucked that up, and not just my family. But that code still exists, even when people break it. Laura was in danger, and Maks believed making her his wife was the best way to protect her. In the beginning, he thought people knowing they were together was enough. It wasn't. Anyone who saw them before they got married knew they were pretty much love at first sight. They moved fast, but it was obvious marriage was an inevitability. I believe marriage is our future, but I won't rush you like that because we have an idea where the threat is coming from. Maks didn't back then."

"Can you tell me who or what it is?"

"Not yet. I don't like hiding this, and I don't want to make you fear any and everyone is out to get you. But until we know more, it's not safe to say anything to you."

"I trust you."

"I know you do, and I always want you to."

I pray I never break her trust. My relationship with God isn't any easy one. I was an altar boy until I was seventeen. I was already doing shit a seventeen-year-old shouldn't have to. But I wanted to live. I sinned during the week and repented on Sunday. At seventeen, I had already repeated the same sins so often I didn't feel my repentance was genuine anymore. I knew I would willingly repeat those sins again.

It started feeling more like I was asking God's permission to sin rather than his forgiveness. It felt too hypocritical to continue being an altar boy. My parents understood since each boy becoming a man wrestled with the same thing. I'd seen Luca and Marco go through it. I saw it with Matteo too.

I have never wavered in my faith, and I believe Chellie coming into my life is proof that somehow God truly has the capacity to forgive. I believe in the Ten Commandments. I do believe I shouldn't kill, but I do. I believe in the sacraments, and I pray one day I'm marrying Chellie and another day we're watching our child be baptized.

I just can't live the life of a good Christian, even if I wanted to. And I can be honest with God and myself. I don't want to. If I did, I wouldn't protect my family. And nothing is more important than family. And now that includes Chellie.

"Daddy, we've been up here a long time. People are going to wonder what we're up to. They've probably guessed, but we're being rude."

"Whether they guessed we had sex or not, they know this conversation can't be rushed. It takes each couple however long it takes them. They won't fault us or begrudge us that."

I help her off my lap, and we gather our clothes.

"Um, give me a moment."

She glances toward the bathroom, and I nod. She dashes in, and I hear the water running. She's back out a moment later, and we dress silently. When we get to the hallway, I slide my hand into hers. When will we have a lighthearted conversation again like we did at the coffee shop?

Ours are always so heavy now. But better to get all of this out in the open now because I told my family the truth. The fuck we're letting the Kutsenkos take care of this. I don't give a fuck how good their intentions are. No one is getting between Chellie and me and surviving.

Chapter Twelve

Chellie

I hold my head up and smile as we return to the living room. I'm embarrassed that anyone — especially Massimo and Nicoletta — should guess we had sex. Now, looking back, it seems grossly inappropriate. Both the time and the place. But I don't regret it. I've never felt closer to a living soul than I did while making love to Enzo. I'm over thirty, so I've been in love before. Obviously, none of it lasted. Now I can look back and see I was too young for any of it to be serious enough for a lifelong commitment. I don't think I'm too young now. In fact, I've never felt older than I do right now. The last three hours aged me.

Blessedly, the conversations don't stop when we step into the room. People look over and smile, but no one's staring. That would mortify me. The problem is, I don't know where to sit. Do I join any of the conversations? Do I stay glued to Enzo?

"Michelle, come settle something between Gabe and me."

I watch Sinead wave me over, and I'm not sure what to do. I

mean, I know I should walk over there like a normal person. But I'm suddenly paralyzed and unsure if I can leave Enzo's side. I hear him laugh as he nudges me but doesn't let go of my hand.

"Gabe, admit your wife is right. Whatever she said is probably exactly what Chellie will say."

Gabe glances at the parents in the room, and it looks like he'd say something to Enzo if they weren't there. It makes me assume it would be something profane. That makes my lips twitch. Instead, Gabe focuses on me.

"Who was the hardest professor in law school?"

"Oh, that's simple. Professor Sebastionson. Hands down."

"Ha! I told you!"

Gabe crows as he points at Sinead. I look at her.

"Who did you think it was?"

Sinead grimaces before she answers.

"Professor Hughey."

"Oh, she hated me."

Now both Sinead and Gabe laugh, and Sinead responds.

"That woman hates everyone. She's bitter that she has to teach Harvard's castoffs because they wouldn't hire her."

"I didn't even apply to Harvard, and neither did Laura. Neither of us wanted to go to law school with a bunch of insufferable twats. I had enough of them during undergrad."

The laughter ceases, and Enzo, Sinead, and Gabe all turn to look at Massimo. Oh, fuck me. Fuck me. Fuck me. Did he go there? Did he hear me?

"If memory serves me correctly, your firm made an exception and hired you despite you going to Yale. All the other attorneys there went to Harvard."

Massimo strolls over, and I want to sink through the floor. Fucking hell in a hand basket. Wonder-fucking-ful. Wait. He did a background check on me. He already knows where I went. If memory serves him.

"I didn't want to go to law school with them. I don't mind running circles around them now."

I'm digging my own fucking grave, but Massimo doesn't appear angry. I think he might be a little amused. He looks over his shoulder at Salvatore.

"Big brother, did you know you're an insufferable twat? I've been telling you that for years. Do you believe me now?"

Oh, Jesus Christ. Fuck. Goddamn it. Oh, fucking hell. I'm a lapsed Lutheran. I take the Lord's name in vain way too often, but that was a double. My grandmothers are rolling in their graves. Fucking full three-sixties.

"If I'm an insufferable twat, then that makes you one too because you've always looked up to me, baby brother."

I'm utterly mortified now. Nicoletta, Sylvia, Paola, and Carlotta are staring at me. Not only did I insult two of their husbands and brothers, they now know I have a foul mouth.

"I've been telling you both that since I could talk."

Domenico joins this little convo, and my humiliation is complete. They might tease one another now, but I started it. Matteo calls out from where he sits next to Maria, who's trying to shut him up with her hand over his mouth.

"And I only got an MBA from there. I told you I was smarter than either of you. I knew I didn't want to become an insufferable — Ouch, Mama."

I watch Carlotta move to stand beside her son, where he sits at the end of the sofa. She put her hand on his shoulder near where it meets his neck. I think she's pinching him, but I can't tell for sure.

"When you're as old and gray as your father, then you can swear because by then you will have found another way to put me in my grave."

"You called me a silver fox just this morning, Lotta."

Domenico waggles his eyebrows, and Matteo looks like he's going to be sick. Domenico shifts his gaze to his son.

"Where do you think you got your charm from? You certainly didn't find it on your own."

Maria jumps in at her husband's expense. "You know you inherited it from your dad, my love. I've known you since I was five minutes old. You definitely weren't born with it."

Maria gives him a smacking kiss on the cheek. I think I might be in the Twilight Zone. What the ever-loving fuck did I step into? This is the most fucking normal family I've ever seen. Except for the part where three of them went to Harvard and two went to Yale. I can only imagine where the others went. There isn't an ugly or dumb one in the bunch.

Sinead leans over to whisper to me.

"What they do only exists in Salvatore's office down the hall. Out here, they're normal family men who tease one another relentlessly. It's the women who are merciless. You did nothing wrong. Just the opposite. We've been worried about you and Enzo. This eased the tension."

Now, I feel super guilty that they worried about us while I was riding my boyfriend's dick. I can't imagine any of them would think it was more than that if they found out. Enzo lets go of my hand, and I dig my nails into the back of his. He shakes free only to slide his arm around my waist. I sag against him, and he kisses my forehead. I want to encircle his waist with both arms, but I don't dare in front of everyone else. I settle for one around his lower back.

Gabe harrumphs.

"Michelle, I'd still like to hear you explain why I'm right, and she's wrong."

He dips his chin toward his wife and smirks.

"Dr. Sabastianson was the hardest because I couldn't

understand a word he said. He always sounded like his false teeth were about to fall out. He never tested on anything out of a textbook, only what he lectured in class. I prayed more that semester than I did all my years of Sunday School."

"Ha! I told you!"

That came from Sinead, and I didn't expect it.

"Why are you cheering?"

"I told him that not understanding the man doesn't count as a hard class. The man may have had a Doctor of Philosophy and a Juris Doctorate, but he wasn't that hard. All you had to do was copy the notes from the board and piece that together. I don't remember a thing the man said, but I could read his handwriting. Professor Hughey purposely worded her questions, so there'd be no right answers, but none of the above wasn't an option."

Gabriele's eyes twinkle, and I know he's about to tease his wife a little more.

"Maybe it was hard for you, *amore mia*. Deductive reasoning always gave me the right answer."

"I doubt that. You got through that class with your charm and looks. I bet she stared at your chest more than she did your eyes."

"And I made sure to flex a lot."

Gabe does that, and I have to admit, it's impressive. The man is enormous, and he looks like he's about to Incredible Hulk that shirt. Sinead's standing where only Gabe and I can see her expression, and his wife certainly appreciates the show he's putting on. I might have too before I met Enzo. But I prefer him. He's got a swimmer's build, which makes his suits hang on him as though he was born to wear them. Naked, he's magnificent. Muscle upon muscle.

I'm trying not to look at Gabe because everyone can see my expression. If I don't get my mind under control, they're going to think I'm thinking the same thing about Gabe as Sinead is. I lean between them.

"I recant. I agree with Sinead now that I've heard her explanation."

Gabe shakes his head as I speak. He grins as he leans forward to be eye to eye with his wife.

"Too late. The verdict is in. The jury can't change their mind."

"Then I motion for a mistrial. The juror decided without the full scope of the evidence."

"Sorry, counselor. You should have started with your best piece instead of saving it for last."

Gabe finishes the argument by lifting Sinead off her feet and kissing her. With his back to everyone else but me, it's definitely not a kiss anyone else should see. He whispers something in her ear, and I could swear he calls her *piccolina*. I look up at Enzo, who must have heard him too. The look he shoots me tells me not to ask right now. I won't, but it hurts. I thought that was a name just for me. Is it a common term of affection?

He draws me away as the couple continues to whisper to each other. We walk over to where Domenico, Massimo, and Paola are standing together. Massimo offers me a fatherly smile, and my heart slows. I didn't realize it started racing as we approached.

"You aren't wrong. We are insufferable. They drill it into us. But my brother was that way before he got to law school. We didn't take it personally."

Domenico elbows Massimo before he takes a dig at his best friend.

"You didn't need to have it drilled into you. You led by example."

"How would you know? You only went to Princeton for a graduate degree in — dare I say it? — Mathematics."

"But you could only manage two little degrees. I got a second masters in engineering from MIT."

All I know about Domenico is that he used to be a *capo*. I never thought to ask what he did when he wasn't *capoing*.

"You're just bitter that your son followed me to Harvard, Dom."

"Bah. I got my son *and* your nephew to follow me. One's an architect, and the other is structural engineer. Matteo may have an MBA from Harvard, but he's still an architect with a mind for business. Carmine still makes sure everything we build stays standing. So it's engineering for the win, my sourpuss old friend."

"Ignore them."

Paola interjects and rolls her eyes.

"Neither of them could find their ass with a map. The only thing that ever proved either of them was intelligent was that they married women far smarter and wiser than them."

Domenico and Massimo stop their playful bickering to look at Paola. Massimo tugs Paola's hair playfully.

"With tact like that, I don't know how you've lasted in politics."

"I only tell clients what they want to hear. You two — well, honesty is the best policy."

Flummoxed. That's the word for how I feel. Flummoxed.

None of the bickering or rivalry has any kind of edge to it. It's a loving family joking with one another. It's not like the movies. They aren't sitting around tables with their Stogies, counting their money or planning their next hit. They're fucking normal. I need this after finding out that someone wants to target me.

As my gaze sweeps the room, I see how everyone else is with each other. None of this is staged. It's all heartfelt. But I have to wonder if it's happening at this particular time to take people's minds off the fact I've brought a threat to their doorstep.

"Michelle, maybe you would like something to eat. Why don't I show you what we have in the kitchen?"

Sylvia gestures for me to follow her. Enzo gives my waist a squeeze before he lets go. I watch him drift over to Carmine and Marco as I go with Sylvia. When we get to the kitchen, she gets me a glass of water before doing anything else.

"Please sit. They can be too much at first. I only had two sisters, but I still come from a big family. I'm used to the noise. But the joking — that's just them. My family loves each other, but we are not so funny. It overwhelmed me at first, and not just because I knew so little English. They welcomed me and spoke Italian or Sicilian mostly for the first two years while I learned. They aren't any different regardless which language they speak."

"You didn't speak English? That must have been a shock moving here."

"It was. Michelle, Salvatore and I had an arranged marriage. He'd refused everyone before me, but something about the way my papa and *zios* described me was enough for him to agree to me specifically. He knew he needed a marriage that could keep us connected to Sicily, but he accepted Papa's offer because he said I sounded perfect. I was not so convinced. I didn't want to leave Sicily for America. If I had, I would have come here for university. I went to France instead. Did Lorenzo tell you I'm a lawyer, too?"

"I don't think so."

I've taken in a lot of information in the past two weeks. Fuck in the past two hours.

"Yes. I went to the Sorbonne. Three years studying law as an undergrad, two years in an LLM, and then three years for a PhD. The French system is very different. I was able to return and practice in Italy because I worked in public international law. When I came here, I continued to work for my family until I knew enough English to pass the bar and go before the review boards. Now I practice corporate law and represent our family."

I want to go back to the part about the arranged marriage, but I don't feel like I can. Thank heavens she does.

"I told you about my career because this wasn't some old-fashioned arrangement with a dowry and me shipped off to a foreign land. When I met Salvatore, it was lust at first sight. I have never met a man I've been so attracted to before even saying a word. It took me longer to admit I loved him than for him to admit he loved me. But it wasn't because I didn't feel it. I wasn't used to such an expressive and demonstrative family. I spent eight years living on my own in Paris. I came home just long enough to find out my father and *zios* played matchmaker. I'm eternally grateful that they did."

"Are they really always like this? Or are they trying to ignore the threat I brought to your family?"

"We're always like this whenever we all get together. My daughters are asleep, but they are just as bad as the rest of them, and they're only eleven and nine. You'll see on Sunday if you can make it."

"Sunday?"

"We have Sunday dinner together every week. I'm going to need a new dining room table soon. It's getting crowded. When the weather is nice, we eat outside. I think we can do that this weekend. Would you like to join us?"

If I don't, I'll be keeping someone from their family. If I do, am I really imposing despite the invitation?

"Michelle, if I didn't genuinely want you here, I wouldn't have told you about it. Lorenzo would have. And if you can't make it or don't feel comfortable coming, no one will blame you for Lorenzo not coming. They can all manage missing one feast. None will starve."

"Thank you."

"Think about it."

Her hand squeezes my wrist before she goes to the fridge.

"What would you like? It's been a long night, and they never feed you probably at those snooze fests."

Snooze fests? I guess she's been here a while if her older daughter is eleven. But her accent doesn't sound like she should know that slang. I laugh and join her at the fridge. I spot the chocolate cake, but I force myself to look down toward the vegetables or something like that.

"Chocolate cake it is."

She shoulder bumps me. I look up at her.

"I was hoping you'd spot that. There are two slices left, and I'd rather you have one than let Salvatore. He's already had four. The man is a bottomless pit, even at his age."

The affection in her voice makes me think they have the same type of relationship as the other couples. I didn't miss the part about Nicoletta and Carlotta having the same due dates with their second sons. I can see where Lorenzo gets it from. I doubt Salvatore needs the gym with a gorgeous wife. She pulls it out and serves both of us. I'm about to take the second to last bite when Lorenzo joins us.

"I asked you to save me a slice!"

I look at the last bite, and I really, really don't want to share. I saved the last bite with the most frosting. Hell, I can ask for a spanking later. I savor that final forkful, and I can't help it. My eyes close for a moment.

"Sylvia, did you make this?"

"No. Serafina did. She owns two bakeries."

"It's amazing."

Lorenzo huffs.

"And that was supposed to be mine."

Lorenzo puts his hand at my lower back and kisses me. I'm certain he can taste the chocolate.

"It's a good thing your cousins are in bed, or you could explain to your uncle why his daughters have kissing questions."

Sylvia says it as she walks past us to leave the kitchen. He spins me on the stool I'd taken to eat the cake. He steps between my legs.

"Do you want to go home like we planned, or would you rather spend the night here? Where would you feel safer?"

"Where will you be?"

"Beside you in whichever bed you choose."

"What do you think is smarter?" Safer.

"You're safe at either place, but there's more security here."

"But more privacy at my place."

"Yes."

"You didn't tell me which one you think is smarter."

"Either. I wouldn't have given you a choice if I didn't think I should."

"Then can we go home — to my place?"

I tack that on at the last minute.

"*Piccolina*, you've been to my place. If yours feels more like home, then we call that home. I'm not assuming you want to live together yet, but home, for me, is wherever you are."

"You say the most romantic things. But— uh — is —"

"*Piccolina* isn't a common term of endearment in Italy or Sicily. But it is one in this family. It's private between husband and wife, boyfriend and girlfriend. I suspect the other couples are like us. I've heard a couple of the women whisper Daddy when I didn't mean to overhear them. I have never called another woman *piccolina* or *cuore*. I've never used any terms of endearment for women who aren't already in my family. You're the only one, little girl."

"I've never called a man I'm dating Daddy."

"I know. These things are special between us. While we might be like the others, what happens between us is our business. No one else's."

I want us to have a home together. This night has shown me a lot. It's almost too much to take in. It's overwhelming like Sylvia said. But I feel safe with them. Everything Enzo told me about family being the most important thing to him was evidenced here tonight. He didn't exaggerate. I want to be a part of this as much as I want Enzo for the man he is separate from his family.

I assume there's a crib somewhere for Petra because Olivia wasn't holding her baby when we came back downstairs. They all have rooms here even though I don't think any of them have lived here besides Salvatore, Sylvia, and their daughters.

Whatever shit is happening because of my involvement with Laura and her in-laws, I trust the Mancinellis to protect me. And I trust Lorenzo to love me. I just hope it's all enough.

It's been a week and way more normal than I expected. I've had lunch with my sister twice, and I was nervous at the beginning of both meals. But she says I'm happier than she's ever seen me and wants to meet Enzo. I told her he was a lot like Maks and left it at that. Her eyebrows shot up to her hairline, and she looked disapproving. When I told her more about what it's like when it's just the two of us, that's when she realized how happy I am. I think she's on board with it.

I've told my parents about Enzo, but I've avoided using his name. I suspect the moment I say Lorenzo and not even

Mancinelli, they would know who I'm dating. I've told them he's a restaurateur, an entrepreneur, and an accountant. I've alluded to his wealth, which I can still only guess at, and that his family is among the richest in the city.

When they asked if he grew up in the city, I said yes. I gave a not so subtle hint when I said his family is from Sicily. Their faces were mirrors of Liz's, but they said nothing at all. Imma go with silence is consent on that one. I haven't told my brother a damn thing. We're close, but I don't want to know who he sleeps with. And I'm damn sure he doesn't want to know who his little sister sleeps with.

It hasn't been hard getting used to having bodyguards because they are professionals. I believe Enzo when he says they trained him to be one. His men — including the ones in his family — are discreet, but present enough that I feel safe.

Enzo guarded me himself the first two days at the office, and he was practically a ghost. I purposely went to the restroom more often than usual or walked clients to the door just to see if I could spot him. I didn't, but somehow I just knew he could see me.

We had a weekend in there, which we spent together. We went running in Central Park. We had men ahead of us and behind us, so I kinda felt like the president. But again, they were completely unobtrusive. You'd have thought they were everyday runners enjoying the beautiful weather.

We went to the movies, and I usually like to sit in the middle. Too close makes my neck hurt. But I had to relent once Enzo explained why we sat in the back row like I did with Laura and Christina. That just made me want to curl into his lap and never go outside again. We can't have anyone who could sit behind us to stab or shoot us. The upside was his men sat down by the entrances, and he bought the entire back row. Our hands did a lot while we watched the movie.

All in all, it's been wonderful spending time with him, and I don't feel claustrophobic from it. Instead, I feel like I have an attentive boyfriend who makes me laugh, helps me around the house, and is just all around amazing. He's spent the night at my place all week, and it surprises me how little I notice suddenly sharing my space with someone else.

I know it started out as a precaution, but I love it. I dread the idea of him going back to his place and not sleeping beside him every night. Sometimes I get too hot from being curled around him, so I roll over. He follows me in his sleep. I don't get any cooler, but I love that he wants me even when he doesn't realize it.

And speaking of wanting me. Holy shit. The sex just keeps getting better. We haven't done anything kinkier than a few spanks and tying my wrists to my headboard. I want more, but he hasn't suggested it. I guess he's waiting for me, but I don't know what I want to ask for.

The only issue is that I have no idea what's going on. I've come home twice to him suddenly hanging up after saying a couple words in Italian. He's come home three times frustrated, but he's gotten his irritability in check the moment we hug.

I don't know if this is just regular business or about me. I really don't feel comfortable asking him about that. What am I allowed to ask without being too intrusive? Do I want to ask and get the blank stare Serafina gave me the night she lent me clothes? Do I want to hear him brush me off or be evasive? Do I want him to lie by thought, word, or deed? There's the lapsed Lutheran in me.

I don't want anything that could put a dent in what's been blissful. It's been so good that I can almost forget why he's staying with me and pretend we're a normal couple in love. Neither of us has said that yet, but we're getting closer. I can feel it. I've caught myself more than once to keep from saying it, and I think he has too.

I'm in the office and need to focus on my work rather than daydreaming about my smoking hot boyfriend. I gotta admit it was thrilling seeing women check him out when we went to the movies and knowing he was with me. Maybe he intentionally ignored them, or maybe he's so used to people staring that he doesn't notice anymore. But he was wholly focused on me, and it made me feel like the most special woman in the world. He had no qualms about public displays of affection. His arm wrapped around my waist with his hand practically on my ass. It was just the right level of possessive and sexy.

I buzz my assistant through the intercom.

"Haley, do you have my calendar?"

I like a printed version at the beginning of the week, so I can keep track of what gets changed. I highlight moved meetings depending on whether the client rescheduled or I did. I want to make sure I never move things around more than the clients do. It means I'm at their whim, but it also makes billing easier.

"Yeah. I moved your Shapiro meeting to twenty minutes from now. He wanted to be here first thing this morning, but I told him you were unavailable until nine."

She hands me the papers with his appointment box highlighted. Fuck. I didn't realize he was even on my calendar for this week. I haven't had to deal with him since running into him at the event. Enzo was with me then, but Marco's in the hallway today. My nervousness shoots through the roof.

"Can you get Kelsey to sit in with us? Oh, and Murphy too."

I hate thinking I need a man in there, but I do. I don't trust Simon not to say something in front of a female paralegal. I doubt he would in front of a male one. I guess Susan overruled Anderson since fuck face is being allowed back in the office.

"Both?"

"Yes. And send them to me now, please."

I click around on my computer until his files pop up. It's only a moment later that both paralegals step into my office.

"Close the door, please."

Murphy does as I ask as Kelsey comes to stand in front of my desk.

"I'd like you both present when I meet with Simon Shapiro. There was an incident the last time he was here, and I don't feel comfortable being alone with him."

"What did that asshat do?"

Kelsey crosses her arms and looks ready to come to my defense.

"The specifics aren't important. I don't trust him alone or with only one other person. Take notes. Speak up if you see fit. Just look like you're in here to work."

Murphy listens and only nods. He's usually chattier and nosier. When he turns back to the door, I watch him. I dash my glance to Kelsey, who just shrugs and follows him out. I assume they're both going to get their note pads. I move my laptop to my conference table and gather the paper documents I need.

I debate whether I should tell Enzo before or after the fact. If I don't tell him at all, and he finds out, he'll know I intentionally kept it from him. I don't know how he would find out, but he's resourceful. I'm at the table answering emails, my nervousness turning to resentment, when Haley announces he's here and shows him in. Kelsey and Murphy follow him and slide into chairs at the table.

"Good morning, Mr. Shapiro."

"Good morning, Michelle."

The informality rankles since we've always addressed one

another professionally. At least before he tried to molest me. Unfortunately, New York requires actual physical harm to claim assault. In other states, intentionally making someone reasonably in fear of physical harm is grounds for the charge.

He touched me, but the marks on my throat faded quickly. It would have been difficult to prove it, so it left me with little recourse. I didn't want to push the issue and bring Enzo into it as the only witness. It would open the door to Simon claiming Enzo threatened his life. That would end up dominating the situation, cause more problems for my boyfriend, and remedy nothing for me.

"The contracts for the new building are available for your review. The property owners increased their demands and want thirty percent down payment for the sale."

"Twenty percent is standard."

"In residential purchases. Commercial is fifteen to thirty-five of the fair market value. Twenty was a courtesy. Thirty is a compromise."

"If I have to produce thirty percent, that ten percent will come out of the donation to the actual building."

"You didn't earmark it as a donation, Mr. Shapiro. This isn't a donation to serve as a tax write off. Only one million eighty thousand dollars can be written off for a property put in service for that tax year. If you try to stretch this over two, you won't be able to claim it that way either. It's not considered in service while under construction. I'm not a tax attorney, so I can't give you specific advice beyond that."

"Then maybe you're wrong."

"I am not."

My tone is decisive, but it's bordering on defiant. I need to rein in my temper. Arrogant son of a bitch piece of shit.

"Michelle, the ten percent still has to come out of some-thing. I suppose it'll have to come out of my cash donations."

That's going to rip a massive hole in the organization's budget. He can afford it without batting an eyelash. He's doing this on purpose. He's punishing me.

"Then you will lose your position as the chief benefactor. You will not be in the ribbon cutting, and your name won't be on the plaque in the entrance."

That's why he's really donating. He wants the publicity, and he wants to be immortalized on some brass rectangle no one's going to bother reading. He doesn't give a shit about the charity. When I continue, I know I'm pissing him off even more.

"If you are no longer the chief benefactor, my client will name the building after the person who is."

"Who?"

"I'm not at liberty to disclose that at this time. That is a separate contract negotiation."

"This is my project."

"And it will remain that way as long as you continue to contribute the most. I clearly outlined the limitations of your influence and control in the contract you signed. You had your lawyer review it, even redline it. Once I adjusted it to accommodate *some* of his requests, you signed."

He's fuming. He keeps glancing at Kelsey and Murphy, who alternate between watching him and taking notes. If they weren't there, he'd be spewing vile shit at me. He'd probably throttle me.

"Michelle, would you really derail this project because I rejected you?"

"You have a poor memory, Mr. Shapiro. I believe my boyfriend, Mr. Mancinelli, had to intervene. I guarantee his memory is far better than yours. Now let's review this construction contract, knowing you will pay the thirty percent down payment. If you're going to refuse, we're done for today. I'll be calling another investor to take your place."

"Give it to me."

I feel like holding it back and saying "please," like you would with a child who's forgotten their manners. I slide it across the table to him. I could lean forward and hand it to him, but I'm not giving an inch to meet him. I watch him skim it before he slides it back to me.

"No."

"Such a pity. Have a good day, Mr. Shapiro. I have someone else to speak to now. I won't slow the project, so I will move on to the other investor."

I have no fucking other investor. My firm's fucking senior managing partner refused to consider it. She said it would be an insult to Simon and a show of bad faith. She fucked us and our client.

I stand and step around my chair as I gather the papers. I turn away from him and return to my desk. I hear him stand, muttering something I can't understand.

"Leave. I'd like to speak to Michelle alone."

"Mr. Shapiro, my paralegals work for me. You do not command them. They remain since we have more work to do. Good day."

"Michelle, you're being—"

My cell phone buzzes on my desk, and thank heaven for small mercies. I answer it.

"Hi, Lorenzo."

"Chellie, what's wrong?"

He must hear something in my tone even though I tried to sound neutral. Maybe that's it. I usually sound as excited as I am whenever I see his name on my phone screen.

"I'm just wrapping up a meeting with a client who's just leaving."

"Chellie, are you all right?"

"Yes. It's just taking a moment, but I won't be late like last time."

"Motherfucker. What did Shapiro do?"

"Nothing."

My gaze locks with Simon's, and he knows exactly what's happening. Kelsey and Murphy do too. At least, they understand the part about why I asked them to join us.

"I'm sending Marco in."

I hear him tapping his cell phone as he speaks. No chance of me stopping him now. I try to keep the conversation sounding normal.

"Are we still on for lunch? I have a couple calls to make, then I'll be ready."

I hear the receptionist call out to someone, so I glance out of my office. Marco is making a beeline to me, and people are staring.

"Your brother is here."

"Good. And yes, we are on for lunch. I'll be there in thirty minutes. You're going to tell me every fucking word that piece of shit said, *piccolina*."

"I know, D."

"I'm not getting off the phone until I hear Marco."

Blessedly, he walks in at that moment.

"Hi, Michelle. I know I'm early, but Enzo asked me to swing by and pick you up before we head for lunch."

"Thanks. My client was just leaving, and I have a couple calls to make. Could you wait in the lobby, please?"

"I'll walk him out."

Simon glowers at me, but he's no match for Marco. He looks like a wilted sapling compared to the mighty oak now planted inside my office.

"Kelsey, Murphy, thank you for joining us. I'll meet with you this afternoon to review the notes."

They're professional, but if ever two people scurried to get out of an awkward situation, it was them. Marco gestures for Simon to follow them, never taking his eyes off the cretin. Marco closes the door behind them.

"Daddy?"

"I'm still here, little girl."

"I don't know if Marco made things better or worse, but I'm glad he was here. Simon had just tried to dismiss my paralegals to speak to me alone. The meeting wasn't going well to begin with."

I can't tell him more than that. I wish I could, so that he'd know what a douche Simon was.

"Chellie, what did he say?"

"You know I can't tell you."

"Is he your client?"

"No. But he's doing business with my client, so anything I'd say connects to their right to privacy. He was contentious about terms he didn't like. He pushed back, which would have been fine until he wanted to speak to me alone. He insisted upon using my first name, which he hadn't done before the incident."

"Incident? The fucker assaulted you."

I'm not getting into legal semantics with him.

"Are you really free for lunch? I wanted Simon to think I was going to see you soon."

"Yes."

"Enzo, are you rescheduling something, so you can say that?"

"Yes, and I don't give a shit. I'm coming to see you."

"Marco used the excuse that he's picking me up so he could come into my office."

"Good. Have him take you to Constantine's. I'm here right now."

"All right. Thank you, Daddy."

"Always, *piccolina*."

Fucking hell.

Anderson will understand, but Susan is going to plotz. How is it my male boss is more understanding than my female one? Does she think I should just suck it up and take it as par for the course? Or is there a reason for her to side with Simon over me?

I need to see Kelsey and Murphy and find out whether they'll corroborate my claim. I grab my purse and laptop, slipping it into its bag. I head toward their portion of the bullpen, the place where the associates work their asses off, trying to make junior partner. I spot them immediately since they're speaking animatedly with one another. But they go mute the moment they spot me. I approach with bravado I don't feel.

"Shit, Michelle. I'm glad I was there for you."

That's the chatty Murphy I'm used to. He doesn't swear in front of many people here. I'm one of the few. I suppose I should be honored. I look at Kelsey, who looks much warier. I wait for her to speak, but she shifts her weight from foot to foot a few times.

"Kelsey?"

"Why did that man interrupt the meeting? Why was he already here?"

"You heard Mr. Mancinelli. He came to pick me up because his brother couldn't make it. We're all having lunch together."

"The three of you?"

I arch an eyebrow.

"What are you implying, Kelsey? Am I not allowed to get along with my boyfriend's family?"

"He's very handsome."

She really thinks I'm cheating or going to have a threesome on my lunch break. If I were, I wouldn't want it done in thirty minutes.

"He is, but his brother is even hotter. I didn't come over to discuss either Mr. Mancinelli. What notes did you take?"

I put my hand out since they're both holding their notepads. I skim Kelsey's, which only note the business portions. That's good. We need a record of Simon's refusal to accept the thirty percent down payment request. We also have notes he wants to withhold the ten percent from the project. She also wrote down that he faced having another benefactor outbid him for the position as the foremost donor.

Murphy's is a word for word recantation of everything said. I'd noticed him scribbling furiously, but he's better than a transcriptionist. I look up at him, and he offers me the kindest smile I've ever seen on the young man's face.

"I have three sisters and a mom, Michelle. He's a sleezoid. I wouldn't want him anywhere near the women in my family. I don't think you should ever be alone with him. I'm glad I was there. It blows, but I don't think he would have held back as much as he did if it was just Kels. He would play he said, she said. He won't do that since I was there. He saw me taking notes."

Kelsey's eyebrows shoot up before she speaks.

"You thought he held back?"

"Fuck, yeah. Kels, that guy can't be trusted. You could tell he wanted to say way more. If Michelle had been alone, I think he would have used being bigger to intimidate her. I'm skipping Anderson. I'm taking these straight to Susan."

He holds up the notepad I'd passed back to him.

"Do me a favor, Murph. Before you do that, type it all up.

Email it to Anderson, Kelsey, and me. Save it on two clouds. Then take it to Susan."

"You don't trust these not to get lost."

That's exactly how I feel.

"I just want you protected. If other people have a copy, and there're copies saved digitally, then I feel better about you stepping forward."

I look at Kelsey as she shifts her weight again.

"I'll type up my observations, too. I'll send it to both of you and Anderson and Susan. He gives me the creeps."

"Thank you. I need to go, but I'll be back in a couple hours. I have a meeting downtown."

I leave the bullpen and swing over to Anderson's office. I knock, and he invites me in. If he didn't have windows that look out to the bullpen, I would leave the door open a crack for propriety, considering why I'm here.

"Michelle, why did I see a man head to your office while you were meeting with another client?"

"That was Marco Mancinelli."

I see his shock then his recognition. He at least recognizes the last name. I pray that's for the better, and I'm not about to get fired.

"I'm dating Marco's younger brother, Lorenzo. He was here to pick me up for lunch because he was closer than Lorenzo. My boyfriend called to tell me Marco was coming, and it happened to be while Simon Shapiro was in the process of telling Kelsey and Murphy to leave him alone with me."

"What?"

He pops out of his chair, his hands fisted.

"He's not pleased that the landowner wants a thirty percent down payment. The long and the short of it is he's threatening to withhold ten percent from us to make up for what he claims is extra for the down payment. I told he could do that, but he wouldn't remain the top donor. It didn't go over well. He started the meeting by calling me Michelle while I continued to call him Mr. Shapiro. It went downhill from there."

"Will Kelsey and Murphy back you up?"

"Yes. Murphy transcribed the entire meeting and is typing it up. Kelsey took notes on everything connected to the actual negotiations. She said she'd type those up too."

"Are you headed out?"

"Yes. Marco's waiting for me over by the elevators. He escorted Simon out of my office. My boyfriend is already at the restaurant. He's going to be upset if I don't get there soon."

And I'm not sure what "upset" entails for Simon. Does he threaten him again? Does he do something to go along with the threat? Does he send someone? Enzo won't overlook this. I have to admit I'm glad. If Simon died today, we'd actually be in better shape. He's bequeathing a shit ton of money to the organization I represent, and there's no way he can amend his will before Enzo can get someone to him.

"You have your computer. Do you have an afternoon meeting?"

"No. I was hoping I could work from home."

"He really rattled you."

"Yeah."

And Enzo probably won't let me come back. Ever.

We say our goodbyes, and I hurry to the elevators. Marco and I head out to the car. It surprises me when he gets in the front seat after holding the door open for me. I haven't ridden in the car with any of the men in Enzo's family. They've all met me at the office after a driver picks me up. They walk me to the car at the end of the day, but it's only a driver who takes me home. When we reach the restaurant, he opens my door. He must see the confusion on my face.

"I'm not your boyfriend's brother right now. I'm your body-guard. It's work."

Well, that makes me feel like shit. I'm just another job.

"Michelle, that means I need to pay attention to everything around me. The windows are tinted much darker in the back, which makes it harder for me to see out. I can't see the wind-shield or the rear and side camera views in the backseat. Enzo would kill me if I rode back there. I can't protect you properly if I'm there."

"That makes sense. Thank you for explaining."

"It may be work, but Enzo trusts me with your life. I'm his brother, but that doesn't automatically mean he'd trust me with someone he loves."

"He—"

I have no chance to correct him because Enzo comes storming out of the restaurant. Before I know what's happen-ing, I'm swallowed in his arms. His hold is so tight, I'm suffocating.

"Can't breathe."

I pant the two words, but he loosens his hold infinitesi-mally. He kisses the top of my head before he leans back far enough to swoop in for a kiss that makes my toes curl. When we come up for air, I don't see Marco anywhere.

"*Piccolina.*"

He sighs the word, and his relief is almost palpable.

"Daddy, it's fine."

"No, it isn't. But I'm going to make it fine."

Chapter Thirteen

Lorenzo

I feel like a caged lion as I sit across from Chellie, having lunch as though my brother didn't have to just escort a man out of my girlfriend's office. A man I found trying to rape her. He may not have touched her this time, but he would have threatened her once they were alone.

I'm trying super hard to act normal, but it's a struggle. She's not as animated as she usually is, but we're both holding up our side of the conversation.

When the waitress takes away our last plates, I stand and hold out my hand. I lead her back to the office, and Manny hurries out the moment I open the door. He won't come back. Not just because Chellie is with me. Everyone who works for me knows that once I'm in here, no one joins me unless they're invited. But I lock the door, nonetheless.

The moment I do, I press Chellie against the wall. I feel her sigh, and for a second, I think it's going to be okay. Then I see the tears she fights to keep from welling in her eyes. I'm ready to lose my fucking mind. I can't leave her, but I want nothing more than to find that shitbag and kill him. It's not like I don't know how to make it hurt while I do.

If any of our enemies discover how easily I lose my shit when Chellie is at risk, they'll use that against me. I'm known for my detached reputation. Going on a rampage will give our enemies way too big an insight into what will set me off.

"Daddy."

"Baby, I'm here."

Our kiss is frantic. She clings to me, and I taste her tears. I press her harder against the wall, and I feel her sigh again. The more I confine her, the more relaxed she gets. Any harder, and I'll be putting all my weight onto her, and I will crush her.

"Just keep holding me like this, please."

"As long as you want. I'm not going anywhere."

"Do you understand why I like it when we stand like this?"

"Yes. No one can see you or get to you without going around me. No one can sneak up and scare you or take you. I'm completely shielding you. I will always shield you, Chellie. But if this is what you need when you're scared, then I'll give it to you. I won't turn down the opportunity to hold you and be the one who comforts you."

"Daddy, I'm not scared anymore. You described it exactly right, but right this minute, you're keeping me from finding that asshole and going after him myself. You're restraining me because I want to take everything from him like he's trying to do to me. He thought he could strip me of my dignity and my freedom when he cornered me. He thinks he can intimidate me and make me fear him. That bag of shit doesn't realize how much I know about him. He runs a publicly traded company, and I have a lot of day trader friends. Telling them to target him wouldn't be insider trading, and it wouldn't be colluding if I get nothing back. No one can quantify personal satisfaction."

"If that's what you want, I can do that. I'm a CPA, but I have my series seven and sixty-three. That means I'm a licensed stockbroker in New York. Between Carmine and me, we have the resources to track down all his financials, find out where all his money comes from, and make it go away."

I'm not testing her, but I'm watching to see how she reacts to that admission and offer. I can tell she's considering it. When she nods, it's without hesitation, and it doesn't take her long. It's not a knee-jerk reaction. She thought about it, and this is what she decided. It's the thinking on her feet that good lawyers do.

"Don't take anything yet, but I'd like to know just how he built his wealth. Some of it is generational, but I want to know where the money his company uses to fund these types of projects comes from."

I can hack the IRS system. It's supposed to be impenetrable, but it's not. People have breached it more than once. I can also track trades and investments and look into his bank accounts. I have the hacking skills and ability to understand the reports. Carmine has the intelligence gathering skills to point me in the right direction. We've made little progress in finding out who's targeting Chellie. Nothing's happened — thank God — but it also means there's not a trail to follow. This gives me something to do.

I take a step back, and she follows. It allows me to wrap her in my arms and hold her. I need the comfort now. She runs her hand over my back as her fingers tunnel into my hair. Our kiss is so tender, it makes my heart ache. I wish we could stay like this forever. I'd be able to keep her safe here. But I can't. I can't because it's not realistic, and I can't because she can only take an hour for lunch.

"We should order, *piccolina*. I don't want to make you late back to the office."

"I told Anderson I'm working from home for the rest of the afternoon. Do you need to stay here?"

"No. Do you want to go to your place or mine?"

"I can work from either. Where do you need to go?"

"Either, but I like yours better."

Her brow furrows. I have an enormous penthouse loft. It's far bigger than what I need for just me. All of my furniture is designed for comfort because it's my escape. But it doesn't have the same homey feeling her smaller condo does. I prefer it there. I know I need to explain.

"I like your place better. It's cozy."

"It's small."

"Only compared to the ridiculousness of my place. You have three bedrooms and live alone. It's not small."

She looks like she's building the confidence to say something, but she's in two minds whether she should. I tilt my head and kiss her temple, her cheek, then her lips before prompting her.

"What is it?"

"Would you ever consider living there with me?"

"Yes. I can move today."

I grin, hoping it masks some of the desperation I feel. I want to live with her now. I want to declare myself, move in, and start talking about a future for real.

"How about we start with you keeping some clothes at my place? You already have a toothbrush."

I like that idea. I can live with it. I unlock the door, and we head into the dining room. There're menus already on the table I favor. It keeps my back to the wall, but I can see the door and out the windows. It's also angled, so Chellie's back is to the kitchen. No one can approach her that I don't see. And I will have watched them arrive.

After we order, I offer her my hand, palm up. She rests hers in mine.

"How much work do you have?"

"Too much."

She smiles ruefully and shakes her head.

"I'll work at your place. All I need is my computer. I have some trading to do as well as review some P&L statements. Nothing exciting, but I'd enjoy your company. This is a shitty reason to have it, but I won't turn it down."

Lunch progresses, and we share stories about our childhood. I think mine always shock her by how normal they are. Yes, we went on luxury vacations to places most people don't. But otherwise, it was totally typical.

I have three siblings, so something was always happening. Toss in Carmine, Matteo, Gabriele once I was thirteen, and Emilio until I was twelve. It was a happy childhood filled with playing at parks, swimming in the summer, and food. Always lots and lots of food.

She tells me stories from before and after her brother died. Her voice changes, and I know that despite it having been several years, the pain is still close to the surface. I haven't lost a sibling, but I've lost people I was close to. I can only imagine the amplified version of my grief.

I realize just after we leave the restaurant that I need documents I have in my safe at my place, so we change our plans. Once we're there, I have calls to make, so I head into my office where I can close the door. She works on the sofa in the living room. I get through them as quickly as possible, then I move into the living room. We occupy opposite ends of the sofa until we both shift and work toes to toes.

When she isn't typing, she rests her hand just above my ankle. It feels amazing to receive such a simple gesture of affection. I didn't think I was emotionally deficient, but I was certainly emotionally closed off to everyone outside my family. She draws something out of me I've never felt for someone because all this newfound affection is tied up with romantic desire.

We've been working in companionable silence for three hours, but my phone just rang three times then stopped. It's on the second of three rings. If I don't answer it, whoever it is will continue the pattern until I do. I pull it from my pocket on the third ring. It stops. Michelle's watching me. This isn't a family member calling to chat. It's work. I get it on the first ring, seeing it's Marco.

"*Cosa c'è?*" What's up?

I answer in Italian, so he knows I'm not alone.

"*Ehi. Dove sei?*" Hey. Where are you?

He responds in Italian in case whoever I'm with can hear him.

"*A casa sua.*" At her place.

He knows who "*her*" is.

"*Abbiamo bisogno di te da zio Sal. I Kutsenko hanno colpito una delle nostre spedizioni. Hanno preso le armi dirette in Venezuela. Dato che i numeri di serie sono spariti, non possiamo provare che siano nostre. Non ci venderanno. Le prenderemo.*" We need you at Uncle Sal's. The Kutsenkos hit one of our shipments. They got the guns headed to Venezuela. Since the serial numbers are gone, you know we can't prove they're ours. They'll under sell us. We're going to get them.

"*Bene. Voglio altre guardie qui. Non me ne andrò finché non saprò che sono al loro posto.*" Fine. I want extra guards here. I'm not leaving until I know they're in place.

"*Luca sapeva che l'avresti detto. Stanno arrivando. Ma sai che vengono dal Queens. Non c'è tempo per aspettare. David è già lì.*" Luca knew you'd say that. They're on their way. But you know they're coming from Queens. We don't have time for you to wait. David's already there.

David was Serafina's guard before she married Carmine. Three of her guards jumped ship and came to work for us after she joined our family. They usually guard her, but they're in the rotation for everyone. He's good, and I trust him. But I don't like the idea of leaving her with only one guy in a car parked outside the building.

"*Lo voglio fuori dalla sua porta. Te lo spiego io.*" I want him outside her door. I'll explain it.

"*Qualsiasi cosa vi porti qui prima.*" Whatever will get you here sooner.

"*Cosa non mi dici? Perché è così urgente?*" What aren't you telling me? Why is this so urgent?

"*Pensiamo che siano coinvolti gli uomini che hanno rapito zia Sylvia. Questo potrebbe significare che i Kutsenko hanno ordinato il suo rapimento.*" We think the men who took Aunt Sylvia were involved. That could mean the Kutsenkos ordered her kidnapping.

That makes no sense. The bratva don't target women. Ever. It's the one line those sociopaths don't cross. Some shit happened to the moms while they all still lived in Russia. They swear they'll never subject any woman to what the women in their family endured. But that hasn't stopped people — including my family — from using their wives for our gain. Have we finally pushed them too far? Have they changed their minds?

"*Sto arrivando. Ciao.*" I'm on my way. Bye.

"*Ciao.*"

"Is everything all right?"

I lean forward and take her hands in mine. I know she's guessed I've been to the garage while she's been at work. She hasn't asked, and I haven't volunteered. But she's seen my busted knuckles. This is different. I'm leaving her to deal with this, and now I could be leaving her vulnerable.

"I have to go, *piccolina*. It's work. David's going to come up and stay outside your door. If you want to go somewhere, just let him know. David will go with you. Text my mom, too. If anything happens, she knows how to reach me."

She nods, but I watch her swallow.

"How long will you be gone?"

She whispers the question.

"I don't know. Hopefully, not long. But there may be times when I disappear for days. The last thing I want is for you to assume I ghosted you or that I'm dead. I'm always coming back to you, Chellie. If something happens to me, my family will get you. I promise. If I'm going to be gone for more than three days, I want you to go to my parents."

"Three days? Could it really take that long?"

"Sometimes I have to travel unexpectedly. If that happens, it's a bigger deal than I thought. I don't want you alone and worried. I also want you guarded more if I'm away. The last time I had to travel unexpectedly was for business and before the threat."

"Will it always be that way? If you travel, then I have to stay with your parents?"

"If it's regular work and planned, no. But if it's more than an unplanned three days, then yes."

"Should I be scared?"

"No, little one. Come here."

I open my arms to her, and she crawls forward to lie against my chest.

"Daddy, I am scared. This sounds so ominous."

"I hate that I'm frightening you, but I need you prepared. I don't think it'll come to all that, but in case it does."

"Please be careful."

"Always. I have you to come home to. Nothing is more important than that."

I'm not exaggerating. Finding out who's fucking with my family is a top priority, but nothing is more important than Chellie.

"You have to go."

She says what we know, but neither of us moves. Our mouths move together, our kiss starting as equals. But I soon take the lead, and her body goes limp against mine, even as she drives me crazy with her tongue. Then it's over too soon, and I'm walking out the door, giving David instructions. He knows what I expect. If he moves before one of the men in my family arrives, I'll kill him.

I head down to the underground garage since I'm going to drive myself. I don't have time to wait for a chauffeur. It's nearly driving me nuts knowing I'm leaving before her other guards arrive. David is good, but he's only one man. As the elevator opens, I consider which car to take. My Range Rover is a tank despite its sleek exterior. It's got a lot of aftermarket shit to reinforce it. But my Porsche 911 Turbo is the fastest modern-day version of their cars you can get your hands on. I opt for that. I want to get to my family as soon as I can. The sooner I'm there, hopefully the sooner this is done, and the sooner I get back to Chellie.

As I pull out of the garage, I look both ways. Are there any dark sedans or SUVs? Yes. I watch as Luigi and Alonzo get out. I breathe a little easier, but I want someone from my family there. Someone has to be available. If they aren't, I want our men to take Chellie where someone is available. I keep looking around as I merge onto the street. I see no other cars that look like ours but aren't.

One of the very many fucked-up things about this world is we all get our cars souped up at the same shop. The guy who owns it is the best, and we all know it. The only way to tell the vehicles apart most of the time is the hubcaps. They're just as custom as everything else, but they indicate which family they belong to. When shit's literally blowing up, it's often the only way we know where to run. That shop is Switzerland. The owner tries to make sure our appointments never overlap, but sometimes we end up there. The deal is we go in peace. The moment someone causes problems is the moment the guy shuts us off.

I don't take the most direct route to the bridge because I want to see if anyone else is taking the same nonsense route. It wouldn't be a coincidence. I see no one, so once I enter Queens, I head straight to Uncle Salvatore's. I catch like every fucking red light. It's almost enough to make me paranoid and think someone's slowing me down. I nod to the guards as I pull through the property's gate. I've already gone through the community gate. I passed four fucking Kutsenko houses just to get to my family. They've all moved in here. Motherfuckers are taking over.

"Uncle Sal?"

I don't hear anyone when I enter, which is unusual. The only time it was this quiet was when Pia and Natalia were babies. I head toward my uncle's office, and I finally hear people. The voices are hushed as though they don't want to be heard. I see none of the women, so why are they whispering? I don't knock on his door, just like I didn't knock on his front door. We all come and go from one another's houses for the most part. Though that's not as frequent now that so many of us are married. No one wants to walk in on shit we shouldn't see. Especially Maria and Matteo since that's my little sister.

"Enzo, about time."

"Nice to see you too, Papa. I came as soon as Marco called. The lights weren't on my side. What the hell did

Marco mean that these men might have been involved in Aunt Sylvia's kidnapping? Does that mean Maks sent those men?"

"No."

I turn toward Carmine, who's sitting in an armchair with his computer on his lap. He's tapping away on the keys, and he didn't look up when he spoke. I wait, but he offers nothing else. He was a nosey fucker when we were kids, and that led to him heading up our intelligence gathering. I look back to my dad, then my uncle.

"What is going on then?"

It's Luca who answers.

"We think these are the same men, but someone else sent them when they came after Aunt Sylvia."

"How do you know they're the same?"

Uncle Salvatore drums his fingers as he speaks up.

"Because one of those fuckfaces had the balls to call me and brag. I was in the kitchen making dinner with Sylvia. My hands were full, so I told her to answer and put it on speaker. She immediately recognized the voice. She said it was the one who'd ridden in the back of the car and spent more time on his phone than paying attention to her grabbing the gun from the dead man next to her. He hadn't been prepared for her to shoot the two up front and to bolt from the car. She said she'll never forget that voice, so I'm certain she's right."

"So, they were hired."

I state the obvious. What we need to know is why. Carmine sits back and looks around the room.

"I think Maks hired these guys to do tonight's job. The guy who called figured Aunt Sylvia wouldn't hear him, or he figured she wouldn't recognize his voice. I don't think Maks had anything to do with Aunt Sylvia. Whoever hired them before is probably hoping we'll believe these jackasses did both jobs.

They're probably hoping we think it's the bratva behind taking Aunt Sylvia and stealing our goods."

That sounds ridiculous to me, so I say as much.

"Does that mean Maks hired men who don't know him? That seems highly improbable. Anyone who knows them knows they don't go after women. They'd know they couldn't possibly pass the blame for both jobs to the Ivankov bratva."

Gabriele mutters something under his breath. When no one else speaks up, I do.

"Aleks didn't go after Sinead directly."

"The fuck he didn't. Maybe it wasn't a direct attack on her, but he did nothing to stop it. He asked too many fucking questions."

The rage on his face must match the look Niko has whenever he thinks about Gabe and his role in Niko's wife getting hurt — twice.

"Did you pick them up?"

Uncle Salvatore shakes his head. He stops drumming his fingers as he locks gazes with me. He's as pissed as Gabe, but he isn't showing it. These men actually took — touched — Uncle Salvatore's wife. Gabe rarely wears his heart on his sleeve, but he does where Sinead is concerned. At least, in front of us he does.

"Marco and Matteo are going. Once we know who they are, we need you to hack their accounts. Follow every penny. Find out everywhere they go. Find their families. Find other jobs they've done."

"Carmine, I'm going to need your computer. I didn't bring mine."

His computer doesn't run all the financial software mine does, but he has what I need to hack. I can day trade, but my primary job is as a CPA. As part of that, I've studied forensic accounting. I don't want anyone tracing our shit, and I need to know how to find everyone else's. I can do all the same shit Sergei Andreyev can, even if I "only" went to Rutgers and not an Ivy League for computer science.

I'd already started hacking in high school, but the guy who taught me died my senior year. Rutgers was the compromise I had to make for my family. I got accepted to every Ivy League and then some. But I had to stay close to the city because there were times the skills I had and the ones I was learning were needed. Rutgers was just far enough away in Jersey for me to justify living in the dorms. I just wanted something semi-normal for a few years.

Carmine hands me his computer as I sit down at the end of the sofa closest to him. He's already logged out of his profile, so I log in to mine. I hear the others talking around me, but I focus on planning where I'm going to look. The obvious place to start is hacking the FBI and DOJ to see if there's anything in their background.

I'll also hack the IRS to see what they've claimed and to figure out what they are hiding. But I don't know their names yet, so I can't find their social security numbers. That means I can't start checking their bank accounts or their backgrounds. I'm antsy to get started, but I have a very limited amount of time I can spend on each site before I risk their security programs noticing me. They won't find me because I'll jump from so many satellites they'll assume it's a foreign hacker. But I don't need to draw attention.

While I wait to find out their names, I think about how much I want to take Chellie somewhere away from all this bull-shit. Somehow, she's connected to this. I'm sure of it. I don't know how, but I feel it in my bones. I want her far, far away. I want to take her mind off knowing she's a target and from this world she's catapulted into. I want us to have time as a couple. So, instead of the conversation going on around me, I pull up travel websites. I'm not browsing flights or even hotels. I don't need either of those. But I want to come up with a destination.

It's my phone that buzzes, and I recognize Marco's number. "Who are they?"

I launch my question with no preamble.

"Hired guys. Only one of them knows anything about the job that took Aunt Sylvia. He's also the only one who's held out. The others know nothing about who hired them. It's the typical find an envelope of cash in a trashcan as a down payment, then a second one once the job is done. These guys are professionals who don't ask questions from their employers. They all agreed that the person who contracted them only used email."

"Email? That's traceable. Does this person want us to find them?"

"I asked them that, but none had a good answer. They're just hired muscle. They don't think for themselves."

Marco rattles off a list of six names. I type them into a digital notepad that's so fucking encrypted even God couldn't see it. Once we hang up, I share the names to see if they mean anything to someone else, but everyone draws a blank. I start digging.

I don't know how much time passes until I glance at the clock on the computer. It's been nearly an hour and a half since I arrived. It doesn't take me long to find everything about these guys from the obstetrician who delivered them to where they got laid for the first time.

Amazing the trails you can find when you have the patience to dig. I filter through their bank accounts and tax returns. I looked up their personal shit in case Marco could use something for leverage. Now I'm ready to roll up my sleeves and really get to work.

Gabe brings me three cups of espresso as I work through

the night. I hate the shit, but it keeps me going. While I work, my mind tries to drift to Chellie, but I force myself to concentrate. I crawl through the various government databases until I find what I'm looking for. The one thing that links them together.

It's six in the morning by the time I have anything. I camped out in Uncle Salvatore's office while everyone else slept. Only Gabe stayed up with me, getting me coffee and making a couple of snacks. We head into the kitchen where everyone else is making breakfast.

"Everything is coming through Russia. I don't know if the person who started this is there. If they are, they weren't careful enough. But my guess is they aren't, but want us to think they are. That might explain why Maks hired them."

Uncle Salvatore stands up from his place at the kitchen table and paces.

"Could it be the bratva the Kutsenkos have history with? Could they have gone after Sylvia, hoping to pin it on Maks and his family? Are they who's targeting Michelle?"

Carmine's brow furrows. He doesn't look convinced, and his comment confirms it.

"Maybe. They might not have claimed taking Aunt Sylvia because they failed to keep her. But they know better than anyone that the Kutsenkos don't involve the wives, definitely not *la madrina*."

The matriarch or the godmother. That's Aunt Sylvia's role as the don's wife. Uncle Salvatore lost his shit in a way I've never seen before when he discovered Carmine, Gabe, and Luca's involvement in going after a Kutsenko woman. He has always said that if we target the women in another family, it opens the door for people to come after the women in our family. Did a bratva from Moscow step across the threshold? It seems unlikely, but that's what often turns into the most obvious answer.

My dad looks at his older brother and raises his eyebrows.

"What now?"

"Enzo, keep digging. We keep this to ourselves until we know something more definitive. For all we know, it's the fucking Diazes or O'Rourkes fucking with us. Maybe they meant no harm to come to Sylvia, but they wanted to scare me. And maybe it's a coincidence that Maks hired one of the same guys. I don't think it is, but maybe. Until we have no doubts, we sit tight."

Sit tight means me working throughout the day and likely into another night. Fuck me.

Chapter Fourteen

Chellie

I don't know what to make of Enzo getting a call and suddenly having to take off. He shared enough to prepare me for him being away, but he told me nothing about why he's gone. Is this going to become my new normal? His phone rings in that odd interval of three, then he tells me has to go. Then he disappears for however long.

Can I live with that? What if we get married and have kids? How do I explain why Papa suddenly vanishes? I'm certain there's already a system since Enzo's parents must have told him something when he was too young to know. That's both reassuring and fucked-up in the same breath.

Laura called this morning to see if I wanted to go out to lunch. Luca showed up late last night and is my family member guard today. He assured me it was fine, so I accepted Laura's invite. I'm headed to meet her now. This will be the first time Laura and I have seen each other since I really entered this world.

Enzo being God knows where, doing God knows what makes me empathize with Laura. I thought I had before, but it wasn't possible because I didn't truly know what her life was like. Now I do. How does she watch Maks leave, knowing he'll be in danger while she stays home with their twins?

"Hey."

I wave when I see her. She's got her son and daughter with her, and her brothers-in-law only a step behind. Each toddler has their own guard, and Laura has one too. I look around, and it wouldn't surprise me if there aren't more bratva men hiding out in the open. I'm certain Maks is being overly cautious with the threat to me. Laura's in danger all the time already. Now she's going to spend time with me in public. It makes me second guess the wisdom in this lunch date.

But she hugs me, and I blow kisses at Konstantin and Mila. It feels so normal. It's like it was before I started dating Enzo and before I found out someone is using me to get to Maks and his family. She points to the restaurant she suggested.

"Are you hungry?"

"Starving. I wasn't hungry this morning, but I am now."

She shoots me a sympathetic smile.

"Stomach hurt too much to eat?"

"Yeah. You make it look like you never worry when Maks is away."

"We're both lawyers. You know how to hide your thoughts as well as I do. I don't want Maks worrying more than he already will. If he knows I'm upset, it'll distract him. So, I bottle it up, shove it way, way down, and get on with the life I chose."

"Does it get easier?"

"Sorta."

We pause our conversation as the host shows us a table, and two servers bring highchairs. It takes Laura about thirty seconds to get her toddlers both strapped in with graham crackers in each little hand. She makes it look so easy.

"Chelle, it's scary when I don't know where he is or how long he'll be away. It would be easy to let my imagination run away from me. But Maks was fourteen when they forced him into the bratva. He's thirty-four now. Twenty years is a long time. I remind myself he survived all those years before we met, so I have to trust he knows what to do. I trust his family will always protect him. I trust he loves the twins and me so much that he will move Heaven and Earth to come home to us. Remembering that makes it bearable. When it isn't, I go to Galina's. That woman carries the weight of the world on her shoulders better than Atlas. But she also has a kind heart. She knows how I feel because she felt the same things when her husband would leave."

Except her mother-in-law's husband left to fight in a war and never came home. I don't want to imagine someone telling me Enzo didn't survive.

"I bet Lorenzo is going to whisk you away on some romantic getaway."

That draws me back to the present.

"Huh?"

"With all this going on, he'll want you away from the city. I think he'll also want a chance to spoil you. Away from all this shit, you can have his undivided attention."

She waggles her brows, and I get what she means. No quickies or work getting in the way. Instead, we'll be able to take our time. I feel my cheeks heat as I imagine Enzo tying me to a bed, blindfolding me, and having his way with me, using a vibrator to drive me crazy.

"Sex that good, huh?"

"What? Shh. Laura, stop laughing."

"Then don't look like you're fucking him in your mind."

"I look nothing like that."

"Really? How about you turn to face Luca with that look and see how he reacts? I bet he won't see you picturing fucking his little brother as entertaining as I do."

"Shh. You've looked the same damn way plenty of times. I know why you're not listening to me and thinking about Maks instead."

She shrugs unrepentantly. Before either of us can say more, the server takes our order. Then Mila chatters, and Konstantin drops both crackers on the floor. They keep us amused until the food comes. We catch up on our families. Her sister, Madeline, is getting married soon. She's a nurse up in Rochester, so the ceremony will be there. Laura's excited, but I know she's worried about people asking too many questions about Maks. I notice Luca and Bogdan striding toward us, and neither looks pleased. Is it because they're near each other?

My potential future brother-in-law speaks first.

"Michelle, we need to go now."

"You too, Laura."

Bogdan's already packing things into the diaper bag, and Luca's putting money on the table. I help Laura get the twins buckled into the stroller before Bogdan, Niko, Aleks, and Luca hustle us out of the restaurant. I try to stop to say goodbye, and Laura reaches for me, but the men give us no chance. Laura's rushed toward an SUV while Aleks pushes the stroller. Luca's practically dragging me to a sedan. He's careful as he helps me in, but he slams the door. I hear him get into the front passenger seat before the privacy glass lowers.

"I need to take you to my parents. Something's come up."

"Is it the same thing that came up with the Kutsenkos?"

"It's about us. When Aleks saw me getting ready to go to your table, he demanded to know what was happening."

"What is happening?"

My heart is racing, and all I want to do is reach into my purse, pull out my phone, and call Enzo. I want his voice to explain what's going on. I don't want to listen to Luca. I want to listen to my boyfriend. But that's not an option, so I try to make sense of what Luca's telling me.

"Whoever made the threat to you knows you're with Enzo now. They broke into your place and trashed it. I'm sorry, Michelle. There's no nice way to say that they left next to nothing unbroken. We're certain they know you're with him because they left a box of pasta and a bottle of chianti on the table."

"That's — bizarre."

"It is. But it doesn't get much more stereotypical about Italians. They want us to know they know."

"Are you taking me to your parents' place because Enzo's going to be gone longer than three days? He said that's when I would need to go over there."

"I don't know how long he'll be away, but no one feels comfortable with you being anywhere that doesn't have a full contingent of guards. Even Enzo's place is vulnerable compared to where Mama and Papa live. It's similar to Uncle Salvatore's."

"Similar?"

"Yes. There are guards that patrol the property, and there's a twelve-foot wall around the entire place. Everyone wants you safe."

"Was it Enzo who called you?"

"No. It was Marco. Enzo's busy."

That's not at all cryptic. Busy doing what? Shit I probably never ever want to know and refuse to allow myself to imagine. I have nothing else to ask since I doubt Luca will tell me much more. He volunteers nothing, so I sit back and watch the buildings go by as we cross over to Queens. I try not to gawk as we pull up to the home where Luca and Enzo grew up. It's a fucking castle like Salvatore and Sylvia's. It might even be bigger, which would make sense since there were four children growing up here at one time.

Luca opens the car door for me, and I try not to walk to the house looking like I'm catching flies. My family is more than comfortable, and I grew up in an affluent neighborhood in northern New Jersey, but this is some next level shit. I didn't even know there were homes like this in Queens. It's even more impressive with each step I take. I follow Luca inside and look around the foyer. I feel like little Orphan Annie waiting to meet Daddy Warbucks. Make that Daddy Enzo. That makes my lips twitch, but I stifle it as Massimo and Nicoletta approach.

"Michelle, are you all right?"

"Yes, Mrs. Mancinelli. Thank you for letting me come over."

"It's Nicoletta and Massimo. We're happy to have you here. We feel better knowing we're able to keep you company."

Keep me company. Or babysit. Or keep me alive from some crazy asshole that's decided to wage a vendetta through me.

Fucking hell. That makes me want to see, or at least hear Enzo. Something in my expression must reveal at least some of my thoughts because Nicoletta steps forward and offers me a hug. I don't hesitate, but I'm unsure. That is until she wraps her arms around me. It's the most maternal hug I've ever gotten. It rivals any my mom's given me, and her hugs are amazing. I give in and rest my head on her shoulder. Enzo, his brothers, and his sister are lucky to have her if this is how she comforted them.

"Did you have time to finish lunch?"

"Mostly."

"Do you want to eat?"

I can't help but smile. She's so Italian, and I'm here for that.

"No, thank you. I—"

I don't know what I should want or what I'm going to do here. I don't have any of my work with me, and I don't have my laptop. Shit. Shit. Shit. How could I forget that I'm supposed to be back in the office right now? Anderson is going to lose his shit. The one thing he doesn't waver on is punctuality. He'll let me work remotely if I ask, but if you don't give him a heads up, heads will roll. I pull out my phone just as it starts to ring. Speak of the devil.

"It's my boss." I swipe the screen. "Hi, Anderson. Something unexpected came up while I was at lunch. I was just about to call you."

"Where are you?"

"Queens."

I don't know if I'm allowed to say that. I look at Massimo, and he nods. But his expression is so reserved that I don't know if he's nodding because it's too late to take it back or if he really believes it's okay.

"Why are you there and not in the office? What unexpected thing came up?"

Fuck. I don't know what to say. I look at Massimo then Luca. I feel like a deer in the headlights.

"Michelle?"

"Yes, sorry. A family matter came up that I need to tend to."

"Your family is in Jersey."

Massimo keeps his voice low when he speaks.

"Tell him you're with us. Anderson will understand."

When he arches an eyebrow, it makes me wonder if he knows Anderson or if he's banking on their last name ending this conversation.

"I'm with my boyfriend's family. I'm with Massimo and Luca Mancinelli."

There's a long pause, during which I can't even imagine

what my boss must be thinking. He's practically whispering when he speaks.

"Are you safe? Do you need me to send a car or someone?"

"Thanks, but no. I don't need anything. I'm where I should be."

That sounds rather presumptuous to my ears, but Nicoletta's smile makes me feel like I just offered her the sun and the moon and all the stars. I feel accepted by my boyfriend's parents. I didn't expect it to mean so much to me, but it does. It was a worry that I must have buried, but now that it's gone, I feel lighter.

"Are you taking the afternoon off?"

"I don't have my laptop, so I guess I am."

Nicoletta shakes her head, and I frown.

"Matteo went into Manhattan to meet Maria after her shift. They can swing by and get it. I can call them now."

I nod.

"Anderson, Lorenzo's sister and her husband will stop by to get my computer. It'll probably take about an hour and a half, but I'll be back online soon."

"And there's somewhere you can work?"

"I'm sure there is. Massimo's an attorney too. He understands."

"I don't like strangers taking your computer, but if you trust them..."

"I do. Completely."

It's not strangers. It's Mafia. I can't blame him to be honest, but it is what it is. We hang up, and I slide my phone into my pocket. Massimo points toward a hallway.

"You can use my office when Maria and Matteo get here."

That surprises me. He's letting me into his inner sanctum. He must trust me. That or he keeps absolutely nothing there. Massimo ushers me into the living room while Nicoletta gets us drinks. Luca disappears before I realize he's gone. Massimo explains Petra has her first cold, and Luca's been hovering like a ruffled mother hen.

It sounds rather sweet. His scar that runs from beside his eye down to below his shirt collar has clearly faded with time, but it's still wickedly noticeable. It must have been excruciating. It lends an air of danger to him that's even more — ominous — than the other men have. That he's hovering over his baby girl is sweet. As I listen to Massimo explain, I realize he was probably exactly the same.

I'm surprised how easy it is to fill the time chatting with him and Nicoletta. I share stories about my siblings and me, and they tell me outrageous tales about their kids.

"Mama! Papa! We're here."

Maria's voice rings out as the front door opens. I turn in her direction, and I don't know what I expected. But it wasn't her completely bare faced, with her hair pulled up in a bun, and in scrubs with rubber clogs. I knew she was a radiologist, but she looks so — well, not what someone would expect from a Mafia princess. Her makeup and clothes were understated the other night, but this shows how naturally beautiful she is. From the way Matteo's looking at her — like he wants to devour her — he agrees.

Nicoletta stands and tsks.

"When are you going to learn inside voices?"

Matteo snorts. Maria ignores him.

"Hi, Michelle. We have your computer, and your assistant added some files she thought you'd need."

Anderson is going to have an aneurism if he finds out confidential client files passed through non-employee hands without being in sealed envelopes. I walk forward and accept the bag.

"Thanks so much for getting this. I appreciate it. I know it was out of your way."

"It wasn't a big deal. I work in Manhattan, so it's not that far."

That might be true on a map, but in traffic, it could have taken them more than an hour. Massimo shows me to his office, where I set myself up. The time flies, and I'm two hours into drafting motions and reviewing a brief Kinsey prepared. Was she sleeping when she did this? There are so many errors. It's not like her to be this sloppy.

My phone vibrates on the desk, and I answer. I don't recognize the number.

"Hello."

The moment the caller begins to speak, I'm out of my chair and hurrying to the office door. It's some type of voice filter because it sounds like machine.

"Hello, Michelle."

Even with the altered tone, I can hear the menace. This might as well be Hannibal Lecter saying, "Hello, Clarice."

"Who is this?"

I rush down the hall toward Massimo's and Matteo's voices. They go silent the moment they see me. I suspect it's more about ending their conversation than wondering what I want. I put a finger to my lips as I pull the phone from my ear and put it on speaker.

"I'm a concerned friend."

"None of my friends change their voice to speak to me. Who is this?"

"Hello, Massimo."

He ignores me but knows I must have gone straight to the *consigliere*. Massimo gestures for me to keep talking, but he says nothing.

"Massimo's not here."

"Really? Because I'm certain I heard you walking toward men's voices, and now I'm on speaker."

"The TV's on. I was coming out of the kitchen. I muted it, so I can hear you. I have my hands full, so speaker is easier. Otherwise, I might drop you. What do you want?"

"You make poor choices in friends and lovers."

I will myself not to blush in front of Massimo. I remain quiet, waiting for this caller to tell me something useful. He or she will if I give them the chance.

"Michelle, you're as stubborn as I was warned. I'm not interested in seeing who can out-wait the other. You put yourself between two powerful families who hate each other. They're going to bounce you around like a pinball, claiming they can each protect you better than the other. But you wouldn't need protecting if you walked away."

That implies I'm getting in the way of something. Why doesn't this person want me around?

"What if I picked sides?"

"You mean the Mancinellis because Lorenzo's banging you? You can try."

There's a note of humor even though the voice is completely distorted and doesn't even sound human. This person is mocking me. They're certain Massimo can hear, and they're trying to humiliate me.

"If you know I'm involved with Lorenzo, then you know he and his family won't be pleased if anyone ruffles even a hair on my head."

"Involved. You may as well be one of those sluts he's fucks at his club."

"You sound jealous. Are you mad he picked me?"

Something makes me think this is a woman after all. There's a bitterness that's replaced the mocking humor.

"You might be the flavor of the week, but you won't last. You're a distraction. A way to get back at the Kutsenkos. He's using you for a good lay and to manipulate Maks."

247

"Are you speaking from experience? Did he cast you off for someone else?"

"Ha. No."

"Then someone you care about."

"You aren't going to analyze me and read into shit."

But I already have.

"You work for someone who wants to cause trouble for the Mancinellis. You've had sex with Lorenzo at his club, hoping to gain something from it. Now you're bitter because not only did you get nothing for whoever you work for, you fell for him, but he doesn't want you. He wants me."

"You think you know so much? You don't—"

"But I do. It won't be hard for Lorenzo to know where to look. You shouldn't have called me, thinking you could taunt me. You're not good at this game."

"I—"

"Enough. I don't know whether someone hired you or you're doing this on your own. If you are working for someone, remind them the Mancinellis didn't become the most powerful family in New York because they manifested it from the universe. They earned it. If you're not working for someone, then leave me alone because I promise you, if it comes down to it, I will bury you so far underground even worms won't find you."

"You don't scare me."

"I should."

I hang up. My heart is racing, and I'm not feeling any of the bravado I showed. I'm scared I made it worse, but I refused to let anyone think they could intimidate me. I didn't want to appear weak in front of my potential in-laws. I didn't want this person to think they had the upper hand. And it just pissed me off.

"You handled that well."

I offer Massimo a wobbly smile. The adrenaline is wearing off fast, and I'm trembling. He hugs me, and it's as good as Nicoletta's. I sag against him, and it reminds me of hugging Enzo when he's comforting me. Massimo isn't as big as he probably once was. I don't doubt he once carried the same amount of muscle as his sons. But he's in shape. This is no dad bod. I feel safe with him, and that's exactly what I need. Matteo offers me a smile, but he's been texting someone since I came into the room. I'm pulling away from Massimo when my phone vibrates again. I'm almost too scared to look at it.

"Enzo?"

"Yes, my sweet *piccolina*."

Massimo points toward his office, and I don't need to be told twice. I hurry back down the hall and shut the door.

"Daddy."

"Yes, little one, I'm here now. Are you all right?"

"Yeah. I don't understand what's going on."

"I wish I was there. There was another threat to you. Whoever this is wants to pit the Ivankov bratva against us. They seem to think we and the Kutsenkos will take their bait. Matteo just told me about the call. I'm so sorry you had to hear any of that, especially in front of my dad."

"Did he know you belong to a BDSM club?"

"If he didn't, he does now. But I'm cancelling the membership. I don't need to go there, and if this is someone from my past there, then I don't want to be anywhere near them."

"That second part makes sense. But don't cancel it because of me. I was hoping we..."

I can't finish. I want to explore this part of our relationship. But I really don't want to have any run-ins with women from his past.

"Chellie, we can join another club if you want to try more than what we can do at your place or mine. But it won't be the one I belong to now. I don't want any of my past touching what we share privately."

"Thank you."

"Will you stay with my parents until I can come home?"

"If that's what's best, and they don't mind."

I don't really have a choice since someone apparently trashed my place.

"They definitely won't mind. I wish I could come home tonight, but it's going to be a few more days."

Days? That's not what I want to hear. I don't know if I can ask anything, and I hate this limbo. Will I get used to it?

"Chellie, I'm not in the city anymore. I can't say where I am, but I left early this morning. I think I can be back in about four days. I don't know if I'm going to be able to call you again. I'll try."

"Will you have your phone on? Or is this one of those times you can't be tracked?"

"I'm not sure yet."

"Are you alone? Is there anyone there to protect you?"

"Carmine is with me."

That surprises me. What are they doing? I expected him to name some guy I don't know who's just a bodyguard. I didn't think he'd be with his cousin. It makes me feel better though. I know some of Carmine's history, and I know Enzo didn't like him for a long time, but they'd gotten along better than Carmine had with anyone other than Gabe and Maria.

But even when things were at their worst between them, I'm certain they would have given their life for each other. That reassures me Enzo will survive because Carmine would do anything for him. But it also terrifies me because Enzo might die protecting Carmine. I don't want anything to happen to either of them, but I don't know what I'd do if I lost Enzo. I can't picture a future he's not in with me.

"Are you alone, *piccolina*?"

"Yes, Daddy."

"What're you wearing?"

"Gray trousers with a green silk blouse."

"What color is your bra?"

"Black."

"And your panties?"

"You know I'm not wearing any, Daddy."

"Good girl."

Why do those two words make me shiver, then send a bolt of heat straight to my pussy? If anyone else said it to me, it would feel like a condescending comment better suited for a dog. But when Enzo says it, it makes me want to get off.

"You told me not to wear them anymore, so I'm not."

"But you could since I'm not there to check."

I hurry to unbutton my pants and tap my camera app at the same time. I pull back the side with the zipper to show my bare hip. I take a quick pic and text it to him.

"What's this, little girl? Are you teasing me?"

"No. I'm showing you I have integrity."

I try to sound as earnest as I can, but his dark chuckle makes me want to squeeze my thighs tight.

"You can show me a lot more, baby girl."

"Phone sex?"

"If that's what you want."

"Will you send me a dick pic?"

He laughs again. This time, there's a lightness to it I think he hasn't felt until now. He was worried about me. My phone pulses, and I know a text just came in. I pull the phone away from my ear and see it's a message from Enzo. I open it, and there, in all its majestic glory, is his cock. He's hard, and I don't think it's been from stroking himself.

"Do you see what you do to me? All I have to do is hear your voice or think of you naked. I'm so fucking hard it hurts."

"I'd kiss it better if I were there."

"Just a kiss?"

"I'd suck you off until you came down my throat."

He groans, and I know what I'm saying affects him just as much as what he says to me makes me wet and horny.

"Touch yourself, Chellie. Let me see how wet you are."

"Enzo."

I hiss his name as I look toward the door. I glance down at my phone and realize he's trying to start a video call. I toggle over, and I can see he's in a hotel room. Nothing that I can see gives a hint where he is.

"No one's going to bother you in my dad's study."

"But it's your dad's. Integrity is doing the right thing even if no one knows. The right thing is *not* getting myself off in your dad's office, even if he never knows."

"Show me, Chellie. Now."

I can't disobey him. I don't want to. I angle the phone so he can see me slide my fingers down my pants. I slide them along my pussy before pulling them out and showing him they're coated.

"Suck them clean."

Hmm. That doesn't excite me. I don't want to taste myself.

"Taste what I do to you. Taste what I can't have right now, but I will as soon as I'm alone with you. I'm going to bury my tongue inside your cunt and suck your clit until you beg me to let you come."

"Yes, Daddy."

It's a breathy whisper before I tentatively stick my fingers in my mouth. It's not horrible, but I don't know why he enjoys it as much as he does. Then again, maybe he wouldn't enjoy tasting his cum as much as I do. I watch him fist his cock and stroke.

"Push your pants down so I can watch you rub your clit."

"Yes, Daddy."

I want to obey his commands. Focusing only on what he tells me is pushing everything scary out of my mind. It's giving me peace. I do as he says, and I rub.

"Go lie down on the sofa and unbutton your blouse. I want to see your tits while I picture sucking them."

God. I miss the feel of his mouth on them. The way it turns me on. The way it makes me feel like I'm doing something good for him since I know it relaxes him, even when we're in the middle of the hottest sex I've ever had. I hurry to do what he says.

"Will you move your hand slower, Enzo? I want you to tease me with it and ache as much as I do."

"Since you asked, little one."

He draws out each stroke, and his groans tell me he likes my suggestion. It makes me work my clit harder and faster.

"I'm getting close. May I come?"

"No."

I struggle not to moan in frustration. Orgasm denial isn't something I'm used to. I like it, but I hate it. I think that's exactly what it's supposed to do. I try to slow my hand, but he grunts.

"You will not come, *piccolina*. But you also don't get to ease off. Keep going. Rub harder and faster."

"If I do, I won't last. I can't help it. I can practically feel you inside me. The moment you thrust into me, and I feel you for the first time. The way your pelvis grinds my clit. The way you make me feel so full I could burst, but all I want is to take more. I need you, Enzo. I need to come because of you."

"I know. Your orgasms belong to me, Chellie. I decide. Your

body is mine to do with as I please, even when we're apart. Obey me, or I will punish you when I get home. Do not come."

My toes curl inside my shoes. I'm fighting back a tsunami with sand toys. I'm no match for the need to come. I squeeze my eyes shut, but then I remember I'll miss seeing him if I close my eyes. I watch him work his cock as I tease myself.

"Put the phone closer to your pussy. I want to watch exactly where I'm going to fuck you the moment I see you."

"What if we aren't alone?"

"You'll have ten seconds to get some place where we're alone. If not, my entire family will know what I intend to do because I'll sling you over my shoulder and carry you off like a conquering barbarian."

"Promise?"

"Definitely. Is that a roleplay that appeals to you?"

"Yes. I like the idea of being at your mercy. I won't know where you're taking me. Only that you plan to take me hard."

"Come for me, sweet one."

I rub with even more purpose until I feel it. It's the wave that starts as a tingle before it spreads from deep inside my pussy up to my core. Then it shatters outward, sending pleasure coursing through me.

"Daddy, are you close? Do you want me to suck you off? Or do you want to fuck me in the ass?"

"Fuck, Chellie. Say shit like that, and I'll run away with you. Chain you up in a room and spend the rest of my life fucking every inch of you. I'll only leave you alone long enough for you to eat, drink, and sleep an hour at a time. I won't stop touching you."

I roll over and hold the phone behind me. The angle is awkward, but I think he can see when I pull one ass cheek open.

"Fuck!"

I shift the phone so I can see him. I watch as his cock squirts cum over his abs. He strokes fast, and I can tell he's squeezing.

"When I get back, you better clear your calendar. I'm going to tie you to our bed. I'm going to fill your ass with a plug. Then I'm going to put a vibrator in your pussy as deep as it goes. Then it's nipple and clit clamps. I'll sit back and watch as you fight the need to come. I'll listen as you scream and beg. Only when I know you can't take another moment will I unclip your clit and take out the vibrator. I'll fill you with my cock and plant my seed in you. You'll feel it filling you until the next time I fuck you. Do you understand me, little girl?"

"Yes, Daddy. Come home soon."

"I'm trying, *piccolina*."

I guess that's the most I can ask for. He did just what I needed. He distracted me and made me feel safe with his dominating personality. I'm still embarrassed that I just got off in his dad's study, but I feel much calmer. I feel like I can face the world again. I suspect this will be my last chance to hide for a while.

Chapter Fifteen

Lorenzo

I fucking hate Chicago. Not the city itself so much as the pricks filling it. They have fucking chips on their shoulders. Everyone loves to point out this isn't New York, and how they don't do things like in New York. No shit.

They have no finesse. It's like a bunch of spoiled toddlers who need naps. It's like everything is a tower of building blocks they can't wait to go King Kong on. They build it just to knock it down. The bribes are out in the open, and no one realizes trying to strong arm me won't get what they want. They think they can intimidate me. Fuck them little shits.

I run in a class they can never join. While I rub elbows with the most powerful people in the world, they're here thinking they can be the modern-day Al Capone. Well, that fuck nut went down for tax evasion. I'm about to make sure the same thing happens to the Rizzos. Don Edoardo is about to understand Luca might look like the scary one, but I'm the one he should really fear.

Since we have a rocky alliance when it suits us, I can't go after him physically and in the open. But I can take everything from him. Every time Edoardo tries to increase his influence east of the Mississippi, we slap him down. Except this time, he got in bed with the bratva here.

He thinks that because Luca considered marrying his daughter, that he has some control over us. He expected Luca to prove himself worthy of Cecelia — a woman who had about as much genuine interest in Luca as he had in her — which was none. At the same time, our dad was pushing Luca to prove himself as underboss. Luca thought he could do that by using the Chicago Oskolki to stir up shit with the Ivankov bratva in New York.

All it did was get Niko's then-girlfriend-now-wife kidnapped by the Moscow bratva the Kutsenkos escaped. Unlucky bastards. They fled the Podolskaya in Moscow only to be sucked into the Ivankovs in New York. Anastasia survived, and Luca escaped the parson's noose. There's a phrase no one uses but seemed apropos when I learned it in an English Lit class. It's a good thing Luca didn't marry Cecelia because he would have been miserable with a woman who loves another man, and he couldn't be with Olivia.

But all of this is to say, Edoardo thinks he's hotter shit than he is. He doesn't know that I've just arranged for the drugs coming up from central Mexico to somehow fall off the back of a truck. Who's going to clean that up? My guys I brought with me. That's not nearly enough for him to understand he can't encroach on our deals in Indiana, Ohio, Pennsylvania, Tennessee, or Kentucky. We have eastern Pennsylvania, but let the Philadelphia *Cosa Nostra* have everything around their city and Delaware. It's not a big enough market for us to do more than keep an eye on.

He's also going to lose all the warehouses where he keeps

his shit. Guns, drugs, counterfeit money, and counterfeit lottery tickets. Dumbass him. He took Luca to them when Luca went there to negotiate the blessedly unsuccessful marriage contract. Cecelia was never horrible, just spoiled. But her husband is a douche bucket. She's going to be a widow by dinner tonight.

"Luigi, are we ready?"

"Yeah, boss. We made sure no one at the airport is tipping them off. We can roll."

We have someone on our payroll who works at O'Hare. We only fly private, but they still have to log flights. At least, ones that aren't ours. We know when any other syndicate leaves or arrives. The guy won't cross us because we know where his eighty-year-old father lives. He doesn't need to know we wouldn't actually kill an elderly man.

Luigi opens the door for me, and I climb into the nearly illegally over tinted window SUV. We don't want anyone seeing in, but we also don't need the fucking po-po pulling us over. He shuts the door behind me and slides into the front passenger seat. Carmine is back at the hotel, coordinating where we send our men who aren't with me.

I have three other guys here, and we ride in silence toward our first target. I watch the buildings whizz by while we're on the highway. I'm lost in thought, my mind filled with Chellie. I miss her. I hate that I haven't seen her in days. This longing is why, lately, Marco and I have done the bulk of any traveling. We don't want the newly married guys to leave their wives. I'd rather be tucked in bed with my girlfriend than dealing with this shit.

"Rocco, over there. On the right. Back into that alley."

We've pulled off the highway and are on a side street in the middle of Near North Side Chicago, aka Little Sicily. From here, we'll see the truck pull out of the warehouse. We can slip out ahead of them and set up a roadblock. We won't wait for them in the middle of the street like some shitty mobster movie.

Sit around, waiting for someone to get nosey and call the police? No, thank you. We're there for fifteen minutes before we see the door open and can spy the hood of the truck. We wait for the truck to pull out of the warehouse bay to be sure it's really leaving. Then we get on the road just as they leave the parking lot. We head three miles down the road before we pull into a parking lot and turn around. We make it look like we're about to leave. The truck will drive past us as we take out the tires. Then there's nothing they can do. They'll shoot, but we're ready.

"They're following us."

Rocco's gaze keeps darting to the rearview mirror, so I know he's keeping an eye on them. We wait with bated breath as the truck crosses our path. We're close enough that I can see the driver with his dumbass vape cigarette. Disgusting. The moment they're just far enough past us that they won't see us coming, we slip onto the road.

Then all bets are off. I wind down my window, and the muzzle of my gun passes through just enough to aim and fire without getting my head blown off. I take out one tire while Luigi takes out another. The truck careens onto the shoulder before the driver can get it back under control.

I'm out of the vehicle before our SUV even comes to a full stop. I inch closer, my gaze scanning our surroundings. This isn't a time to trust anything but the men I brought.

"Get the swing door open. Dump it all. Get what we came for, and we go."

Rocco leaves the engine running while he dashes to the driver's side of the truck. He yanks it open, then is even rougher with the driver. The man drops to the ground and curls into a ball. Rocco drives the tip of his steel-toed boot into the man's ribs. I hear the howl of pain.

If I were any more fucked-up than I already am, it might amuse me. I don't take pleasure in other peoples' pain, except for what I'll share with Chellie — the kind that'll bring pleasure. But knowing Edoardo will discover my family's anger during the autopsy is satisfying.

Luigi and my third guy, Giovanni, are pulling the boxes of stuffed animals out. How motherfucking original. They tear apart one after another and grab the kilos. They leave the teddy bears and giraffes with their stuffing innards strewn along the road. It looks like a massacre. Once we're certain we have the right boxes, they hurry to move the stacks of coke to the back of our SUV. I approach the driver, and I glance into the cabin. He's alone. There's the first mistake.

"You know you're going to die. Tell me how you'd like to go. Slow and painful or quick and merciful."

"Quick."

The man croaks just before Rocco's boot lands against his kidney. The man howls again, and I roll my eyes. I don't doubt it hurts, but for fuck's sake. Really? It wasn't nearly as bad as it could be. As bad as it will be.

"Then you tell me what I need, Giacomo."

I see the shock on his face as he registers that I know exactly who he is. Edoardo's nephew. He stares up at me, and I know the moment he realizes who I am. People consider me the pretty one in the family. But all the men look enough alike that there's no doubt we're related. He met Luca, so he knows I must be his brother.

"Clock's ticking, Giaco."

"What? I don't know what you want me to tell you."

"Oh, I think you do."

I fire directly at his left kneecap. Now his cries of pain are real.

"You chose the slow and painful."

"I'll tell you."

I shoot his right femur. If I let him live — which I won't — he'd never walk again. Between the two injuries, he'd be wheelchair bound for life. I knew it would only take a few broken bones to make him crack.

"Edoardo wants to make a move in NOLA. He knows the only way he can afford to do that is to build his business between here and Kansas City. He wants to take over the meth market."

"So, he's trading these kilos of coke to the Grassos for their meth."

It's what we suspected, and what Carmine's investigating. But even before the guy responds I know it's the truth. There's not a chance in hell we're letting them get a port city like New Orleans.

"Yeah. They have a deal where the don trades twice as much coke for meth for the next two months. Then they call it even, and the don can take over the production in Missouri."

That sounds like the dumbest deal I've heard in ages. Once upon a time, Missouri was the leading producer, but they've lost the title to Indiana. Woe is them. A kilo of this coke will go for twenty-two K. A kilo is about two times as heavy as a pound. So, it's basically eleven K per pound.

Meth in Missouri goes for about twelve K per pound. The thing is, cocaine is one of the most valuable illicit drugs in the world. Meth is for junkies and street hustles. The upsell on coke is way higher than meth. The street value for one of these kilos once packaged into eight-balls could be upwards of thirty grand. The meth value isn't going up. Giving up two months revenue to take over the meth production doesn't make it a long-term gain. There has to be another reason.

"Who's Edoardo selling the meth to?"

"I don't know."

I shoot near his head, careful not to hit him but close enough to make him piss himself.

"I think you do."

I fire my gun again. This time the bullet lands in the dirt between his legs. I think he's about ready to shit himself.

"It's Tony. He wants to take it on. He thinks there's more to be made in meth. He thinks they can make the profit through the quantity sold rather than the price it's sold at. I don't know whether that's true, but he insists meth is more popular than coke since it's not the eighties anymore."

Edoardo's son-in-law isn't wrong. Coke's popularity has waned, but that's in the U.S. It's still more profitable in other parts of the world. Hell, with pot now being legal in so many places, even that would be a better deal. But this is short-sighted.

"Where's the handoff?"

"I—"

"If you say I don't know, I'll beat the shit out of you."

"Aren't you already doing that?"

My shoe rams into his junk.

"I am now." I kick him in the other kidney as he rolls onto his side again. "Where's the fucking handoff?"

"Urbana."

Why the hell there? There's not a whole lot there except a university. As I stare at Giaco, it dawns on me. The Grasso don's youngest son is a student there. They want to set up a cocaine ring there and make money off the students. He wants his kid to be a drug dealer. Some might say I am and so is the rest of the family. I disagree. I sell to distributors. What happens after that and whose hands the drugs wind up in isn't my problem.

I want to know how this connects to New Orleans. I suspect Edoardo plans to sell the meth down there. Its street price is way cheaper than coke, and there's a large transient population in the city. But I've learned over the years that selling to the homeless not only exploits them — which I find reprehensible since life is already difficult enough without creating or feeding an addiction — it's an unreliable income source.

This still doesn't all add up. Edoardo may be ambitious, but he's not stupid. And neither is the Grasso don. I don't know him, but I've heard of him. He's certain he's the second coming of Marlon Brando. Fucking Don Corleone in the flesh. Asshat.

"You have a choice. Tell me the rest of what you know, and I'll put a bullet between your eyes. Act like you know nothing, and I'll make you into Swiss cheese before I put a bullet between your eyes. What'll it be?"

I point my gun at his hip. I'll shatter it, but it won't be lethal. I'm watching him, but I'm aware of what my guys are doing. They're done loading our vehicle, so now they're keeping watch. I need to wrap this up. I'm tempting fate right now.

"Edoardo thinks that if he can score deals in Kansas City and New Orleans, then he'll make enough to impress the Mexican Cartels. He wants in on more than the drugs."

"Human trafficking?"

"Yeah."

Motherfucker.

"Why?"

"He got a taste for it after what happened to that bratva cunt."

"You mean he approved of what Luca and Carmine started?"

"Yeah. The Podola-whatever-the-fucks paid the Oskolki good money for the info. Edoardo knows because he's been tapping their phones for years. With people frequently disappearing in Mexico, he saw an opportunity to make money by buying and then ransoming them back to their families."

"That is the dumbest shit I've ever heard of. If the cartels want someone gone, they want them gone. Having their victims show up again only ensures the poor fucks die. He'll make a serious enemy, and he'll wind up dead."

"He figures the cartels can do whatever the fuck they want with the people once they're back. He'll have made the ransom money."

"There isn't a snowball's chance in hell that he'd ever get enough from a ransom to cover the cost of buying them."

Giaco shrugs. I know that's above his rank and paygrade, even if he is Edoardo's nephew. Obviously, he's nothing more than a Made Man. While that's nothing to sneeze at, he's not a *capo*. He has no pull in any of his branch's decisions. He's a glorified errand boy.

"Anything else?"

"Yeah."

I wait, but he says nothing. I cock any eyebrow, but he holds out. What the fuck does he think is going to happen besides pissing me off?

"I'll tell you what you want, but only if you let me go, then I disappear."

"The fuck I am."

"Then you won't know what's going to happen to that pretty little bitch you've been humping."

I stick my free hand out by my hip. I hear a car door open, then Luigi's handing me a pair of pliers and a hammer.

"Strip him."

The guy is bleeding all over the road. I'm actually shocked he's still conscious. He's struggling, for sure. But he's still talking. I almost have to admire that. My guys wrangle him and leave him naked. I survey the wounds I've already given him. I holster my gun, knowing my guys all have theirs trained on him.

I squat beside him, and I use the needle-nose pliers to dig out the bullet I put in his thigh. I can't even imagine just how much pain I'm causing him. I pray I never experience it. I dig out the one in his knee next. Then I take the hammer to his feet. It's a shame it isn't a sledgehammer. Then I could go all Kathy Bates from *Misery* on him.

"Speak."

I use the pliers to pinch his balls.

"It's too late. She'll be dead within the hour, and it'll look like you let her die. The bratva won't forgive you."

"How do you know?"

"A little birdie told me."

"Did Edoardo order this?"

"No."

I believe him.

"Then why do you know?"

"I heard Tony talking to some guy on the phone. He was ordering a hit put on some associate in Kansas City to make sure the Grassos know we aren't shitting them when we say we want this deal. The guy said he couldn't get to it because he had another job. Tony demanded to know what came before his request. The guy told him."

That's not how mercenaries work. They don't tell anyone what jobs they have lined up. Either Giaco is fucking with me, or this gun-for-hire is fucking with Tony. I'm leaning toward the latter. Whoever this is, is going after Chellie since we already know the threat exists, and Giaco's explanation is too close to what Maks told us.

But there has to be a reason this mercenary would share that with Tony. And Tony's an idiot for having a conversation like that where anyone could hear. Not everything is adding up yet, but I'm seeing the pieces and pushing all the corner and outside ones out of the way while I sort out the center ones. I'll have the puzzle put together, but I'm not there yet.

"Who's the guy?"

"I don't know. Truly."

That much I can tell is true. If he overheard a conversation, the guy wouldn't have introduced himself. And Tony has to have at least enough sense not to say it where anyone could hear. There's always a snitch somewhere.

Each word is getting weaker and weaker as he gasps. His voice is almost impossible to hear. Between the pain and blood loss, he's almost useless now. I know I won't get more out of him, so I put the muzzle of my gun to the space between his eyebrows. I look away to avoid the blood splatter on my face, then I pull the trigger. I make sure I leave nothing to identify us after I pull out that bullet. He's sprawled, naked, on the street with annihilated stuffed animals surrounding him.

I didn't get blood on my face, but it's on my clothes. I walk to the back of the SUV and open my bag. I strip and scrub myself with the wipes doctors use before surgery. I don't care if my guys see me. Not the first time. Not the last time. Rocco gathers everything up, along with Giaco's clothes. He pours lighter fluid on the pile and sets it ablaze. The flames won't grow big enough for anyone to notice in the industrial park. But it ensures nothing remains to identify us.

By the time he's torched everything, I'm dressed again. We can't linger any longer. We've already been here long enough to risk being seen. I just want to go home, but it looks like Urbana and New Orleans are on my travel plans. Thank God for private planes. At least I'll get to each place fast. I just pray I don't have to extend this and go to Kansas City, too.

I dig out my phone and tap on Marco's contact. I let it ring three times, then hang up. I do it a second time. On the third round, he answers. He knows this is business, so he should answer. He gets straight to the point after we both say hello.

"Is it done?"

"Yeah. But shits not adding up. Edoardo's nephew was the driver. He said Tony tried to take a hit out on one of Grasso's men. The guy said he couldn't take the job right now because he's going after Michelle. I don't want her out of our sight. She goes nowhere, Marco. If she has a problem with that, too bad. Tell her I ordered it."

"That's not going to go over well if I tell her, and she doesn't hear it from you."

"You know it's safer if you tell her in person."

"I will. I'm just saying you'll come home to a shitstorm."

"I know. Do it. I'll deal with the fallout when I get back."

"All right. *Ciao*."

"*Ciao*."

I want to call Chellie tonight, but I can't. I have a burner, but I won't risk any calls to her. I miss the way she smells and feels. I miss the soft moans she whispers against my ear. I miss looking in her eyes as I make her come, as she makes me come. Fucking hell. As if I didn't already hate this life enough. Now I'm in love.

Chapter Sixteen

Chellie

I look up from my desk, surprised to see Marco standing in the doorway.

"Hey."

"Hey. I need to talk to you. Do you have a minute?"

"That doesn't sound ominous or anything."

"Can I shut the door?"

Now he's freaking me out. He doesn't want anyone to hear, and I think he's asking for propriety's sake. My office has a glass wall and door. Anyone can look in and see who I'm meeting with. I nod. I'm slow to stand; somehow, I don't think I should be at my desk for this. I gesture to the chairs near the small conference table.

"What's going on, Marco? None of you come into my office. You always stay out of sight."

"I know. I just spoke to Enzo."

I keep my face neutral, but that hurts. I haven't heard from him in days. I know Marco's his brother, and it probably had to do with business and not pleasure. But the emotional side of me wants to demand why he has time to call Marco and not me.

"Michelle, he called because there's a problem. It wasn't a social call."

"A problem? Is he okay?"

"Yes. But it's going to extend this trip. He wants to increase your security detail. Can you work from home until he gets back?"

"How long's that going to be?"

"I honestly don't know."

"I can't just not show up here indefinitely. I have client meetings. I can do a day or two max."

"That won't be enough."

"Does this have to do with the threat already made against me?"

"Yes."

I wait for him to say more, but I should have known nothing would be forthcoming. We sit and stare at one another, both willing to wait the other out. It's my office phone that interrupts the standoff. I walk back over to my desk and answer it.

"I'll have to check my availability. I may have a conflict."

I watch Marco as I make an excuse to one of my biggest clients. I tell her my secretary will call hers. She's not pleased, but what can I do? I return to the table once I hang up.

"See. I can't just disappear. Why can't you add men to the detail rather than locking me up?"

"No one is locking you up, but I'm certain Enzo would feel much better if you stayed with our parents."

"No."

I'm not staying indefinitely with people I barely know. This is going too far. It was one thing to agree to it in theory. It's entirely different now that it's being forced upon me. I've been there four days. I thought I might even go back to my place tonight. I want to see if there's anything I can salvage.

"This isn't a request, Michelle."

"Are you going to manhandle me into a car and lock me in Enzo's room?"

He cocks an eyebrow. This is a man used to getting his way. This is a man who'd have me pinned against the table, begging for my life if I weren't a woman. This is a man who won't relent until I bend to his will. Is it worth the argument? Yes.

"Marco, unless you can give me a clear and persuasive reason, I'm not staying with your parents any longer. I'll agree to staying at Enzo's place instead of mine. Since someone trashed it, I don't really have much choice. Either way, I know he has security there, and I don't. But I'm not imposing on people I don't know any longer than I already have."

"You don't know? They're going to be your in-laws."

I stare at him, then narrow my eyes.

"Don't manipulate me."

"What's manipulative about stating the obvious. Michelle, you wouldn't know any of us if Enzo wasn't going to marry you. You sure as shit wouldn't be the only thing he talked about when he called. You sure as shit wouldn't be what'll end up as distraction when that's the last thing he needs. If he doesn't know you're safe, he won't focus. Is that what you want?"

"That. That's the manipulative part. If it's that serious, then he can tell me himself. If he has access to a phone to tell you to issue me orders and try to scare me into following them, then he can call me."

"That's not how this works."

"I'm just supposed to be the submissive little woman."

"No. You're supposed to love him enough to put his safety first just like he's putting yours. He won't call you because he's terrified it'll connect you to us even more than you already are.

He won't do it until he's certain you're somewhere no one can tap the phones or trace you. This isn't some shitty Mafia movie, Michelle. There isn't a single submissive woman in my family when it comes to this shit. They can defend themselves long enough to get to safety because that's fucking common sense."

"Don't swear at me. This isn't common sense to someone who knows nothing about this. If Enzo is safe where he lives, then why can't I be?"

"Because he lives in the city where it's easier for someone to slip in and get past even the best security. Because he's trained to defend himself, and he has no limits on what he'll do to survive. You aren't trained, and I assure you, there are things you couldn't make yourself do, even if you think you can."

"What does that say about Enzo and your entire family if that's the case?"

"It says there's a reason we're all alive."

Anger seethes from every pore as I watch Marco restrain his temper. I'm pushing back because I'm scared. Instead of agreeing with him, my fight and flight instincts are pulsing through me. I'm fighting him, but I'm ready to flee all of this. But where do I go? Laura's. Somehow I know that would wound Enzo far deeper than I'm willing to go. If I pick the Kutsenkos over the Mancinellis, I'll end my relationship, and I'm certain that isn't what I want. I just want Enzo home, safe with me, and making me feel safe.

"I've already taken off unexpectedly more than once. I'm going to lose my job."

"Then open a private practice."

I snort.

"For starters, I have a non-compete clause, so I can't take a single client I've spent countless hours cultivating. And what major organization is going to follow me to a one-woman practice when they can have the resources of one of the top five firms in the country? Not just New York. The entire country."

"Is any job really more important than your life? Is it more important than Enzo knowing he can concentrate because you're completely protected?"

"Back to manipulating me. You know the only answer I can give to those questions, but you're forcing my hand. You're trying to guilt me and make me feel shitty."

"Now who's swearing?"

"Fuck off."

I go back to my desk and sit down. I'm stubborn, but I'm usually not this stupid. I know I'm making a mistake, but I can't bring myself to go anywhere with Marco. It's like I'm frozen here. I don't want to leave my office because that means entering the real world without Enzo. I trust Marco, but I don't trust anyone as much as I do Enzo. Which I know means I should listen to Marco since Enzo sent him. But I'm too fucking terrified to go anywhere. I might just move in here and sleep under my desk. I watch as he approaches me.

"Look, I know I'm strong arming you, and obviously, that isn't the right way to convince you. Please, Michelle. Enzo gave this order — and yes, it is one I will obey, even if he is my baby brother — because he loves you. I don't know if you've told each other that, and if he hasn't, I'm sorry to ruin it. But he does. He won't stop until he's certain the threat is gone. That means he can't come home. If you refuse, then he will come back, and the threat remains. Don't tear him in two."

Marco's tone is much softer now, and just that is enough to make his words feel less coercing.

"I'm scared."

"I know. So am I."

That's not what I expected him to admit. It's both reassuring and nerve-racking.

"Can I stay until the end of the day? Then I can call in sick in the morning."

He hesitates, but then he nods.

"Are you going to tell Enzo that I argued with you?"

"He already knew it was coming. I warned him, but I didn't need to."

That just makes me feel dumber and like a monumental bitch.

"Michelle, don't feel badly. We both knew because this isn't a life you're familiar with yet. It's a lot."

I snort. A lot. Master of understatement.

"I'm still sorry. I don't want to be an inconvenience, and I definitely don't want to distract Enzo. We haven't said anything yet, but you know I feel the same about him."

I won't say it out loud until I say it to Enzo first. Marco offers me a tight smile, and I know he understands.

"What about clothes? I can't keep borrowing stuff."

"We'll swing by your place so you can grab what you need. Pack for at least a week, if not two."

Two? That makes my panic want to rear its ugly head again. But I remind myself this is a precaution. It doesn't mean it's absolute.

"Thanks. I need to get stuff done that I won't easily be able to do from your parents' place."

"I'll be in the hallway."

I offer him a smile that matches his before he leaves. I stare at my computer screen for a solid five minutes before I can concentrate. My mind is blank. You would think it would be racing, but I can't seem to conjure a complete thought to save my life. When I finally can, it's sluggish. But I pull my head out of my ass and get back to work. The moment my fingers touch my keyboard, the phone rings.

"Hello."

My calls get routed through my secretary, so I never feel the need to announce my name.

"Hello, Michelle."

The hair on my arms goes up. It's another voice like Hannibal Lecter saying "Hello, Clarice." I've thought about that movie more times since I met Enzo than I have in like twenty years. It's not the same voice as last time, but it gives me the same feeling.

"Who is this?"

"A concerned friend."

"Concerned about what?"

The last caller said that too. But I don't get the feeling it's a woman like last time.

"Concerned about how I'm going to kill you. Should I stalk you for a few months, making you look over your shoulder? Should I sneak up on you and dart out of the shadows? Should I torture you for days?"

I fumble for my phone as this psychopath threatens me.

"You can text Marco and beg him to come back. You can realize that he was right. You can do any number of things, but you can't stop me."

ME

> 911 come back on the phone with someone threatening me he knows we what we just argued about.

"Did you send that text to Marco? You wouldn't want to distract Lorenzo, would you?"

"Why me?"

"Why not you?"

"My question wasn't rhetorical."

"Then make up a reason. I don't owe you one."

"But you do. You're going to kill me and won't tell me why. Seems rather cowardly. Will you shoot me from behind?"

"I'll look you in the eye as I slit your throat. Then I'll send you to Lorenzo and Maks in pieces. They'll have to work together to put enough of you back together to bury you."

This person knows I'm more than just Laura's friend. They know I'm more than just some girl dating Enzo. They're going to wage war on two syndicates by coming for me.

"Killing two birds with one stone. How convenient for you."

"You think I'm doing this to cause trouble with both families. I'm doing this because neither family will forgive the other for failing to protect you. But you're Lorenzo's problem more than Maks's. After all, you're only fucking one of them. Though Maks and Laura like it kinky. Maybe they'd let you join."

"There's not a snowball's chance in hell of that, and you know it. You're just being a pervert to add to your threats."

Marco rushes back into my office, and the man on the phone laughs.

"Time to go, Michelle. See you in your nightmares."

Then the line goes dead.

"What did he tell you?"

"He wants me to fear how he's going to get me. He wants your family and the Kutsenkos at war with each other over failing to protect me. He's going after both your families by doing this. He said he'd slit my throat and send me to Maks and Enzo in pieces they'll have to put together to have enough of me for a funeral."

He says nothing to me as he unlocks his phone and taps something.

"Carmine, I need you to trace a phone call Michelle just

received on her office landline. Whoever has the job just called her. What's your number?"

"Two-one-two, five-five-five, two-six-two-seven. He had to be routed through my secretary to get to me. I never give out my direct line."

"Ask her."

I tap the intercom button.

"Haley, what was the name of the man who just called me?"

"It wasn't a man. The woman said her name was Sally Kuntz. She said she's a prospective client you met the other day."

"Are you sure it was a woman's voice and not just a soft or high-pitched man's?"

"Yeah. What's going on, Michelle?"

"I don't know. It was just a weird call. Don't put them through again if they call."

Marco shakes his head. He wants me to talk to this fucker. What the hell?

"Actually, Haley. You know what? Scratch that. Make it the opposite. Connect me no matter what I'm in the middle of."

Marco nods.

"Are you sure? What's going on?"

She's asked me twice, and I can't say a damn thing to her.

"I wasn't going to take her as a client, but I just changed my mind. I think I can make it work."

"All right. If you say so."

The light stops blinking, so I know she's turned off the intercom. Marco is still on the phone, and Carmine must be talking. He walks around my office, running his hands along the baseboards. He heads to my bookshelf and starts pulling out one book at a time, holding the covers out and flapping the pages before running his hand along the shelf. He keeps doing that as he switches to Italian. He's looking for bugs. I'm certain.

How else could this guy know what I just said to Marco or that we even argued?

I look up as a siren blares, and the emergency lights flash in my office. I grab my purse, but Marco signals for me to wait.

"Carmine, find out who did this and call me back."

As people try to hurry out of the office suite, I see the other guards assigned to me today pushing through the crowd.

"Someone manually pulled it on the seventh floor."

David blurts out the explanation as the four men, including Marco, surround me.

"How do you know?"

Marco's the one to answer.

"Because we made sure the security company hired eight of our men to work here. We have someone watching the security monitors and at the front desk around the clock. Did they see who it was?"

David shakes his head as we join my colleagues and staff, trying to get into the hallway. We're on the thirty-eighth floor. It's a long way down by foot. If there really is a fire on the seventh floor, it will trap everyone above it. This isn't something to fuck around with when it comes to New Yorkers in Manhattan. We enter the stairwell, and I don't hear any panicked voices, but that doesn't mean there aren't a bunch of people reliving that day.

I'm in shape for the most part — at least I thought so before today — but I'm struggling by the time we reach the twenty-first floor. I'm winded, and my knees feel like they'll give out. But the Mancinelli men haven't broken a sweat, and they're all in suits and ties. I know Enzo worked out twice a day before we started dating. He still works out at least once a day. Is it for shit like this?

I don't know how Marco feels or hears his phone, but he pulls it out.

"Carmine, what's going on?"

Marco's quiet, but there's no way I can hear anything other than footsteps on the stairs and everyone's labored breathing. I don't even notice when he hangs up because I'm clinging to the handrail and clutching David's suit coat to keep from sliding the rest of the way down the stairs. Our progress is slowing as people struggle to keep going. Pure adrenaline propels me every time I think I can't take another step.

It takes us nearly forty minutes to get to the lobby. That proves it was a false alarm since we're all still alive to make it there so slowly. But that doesn't seem to have registered with anyone but my guards and me. The panic and pushing started around the twelfth floor when we were so close yet so far away from the ground floor.

"We have a gathering place. I have to go, or they will list me as unaccounted for. The firefighters will have to search for me."

I point toward Imogene, our office manager. The woman is in her sixties and sweating profusely, but she has her clipboard with the company roster. She's calling off names, and I arrive just before she gets to mine.

"Michelle?"

"Here!"

I raise my hand and wave it over my head. I feel a hand wrap around my wrist and yank it down. I'm staring up at Alonzo, who looks at me like I'm an idiot. It's his brother, Afonso, who explains.

"Don't make it obvious where you are. We need to keep you lost in the crowd."

I look over my shoulder at Marco, and his expression is grim, but I can tell he agrees. I look around as firemen flood the sidewalk, some going in and out of the building. Traffic's backed up for blocks. Am I being watched? How long do we hide here?

Out of nowhere, Afonso staggers backwards as blood seeps through his sleeve. People notice and scream, but I don't know what just happened. David just bolted in the direction the shot came from. Marco and Alonzo are dragging me down and away as more blood appears, soaking Afonso's middle.

"Your brother! Go!"

I try to shake Alonzo off me, but he's still pushing me through the mass of people. I trip, and Marco loses his hold on me.

"Go back!"

Alonzo still has hold of me, and I can't believe he's putting me ahead of his brother, who's just been shot twice. His oath to the Mancinellis supersedes his love for his brother. I know how close they are. I twist away until the momentum of the crowd forces him to release me.

Marco shoves to get to me, but as I look around, I spot a cab that's about to pull away from the curb when traffic opens up enough for his lane to move. It's my turn to shove as I break out of the masses. I sprint to the cab and am in it before I know what I'm doing. I hear Marco and Alonzo calling my name. Then I see Alonzo turn back for his brother as Marco barrels toward me.

"Drive."

"Where to?"

"Anywhere for now."

I need to think for a moment. Was all of this done because of me? A fire alarm pulled only minutes after I get a threatening call. Then one of my bodyguards is shot twice. The preponderance of evidence would say I'm the reason. As much as I don't want to die, the idea of putting Marco in a position where he might get shot too is so abhorrent that I had to get away from him. He's a target as long as I'm near him, and I can't be the reason one of Enzo's brothers dies.

An idea comes to me as I think about what's around me.

"Thirty-fifth, Midtown between tenth."

I watch out the window as the chaos vanishes. It's slow going, but we're inching along. It's not too long before I see the sign for the rental car place. I pay the driver and head into the business.

"Hi. I'd like to rent an SUV, please."

Part of me thinks I should get a tiny, unobtrusive car. But the stronger part of me says get as close to a tank as you can in case someone tries to run me off the road. I give them all my information. While they process the reservation, I go to the vending machine and use almost all the cash I have to get snacks.

I know they'll have the car gassed up, and I have an idea where I'm going. Even with a vehicle that'll be about as fuel efficient as a Howitzer, I'm confident I'll reach my destination on one tank. I can't get around giving them my credit card information, even if I was going to pay in cash. I don't doubt the Mancinellis will track that. But even Enzo doesn't know about the place I'm going.

"Here you go, Ms. Russo. One of our guys will pull the car around for you."

"Thank you."

I force myself to appear relaxed when I'm nervous as hell. I'm trying not to draw attention to myself, but am I being watched? As soon as I get where I'm going, I'm calling Enzo. I don't care if all I can do is leave a message. At least it'll be there when he can listen to it.

It's not long before I'm on the road. Once I cross the George Washington Bridge, I'm on Route 80. It'll take me two and a half hours to get to my hiding place, but even with traffic as I leave the city, I feel calmer. By the time I approach the Poconos, I'm breathing easier. I'm constantly checking my mirrors to make sure no car follows too close or for too long. I even get off the highway at a few exits and make detours before getting back on. I'm alone.

When I pull off the gravel road to open the gate, I wait to see if any cars approach. I get as close as I can before I leave the door open and engine running. Even if I didn't fear needing to make a hasty getaway, I'm always nervous about closing all car doors with the keys inside. What if I somehow lock myself out?

Once I'm onto the property with the gate shut again, I pull around back until I can get inside and open the garage door. This place — my grandparents' hunting lodge where they never actually hunted — is isolated enough that people who don't know where to look won't find it.

Once I'm inside and I've tucked away the car in the garage, I collapse on the sofa and shut my eyes. I rest my head back and exhale. The adrenaline and whatever else I've been surviving on for the past three hours vanishes, and I'm suddenly shivering. Goosebumps form on my arms, and I can feel them under my skirt. I drag the blanket off the back of the sofa and wrap myself in it, allowing myself to catch my breath. Then I gather my last burst of courage and find the satellite phone. Reception is shit out here.

"Enzo, it's me. I'm safe. I'm sure Marco's already called you. And I'm certain you're more pissed at me than you've ever been at anyone, but I don't want you to be panicking. I'm somewhere few people know about and even less would know where to look. I don't want anything to happen to your brother. Whoever this is already shot Afonso. I didn't want Marco to be next. I'm not taking this to your parents, either. Right now, hiding is best. I don't have reliable cell service where I am. I'm not leaving for at least two days, so if you call or text, I can't promise I'll get it. It doesn't mean I'm in danger. It means hiding is working. I hate saying this over the phone. I love you."

I feel the tears welling, and the lump in my throat threatens to keep me from saying anything more. But I persevere.

"There's nothing I won't do to keep you safe, and the same goes for your family. I know they're trained for shit, but I still refuse to force them anywhere near this. I pray you understand because I love you more than anything or anyone. Bye."

I don't know what else to say, so I hang up. I'm completely drained.

Chapter Seventeen

Lorenzo

Success. Fina-fucking-ly. A trip to New Orleans ensured the Grassos and Rizzos now understand that nothing happens without my uncle's permission. Ships they both depend upon are at the bottom of the Gulf of Mexico. No one is even going to look in their direction after the fear of God I put in them. Kansas City wasn't so easy.

The Grassos had the means to put up a fight there, so I had to use logic and not brute force since I don't have the men to wage a war. Watching his bank accounts drain in real time can be very convincing. Seeing photos of how I fucked up Tony while holding his own son hostage in his dorm room convinced the Grasso don to agree to my terms. Clothes hide his son's injuries. Not so much for Tony. He won't be recovering from his.

"Luca—"

"You need to get home now. It's Michelle. We can't find her."

I stare at my phone for a second. I've only just turned it back on for the first time in four days.

"What the fuck do you mean?"

"Right after you talked to Marco, someone pulled the fire alarm in her building. She got separated from Alonzo and Marco after someone shot Afonso. David searched for the shooter. The crowd panicked, and it was a near stampede. They saw her get in a cab, but no one could get in a car fast enough to follow her. Our drivers were on the other side of the building, jammed up in traffic. We know she rented a car from her credit card record."

"What about the vehicle's tracker?"

"It only has GPS, and she isn't using it."

"Then she knew where she's going. I'm calling Laura."

"Fine. I'll call back when we know more."

I hang up and notice the voicemail icon. I know she called. Whatever she's done is rash and driven by fear. It's naïve, which makes it foolish, but I know she has a plan. I skip over the ones I don't care about until I hear her voice. My chest aches so much that I rub it. I finally hear her say she loves me, and it's over the phone somewhere I might not find. Fuck that. I'm finding this hiding spot. There's no two ways about that. And when I do, I'm turning my *piccolina* over my lap and reddening her ass — after I make love to her until next week.

I listen to the message three times before I hit save.

"Laura, it's Lorenzo. Where would Michelle go if she didn't want anyone to find her?"

"What? Lorenzo, what happened?"

"She got a threatening call today at work while Marco was with her. Then someone pulled the fire alarm in her building. Marco and our guys got her outside, but one of them got hurt. She took off, and all we know is she rented a car. She left me a message saying she's safe, but her reception will be shit. Where did she go?"

"Her grandparents' lodge in the Poconos. It's small and hidden. We used to go all the time as kids. We would pretend we were Tom Sawyer and Huck Finn searching for the right old tree that would have treasure. She probably called you from the sat phone. Lorenzo, no one will find her up there unless she wants to be found. It really is remote. Her family keeps a ton of nonperishable food, and she has winter clothes too. The garage is big enough for even a large SUV. Her grandparents don't hunt, but they have a couple rifles and a shotgun in case of bears, coyotes, or bobcats. She knows how to shoot to kill, even if it's only large animals. Push comes to shove, Michelle will shoot to kill a person. Don't doubt that."

"I don't want it to come to that. How do I get there?"

Laura hesitates, and it pisses me the fuck off.

"If you're thinking about sending Maks, I will find him and follow him. She didn't fucking run from me. She ran from whoever the fuck is doing this. And they only noticed her because of her friendship with you not her relationship with me. I'm not blaming you, but I want to know where my girl-friend is. Believe me, I'm no less determined than Maks was to find you."

"I wouldn't stop you. I don't want you storming up there and laying into her."

"I'm not going to. I just need her, Laura. She and I will decide what happens because of this naïve decision, but I'm not angry. I'm terrified."

I will punish her, but that's no one's business but Chellie's and mine. I listen as Laura gives me directions. It's going to take me at least three hours to get near the Poconos. Then it'll take an hour to get from the closest airport to where she is. I'm firing off a text as Laura continues to talk.

"There's a gate, and the code is six-three-eight-one."

"Sixty-three-eighty-one?"

"Yeah. There isn't an alarm system, but the lights are on motion sensors."

"No alarm?"

"No. Even the satellite phone isn't always reliable. There's no ethernet or Wi-Fi there. It's too remote."

"Does it have electricity and running water?"

"Yeah. It's off a generator, and the water is from a well. The property has been in her mom's family for generations. It goes back to the settlers."

"I'm going to be wheels up in thirty minutes. Do you know the satellite phone number?"

"No. I've never called it before. I only used it as a kid to let my parents know I arrived. Lorenzo, please find a way to let me know she's okay."

I hear the distress in Laura's voice with her plea. She's sounded direct until now. I know her emotions are there, even if she doesn't want me to know. I soften my tone.

"I will, Laura. I'm certain she'll want to talk to you as soon as she can. Thank you."

"You're welcome. Bye."

The last word comes out choked.

"Bye."

There's a fence that runs the entire perimeter of the property. It's electric, so at least there's that. I don't know if they run it all the time, but I threw a rock to test it. It's live now. My men are going to hang back and surround the place on three sides. The property backs onto a ravine, so there's no need for fencing along the fourth side. We've had no sign that anyone's followed us, but I'm going in alone.

I don't want to scare Chellie since I don't know if she'll have one of the guns with her. I dressed casually for the rest of the mission, and I'm still in jeans and a polo shirt. My clothes were dark when we waited for Giacomo, but now my shirt is baby blue. Nothing intimidating.

I punch in the combo for the gate and ease past it. I'm walking up to the house in case she isn't alone. I don't want to alert a captor. I inch along the side of the house until I get to a living room window. I peek inside. My fists clench along with my jaw. I stalk to the door and try the doorknob. At least, that doesn't turn. I think about ramming my shoulder into it to get it to open, but that'll just break the hinges. I pull out the lock picking kit I brought with me. I have the door open with a thud against the window.

"Take your shirt off now, *piccolina*."

She jumps, and her bowl of whatever goes flying. Her book drops to the floor, and her feet that were resting on a table kick a bowl of chips and a cup of something.

"Enzo?"

"Get that fucking shirt off before I rip it off you. Take your fucking bra off, too."

Her eyes are enormous as I slam, then lock the door. I'm pulling my belt off as I approach, and it's only her certainty that I won't harm her that has her obeying rather than running. I'm looping the belt through the buckle by the time I get to the sofa, where she's sitting topless. Fuck. Her tits are amazing, and I'm about to enjoy them. I pull her off the sofa, pushing her skirt to her waist as I sit, pulling her down to straddle me.

"Take me out, then put your hands behind your back."

She fumbles, but she unbuttons and unzips my pants. She pushes them and my boxer briefs down as I lift my hips. She lets go and immediately puts her hands behind her back like I commanded. I have the belt around them and pulled tight enough for her to know she better not move them, but not so tight as to hurt her. It's far too snug to use any of the holes.

"At least, you got the no panties part right."

My hand lands across her ass before I impale her with my cock. Then I'm latched onto her right nipple like a starving baby. I suck until she moans. I bite, but only enough to make her inner muscles clench my dick. I fist my hand in her hair, pulling her down to kiss me. She's as desperate as I am. I feel her tugging at her restraint, but I won't let her go yet.

When we come up for air, I tug on her hair, tilting her head back. I know she can't see me, and I know how much she likes to watch. I dive in and take her other tit in my mouth and suck until I finally start to relax. My free hand cups and holds it while I worship it. My tongue flicks her nipple as I keep the suction tight. I don't know why, and I don't feel like examining my psyche to understand how sucking her tits eases my tension, but it does.

I thrust into her three times before I come. I pull her off me and practically dump her on the sofa as I fish out my phone. I tap the camera and turn the focus to a selfie. I hold it between her thighs, and I know she can see my cum.

"You are mine, Chellie. My cum in your cunt proves it. You didn't do a damn thing to stop me, and it's not because you fear me. You know it's because your heart, body, and soul are mine as much as I've given you everything of me. You aren't fighting me or looking away. No. You love seeing it. You love knowing I love you. I will always come for you, but you never ever hide from me again. You trust my family just like you trust me."

I unfasten the belt and strip off her skirt. She's already barefoot. I rip my clothes off before I cover her body with mine. I'm still hard. I ease into her and hold still.

"Touch me, *piccolina*. Please. I need you. I love you."

"Enzo, I love you."

Her touch is gentle. It soothes my anger over seeing her happy as a clam, sitting on the couch with her snacks. It reassures me she's okay, and we're okay. She caresses my hair back from my face, then over my cheek, down to my shoulder, and along my back. She tilts her hips to take all of me.

"Come in me again, Daddy. I want to feel it as it drips down my thighs for the rest of the night. I want you to keep claiming me, even if I give myself to you freely."

"I'm not pulling out until my dick refuses to stay. Then I'm going to get myself hard again as fast as I can, so I can be inside you again. Some part of me is going to be touching you until you can't stay awake."

"Do you promise, Daddy?"

"Oh, *piccolina*. Don't you know by now that I keep my word?"

"Enzo, I was scared. That's why I ran. I wasn't actually reading. I just kept staring at the page. The moment I saw it was you, I stopped being afraid. Even with how pissed you are, I'm not scared anymore. I don't want you to let me go. Please don't restrain me again tonight. I need to hold you."

We move together until she tenses beneath me. She claws at my back as she comes. But I don't relent. I keep thrusting until she comes two more times before I unload my cum in her. It isn't until after that I realize she doesn't have her pills with her. I'm certain she took it this morning, but she won't be able to take it tomorrow. I don't have any condoms on me, and I doubt there are any here.

"Daddy, I know what you're thinking. I don't have my birth control with me. I wish you could keep coming inside me, but I won't risk trapping you."

"Do you want your spanking even sooner? Never say that

again. Having a family with you is not trapping me. Chellie, we're getting married as soon as we're back in the city."

She just stares at me for a moment, then there's a tentative smile.

"Is it because of the no women and children rule?"

"I'd be lying if I didn't admit that's part of it. But there's no point in waiting. We both know neither of us would have committed unless we wanted to get married. There's not a chance in hell you'd enter this world if you didn't mean to stay. I wouldn't have brought you in if I didn't want you by my side for the rest of my life."

Her gaze drifts down between us, and I know she's trying to piece something together. I give her time to work out her thoughts and emotions.

"Enzo, I'm going to quit my job."

"What? No—"

"Wait. Hear me out, please. Laura got fired for needing indefinite time off. The same will happen to me. It's not fair to my clients or colleagues to keep vanishing. Every time you suck on my breasts, it brings out something in me that wants to burn the world down to protect you, to take away whatever's troubling you. It's not maternal toward you, but I want to look down at our kids nursing. I want to know that we made the life together that I'll be nourishing. That all the love I feel for you is amplified by loving our children. I can't do that easily working eighty-hour weeks. I've slacked off since we got together, but if I stay at my firm, I won't be able to do that for much longer. I want a family more than I want to make senior partner."

"Are you agreeing to marrying me?"

"Yes."

"You know this is just a conversation. I am going to ask you properly."

"That would be wonderful, but I don't need it. I want to

head back into the city, call my parents while you call yours, then call my siblings, Laura, and Lanie. I want to be in City Hall or a church as soon as they open in the morning. I want to be your wife by midmorning. If I'm pregnant before the end of the month, all the better. But I can wait for nature to make that happen."

"Do you have a bedroom here?"

Her brow furrows, but she points down a hallway. I pull back to kneel, bringing her with me. She wraps herself around me as I stand.

"Good. I'm not making love to you in your grandparents' bed. But I am going to find a spot for us where we aren't so cramped."

"Are you going to punish me?"

"I am. But not right now. I want to keep making love to my soon-to-officially-be fiancée."

She shakes her head.

"I want the punishment now."

"We—"

"No. Please, Daddy. I know I scared you. I know I defied the order you gave Marco to give to me. I argued with him about it. I ran from your brother, and even if I stand by that decision as the right one, I know you don't see it that way."

"Do you need the absolution? You know we're truly all right, don't you? We aren't just talking hypotheticals."

"I know. But it's going to weigh on both of us until it's done."

"What do you think is the appropriate punishment?"

She looks at the belt where it lies on the floor.

"Chellie, no. You are not used to the pain that will come with that. We haven't gotten into any real kink. That's a big jump to make from my palm to a belt."

"Enzo, I know you won't harm me. I want this."

"I don't like—"

"The moment I saw you stripping it off, I wanted to feel it across my ass. I thought that's what you were going to do. I doubt I'm going to like it, but thinking you were going to spank me with it actually brought my mind peace."

"You need to know I care enough to punish you that hard. That I care enough to make sure you learn your lesson."

"Yes."

"You need me to let go of my fear and frustration, and you know punishing you will reassure me you understand the rules. You know it gives me back the control I didn't have from the moment Luca called me until the moment I was inside you."

"Daddy, I want you to be in control. I want to submit to you. I'm sorry I scared you and your brothers. I'm not sorry I came here. I told you. I stand by that decision. But I don't enjoy knowing I caused you a moment's worry, and I knew I would even as I drove here."

"I won't fuck you or make love to you afterward."

"I know. This isn't about pleasure. This is for real. There are no rewards for accepting what I did was wrong. Will you let me suck you off instead?"

"No. You might submit to this, but you are not my sub. Your forgiveness isn't contingent upon anything. Once the spanking is over, so is the transgression. You never service me, Chellie. We might fuck, and we might make love. But you don't have to do anything to me or for me to earn my love or my praise."

She gazes into my eyes for a long time, and I can't tell what she's thinking.

"You're a possessive and protective man, but you don't smother me or intimidate me. Other people would say you talk to me as though I'm a possession. I've never once felt that way. I feel precious to you. I feel loved. You make me feel like there is nothing more important to you than me — than us. I'm entering a world most people believe is morally devoid. I see it as the exact opposite. I think you're a man who holds himself to a high moral standard. Because of that, you will stop at nothing to protect me and love me. So, no, you don't objectify me. You make me feel alive."

"Come, little one. I'm going to punish you, but I'm going to break my own rule. I'm sticking with what I said earlier. I'm making love to you until you can't keep your eyes open."

I grab the belt, then carry her into the bedroom she points to. As I lower her to her feet, I'm having doubts I can go through with this. Not only have we not built up her experience and tolerance, but I haven't learned enough about what she can handle. I don't want to ruin what we could have by jumping ahead about a hundred steps.

"Daddy, I know I don't have experience in this. I know you're worried that you'll traumatize me or something. Have as much faith in me and yourself as I have in you."

She goes up on her toes and kisses my cheek. I swallow before I nod. I sit on the edge of the bed and open my thighs. She steps between them, and I help her lie over my lap with most of her upper body supported by the mattress. I squeeze my thighs to trap her legs. I don't want her moving around lest I miss my aim. I wrap most of the belt around my right hand.

"Do you remember your safe word?"

She chuckles.

"Prunes."

My left hand skims down her back and over the most perfect ass I've ever seen. I know there are parts of her she doesn't like, but she's good with her shapely backside. I plan to be good with it later tonight, assuming I can find something — anything — that could serve as lube. If not, that'll have to wait until we get back to the city.

I bring my bare hand down across both cheeks, and it makes her lurch forward. She grabs the comforter and braces herself for the next spank. It lands on her left ass cheek. I alternate sides, giving each ten slaps. Her skin is turning a bright and beautiful pink. I lean over her and kiss her right ass cheek.

"I will give you five with the belt, *piccolina*."

"Ten."

"*Picco—*"

"Daddy, you decide how hard they are. But five won't feel sufficient. It'll feel like you did this to placate me. If I'm going to be absolved, I want to feel fully absolved."

That makes me laugh. She turns her head to see me, her brow furrowed.

"Maria says that's why she wants bells and smells at Mass. She wants an organ, the bells, and incense at every service. She figures, if she's going to be absolved, then she wants the whole shebang to feel like she did it properly."

"She does get God's forgiveness isn't contingent on how much smoke and noise are made, right?"

"Of course she does. She's been saying that since we were kids. Back then, she was serious. Now it's just stuck because that's why she likes formal services. She'd go to an all-Latin service if she could. When she does church, she does church."

I shrug. We all have complicated relationships with God and Catholicism. We all believe in our faith, but we all harbor guilt because what we do is the antithesis of everything we should. Even though we grew up in Queens, my family has been going to the same church in Manhattan for generations.

All four of us, plus our cousin and friends were altar servers. We sang in the children's choir and went to Sunday School. We believe in all the Sacraments, but the men struggle with believing in our redemption when we continue to sin willingly and knowingly. One of the many contradictions in this life.

I'm lost in thought until Chellie pulls me back to the present. I know she did it on purpose. I don't need to grow morose or even contemplative right now. I want to be present and in the moment with my girlfriend.

"Ten, Daddy."

"Fine. But the second it's too much, you will use your safe word. We'll never do anything like this again if you don't speak up, and I harm you."

"Enzo, I will never put you in that position. I never want you to lose your trust in me. That would devastate me. Nothing is worth that."

I raise my right hand and bring the tongue of the belt down across her ass. Her body jerks and goes rigid. She clutches the comforter and buries her face in it.

"Chellie?"

"I'm all right, Daddy. Keep going. I knew it would hurt, but that's worse than I expected."

I run my left hand between her shoulder blades. Then I massage each ass cheek until she relaxes. I bring the belt down on her right cheek, then her left in quick succession. She tries to kick her feet, but I pinned her legs between mine. The next one lands across her horizontal crack and pushes her forward. I feel her clit rub against my thigh. I'm already hard from having her touch me and having the view that I do. Her hip rubbing my cock doesn't help. I land another spank in the same place. She moans, and it's not entirely from pain.

"Put your right leg over my left."

I move mine enough for her to adjust her position. I have a clear view of her pussy, and I can see my cum still dampening her folds. But I can also tell she's wet from her own arousal. I adjust the belt and thrust three fingers into her.

"Fuck, Daddy."

"Naughty *piccolina*. This is a punishment, not foreplay."

I rub my thumb over her clit as my fingers stroke her g spot. She shifts restlessly, searching for relief. Searching for release. I pull out and immediately bring the belt down on her ass.

"Ow!"

I'm careful how much force I use, but I don't ease up for the next four on each side. She's dripping, and I know her clit must ache from the way she's purposely rubbing my thigh with each spank. This time, when I thrust my fingers in, I press my thumb against her asshole. The tip enters her, and she clenches.

"You like that, don't you?"

"Yes."

She croaks her answer. I pull my thumb away, but she pushes her hips up, chasing it. I bring the belt down again with the hardest spank yet.

"I decide what your body gets, little one. I decide whether I'm going to finger fuck you. I decide whether I'm going to play with this perfect ass. I'll fuck it when I'm good and ready."

"You feel ready to me, Daddy."

I'm extra careful with my aim, but I land the belt against her pussy. I made her reposition herself for this. She howls with the unexpected and unfamiliar pain. That makes ten. I regret I'd wasted four on each side. I can tell from her breathing and the way she's trembling that it's not out of genuine pain. It's need. I've aroused something in her she doesn't know how to manage yet. I help her up and turn her as she pushes hair out of her face. I sweep her into my arms and position her, so her ass is between my thighs.

Tears started streaming down her face around the third or fourth one, but she never sobbed. Now she does. It's the aftermath of too many emotions today. I cradle her and rock her as she cries. I let her. I don't offer platitudes or try to convince her to stop. If she's crying this hard, she needs it.

I just hold her. She wraps her arms around me and clings to me for dear life. As though I'd go anywhere. I can't bear the idea of not touching her right now. Fuck. I need to be inside her, but I told her no rewards after a punishment. She sits up and cups my cheeks. The kiss she gives me is like nectar from the gods. She's not holding back. It's passionate, but it's not meant to be lustful. It's filled with love. She shifts, and I know she wants to straddle me. I help her, then I'm inside her again.

Neither of us moves. We watch each other, our gazes locked. The goal isn't to get off. It isn't even to pleasure the other. We are one. Our bodies and our souls. I've enjoyed the moment I enter a woman plenty of times. But it's never been like it is with Chellie. It's never been like it is right this minute.

"Can we just stay like this forever, Enzo?"

"We can imagine we can."

She rests her head on my shoulder, and I press my cheek to the top of her head. I shut my eyes, blocking out the world. I know my guys are outside on patrol. I know my family wants to know where I am, and that Chellie is safe. I know Laura must be bouncing off the walls with worry. But nothing matters more right now than this intimacy.

We stay like this until she comes down from the heightened emotions, her soft trembles turning into real shivers. I carry her into the bathroom, but she lets go as she gathers what we need for a bath. She plugs the tub and reaches under the sink to retrieve bubble bath. She moves around, grabbing towels. I keep testing the water until I'm confident it'll stay warm for a while without scalding either of us.

I help her in, and once again, she sits on my lap, her knees and shins resting on the tub floor. I splash water over her shoulders before I sink farther under, bringing the water to her neck.

I barely filled the tub to halfway, but displacement has the water nearly spilling over. We soak until we're both falling asleep. She lets the water out, and we pull the shower curtain closed after we stand. She adjusts the water temp this time until it's comfortable.

"You know what I said earlier about never feeling like a possession when you speak to me?"

"Yeah."

"Would you say that sort of stuff every time you're inside me? Even when we're just together like earlier."

"If that's what you want, I'm happy to say it all the time."

"I don't know if it's just because I'm freaked out by what's going on or what. But I need to hear it. I know it's all true, even if you don't. But it stops my mind from spinning. You're always so certain."

I pull her close to me, and this time the kiss is passionate and lusty. I turn her to face the wall, and I lift one foot onto the edge of the tub. I pull her hips back as I thrust into her.

"All of you is mine, Chellie. There isn't a part of you I won't possess. I won't share you, and I won't let anyone take you from me. I know you can guess what I do, but you can't imagine the extremes I will go to, to keep you. We're getting married in the morning, and you're throwing out your pills. I'm going to fuck you full of my cum every chance I get until I get you pregnant. We are going to have a family and a long life together. I'm going to suck your tits until it's our baby's turn. Then I'm going to watch you and hold you while you hold our son or daughter. No more you or me. Only us."

I'm not sure if I went too far with that, but it tumbled out once I opened the gates.

"Enzo."

She moans my name as I watch her fingers bend and

straighten against the wall as though she'd fist it if she could. I press my chest against her back as I thrust over and over.

"Come, *piccolina*."

"Yes, Daddy."

"I'm going to count down, and you will come all over me. Five. Four. Three."

"I'm so close, Daddy. Harder."

"Two."

"Harder!"

I slam into her hard enough that her face bangs against the wall as I say one.

"Fuck. Chellie, are you all right?"

"Don't stop. I'm coming. Fucking come in me, Enzo. Fill me like you promised. Fuck a baby into me."

I grip her hips and pound into her. I fist her hair and pull her head back.

"Is that what you want, little girl? You want Daddy's cum dripping out of your tight little pussy."

"No. I don't want any of it to drip out. I want it all inside me. It's mine. I want it all."

"You're going to have it. Over and over until you beg me to stop because you're too sore for another round."

"You're going to fuck me until you have no more cum. Your dick is mine, Daddy. I'll suck you off, or you can fuck my ass if I get too sore. But you promised me all fucking night. I demand it."

I pinch her nipple hard as I tug her hair again.

"Demand it? I don't think you understand how this works. I decide what we do because I'll always take care of you. If I say enough, then we stop. Don't push me, Chellie."

"I know what I can take, Enzo. I want you to fuck me all night. We're only stopping or slowing down if you need to. A woman's body recovers faster than a man's, and you're no teenager anymore."

She's goading me, and I can see her smile. I thrust as hard as I dare and spill inside her. I wrap my arm around her waist and lift her off her feet as I keep rocking my pelvis.

"I'm no boy, *piccolina*. I'm going to tie you to that bed and edge you all night if you give me one more order. You said you didn't want to be restrained because you want to touch me. I'll take that from you and make you beg. I'll drive you crazy with how badly you need me to make you come — let you come."

"Promise?"

I hear the humor in her voice, and she looks back at me and winks. If her ass weren't still red, I'd spank it. Instead, I grab a handful and squeeze. It makes her Kegel, and my dick pulses. I pull out and put her back on her feet. A moment later, we're shampooing our hair as though we didn't just fuck like bunnies.

"You're good at the dirty talk, Enzo."

Is she fishing?

"Do you want to know if I spoke dirty to the women in my past?"

"I assumed you did since you always know what to say. I'm not trying to pry. I just meant it as a fact. I like it. I think it's hot. I told you I need it right now, but I liked it before all this. I want you to keep talking like that even once everything is back to our normal, even if I get pregnant."

I want to correct her and say when, but I know it's not always that simple. She sticks her head under the water to wash out the suds. With her arms raised over her head, her tits stick straight out, calling to me. I'm obsessed. There's no other way to describe it. I latch on and suck. Her hand rests at the back of my head, pressing me closer.

"I think my daddy loves my tits. I think he wants to fuck me all night. I think he wants to suck them and wishes I never wore another shirt or bra. You're going to keep sucking them while I ride your cock. It makes my cunt ache to feel you inside me. It makes me want to push you down on the bed, climb on over you, and make you take my tits. You don't get a choice. I know how badly you need to suck on me, and I'm going to give you that until you're ready to crawl out of your skin because you need to fuck me."

She reaches between us and strokes me. When I groan, she lets go. I'm not used to this kind of power exchange. I never thought I'd let her take control, but it's hot as fuck. She pushes her tits together, and I alternate sides until they're as red as her ass.

"I can't wait to get home and order clamps for these. You're going to wear them whenever I tell you to. You'll leave the house wearing them, knowing no one can tell but us. You'll wear them when we make dinner. You'll wear them while you work at your computer. You'll wear them until I say they can come off. Then I'll suck your nipples as all the sensation rushes back, and you beg for relief."

"In all seriousness, can we go home tonight, Enzo?"

"Yes. Once we're done, we'll get dressed. Two of my guys will drive the SUV back. We'll take the town car since it has the privacy glass. We have two hours to fuck in the backseat."

We hurry to finish the shower. We towel off, and I fetch our clothes from the living room. I stay out of the way as she moves around the cabin, putting everything away. She's on the satellite phone with Laura as she does it.

"I promise I'm okay. I was having a snack and trying to read when Enzo arrived."

She grins and waggles her eyebrows. That's one way of putting it. She walks past, and I'm close enough to hear what Laura says next.

"Arrived? Let me guess. Kicked in the door and had you bent over the sofa before the door closed."

She winks at me.

"Something like that."

"And I bet you two have been going at it since that moment. That's why it took so damn long for you to call me. I'm certain Lorenzo's been there for a few hours."

"He has."

"Good for you."

Chellie laughs. I wrap my arm around her waist and pull her back against me. When I speak, I make sure Laura can hear me.

"Say goodbye, Chellie. We need to go, and I haven't touched you for five whole minutes. I don't know if I can last."

"Bye, Lorenzo. Bye, Chellie Belly."

"Bye, Laura Snora."

I think their nicknames are adorable. It's not long after that we've locked up the place and are in the car. Best laid plans of mice and men. We're both asleep within five minutes. I wake as we cross into Manhattan. I glance down at Chellie as she continues to sleep. Clearly, we both needed it since neither of us stirred the entire ride. My driver knows where to take us, and it's not to either of our places.

"Chellie, wake up."

"Huh? Are we home?"

"Not yet."

She sits up and peers through the window.

"Where are we?"

"You'll see."

We pull up to the curb, and Rocco opens the door. He was in the front passenger seat as our guard. The other guys broke off and went to return the rental. Once I'm out of the car, I reach in for her. It's already late, and all the other shops are closed. But I told Rocco to make sure this one stayed open at the same time as I told Luigi where to take us.

"Mr. Mancinelli, I'm glad you made it. I wasn't going to be able to stay much longer."

I shoot the man a scowl, and he quickly plasters a smile on his face. For what I've already spent, he'll fucking stay until the cows come home.

"Is it ready?"

"Yes, sir."

"Enzo?"

"Shh, *piccolina*. Good things come to those who wait."

Chapter Eighteen

Chellie

My gaze sweeps the jewelry store before settling on the salesman, who's beaming at Enzo. It takes me a moment before I realize they must know each other. Enzo guides me toward the wedding ring display. I glance toward the engagement rings, but he nudges me in the opposite direction. I can only stare up at him. It was only a couple hours ago that we were truly talking about getting married and soon. Now, we're bypassing engagement rings and moving straight to wedding rings. My head's spinning.

"Pick whichever one you want."

All I can do is blink at such a blanket statement. Whichever one? This is a high-end store in the Diamond District in Manhattan. Nothing in here starts at less than at least twenty-thousand dollars. I know he's wealthy, but this not only hits me in the face but shoves it down my throat that we run in very different circles. I may have come from parents who are well off, but this is another level.

"Chellie, what style do you like? Eternity bands? Vintage?"

"I — I don't know."

I do. I'm just too stunned to remember I have a preference. I look into the cases, and I can't form a thought. Everything looks pretty. But the longer I look at them, the more my mind clears.

"I don't like emerald cut or baguette. I — I don't like lunette either."

"What's that?"

I turn my head to meet Enzo's gaze. He looks nervous for a moment, as though he might have already made a mistake.

"It's a style that would allow an engagement ring to nestle against it. It's like a crescent or semi-circle that the engagement ring stone would slide into."

I don't care for how they look to begin with. If I don't have an engagement ring, then I think it would look — it would detract from a single band. I'm not going to knock the style since some women like it. It's just not for me.

"Ms. ..."

The jeweler trails off, not knowing what to call me. Enzo is quick to jump in.

"Mrs. Mancinelli."

His arm wraps around my waist as I realize I'm bracing myself against the display case. I've never heard anything better — or more shocking. I twist and encircle his waist with my arms. I lean against him and sigh. It's truly the most at ease I've felt since he went out of town. He tightens his hold on me and kisses my forehead.

"Anything you want, *piccolina*."

"Really?"

"Absolutely anything."

I inhale, then nod. I point to different trays, and the jeweler pulls out displays laden with scalloped pavé, French pavé, and shared prong diamond rings. I try on several and almost lose myself in it. I'm suddenly a fairy princess with my Prince Charming texting beside me. I glance over at him a few times when I'm certain he's on his phone. But the moment I take my eyes off the rings, he's back to being attentive. Even if he's on his phone, he's following the conversation and doesn't miss a beat when he offers his observations — never suggestions.

I know he just came back from a work trip that I didn't think to ask about and wouldn't dare even if I had. He must have things he should have taken care of instead of chasing me into the mountains, then fucking me senseless for hours. He's trying to be discreet, and I appreciate that. Even when he's distracted, he still pays more attention to me than any man ever has.

"This one, please."

I hold out my hand and pray I didn't pick something too extravagant. I have no idea how big a ring this is, so I can't even wager a guess at how much this must be.

"Perfect. We'll take it."

The ring is still on my finger when Enzo pulls me in for a kiss that no one should watch. But I don't pull away. I soak up every moment of this.

"Excellent. This nine-and-a-half carat shared prong ring will match the five carat—"

"Thank you so much for your help. If you can clean it, we'll take it now."

Enzo practically rips his mouth from mine to cut off whatever the man was going to say. I'm stuck on the nine-and-a-half carats part, then picking out a band for Enzo. It isn't until we're about to leave that I realize he was going to say something about a five-carat piece of jewelry. I'm about to ask when we step outside. Instead of a town car or SUV waiting for us, it's a horse-drawn carriage. And not the kind that are waiting on a corner near Central Park for anyone to hop in. This is way, way nicer. Enzo's hand at my elbow guides me forward.

"Daddy?"

I whisper the single word.

"Get in, *piccolina*."

"Is it safe?"

After watching Afonso get shot today, I'm not so certain I want to be in an open air anything.

"No one knows where we were or that we came into the city. It won't be a long ride. I promise."

That's a bit disappointing. I mentioned never having ridden in one of these and how romantic they look. That was not long after we got together. It was a comment made in passing. I can't believe he remembers. Once we're settled in, he leans over to whisper in my ear.

"I remember the things you say that you don't think matter. They matter to me."

"I love you."

The words tumble out of my mouth, but the happiness I see in Enzo's eyes is worth its weight in gold. I nestle closer to him and close my eyes for only a moment. I want to bask in this perfection and how loved I feel. I also don't want to miss a moment of this carriage ride. But I'm not relishing the moment like I thought I would.

"Daddy, I'm sorry I made you come home early. You probably still had things to take care of."

"The only thing that matters is you."

I twist to look up at him.

"We both know that isn't true. Did I cause problems for your family? For your businesses?"

"Chellie, you did nothing wrong. You didn't ask to be targeted or for someone to attack. Running might not have been the best response, but it was human nature to flee. We resolved all of that back at the cabin. Whatever I had left to do isn't going anywhere."

I can practically hear the word unfortunately hanging in the air.

"I don't want you to fear that whenever you travel, you're going to have to rush back because I freak out."

"I don't think that and never have. This was an extraordinary situation. But I'm glad to be home and with you. There's no part of my work that I prefer to spending time with you."

That makes me want to picture what he does, but I push the thoughts from my mind. I don't want to know if he extorts people or hurts them. I don't want to know what he sells and buys. I don't want that part of his life to intrude upon the one we share. Strike that. I don't want that part of *our* life to intrude upon what we share. I am marrying him. I don't think I've ever had a more decisive and definitive thought in my life. That means his life is mine as much as mine is his.

His kiss is gentle as his thumb and index finger hold my chin. All of this feels like something out of a movie. The people hurrying along the sidewalks, the car horns, the permanently slightly off smell of the city all disappear. It's just the two of us. When we sit back, I realize we're approaching Enzo's place near Hudson Yards. I figure we're heading to his penthouse, but we stop outside the Edge.

It has the highest observation deck in the Western Hemisphere, with three-sixty views of the city. It has a glass floor and angled glass walls. I've only been up there once and loved it. They have some type of climbing challenge in case you want to go all Mission Impossible. I would in a heartbeat, but the only person who would ever agree to do it with me is Laura. Now that she's a mom, it seems irresponsible to ask her.

Enzo helps me out of the carriage, and we head inside. I

look around and realize it's quieter than I expected. The observation deck is open until like midnight. It's only nine-thirty. We must have spent nearly two hours at the jewelers, and I didn't even notice. Enzo slips his hand into mine, and we head to the elevators.

"Mr. Mancinelli, this way, please."

I look over at a young woman in a dress I would never wear to work and heels that are better suited for a nightclub. She's devouring my boyfriend and practically eye fucking him.

"Thank you."

Enzo barely glances in her direction as we change course and head toward what looks like a private elevator. When the doors open practically on command, we step in. The woman takes a step to join us, but Enzo hits the close door button.

"I know the way."

"But—"

The door closes on the woman mid-word, and it makes me want to smirk. But I have no time for that since Enzo hits the stop button and presses me against the wall. My skirt is practically at my waist as I fumble for his belt.

"Enzo, what about cameras?"

"My men have taken care of that. Seeing you wear a wedding ring is the most arousing thing I've ever witnessed. I'm going to fuck you, *piccolina*, because I can."

I push open his pants and practically rip his boxer briefs in my haste. He lifts my right leg and thrusts into me.

"Daddy."

It's a breathy moan that elicits a groan from him. Then we're clawing at one another as he thrusts over and over. This is definitely going to be a quickie, and I love it. Watching him trying on wedding bands had the same effect on me. I wanted to jump his bones right there in the store.

"Come, little one."

My pussy is under his command. It's only one thrust more, and I'm clenching around him. I feel him pulse inside me, and I know he didn't hold back. I know without panties, I'm going to feel his cum on my legs when we step off this elevator. He'll know that, and I'll know that. But no one else will. I love that shared secret. We adjust our clothes, and Enzo hits the button to send the elevator up to the observation deck. I look down to make sure I'm fully covered again. When the doors open, I freeze.

"Chellie?"

"What's this?"

"It's for you."

I follow Enzo off the elevator. I expected there to still be people up here, but there's only one man. There's a beautiful table set with candles on the ground along each glass wall. The man pulls out a chair for me, and I take my seat as Enzo walks to his. The breeze lifts my hair, and it's refreshing. I don't know where to look. The spectacular view or Enzo. I should clarify — the spectacular view of New York City or the spectacular view of Enzo. My God, he's hot. The way he's smiling at me, I could almost forget where we are.

He reaches for my hand as the man steps forward to pour us wine. I barely have time to blink before the elevator opens, and a line of servers brings trolleys of covered dishes. It's not long before I realize it's a four-course meal, and I'm soon stuffed. We chat over dinner, but I can't help but wonder why he brought me here. I would expect a proposal at somewhere like this, and he said he would ask properly. But he doesn't have any ring except for my new wedding band.

"Come here, *piccolina*."

Enzo stands and holds out his hand to me. We walk over the glass floor to the corner. The observation deck is an overhang that protrudes from the building. The view down is almost as amazing as the panoramic view. It might make some people nauseous or terrify them. I love it.

"I love you, Chellie. The moment I saw you at the theatre, I knew I needed to get to know you. I knew I wouldn't let you go. I fell in love with you that night. I'm certain of it. This life isn't easy, and it'll take time for you to get used to. But I'll be by your side just like you're beside me. You're my sanctuary, my haven. You're who I look forward to seeing the most. The person who gives me a sense of peace I haven't had since I was a kid. I've never wanted to spend time with someone as much as I do you, and I've never desired a woman the way I do you."

I watch as he gets down on one knee and pulls out a small jewelry box. It's a different shade of red from the one the jeweler placed my wedding ring in.

"Chellie, will you marry me?"

He has the closed box in one hand and is holding my left hand with the other.

"Yes."

I don't have to think about my answer. Obviously, it's yes since we just bought wedding rings. But even if we hadn't, it wouldn't take me longer than the time needed to say it. He flips the box open and takes out the ring. My eyes almost fall out of my head. The ring is gorgeous. It's exactly what I would pick out. Except the stones are way bigger than I would have dared consider. Between this and the band, I'll be wearing at least thirteen carats of diamonds. I don't know if my finger is even long enough to carry this off. But I practically want to jump up and down when he slides it onto my ring finger. I fist the front of his shirt and tug.

"Enzo, you're perfect."

I kiss him with all the love and passion I feel that I can't contain at this moment. Would most people say we're moving way too fast? I'm certain they would. Most people would think this is infatuation and lust. I'm sure it's not. This is something I feel to the marrow of my bones. Infatuation and lust sure as hell wouldn't be enough to make me agree to the life and world I'm entering. Love is.

"I don't know about that. But I'll try."

Enzo's smile is everything. It's boyish and even a little tentative. It's not the brash one I've seen; the one that dazzles everyone around him. It's not the playful one I see sometimes before he grabs me and kisses me senseless. He's worried he won't live up to my expectations.

"Enzo, this is beyond amazing. I will never forget this day. Yes, it started out horribly. Nothing is going to erase that. But the way you burst into the cabin like the devil on a mission, then the way you needed me, the way you made my body come alive. The spanking, the making love, the falling asleep in the car knowing I was safe with you. And now this. Shopping for our rings, the carriage ride, the dinner, the proposal. It's something out of a movie. It doesn't happen to ordinary people like me. You made it happen, and I've never been so happy as I am right now. I love you because you make me feel whole."

"I feel the same way. I'm sorry I was away from you this morning and not there to protect you myself, not there to comfort you when it went down. The moment I heard what happened, nothing could have kept me away. I couldn't get to you fast enough. I didn't know what to expect when I peeked through that window. Seeing you reading with snacks around you was not it. I thought my head might explode. But the moment I was inside, and I could see you with nothing in the way, all I wanted was to hold you and be held by you. I've never felt a need so consuming as that. The moment we touched, even before I was inside you, I felt whole."

I notice we're alone on the deck. It's like we're in a world made only for the two of us.

"In a city of eight-and-a-half million people, with thousands of buildings and cars and buses, you've managed to make it feel like there's only the two of us."

I turn to look out at the view. He kisses my neck and pulls my shirt collar so he can kiss my shoulder. I press back against him and rub my ass on his dick. I can feel how hard he is again. I step toward the glass barrier, and he follows me. The city lights of Queens, Brooklyn, the Bronx, and Staten Island twinkle in the distance. The sounds of busy city life are muted this high up, but it's the reminder of a vibrant city life continuing on, even though we're in our own fairytale.

I feel him unfastening his pants again, then lifting my skirt. I widen my stance and pray no one comes up here. I'm certain he's made sure that won't happen. I place my hands on the glass as he pulls my hips back and slides into me, then his hands cover mine. I'm pressed between him and the rest of the world. He knows how much I like being pinned by his weight. He's not moving, just keeping me in one place. He's kissing my neck again, but that's it.

"I know you said you want to get married in the morning, but I think you'll regret not giving your family time to be part of this. I know you'll want your sister as your maid of honor. Can you have two? Could Laura be your matron of honor? Do you think Lanie would be a bridesmaid?"

"I don't know about her. She refused to come to Laura's wedding, and she's been really pissed at me."

I haven't told him about the arguments she and I have had or the angry texts she's sent me. I've tried to be understanding because I know she's as scared for me as she was for Laura. They've made peace, but their friendship is nothing like it was. I know she's going to feel even more alienated now that I'm joining the same world Laura entered. But I don't want to think about that right now.

My sister, on the other hand, has been incredibly support-ive. Things with Enzo have been such a whirlwind that I haven't seen her much since Enzo and I started dating. We had lunch again while Enzo was away. What I haven't told her, I'm pretty damn certain she's guessed. She worries about me, but she accepts my choices. I think seeing Laura and Maks makes it much easier.

"You'd be okay with Laura coming?"

"They can all come, Chellie."

I freeze.

"You'd let all the Kutsenkos come to your wedding?"

"Maybe only Laura and Maks to the ceremony, but they'd all be invited to the reception, anyway. You saw how things were with them at theirs."

"Yeah, Maks almost ruined their night because he didn't explain how things would be in public."

"I noticed he wasn't exactly the doting husband that we all assumed."

"Will you be like that?"

"Distant and cold for appearance's sake? Fuck no. Besides the fact it would be pointless since so many of us have married for love that it's no secret to anyone, I have no desire to hide how happy I am. I sure as shit don't plan to stop kissing you and touching you on our wedding day. Fuck the world if they think I'm suddenly a sap. I love my wife."

"I'm not your wife yet."

"But you liked hearing me call you Mrs. Mancinelli."

"I did. There are a lot of Mrs. Mancinellis, though. Maybe I should be Mrs. Lorenzo."

I shake my backside against him, and he growls, pressing me harder against the wall. He thrusts as I splay my fingers. He entwines ours, and I wrap mine around his. This isn't the rough quickie from a couple hours ago in the elevator. As the minutes pass, I let go of his fingers and slide my hands out from under his. I'm quick to squeeze them between us and cross my wrists at my lower back. I don't want him to think I want to stop. Just the opposite. He gets it because he fists my hair and pulls my head back.

"You've had enough vanilla. Now you want me to lead."

"Yes, Daddy."

"I ordered some things for us on my flight out. They should have arrived by now."

"What?! All the packages get scanned and opened at your place. People will have seen whatever it is."

Sex toys. That's what it is.

"Yes, they had to scan them. Nothing comes near you without being checked. But they didn't open them. When we get home, we're going to introduce you to real BDSM. I was going to hold off, but I think that's what you want to make tonight complete."

"It is."

"My sweet *piccolina,* the things I'm going to do to you."

"Promise, Daddy?"

"Most definitely."

He thrusts harder and harder until I'm on my toes with my cheek pressed against the glass. I meet each of his thrusts.

"May I come, Daddy?"

"No."

So it starts. Orgasm denial. Sweet, sweet torture. His hand is still in my hair, but the one that rested on my hip after I moved my hands is now at my throat. He squeezes enough for me to feel his control without making me panic. I feel so small against him. Some might feel out of control, not being able to move other than to rock my hips. But it's just the opposite.

The control is letting him lead. Knowing I'm safe with him, that he'll do everything I need. Knowing that I'm the most important person in the world to him. Knowing that if I said my safe word, we'd stop immediately. I am someone who likes to be in control, or else I feel anxious. It's part of why I bolted to the Poconos today.

But he knows being like this with him, happily following his lead, gives me back what I need. It gives me as much control as it gives to him. And he's a man who lives by being in charge. He's so used to bearing the weight of the world on his shoulders that his equilibrium depends upon him knowing I'll submit to him. That he can dominate me and the bubble we're in.

"Please, Daddy."

I'm begging, and my pussy aches so much that it nearly burns. I need to come. I don't know that I can stop if it happens. He releases my hair and slides his hand over my breast and down my belly. It forces me to pull back a little, but he finds my clit and rubs. My head falls back on his shoulder, and I close my eyes.

"Come for me, baby girl."

His gruff whisper pushes me over the edge. My hands are still behind me, but I twist them and fist his shirt.

"Enzo!"

Fuck! I meet each of his thrusts and push my hips back until both of his hands come to my hips and hold me while he spills inside me. We collapse against the wall, panting. His left hand strokes that side of my ass.

"Happy, baby?"

We stay like that for I don't know how long, just looking out and enjoying the moments of peace. Little do I know it's all about to shatter.

Chapter Nineteen

Lorenzo

I'm floating on clouds nine, ten, and eleven. I knew I wanted to propose today even before I touched down in New York. The moment I saw her in the cabin, I was certain. She confirmed my decision when she said she wanted to get married tomorrow. While we were at the jeweler, I texted Marco to go to my place and get the engagement ring I got almost the day after we went on our first date. I got the stone while I was in Antwerp and had it set at the same jeweler as where we got our wedding rings. While Chellie was climbing into the carriage, the driver slipped me the box. I saw Marco hand it to him as we came out of the shop. I was afraid she'd spot him, too.

Dinner was delicious, but nothing compares to watching Chellie as I proposed. Her happiness is my happiness. As we sit in the town car on the way to my building, which is only a couple blocks away, I keep running my thumb over her ring. I knew the carriage ride was a risk, but I knew she'd always wanted to go on one. The Edge is so high that I didn't worry about us being a target. The only way to get to us would have been by helicopter or plane, and I would have spotted that. But I don't want to risk walking.

"Are you going to have to fly out again?"

There's no accusation or anger in Chellie's tone. Perhaps it's more resignation than anything else. I talked to Marco while I was in the car to the Poconos.

"No. My brother will handle the rest of this."

"Are you sure? You weren't going to come back today, but I interfered."

"You did no such thing. Whoever is behind this did that."

"But if I hadn't refused your order and argued with Marco, and if I hadn't taken off—"

"Chellie, the moment someone shot in your direction changed everything. There wasn't a chance in hell I wasn't coming home. We're going to spend the night at our place because we just got engaged, and I don't need anyone hearing what I plan for us. But I'm taking you back to my parents' place in the morning. You saw where they live. It's way safer than a penthouse in Manhattan."

She nods. I lift her onto my lap and cradle her.

"I don't want this to ruin our night, *piccolina*."

"It's not. Nothing can do that. I just feel like an imposition."

"You're about to be their daughter-in-law."

"And in-laws are like fish. After three days, they stink, and you want to throw them out."

I laugh and give her a smacking kiss.

"Not in my family. In-laws are like fine wine. The longer we keep them, the better they get."

I wink at her, but as I look up, I spot headlights far too close to her side of the car. I twist and cover her body with mine as we bear the brunt of the impact. The vehicle slams into the middle of the car, ensuring it crushes the driver's door and the back passenger one. The force feels like it pushes the car sideways, but we're in a tailspin.

"Chellie?"

"I'm all right. What about you?"

"Fine."

We stop turning, but immediately, we're rammed from behind. I feel around until I can reach the button to drop the privacy glass.

"I'm working on it, Enzo."

Luigi speaks before I can. Thank God he's conscious.

"Chellie, get down on the ground and do not move. Cover your head."

I sit up enough for her to roll out from beneath me. I pull my gun, something she's gotten so used to that she doesn't even look twice. The moment I do, the window on the crushed side shatters. I feel the pain as the bullet enters my shoulder. I grit my teeth, refusing to make a sound.

Chellie isn't looking at me, and I don't want her to. But the open space now makes aiming easy. I point and fire toward the tires of what I realize is a second car that hit us. Luigi's window is open and firing at the driver of the car. Their windshield shatters as blood splatters it from inside.

Motherfucker! Goddamn that hurts. I press my free hand to my left ribs. This one grazed me, whereas the one in my shoulder is there until someone pulls it out. Fucking hell. Everything is getting blurry. I blink as I try to focus and shoot. I'm bleeding faster than I thought. The pain is worse than I expected. This isn't the first time I've been shot, and morbidly, I pray it isn't the last. That would mean I'm dead. I can hear nothing past the ringing in my ears. Everything is turning black as someone pries the gun from my hand.

"Chellie?"

"Lie down."

I can barely see as I watch her hold the gun like an expert marksman. She fires off a round of shots in quick succession, and I hear a car crash, but it isn't into us.

"Luigi, they shot Enzo twice. Where do we go?"

"Carlotta's."

"Hurry."

That's the last thing I hear.

"Enzo?"

"Mama?"

"*Sono qui.*" I'm here.

"*Dov'è Michelle?*" Where's Michelle?

"*Con Carlotta.*" With Carlotta.

I'm woozy as I sit up abruptly. Stitches tug in my shoulder and ribs. It's enough to make me think I'm going to throw up. I swallow it down.

"Chellie!"

"*Shh. Sta bene. Tutti vogliono solo essere al sicuro.*" Shh. She's fine. Everyone just wants to be on the safe side.

I lean back against the pillows as Mama adjusts them. Everyone. I look around and realize I'm in my childhood bedroom. My entire family must have come here. It wouldn't surprise me if Auntie Carlotta and Mama were already here together. If they have the time, they often bake together. I sniff and smell fresh bread.

"Enzo?"

I look up and see Chellie in the doorway.

"*Vieni qui.* I mean, come here."

I wave her forward with the hand that isn't in a sling. We all learned Italian before English, so it doesn't surprise me to realize I slipped back into that. Unlike my parents' generation, mine learned English before going to school. But I didn't know anyone outside my family who took sardines or bruschetta for lunch. My parents' generation learned English in kindergarten.

I reach across me and pat the edge of the bed. Chellie's tentative, looking at Mama rather than me. When she nods, Chellie perches next to me.

"Are you all right, *piccolina*?"

I don't care if my mom hears me call my fiancée that. I'm certain she already spotted the ring. I'm not the only man in this family to call his woman that. Old fashioned and outdated as that sounds, I love thinking it.

"I'm fine. Carlotta checked me out since I got a minor cut on my hand when the window shattered."

I look down and see the bandage. That's not a minor cut.

"Stitches?"

"A couple. How do you feel?"

"Don't change the subject, Chellie. How bad is it?"

She starts to unravel the bandage, but I reach out to stop her. She smacks my hand away and reveals the neat row of six stitches. Fury boils inside me, looking for a vent like a caldron about to explode. She leans forward and kisses my cheek before she whispers to me.

"Calm down, Daddy."

She sits back and wraps her hand again. She casts her gaze over me, and I recognize her feelings as ones that match mine. When our gazes meet, I see something I never expected. It isn't directed at me. It's directed at the invisible threat. It's a resolve to do whatever it takes to end this. It triggers a memory.

"Did you shoot my gun?"

"Yes. More than once. I hit the driver of the second car and the passenger. They're dead."

I just blink. She might as well tell me what we had for dinner tonight.

"Chellie, I'm sorry. That must have been so hard for—"

"It wasn't even remotely hard, Enzo. They attacked us and shot you. Nothing was going to stop me from keeping them away from you. I ran out of bullets, or I would have shot the driver of the third car. I'm certain he was watching what happened. Luigi spotted him too, but he said he didn't have time to reload. We needed to get away and get you to Carlotta."

"How do you know how to shoot?"

"My mom. I used to go to the range with her and Laura. I'm a better shot than either of them."

That's hella impressive then. I've heard about Laura's aim, and she could be a sharpshooter. I know she killed men who attacked her, Sergei, and her dog on Maks's roof before she married Maks.

"Enzo, I'm not as openly assertive as Laura. I don't command every space I enter like she does. She doesn't intend to, but I'm purposeful in hanging back. I observe like she does, but differently. Don't assume that means I'm meek or mild-mannered in all things."

She cocks an eyebrow at me, and I realize she and Laura could run the underworld without thinking twice about it.

"You like people to underestimate you."

"It has its advantages."

She looks away a moment later, and I know she's thinking about that bastard Shapiro. He thought he could assault her because of it. My free hand wraps around her left hand, and I love the feel of her ring pressing into my palm. We definitely aren't getting married in the morning.

"Enzo, you shouldn't be sitting up yet."

"Yes, Auntie Carlotta."

I watch as my mother's best friend and a woman I've

considered my aunt my entire life walks into the room. Even though there's no blood relation or even one through marriage, she's like a second mom. Uncle Domenico is Papa's adopted second cousin, but calling them Uncle and Auntie has always been easier. I'll never outgrow it.

I try to shimmy down the bed but wince. Chellie leans forward, and I have a clear view of the best tits in the world. Fucking hell. My cock still works better than a fourteen-year-old boy's.

Go down. Go down. Go fucking down.

I shift again as though I'm trying to get more comfortable, but it's so I can pull the covers over my lap more and rest my uninjured arm in my lap. When Chellie glances down at me, I know she's aware of what she does to me. I want nothing more than to be alone with her and her tits.

"Enzo!"

I hear a herd of elephants charging up the stairs down the hall. The calvary — aka my brothers, Carmine, Matteo, and Gabriele — have arrived. Or they decided they don't want to wait any longer. Luca's the first one through the door.

"*Che cazzo?*" What the fuck?

"I'll wash your mouth out."

Auntie Carlotta is the strictest about not swearing. At least not swearing in front of her. Mama glowers at him.

"I'll hand your aunt the soap. Your brother's not only alive, but awake. No need to swear."

Luca doesn't look like a man nearly in his mid-thirties. I snort, and the other guys push his shoulders as they squeeze past him.

"Sorry, Mama. Sorry, Auntie Lotta."

He walks toward the bed, and Chellie tries to stand. He and I speak at the same time.

"Stay."

Luca understands, and I appreciate it. But it means we can't talk about anything unless it's in Italian. Even then, that means Mama and Auntie Carlotta need to leave.

"Enzo!"

Well, fuck.

It's Matteo who responds.

"We're in Enzo's room."

Maria barrels through the five men, my father on her heels. She rushes to the other side of my bed, but she slows down as she climbs on. She reaches for my wrist but sees that hand's holding Chellie's. My fiancée lets go, and Maria drags it over to her. She's checking my pulse, and I know she's looking at my pupils. She's a radiologist and generally lets Auntie Carlotta handle stitching us up since she's a general surgeon. But if this reassures my little sister that I'm okay, then let her check away. She wraps her hand around my thumb and the back of mine. She brings my knuckles to her lips.

"Don't get shot. You know I don't like it."

A moment later, she pinches the back of my hand.

"Ow. I'll remember."

She slips off the bed and goes to stand with Matteo, who envelops her in a hug. Papa comes to stand behind Chellie.

"Carlotta said you're going to be fine. I doubt you feel fine."

"I'm not at my best, but I'll survive." I look at Chellie, who nods. "We got engaged tonight, so I have to live."

Mama and Auntie Carlotta give us matching smiles, which tells me they already knew. Everyone else congratulates us, and I might have heard some muttered suggestions in Italian from the married men other than my father.

Papa shoots them all a warning look, and it's my turn to laugh. Chellie's brow furrows.

"I'm not translating. Suffice it to say, they have advice."

"Oh."

"I'll translate."

Maria chimes in. Of course. She has the same irrepressible smile that she's had since she was a baby. I can't help but feel better when I see it. But I grow serious when Uncle Domenico and Uncle Salvatore join everyone. They might have staggered all showing up at once, but when Mama said everyone, she meant everyone.

Uncle Salvatore stands next to Papa and pats his shoulder. As the older brother, I'm pretty sure Luca learned that from him. He does it to Marco and me. Sometimes it's patronizing as fuck, but usually it's a welcome sign of solidarity.

"Aunt Sylvia is home with the girls. She sends her love."

"Thanks."

I wouldn't want Pia and Natalia to see me like this. I know I don't look that bad, but they're too young for truthful answers to their inevitable questions. It's best they just don't know. Uncle Salvatore looks over at Maria, and I see the slight dip on her chin.

"Hey, Michelle. I brought some clothes with me, and so did Sera. She, Sinead, and Olivia are downstairs. I'm pushier than all three of them put together. Would you like to get changed?"

Chellie looks down and seems to notice her clothes for the first time. There's blood on her skirt and on her shirt. She stares at me before she nods. I know she doesn't want to leave, and I don't want her to. But the only choice is to speak Italian, and that would be rude. She whispers to me, and I realize she gets it.

"You need to discuss this, and I can't listen. Just have one of the guys let me know when I can come back."

She's been stoic so far, but she looks like she's going to burst into tears now. I speak so everyone can hear.

"Get changed, then come back. If you're all right with us speaking Italian, I'd like you here."

"That's fine if it's okay with the others."

Uncle Salvatore rests his hand on her upper back, and I know it feels paternal to her. Her spine isn't ramrod straight anymore.

"You're welcome whenever you're ready."

We exchange a quick peck, and I watch her walk out. Mama, Maria, and Auntie Carlotta follow her, my aunt closing the door behind them. The moment it clicks, I want to know.

"Who the hell did this? Who shot at Michelle, and who the fuck tried to kill her in the car?"

Carmine shakes his head, and he knows I don't want to hear what he has to say.

"We don't know. No one has claimed responsibility. By the time we could get anyone to the accident scene, whoever ordered this or orchestrated this already had people clear it out. You know Luca got the alert the moment the first car hit you. We got it when you triggered your belt."

I forgot I even did that. It's been so drilled into me I didn't even notice it. I must have hit the small button on the inside of my belt buckle. We all wear trackers. The men have them in their belts, and the women have them in jewelry. I must have done it as I drew my gun.

"Who got there first?"

"David."

He's a solid guy, and I know he's loyal.

"What did he have to say?"

"The police and ambulances were already there, but the cars were gone. He listened to the police scanner on his way. Their response time was fast, but the only thing there was the glass from your car and theirs. These people were prepared. They had to have tow trucks waiting, expecting the guys would either total them or be dead."

None of that surprises me, and I say as much.

"These are pros. These weren't some two-bit criminals

someone hired, not caring if they lived or died. This is too well planned to be anything less than one particular man."

We all know who I'm talking about. Robert Simms. He's a fucking ghost. The man comes and goes as he pleases. None of the syndicate heads know that much about him, but we've all used him. He has no alliances except to his money. Until recently, everyone in our business believed he hid his money under a fucking mattress. It was only when he targeted Pasha that we discovered the truth.

Pasha's wife is a forensic accountant, just like him and just like me. At least we all have expertise in the area, even if it's not our day-to-day shit. Evidence pointed to us, but it didn't take her long to realize someone planted it. She also discovered Simms's real identity, which links him back to the Cold War and the former USSR.

I grit my teeth and force myself to calm the fuck down before I keep going. We suspected it might have been him, but our initial leads didn't pan out.

"He went after Chellie because she's friends with all the Kutsenkos. Simms can't touch any of them after he failed with Pasha. But he's still pissed Pasha got involved with his son and made him run off. This is personal. He wants to hurt that family, but he also wants me to blame them. He wants to stir the shit, so we retaliate against the bratva for making Chellie a target in the first place."

Papa's grim expression matches Uncle Salvatore's. They could practically be twins right now. I look at everyone else, and Papa's just about to speak when someone knocks at the door.

"Come in."

I call out, expecting it to be Chellie. It is, but Uncle Cesare and Auntie Paola are behind her. If ever there was a couple made of oil and water, it's Carmine's parents. Now that they're separated, they're actually practically besties. They live their own lives romantically and otherwise, and they don't ask each other questions. But when it comes to our family, especially Carmine, they're entirely unified.

Auntie Paola pushes past Uncle Cesare to walk in alongside Chellie. She doesn't push my girlfriend — fiancée — out of the way, but if Chellie were already family, Auntie Paola would.

"Are you all right, *cucciolo*?"

Little cub. She's been calling all her nephews that, and *cucciola* for her nieces since we were born. She was in a serious accident when she was twenty-five, and we all feared Carmine would lose his mom. So, she's pretty sensitive to anything like this.

"*Sto bene, zietta.*" I'm fine, Auntie.

"You would have thought I was the doctor in the family if you'd seen how I looked over Michelle. I'll spare you that since you're a man."

The way she says that last word. It's a running joke from when I was thirteen and tried to assert that I could make my own decisions about eating eggplant — which I loathe — and told her I was a man. I'd been carrying a knife with me for a year after all.

She gives me a kiss on my temple and hurries out of the room. Chellie looks completely lost now that it's a room filled with men who look like linebackers in custom Italian suits. I kick Marco's hip since he'd practically sat on my feet when he dumped his ass at the end of the bed. He huffs but smiles at Chellie. I wouldn't exactly call him gracious about giving up his seat, but he hurries out of the way.

The moment she's within reach, I can't keep myself from touching her. I've been focused on the conversation, but I haven't stopped thinking about her. I realize how close to my ears my shoulders have been when I wrap my arm around her shoulder and relax. I nudge her closer, and when she inches nearer, I press her head to my shoulder. She takes a moment to relax, likely embarrassed, but she sinks into my embrace.

Uncle Salvatore glances at me before jumping in.

"Michelle, what do you remember?"

Chapter Twenty

Chellie

I had a pounding headache when we arrived. It started the moment we walked through the door. I think fear had me so caught up that it wasn't until I felt safe that I realized how much my body hurt. Carlotta checked me over and gave me ibuprofen the moment she finished with Enzo. She warned me it'll likely be far worse in the morning. She suggested a hot bath with Epsom salt tonight. Now I feel like I'm awaiting the Inquisition. Salvatore doesn't mince words.

"I remember talking to Enzo and noticing super bright headlights approaching. Enzo told me to get down and cover my head. Then it felt like they pushed our car sideways. Then another one rammed us from behind. I remember spinning and not knowing when it was going to stop. Then there were gunshots, and they hit Enzo. I turned around as best I could and took his gun. I shot what I could see."

There isn't a surprised look in the room. Apparently,

women killing is about as commonplace as men. Or, at least, it's not shocking that a woman would defend her family and herself.

"Do you know if you hit anyone?"

"I killed the second car's driver and passenger. I ran out of bullets before I could shoot the man in the third car. He was watching. I think he figured he couldn't get close enough to do more damage to the car, so he stayed put. I saw his gun pointed at us, but I don't think he ever fired. At least not once I had Enzo's gun."

"Did you see his face clearly?"

I shake my head.

"Only through the windshield, and he was too far away to tell. He wasn't in my straight line of sight. I only saw him when I looked around. The men I shot were much closer."

It doesn't surprise me that I shot to kill. It shocks the shit out of me I'm not more bothered by taking two lives. But it was Enzo's, Luigi's, and mine that mattered a shit ton more to me. I wonder how I'll feel in the morning.

Massimo's tone is a little gentler than Salvatore's, but it's still commanding.

"What did you see?"

"Middle-aged man, light colored hair, broad shoulders. I couldn't tell much more than that, and I'm not even certain about age and hair color. It's how he seemed. But I do remember thinking he was as big as you."

I don't think Enzo's dad hits the gym twice a day anymore, but he's still an impressive figure. He gives off a don't fuck with me vibe. He reminds me of Sylvester Stallone in the Mafia TV show he was on. Suave, but he's seen some shit kinda look.

"That could describe who we think it was."

I lift my head to look up at Enzo as he speaks. None of

them are going to name names while I'm in the room. I get that, but I still want to know who the fuck did this.

"Do you know why? I mean beyond your family name?"

Enzo looks down at me and hesitates. He's choosing his words carefully.

"We believe it has to do with Pasha. There's someone who holds a grudge."

"A grudge? This is over someone being bu — angry — so they went after me because they know better than to go after any of the bratva."

I stopped myself from saying butt hurt. No need to be crude in front of Enzo's dad and uncles.

"The man's son was involved, and Pasha encouraged the kid — young man really — to leave before he got caught in literal crossfire. The guy sneaked out of where Pasha was being held, and I don't think the man who orchestrated this has seen him since. I think his son is back in China."

"Triad?"

It's like that single word sucked the air out of the room.

"How do you know about them?"

Enzo's practically demanding an answer to that.

"I have a nonprofit client that has some dubious contributors. Laura did some interpreting for me at a meeting. I'm pretty sure the Chinese representatives understood every word, but they acted like they didn't. Laura's firm had just started representing them for their corporate negotiations. She didn't know them well then, but we both got the impression their money wasn't clean. She confirmed it later when she warned me to keep a close eye on the books. I'm certain they bought themselves four acquisitions with that sizable donation. I figure if there's a Chinese connection to this, given what your family — does — then the Triad are more likely than anyone else."

Enzo takes a moment before he responds to everything I just revealed.

"Do you know which syndicate?"

"Wo Shing Wo."

The silence that greets those words tells me way more than anything anyone could say. I hit the nail on the head. Do I mention I deal with them pretty regularly now? Several other clients have gone knocking on their door for seven and eight-figure donations. The books have always been spotless with every — shall we say — investment, but I think there's been money laundered in both directions.

I don't know where to look, so I keep my gaze on Enzo. No one else is forthcoming, so I wonder if we've reached the part of the meeting they don't want me to hear. Do I excuse myself?

"Chellie, my family and I need to speak. It's either in Italian or English if you leave. I'd rather you stay, but none of us wants to be rude."

Now I glance around again, but my voice is soft when I respond to Enzo.

"I'd rather stay and not understand."

My gaze drops. I'm embarrassed that I've admitted what I want. What if his family was being gracious but don't really want me here? What if I look too clingy? I'm unprepared for Luca to fire off rapid Italian.

"*Chiamiamo Maks e lo coinvolgiamo o cerchiamo Simms da soli?*" Do we call Maks and get them involved or look for Simms on our own?

I hear a last name, or at least I assume it's one that I don't recognize. My gaze shifts to Matteo, even though I don't understand him any better than Luca.

"*Io dico di fare prima la nostra caccia. È impossibile che Sergei non sappia già cosa è successo. Ha uomini che ascoltano gli scanner della polizia proprio come noi. Ma nessuno di loro ha chiamato per chiedere informazioni sul suo benessere.*" I say we do our own hunting first. There's no way Sergei doesn't already know what happened. He has men listening to police scanners just like us. But none of them have called to demand information about her wellbeing.

Enzo's chest rumbles against me when he speaks.

"*Sono doctor.*" I agree.

I expect him to say more, but he goes quiet. The hand of his uninjured arm strokes along my shoulder, and I suddenly feel a wave of exhaustion. I close my eyes, listening to the conversation around me, but no longer worried or even interested in what the men say. I just want to feel safe with Enzo. I tune them out and am almost asleep when Enzo kisses my forehead.

"*Piccolina*, we're done talking."

I open my eyes and watch as everyone but Massimo and Salvatore file out of the room. Massimo offers me a fatherly smile, and I didn't expect something so small could make me feel so much better. I sit up and return it, hoping my expression shows my gratitude. He darts his gaze to his son before shifting his focus back to me.

"Michelle, Nicoletta and I would like you to stay with us until this is over. It's an open invitation that I hope you will accept. We'd all feel better with you staying at one of our homes, and Nicoletta and I already consider you family."

I can't help it when my eyes widen. I've barely been dating their son, even if he and I are talking about marriage. I didn't think they'd be so accepting so soon. I've already been an unexpected houseguest, and now my future father-in-law is telling me I can basically move in.

"One day, Nicoletta and I will tell you the story of how we met. She comes from a *Cosa Nostra* family, so she's known this life since she was born. She knew who and what I was back then and what I would become. She understood how fast men must decide, but the speed didn't mean they rushed those decisions. I knew within five minutes of meeting her I would marry her. We were barely more than kids, but I knew. Some days she says it took her four minutes. On the days I annoy her, she says it took her six. She knew when I asked her out that I wasn't just asking her for one date. She knew I was asking for a lifetime. I wouldn't have brought any woman deeper into my life if I didn't mean for her to be there until my last breath. You aren't from this world, but Enzo is. The moment he said he was dating you, I knew I had another daughter-in-law. We're happy to have you join our family."

I swallow several times as I listen to him. The story he alludes to piques my curiosity. But my stomach knots when he says he already considers me family. I want to believe him since I have no reason not to. But could they really be that okay with an outsider joining them? My mind dashes to Sinead, then Olivia. Both women knew nothing about this life, either. Both seem to fit into the family as though they'd always been members. Maybe it would be all right.

I'm unprepared for what Salvatore says, and it's a bucket of ice water.

"Michelle, we don't expect you to keep anything that happened from your parents. You're going to have bruises and be sore for a couple weeks. But we're asking you to tell your mother not to tell her family. The O'Rourkes can't know."

"The O'Rourkes? They're not family."

Enzo tenses beside me, so I shift to see his face. He looks as confused as I am.

"Uncle Sal, what are you talking about?"

Salvatore doesn't take his eyes off me.

"We ran a background check on you and your family as soon as Lorenzo said you were dating. We didn't ask Carmine, who usually does it. There was something about your name that sparked a memory. Your father's family may be of Sicilian descent, but your mother's isn't."

"I know."

"Your mother and Killian Doyle grew up together."

"My mom and Laura's dad went to school together through high school, but they lost touch for years. It wasn't until Laura and I became friends that they realized they knew each other."

I don't like the expression on Salvatore's or Massimo's faces. I look at Enzo, but he's still as confused as me.

"You're not as closely related to the O'Rourkes by blood as Laura is, but your families are. Your mother's grandfathers were senior members of the Irish mob. Your maternal grandfather was even in line to run the organization here in New York."

"What?"

"How do you think your mother learned to shoot so well? Your grandfather refused to be a part of anything to do with the mob once he met your grandmother. He did everything he could to keep your mom and aunts away from his old life. But it's also why all of his daughters could be sharpshooters. He wanted to be sure they could defend themselves if anyone came knocking and asked too many questions. She made sure you can shoot just as well as her, didn't she?"

I'm too stunned to say or do anything. I remember my grandfather as a kind man who used to take me to the park and let me jump off the swings when my mother would have lost her shit. He was the one who taught me to drive because my parents said I terrified them with my lead foot. He cheered for me at my law school graduation so loudly I remember my mom tugging on his arm to make him sit down. He died last year, and I still miss him so much that hearing about him makes me want to cry.

"You don't want me to tell my mom because you believe

she'll tell the O'Rourkes, and they'll get involved. She's not in touch with any of them. She doesn't even know them."

Massimo's and Salvatore's piercing gazes skewer me to the mattress. They say nothing more, but it's clear I'm the one in the wrong. Enzo's arm tightens around me, and I don't know what to think. I blurt out the first thing that comes to mind.

"You're still going to let me in your family?"

Massimo steps forward and squats low enough to meet my gaze. It's like I'm a little kid he's getting down to eye level with.

"Michelle, no one gets to pick their relatives or the family they're born into. Your mother's family took a different path than ours. They left when we didn't. If your grandfather had accepted the position everyone believed he would, you wouldn't be in love with my son. He wouldn't be in love with you. You definitely wouldn't be sitting here. My family couldn't make that same choice. My father wouldn't have let me or Salvatore leave. Because Salvatore is our don, my sons can't leave either. I won't leave my brother, which means my boys won't leave me. God has a plan for each of us. Many of us ignore it and do what we want because we feel we must. But sometimes God speaks louder than any of us, and that's why you and Enzo are together."

I can only nod. I'm not exactly sure how Massimo believes we're following God's plan rather than ignoring it, but there's conviction in his voice that soothes me. I'm not the most religious person I know, but I still have a deep faith. I just don't think about it that often. I want to believe what my future father-in-law says, so I choose to.

"My parents know I'm dating a Mancinelli. I know they guessed without me saying it, and they took it better than I expected. They don't know it's Lorenzo, but they know we're serious. I haven't been sure what I can and should tell them. If my mother's family is that close to the O'Rourkes, she knew exactly who I'm talking about the moment they deduced I'm with a Mancinelli. I don't know that I could keep her from telling any of them, even if I never mention the car accident. The crash."

I correct myself because nothing about what happened was an accident. Massimo continues to explain how things are going to go.

"We know, and we're prepared for that. It would surprise none of us if the O'Rourkes don't already know, but have chosen — for whatever reason — not to bring your family into this. They probably know you and Enzo are together, but they don't know about the threats to you. If your parents tell them you were in a crash with Enzo, they will insist upon getting involved. They will blame us for you being unprotected, and they will want to take matters into their own hands. It will only make it messier since the bratva is already involved. Two syndicates are a challenge, three syndicates are a powder keg."

I still can't do more than nod. I want to call my parents and demand to know why they never told me any of this. How could they let me go through life not knowing there were people who would probably love nothing more than to harm my grandfather's family? How could I not know there were probably people watching me my entire life? Were they friend or foe? Did that depend on the day of the week? There's so much I want to know. I'm pissed my parents kept this from me. And I'm pissed Massimo and Salvatore felt it was their place to tell me. But they did it for Enzo, not me.

"Is there anything else in my family history I should know?"

It comes out harsher than I intended, but not because I feel badly that I'm demanding an answer. I intended to sound detached, so they wouldn't know how I feel.

"We believe Laura doesn't know any of this, but her

parents do. I'm sure knowing their daughters had an extra set of eyes and ears looking out for them was reassuring."

"In other words, they were happy to know at least one parent from each family would shoot to kill."

Massimo and Salvatore remain quiet. It's not until Enzo takes my hand that I realize how far I'd pulled away from him. It's not him I'm angry at, but I want to shrink into myself. Make myself as small a target from the real world as I can. When I remember he's there, I lean against him again. I don't have to curl into a tiny ball to feel safe. I feel protected when I'm near him. Far more than trying to face this alone.

"Papa, if there's anything else, tell us now. Otherwise, I want to talk to Chellie alone."

"There's nothing else. We'll let you know about the other stuff when there's more to tell."

The two older men leave us alone, and all I can do is turn toward my boyfriend and stare.

"What do you need from me, Chellie?"

I blink several times, my eyes burning with tears.

"You're all right with who my family is?"

"Of course. I'm marrying you, not them."

"That's bullshit. I'm marrying your family as much as I'm marrying you, and we both know that. It's no different for you."

"Yes, it is. My family is the *Cosa Nostra*. You're marrying a man who does things he will always hide from you. You're marrying a man whose family does things that could wind them all up on death row. You're marrying a man who most people would consider a monster, and they'd think no better of his family. That's who you're marrying. I'm marrying a woman whose family has done their best to leave that life behind to protect their children. I'm marrying a woman whose family chose to rise above this life. I—"

"Don't make my family sound like saints compared to yours. My parents kept a massive secret from me."

"Don't you think I'd keep all of this a secret from you if I could?"

"You'd spend a lifetime lying to me about who you are?"

"I already will. There is so much I can't and won't tell you. Half-truths, lies by omission, flat-out bold-faced lies."

"That's out of necessity."

"And you don't think your parents felt the same way, *piccolina?*"

His voice is lower, but his tone feels condescending. Like I should see the obvious. I get what he's saying, but that doesn't help how I'm feeling. I get up, no longer wanting anyone near me. I need space to think. Apparently, my boyfriend doesn't agree. He gets up, and I hear him suck in a breath rather than groan in pain. Then he's sliding an arm around my waist as I look out the window. He moved fast and silently. I almost jump.

"You should be in bed."

"Only if you're in it with me."

"Is that all you can think about?"

"I didn't mean sex, though I think about that a lot now that I know you. Let me hold you while we talk."

"I need to think without being distracted. I can't do that while I'm touching you. I either want to fuck your bones or fall asleep."

"Fall asleep?"

"Yes. I feel so comfortable and safe with you that I can relax. But I need to think right now."

"Talk to me. Let me hear your thoughts as you work through them. Don't shut me out."

I rub the bridge of my nose and between my eyebrows, then scratch my temple before swiping my hand over my forehead.

None of it eases the headache that's back, nor does it make me think any more clearly.

"Can you stand? Or do you need to sit down?"

"I'll stand as long as you want. Chellie, this isn't the worst injury I've had."

"That is not what I need to hear right now. But if you don't mind holding me like this, I can think straight. But I need to do it on my own. I'm not ready to talk yet."

He kisses the temple I'd just scratched. His arm remains around my waist, but he says nothing more. It's the security I need without lulling me to the point where I can no longer keep my eyes open.

I get why they don't want the O'Rourkes involved. They don't need any more hands in the cookie jar. I know that as many problems as the Kutsenkos have had with the Mancinellis, they've had just as many with the O'Rourkes. I don't know all the details, but I know the fucked-up shit that happened to Laura when she was dating Maks involved them.

Laura is the one person I want to go to for advice since she's the only one who can understand my position — an outsider now sucked into the heart of a syndicate. But I can't. Her new family and the one I intend to marry into are enemies. I can't ignore or downplay that. It was childish of me to think that I could.

Will marrying Enzo and becoming a Mancinelli end my oldest friendship? Possibly. Could I walk away from Laura to be with Enzo? Yes. And that makes me feel like shit. But I also know exactly how Laura felt almost three years ago when she made that choice. When she picked Maks. I didn't fault her; I just didn't understand her. Now I do, and that brings me right back to why I wish I could talk to her.

"Do you want to talk to Laura about this?"

I wasn't prepared for Enzo to ask that.

"Are you standing close enough to hear my thoughts?"

"No, little one. I just know she's the one person you know who can understand the position you're in. I wish I was that person. The one you want to turn to. But I know I'm not."

I twist in his embrace and cup his face.

"It doesn't mean I love you any less."

The relief I see in his gaze floors me.

"Do you think I'm going to leave you over this?"

He doesn't answer. He doesn't have to.

"Daddy, I'm not going anywhere but where you go. I have shit to sort out, and I'm hurt and confused. But I want — I need — you beside me through this. I know I'm shutting you out right now because I have to work some of this out, but the only reason I haven't run screaming into the hills is because I know you're with me. That you'll be here while I figure out what I'm thinking and feeling, and you'll be here after, too. I love you, so you're stuck with me."

"Stuck only because I want you glued to my side."

"You say the sweetest things."

I slide my arms around his waist, careful not to touch his injury. I lean against him, but only on the side that doesn't have bandages. His good arm tightens around me as he kisses my forehead.

"I wish I could fix all of this for you, *piccolina*."

"I wish you could too. But this feels too big. Too far beyond our control for either one of us. For people like us, that makes it a thousand times worse. We both love being in control. Except, the only time I don't feel like I have to be is when I'm with you. But I know you have no more control over what's happening than I do. That must be driving you mad."

"I want to crawl out of my skin."

"I wish I could give that sense back to you, so I could feel calmer."

His hand slides down to my ass and squeezes mercilessly. It hurts, and I'm instantly wet. His fingers dig into me, and I know he's leaving marks. Marks I'll relish seeing because they remind me we're all right. That we're together no matter what.

"No matter what happens, little girl. You are mine. We will work through this, whether it's together or you telling me what you need. But don't doubt that I will hold on to you and never let you go."

He says the exact words I was thinking.

"Do you have any idea how much I want to suck you off right now?"

That surprises a deep chuckle from him.

"Not even a clue. How about you tell me?"

"I want to submit to you and suck you while I'm on my knees. But I also want to know I'm the one giving you pleasure. That you're mine, despite finding out my family is who they are."

"There's the tiny amount of control you need while letting me have most of it."

"Yes."

"Do you know how much I want your ass over my lap while I spank you?"

"So that I remember you'll always take care of me. Daddy, I need both, but we're not alone. We're at your parents'."

His hand fists my hair and holds my head in place.

"I don't give a shit where we are. If this is what you need, if this is how you need us, then take your fucking clothes off, *piccolina*. I expect you naked and over my lap in the next thirty seconds. I'm going to spank you until you can't move without thinking about how I own you. Then you're going to get on your knees and suck my cock. But I won't come in your mouth. I won't come on those magnificent tits. I'm going to come in your cunt because I can. Because it's mine."

If any other man ever said he owned me, I'd walk away and never look back. When Shapiro said it, I wanted to claw his eyes out. I know Enzo doesn't see me as a possession, but he knows what I like to hear when we slip into these roles. I know he likes to say it because how we act when we are together is the one thing he can control without the real world fucking it up.

"I want that, Daddy. But I'm scared you're too hurt for that. Seriously, Enzo."

"I won't push myself if for no other reason than I don't need Auntie Carlotta or Maria coming back in here to sew me up again. I don't need to feel that shit again, and I sure as hell don't need them knowing why I opened my stitches. But you know neither injury is as bad as we feared. They're little more than nasty cuts."

The bullet I thought lodged in his shoulder actually only grazed his collar bone. I think it bled so much because it was so close to his neck. That's what made him pass out. Not the pain. The one that grazed his ribs just pushed him over the edge. He has a few stitches, but he's more bruised than anything else.

He slides his fingers over the top button of my shirt and tugs.

"Take this off before I rip it off you. Then we really will have questions to answer."

I unbutton the top two, then whisk it over my head. I unfasten my bra. He snags it before it falls to the floor. Then the rest of my clothes are in a pile. He tugs my arm until I face away from him. He moves my arms, so my wrists cross at my lower back. Then my bra straps are binding them. I don't know how he does it with only one hand. His hand wraps around my throat when he's done.

"Snap your fingers if you need to use your safe word. I'm going to gag you, so no one hears how I make you scream."

The pressure on my throat eases, but he guides me to the bed.

"Stand there. Open your legs and bend over to touch your toes."

I know he wants to look at my pussy, and I'm happy to show him. I widen my stance and turn my toes in as I lean toward them. I can't see him right now, but I hear him moving around. As his feet come into view, I'm unprepared for the feel of his belt against my ass. The spank isn't hard. Just enough to catch my attention. Then he slaps my pussy, and that makes me hiss. He draws the leather between my legs, and I'm sure I'm coating it.

"All I have to do is talk to you, and you're wet."

"Yes, Daddy."

"You're going to be dripping for me by the time I'm done spanking you."

"Yes, Daddy."

My clit throbs, and I need him. My pussy burns with the ache that only goes away when his dick is pounding into me.

"Stand up."

I follow his command, and he lifts his folded belt until it's in front of my mouth. I can see the sticky white fluid that came from me.

"Open."

He wants me to taste myself. He knows I don't love it, but he's in charge. I do as he says, and he sticks it in my mouth. I notice he no longer has his sling on, and I frown. I'm even more alarmed when he uses both hands to fasten the belt around my head.

"Trust me, Chellie."

"I do."

I don't know if he can understand me, so I nod several times.

He sits on the edge of the bed and draws me over. I lean across his lap, still being careful not to go anywhere near his bandaged side. I'm doubting whether this was such a good idea now that he's using an arm that should be immobilized. Carlotta said he should try not to move it too much, even if he can. But he gives me no time to consider that because he lands a stinging slap across both cheeks.

"Stop worrying about me, *piccolina*. I decide everything right now. That's what you want. That's why you submit. You know I need this to feel calm, and you know you need this for the same reason."

I relax against his legs as he strokes down my back and over my ass.

"You know this is strictly for pleasure. There is no punishment at all. This is to make both of us feel better. I love you, and I love that we can share this."

Me too.

I wish I could say that clearly enough for him to understand me. But it would only come out garbled, so I keep it to myself. I brace myself, and the first spanking lands across my right cheek. Then my left. He creates a rhythm that I think I can predict. Left, right, both. But just as I feel like I can prepare myself for each strike, he changes the pattern. Both, two right, both, two left, two right, two left, both. I kick my feet, but I can do nothing with his arm pulling me closer to him. My restrained hands and the belt fastened in my mouth put me at his mercy.

"Put your right leg between mine."

I hook it over his thigh, knowing what'll come next. I still yelp. He spanks my pussy, then taps it three times. He spanks it again, then thrusts three fingers into me just long enough to stroke my g spot. Then he spanks both cheeks before spanking my pussy once more. He pinches my clit. I don't realize I'm trembling until he shushes me and runs his hand between my shoulder blades.

He spanks my horizontal crack twice before delving his fingers into me and keeping them there. He doesn't move them. He just fills me. I want to wriggle and squirm with my restlessness. When his thumb rubs my clit, I moan from deep in my throat. My pussy throbs around his fingers. Then I'm coming. I couldn't stop it if I wanted to, and I most certainly do not.

"*Piccolina mia*, I didn't tell you, you could come. You didn't ask Daddy."

He knows I can't with a belt in my mouth. He unfastens it and helps me off his lap. I want to rub my sore ass, but I can't with my hands still bound. His hand on my left shoulder presses me down.

"But you can ask to suck Daddy's cock."

"Please, may I suck your cock, Daddy?"

He adjusts his pants and boxer briefs until he can spring free. I lick every inch before sinking down to take as much as I can. I breathe through my nose, tell myself to relax, then inch farther. I talk myself through swallowing him, or at least trying to.

"Fuck, Chellie. I want to thrust and fuck your face, but I won't do that. But it's so hard to tell my dick no."

I pull back.

"That's exactly what I want. Fuck my mouth like I'm a porn star. Don't stop yourself."

I love knowing I do this to him. That he needs me that badly. I try even harder to take all of him. His hands grip my head, and he rocks his hips forward. I know he fears hurting me, so he won't thrust. But he presses and pulls back over and over until he pulls out. I squeak when one arm wraps around me just beneath my armpits and hauls me up.

I don't even manage to put my feet on the ground before

I'm thrown onto the bed, landing on my stomach. He yanks the bra from my wrists, then rolls me over. He grabs my left ankle and pulls me back to the edge. He pushes that leg up and out before he thrusts his cock into me. I struggle not to cry out with the pain and pleasure. He stays there, looking down at where our bodies join.

"Daddy?"

"I think I've reached my limit. But I won't stop. Sit up, baby. Wrap yourself around me."

I scramble to do as he says.

"Enzo, we can stop. This is exactly what I feared."

"Do as you're told."

The command in his voice is back the moment I don't comply. I loop my arms and legs around him, and he lifts me off the bed. He moves us almost across the room until we get to an armchair. He hooks his foot around the leg and pulls it around to face a full-length mirror.

"I'm going to watch your ass bounce while you ride me. I'm going to enjoy seeing my handprints move with you. Just before I'm ready to come, you're going to turn around and watch as I fuck my cum into you."

Holy fuck. The things he says to me. Of course, I obey. I've already released my legs, so I'm kneeling as I straddle him. He remains still as I ride him. He pulls me close for a kiss. He lets me move however I want, and I know he wants me to get off.

"Fuck, Daddy... I'm coming... Yes."

He doesn't rush me, but the moment I still, he orders me to turn around. I'm only too happy to oblige. It's awkward, but we figure it out. Once more, he grasps my wrists and holds them behind me. I bounce on his dick, my tits swinging. He sits forward, his good arm wrapping around my belly. He holds me in place as his hips thrust up, and I know he's coming inside me.

"Turn around."

I do as he says, feeling his cum dripping down my leg. Once again, I climb onto his lap, and his cock is still sticking straight up. I slide down it with a sigh. He holds my right breast, squeezing it.

"One of these days, our baby is going to eat from your tits. Until then, they're mine."

He wraps his mouth around my nipple and sucks. My back arches as he leans back, not releasing me. It makes my clit rub against his pubic bone, and I'm aroused all over again. I rock my hips, and his hands move to them, encouraging me to do what I need to get off again. His eyes are closed as he sucks. My hands are free, so I press his head to me. I feel him sigh as my fingers lace through his hair.

"That feels so good, Daddy. Do you like my tits?

"Mmmhmmm."

It's a long groan of agreement. My free hand offers him my other one, pressing it against his cheek. He switches without missing a beat. The way he looks as he suckles me, the pleasure I see — it makes me feel as empowered as when I give him a blowjob. I do this to and for him. No one else. It makes me feel more connected to him than I ever have with anyone else. He actually looks relaxed for once. He eventually pulls back, and I look down. There's a ring around each nipple like giant hickies. I hope we can do this every night. Like I've told him before, it doesn't feel maternal. But it feels like I'm giving him something no one else can that's even more connecting than sex.

"We can't stay up here forever. At least I can't. You should be resting. And I need to talk to my parents."

"Get your phone out of your pocket, then come back here and sit on my lap again."

I stand, and I stare for a moment as he strokes himself.

"Go."

I take two steps backwards before turning around to look

for my phone in my discarded clothes. When I have it, I come back and notice he's still hard. When I ease onto him this time, it feels different. This is about that connection we have when he's worshipping my breasts. Neither of us is trying to get off. I unlock my phone and dial my mom's number.

"Hi, sweetie."

"When were you going to tell me we're in the mob?"

Chapter Twenty-One

Lorenzo

I might not have been as blunt as Chellie. She has the call on speaker, so I'm careful to remain silent.

"What? What are you talking about, Michelle?"

"When were you going to tell me that Grandpa was a member of the O'Rourkes' mob family until he met Granny? When were you going to tell me that the reason you shoot like a sniper is because Grandpa wanted to make sure you could defend yourself?"

"How do you know all this?"

"That's your first thought? Not to deny it or correct me?"

"It's obvious you already know. I want to know how."

"I'm going to marry Lorenzo Mancinelli."

I cringe. What the fuck has gotten into her?

"The hell you are, Michelle. You are not marrying into the don's family. Do you know what those people do?"

"The same things your grandfathers did. The same things Grandpa did until he left."

"Left. That's the operative word. He left it because he loved his family more than money and murder."

"Mom, you should have told me."

"What? Like bedtime stories? Was I supposed to say, once upon a time, your grandpa used to kill people and taught me how to do it because evil men might come after us? How about this story, once upon a time your new boyfriend's grandfather, Vicenzu Mancinelli, shot your grandfather in the leg? Is Lorenzo the guy you mentioned? Is he the one you said you're serious about? I didn't think the guy you were dating was that high up. There are tons of Mancinellis."

"Yes."

"So, you call and unload on me, sliding in there that you want to marry a man you've only dated for what — a month, maybe two — and I'm supposed to share every family secret. Is he pressuring you to do this, Chelle? Are you safe?"

She looks at me, and I can tell she's severely regretting her lack of tact. It's so completely unlike her I don't even know what to think. I think she's shocked at herself.

"I am safe with Lorenzo and his family. But I'm angry that I found out about our family from them. If Enzo's grandfather shot Grandpa, what did Grandpa do to wind up Vicenzu's target?"

"Breathed."

Her brow furrows. I wish the call wasn't on speaker. I would whisper to her, but I can't. The best I can do is shoot her a rueful frown and nod. That sounds just like my grandfather. He was a hard man. Old school Mafia to a T. Papa and Uncle Salvatore are nothing like the man I remember from when I was a kid.

Nonno would have called them both weak for the affection they show their children, but I think they're both far stronger men and leaders than he ever was. He often terrified me as a kid. He had a foul temper. He never turned it on me or my brothers and sister, but that's because we stayed away when he was like that. Not everyone in my family was so lucky.

"Mom, do you really believe no one in this world knows about us? Knows how closely you and I are related to the mob?"

"We aren't close at all."

"Laura's dad is, and you're Susan's best friend."

I didn't know that. Mothers are best friends, and daughters are best friends. That makes my head hurt. Fuck.

"And Laura's parents have nothing to do with the O'Rourkes."

"Not true. They must not have told you that something happened to Laura while she and Maks were dating then right after they got married. I don't know what, but I know it had to do with O'Rourkes who are now dead. Killian was involved somehow because it was his family. You knew who and what Killian's family is, and you let me be friends with Laura. You're best friends with Susan. You never tried to keep our family away from that. You just tried to keep me away from the truth."

"Can you blame me? Chelle, what made you call me so angry? We talked a few days ago. You didn't tell me who you were dating, but you said you were the happiest you've ever been. You keep telling me you're serious, but now you say you're marrying a man you haven't introduced a single member of the family to. You don't even know the Mancinellis. You don't know what you're getting into."

I watch Chellie wince.

"I know the Mancinellis, Mom."

There's a long pause.

"You think you know them."

"There are things I will never know. Just like there are things I'm certain Grandpa never told you or Granny or anyone else who wasn't part of the O'Rourke brotherhood. There are things Laura will never tell any of us, and things Maks will never tell her. But you understand her life better than I did, and you never said a word about it."

"I only know what Killian and Susan, or you, have shared. I know nothing for sure about Laura and her in-laws."

"Mom, you know plenty. You know because of our family's history. They may not have told you, but you know. At least, you can guess pretty damn close to the truth, and you never told me."

"You're angry about the secrets I kept to protect you. How am I supposed to feel knowing everything I did was for nothing if you marry a mobster?"

"Mafioso."

It's my turn to wince. Normally, I'd be the first person to correct that, but this isn't the time.

"What?"

"Our family is the mob. Lorenzo's is Mafia."

"Same difference."

"Apparently, not. If they were so alike, then you would have told me about ours, and you wouldn't be worried about Enzo's."

"Chelle, there's a lot to unwind here, but there is no way you found this out if something isn't wrong. What happened?"

She looks at me, and I nod. There was no way we were going to keep this from getting out, and it's better Chellie tell her parents than they hear it from some O'Rourke.

"Someone put a target on me because I'm friends with Laura. This person holds a grudge against the Kutsenkos, but the guy knows he can't touch them. It started just when Enzo and I began dating. We think the guy now hopes to pit the Mancinellis and Kutsenkos against each other by getting to me. Enzo and I were in a car accident today."

"What?!"

"I'm all right. I'm a bit shaken up, and I'll be sore, but I didn't get hurt."

We both look at the bandages on her hand. I wonder if she's going to be in pain later like I will be. I felt fucking invincible while spanking then fucking Chellie. But I'm sure the pain that's coming will try to make me regret it.

"Someone tried to kill you in a car accident."

"I don't know about kill, Mom. But at least hurt and scare me. And before you say it, I was way safer being with Enzo than alone. I would be kidnapped or dead if I hadn't been with him and his driver."

"Lorenzo, thank you for protecting my daughter."

Her eyes widen, and her mom confirms my suspicions.

"Mom!"

I talk over her exclamation.

"I love Chellie. I've never been more scared than during that accident because I knew she was the target. But I've never been more grateful for being able to protect her than I was then."

"Protect her? The accident happened, yet you said protect her. How many men did you kill in front of my daughter?"

Chellie rests her hand on my good shoulder.

"Mom, Enzo was shot twice protecting me. But you taught me how to protect myself too, didn't you? It wasn't just fun at a range. It wasn't just shooting skeet and clay pigeons. You wanted me to know what to do."

"What are you saying?"

"I'm saying thank you for all those hours we spent together. It's a useful skill."

There's another long pause, and I can only imagine what her mother must be thinking.

"Lorenzo, are you all right? Will you be okay?"

"Yes, Mrs. Russo. Nothing too serious."

"Are you well enough to come over? It's almost dawn, and I'm wide awake now. I think the rest of this conversation should happen in person, and Chelle's dad should be here too."

Chellie's looking at me, uncertain about what's happening.

"Do you want us to come over right now?"

"If Lorenzo is up to it, yes."

I nod.

"Fine. Give us about an hour. Love you."

"Love you too, sweetie."

I hear her inhale and exhale before she hangs up.

"That wasn't my finest negotiating."

"Probably not."

"Are you disappointed in me?"

My brow furrows.

"What? No, of course not."

"I'm disappointed in myself. I handled that like shit. Fuck."

She closes her eyes and leans forward, resting her head on my shoulder again.

"*Piccolina*, you might have come in a little hot, but you've been through the ringer today. Maybe we can be a little less — forthright."

"We. You mean me. I just vomited everything that came to mind. Whoever is targeting me, do you think they know about my family? Are they trying to draw the O'Rourkes into this? I mean, without me going to my parents. Would they recognize my name and come to my defense because of who my grandpa was?"

"I don't know for sure. Maybe."

"Are your parents going to be okay with you going out?"

"I'm thirty-one. I can go out at night."

"You also got shot twice today. Will it upset them?"

"No. They'll understand why we need to see your parents.

This isn't quite how I'd have liked to meet them, but this is what we have."

Once we stand, we head into the bathroom. I dig out waterproof bandages that go over the ones Auntie Carlotta already applied. Chellie watches but says nothing about the fact I have supplies to deal with a wound in a bathroom I don't even use that often. We waste no time washing off the evidence that we had sex in my parents' house. That's a first. Fuck. Now I'm embarrassed. What if someone came up to check on us and heard us?

"Are you thinking about someone overhearing us? I am, and I'm mortified."

"Is it your turn to be standing close enough to hear my thoughts, little one?"

"No. Just great minds think alike."

We finish our shower, and she slips back into the clothes she was wearing. I pull out fresh ones since I still keep some stuff here. We make our way downstairs, and I can hear everyone in the living room. My family has always been early risers, but I'm sure most of the men haven't slept tonight. When people look over, I wrap my arm around Chellie's waist.

"We're going to Chellie's parents'. It's time for me to meet them."

Auntie Carlotta stands up from where she was playing with Petra on a blanket on the floor.

"Do you want anything for the pain before you leave?"

"I probably should."

She hurries to grab something stronger than ibuprofen that no one asks how she got ahold of. Chellie's not sure where to look. I know she's still embarrassed that people might know what we were doing and because we're headed to her family because of their mob connections. It's not just a nice meet my boyfriend brunch. It's meet my Mafioso fiancé. It sounds totally fucked-up to my ear. Luca walks over and leans to whisper to me.

"*Sarà imbarazzante come il cazzo. Ma lasciamo che dicano tutto quello che devono dire. Mamma e papà non sarebbero diversi da Maria se la situazione fosse invertita. Ricorda solo che tutto ciò che hanno sempre voluto è proteggere la loro figlia. Ho dovuto ricordarlo quando ho incontrato la madre di Livy.*" It will be embarrassing as fuck. But let them say whatever they need to. Mama and Papa wouldn't be any different about Maria if the situation were reversed. Just remember all they've ever wanted is to protect their daughter. I had to remember that when I met Livy's mom.

I nod just as Auntie Carlotta reaches out to give me some pills and a glass of water. I take them quickly before we say goodbye and head out to the next disaster.

I don't know what to expect when we walk into Chellie's parents' house. I assume it would be a frosty reception, and I can tell she's just as nervous as I am. She slides her hand into mine just before her dad opens the door. I follow her in, one step behind. I'm prepared to let go, but her fingers don't uncurl when mine do. In fact, she digs her nails into the back of my hand. Unfortunately, she has to let go, so I can shake her father's hand. I ended up putting my other arm back in the sling before we left the house. Auntie Carlotta insisted, and she was right.

"Mr. Russo, nice to meet you. I'm Lorenzo Mancinelli."

"My daughter's fiancé. It's nice to finally meet you."

It could have sounded snide, but he sounds far more welcoming than her mother did on the phone. I don't know if he's more laid back or if he hides it better or he's just had time to gear up for this. When we follow him farther into the house, I rest my hand at the small of Chellie's back. She shifts a little closer to me, the only sign of how nervous she is. Her mom's already in the living room when we walk in. I step forward and extend my hand. She takes it, and I don't sense the same anger as before.

"Mrs. Russo, thank you for having me over."

"Welcome."

Has she accepted it? Or is she as good as Chellie usually is at disguising her thoughts? Chellie leads me to the sofa, and I wait for her and her mom to sit before I do. Old habits die hard. I know her parents notice, but I'm not doing it to gain their approval. I'm doing it because my father drilled it into me.

Her dad looks at Chellie, then me before he speaks.

"How did you meet?"

"I remember seeing Michelle at Laura and Maksim's wedding reception, but it wasn't until my sister, her husband, and I were at the movies. We ran into Chellie, Laura, and Laura's sister-in-law. We went across the street to a coffee shop after the movie, and I fell in love."

I didn't expect to say that. Apparently, I'm the one who doesn't know how to disguise his feelings. Chellie beams up at me. When she speaks, she's still looking at me.

"And I thought you had to catch up to me. I know I fell in love with you there. It was like I'd known you my entire life instead of talking for the first time."

I don't take her hand to hold it, but I cover hers with mine where it rests on her leg near her knee. She moves them when she rests her palm under mine. I look at her parents and gird my loins.

"I'm sure there is plenty you want to know about me, my family, and what life is going to be like for Chellie. I'll answer whatever I can."

That seems to take them both aback. What's the point in beating around the bush? Her dad recovers first.

"What type of security will you have for our daughter?"

"She already has twenty-four-hour protection. Unless it's going somewhere routine, like work, she has a man in my family with her if I can't go. If something comes up, and I need to be away for more than a few days, then I've asked Chellie to stay with my parents. They live in a gated community behind a gated property wall. They have plenty of security."

I can't think of an embassy in the world that's more secure than my parents' house.

"Why can't she stay with us?"

It's Chellie's mom who demands an answer.

"Now that I know how well you shoot, I might not be as nervous. But I'd still feel better with Chellie having a full detail on a fully protected property."

"But don't your parents live in the same neighborhood as the Kutsenkos? Aren't they your rivals? Isn't that the entire reason Chelle's in this mess?"

"They live in the same neighborhood as my aunt and uncle. My parents live in a different one a few blocks away. But it's the same type of community."

Old money with high walls to keep the riff-raff out.

Chellie's mom still presses.

"That's still very close."

"Family homes are off-limits. Anywhere where women and children are remains untouchable."

As kids, we thought of our homes as base. We were safe there during a fucked-up game of tag.

"We can see the ring on Chelle's finger. Where will you live once you're married?"

Her mom could be a mob enforcer with the way she watches me. Each word feels like she intends to make me trip up. I can't blame her for a moment. I'm taking her daughter and dragging her into a world of unadulterated danger.

"That depends on Chellie. We can live in the place she has now, or the one I have, or we can buy a home together."

I'm pretty fucking sure Chellie hasn't told her that someone broke in and trashed her place. Guys who work for my family have already been in and repaired or replaced everything.

"What do you want?"

The woman's gaze bores into me.

"A home we buy together that can offer us the protection I want for my family."

Both of her parents' gazes drop to Chellie's stomach.

"I'm not pregnant, though we'd like to have a family sooner rather than later now that I'm in my thirties."

"Barely."

Her mom mutters the single word.

"Mom—"

Something catches my attention in my peripheral vision. I yank Chellie and push her to the ground.

"Get down!"

I cover her with my body as I call out to her parents. Only seconds later, glass shatters as gunshots fill the air. I reach behind me for my gun and pull it out.

"Enzo, stay down. Please."

Chellie's begging me, but I can't do as she says. I lift my head as I hear the front door and back door both burst open.

"Enzo?"

"*Capo?*"

Two of my men run toward the living room. I look over my shoulder to check on Chellie's parents. They're all right, huddled together.

"*Piccolina*, stay here. Don't move." I press her shoulder

367

down as I move to a crouch. "Mario, stay with them. Cristiano, come with me. Where's Santo?"

"He's—"

Mario has no chance to answer as more gunshots fill the air. They aren't directed at us, but I'm certain there's return fire we can't hear. That's Santo. We all have silencers on our weapons.

"Chellie, don't move until I come back. Mario..."

I don't have to warn him what will happen if he doesn't protect my fiancée and her family with his life. He knew what the deal was when he accepted a job in my family's security detail. I don't look back to see him nod.

"I love you, *piccolina*.

"Love you, Da — darling."

Who knows if anyone else guessed what she was going to say? I don't give a shit. I press a searing kiss to her lips before I stay low as Cristiano while I run out of the room.

Chellie's parents live on an acre and some change, but it's still the suburbs. People will hear us, so we don't have long before the cops arrive. We need to deal with this fucker and get Chellie and her parents away from here in the next two or three minutes. That's what we need to do. That's not even in the realm of possibility.

I spot Santo with his shock of red hair. He blames it on his dad being from the north of Italy. It's his mom's side that's Sicilian. He has a rifle he got from the back of the SUV we traveled in. Until this shit's resolved, Chellie isn't riding in anything else. No town cars. Our SUVs are veritable tanks. We reinforce any and everything, and they're bullet proof. There are steel plates beneath the chassis to protect against car bombs and improvised street explosives. The tires can still roll even if they're punctured.

As I run toward my guy, I yank the sling off my arm. I grit my teeth against the pain that's set in after way overexerting myself earlier with Chellie. Not that I regret a thing we did in my old bedroom, but fuck, I'm paying for it now. Thank God the bullet only nicked my shoulder. If it had gone in, I wouldn't be able to move it at all.

I press the alert button on my belt. It'll send out a ping to all the men in my family. They'll track me. We should be away from here before anyone can make their way out to Jersey. But I just need them to know shit's happening just like during the car crash. They'll start calling, but it'll be awhile before I can answer. As long as my tracker keeps moving, they'll be more confident I'm alive.

I spot a guy in a tree. His rifle has a telescope on it, and from the way he's leaning over the branch, this isn't the first job he's had like this. He doesn't see me coming from behind, so I shoot his leg and arm. He rolls from a branch that isn't high enough to kill him. But it knocks the wind out of him.

"Keep searching."

I command Santo and Cristiano without having to look at them. I use my foot to nudge the sniper onto his back. He groans, and his eyes flutter open. I recognize the guy as some-body we've contracted before. Goes to show you money talks. Someone paid this guy to take out Chellie or me, or even at this point, her parents. He doesn't care that he once did a job for us. He's loyal to the person who pays him.

"Did Simms send you?"

"Huh?"

"Unless you want to bleed to death slowly, answer me. Tell me what I want to know, and I'll end this fast. Don't, and I'll make sure my guys take you somewhere to die in agony."

We're not taking him anywhere. He's as good as dead now, but I want to know things.

"Why should I tell you anything? I'm going to die no matter what."

"And you get to decide how painful it will be."

I shoot his foot, and he howls. This is taking too long.

"Was it Simms?"

"Yes."

"How much?"

"Ten grand."

That's not a huge bounty, but it's nothing to overlook. I don't know if I should be insulted that Simms doesn't think the love of my life's life is worth more.

"Who hired Simms?"

The guy doesn't answer, so I shoot between his legs, barely missing his junk on purpose.

"I don't know. I think this was him going solo. He hates your woman."

That makes it sound personal. I thought she was just a means to an end to hurt Laura and get back at Maks.

"Why?"

"I don't know. Something about her fucking up some deal with the Wo Shing Wo and his kid."

"So, this has nothing to do with the bratva?"

"Maybe. I don't ask fucking questions."

I hear the snideness. *Stronzo.* Asshole.

"Well, I do. Does this have to do with the Ivankov branch or not?"

"If it fucks them over, then that's just a plus. He's pissed at your woman."

Chellie mentioned her work connecting her to the Triad. Does she know more? No. She wouldn't keep it from me if she knew more. She might not have said it in front of my family, but she would have told me in private.

"Who else is coming for her?"

"Don't... know."

He's struggling now, and I can tell he's close to passing out.

"Where's Simms?"

"Don't... know."

There was slim chance he did, but I had to try. I raise my gun and put a bullet through his forehead. A second after I do, there're three gunshots coming from the backyard. What the hell? I run to the side gate and use my shoulder more than the latch to get through it.

I'm unprepared for the sight that meets me. Santo's bleeding from his nose and mouth, and it's obvious someone just tried to beat the shit out of him. Cristiano has his nine-millimeter to some fucker's temple, and Chellie's mother has a smoking gun. Not literally. But it's obvious she's the one who just shot a guy who's now floating in the Russos' pool.

"Chellie? Where's Chellie?"

Something got her mom out here. Where is she?

"Up here, Enzo."

I step far enough off the patio and onto the grass to look up to the second-floor windows. Chellie has her own gun, and it's pointing toward the guy in the pool too. It's not until our gazes meet that she lowers the weapon. What the fuck Twilight Zone shit did I enter? I look around for Mario, but I don't see him.

"He's outside my door. Would you tell him I can come out?"

Did I ask for him out loud and didn't realize it?

"I know that's who you're looking for, Enzo. I'm okay. Tell him to let me out."

"Mario!"

"Sì, *capo*."

I see him step behind Chellie in the window.

"Let Ms. Russo out of her room. Escort her down here."

It's only a moment later that she's flying through the sliding glass door, and I'm running to her. I groan as we slam into each other, jarring both of my wounds. But I don't care. I kiss her, but it's all too brief.

"Get the casings."

I give the order, but when I look around, I realize my men are already gathering the evidence. I look at Cristiano and nod. The moment neither Chellie nor her mom can see, he'll take care of the other guy. We have silencers on our weapons, but these guys didn't.

"Where's your dad?"

"He's in his study at the window there."

"With a gun?"

"Yeah. Apparently, we have more in the house than I knew."

Now I'm the one wondering what the hell kind of family am I marrying into.

"I don't need him shooting me. Send your mother in there to get him. We have to go. Now."

"Wait. Were these guys after my parents, too?"

I hesitate, but I can't hide it from her. Especially not with her mother standing there listening.

"No. It's the man we suspected, but it's personal with him. It's about some deal that didn't go through because of your work connections."

She mouths Triad, and I nod.

I hear someone pull up in the driveway, so I hold my gun up, barrel skyward, as I dash to the gate I passed through only minutes ago. I ease it open just wide enough for my left eye to scout who's arrived. Thank the Sweet Baby J. I step back and open the gate as a team of our men flood the backyard. I follow them after holstering my gun and latching the gate.

"Enzo?"

I wrap my arm around Chellie when I stop beside her. The men are already pulling the body out of the pool and wrapping up the other one. Some of them are sweeping the yard for casings and anything else that shows a sign of a gunfight at the O.K. Corral. Everything is happening in a synchronized whirlwind, and Chellie doesn't know where to look.

"They're cleaners. They'll make sure there's nothing that can answer any police questions when they get here. But we need to go, Chellie. They know what to do."

There's two dozen of them who buzz around, removing any traces of blood or other bodily remains. There are men inside checking the house, and I know some are in the front yard. Chellie's parents join us a couple minutes after the team arrives.

"Where are the guns you both fired?"

I need to know because those can't stay here. Before Chellie or her mother can answer, I hear a voice from above. I look up to see one of our guys in the white hazmat suits with the paper shower cap-looking cover on his head.

"We got 'em, *capo*."

I nod to Tony before I hurry Chellie and her parents out to the waiting SUV. No one speaks as we climb in. Santos drives with Cristiano in the front passenger seat. I'm in the third row with Chellie, and Mario sits between Mr. and Mrs. Russo. I'm pretty certain they know he's in that seat, so he can shoot out of either window easily.

"Uncle Sal's."

I give the instructions as I twist to look out the rear window. The van is already backing out of the driveway. I pull out my phone and hit the group text.

ME

Chellie's with me so are her parents we're headed to uncle sals

LUCA

Do we send more men

It was my tracker and my location that clued Luca in. He knew I'd only hit the alarm there if some shit was going sideways. Those men are just as equipped to make the mess as they are to clean it up.

ME

No

LUCA

How long until u r here

ME

An hour or so

An hour in the car with Chellie's parents is going to be excruciating whether or not we ride in silence.

LUCA

Okay text when u r pulling up. Mama and papa are already headed to uncle sals

I send him the thumbs up emoji before tucking my phone back in my pocket. I didn't hide what I typed, so Chellie saw it. I wrap my arm around her shoulders. When she nestles closer to me, I want to wrap her in both, but I don't have that much range of motion now that the pain is really kicking in. She sinks against me, her head on my chest. I whisper to her.

"*Piccolina*, you're safe now. I won't let go until you tell me to."

She leans away, so she can turn her head to look at me.

"Thank you." *Daddy*.

She mouths the last word. I pull her close again, stroking her back and dropping kisses on her head. If we were alone, I'd pull her onto my lap. Well, alone being without her parents. If we had the backseat of a town car with the privacy glass up, I'd do a hell of a lot more to distract both of us. I'd really reassure her Daddy will take care of her.

That's something I didn't know I'd be into. I get why some people find it a turn off. I knew Olivia, Serafina, Sinead, and Maria call their husbands that. They'd be mortified if they discovered we all know. But it just sort of existed but wasn't anything of interest to me before meeting Chellie.

It's a sign that she trusts me. That she relies on me. That she's comfortable with me taking the lead when she needs a reprieve. It's no different from why I call her *piccolina* or little one. She's smaller than me, and I want her to know I'll protect her. That she can count on me to always be there. That I love her.

I move from stroking her back to stroking her hair in between kisses. She's not asleep, but her body is lax against mine. After a few more minutes, she sits up, and I'm ready to pull away. She reaches for the hand that rests on my lap since I left the sling somewhere in her parents' backyard. She laces our fingers together and rests our hands on my thigh. A moment later, she must think of something because she reaches into her pocket and retrieves her phone. After she unlocks it, she opens her notes app.

I won't feel truly safe until you're inside me. I just want to sit together like that with your arms around me and my head on your chest. Is that weird, Daddy?

I take the phone from her and tap out a response with my thumb.

No it isn't. I want that too. I want our bodies to be one so I know you're part of me. That nothing keeps us apart. I don't know how soon we can be alone but I need that. I thought the accident was the most scared I've ever been but this was even worse.

I pass the phone back to her.

Why?

I lift my arm from her shoulder to type faster and more easily when I have the phone again.

Because I could see who was doing it once our car stopped spinning. This time, I had to search for them. This time we didn't have the protection of our reinforced cars with bulletproof glass. This time your parents witnessed it.

It's her turn to respond, and I feel like kids passing notes in class.

Do you believe they're going to try to break us up?

I don't respond with a message. I nod.

Daddy, they can make their case. But I'm not going anywhere that isn't with you. We didn't have time to talk to them, but we know this isn't about the Cosa Nostra or the bratva. It's only partly because of the mob. It's mainly about me screwing this psycho over. He'd come after me regardless, so I'm way better off being with you. I love you. My future is your future.

She leans back, so I drop a chaste kiss to her lips.

I love you too piccolina. We have to talk to them.

It's her turn to nod, and she sits up. The men with us already know enough that I can trust them to hear more.

"Mom, Dad, we need to finish talking."

Chapter Twenty-Two

Chellie

I was enjoying the silence. Passing my phone back and forth with Enzo let me say the things I needed to privately. Now we have to deal with what just happened. I don't even know where to start, so I just dive in like I have been since I called my mom at the butt crack of dawn.

"I'm up to my eyeballs in this, even without being engaged to Enzo. This man who's targeting me has some kind of vendetta against Pasha Kutsenko, Laura's cousin-in-law. He also has issues with the Mancinellis and the O'Rourkes. Turns out, I'm connected to all three. But Enzo thinks he's going after me because of some of my clients. He's using my connections as scapegoats, so no one focuses on him. He thinks he can pit the syndicates against each other for not protecting me."

My dad looks over his shoulder, his brow wrinkled in confusion.

"What kind of clients are you dealing with? You work for nonprofits, for charities."

"And some of those organizations receive massive donations, and they often come with strings attached. Apparently, I interrupted an arrangement he had with a foreign syndicate, and he's angry."

My parents have twisted in their seats as best they can to see Enzo and me. It's difficult with seatbelts and Mario between them. My dad's gaze is riveted on Enzo when he speaks.

"Do you know who this is?"

"We believe we do. One of the men basically confirmed it."

My dad doesn't like Enzo's evasiveness and presses him.

"Who is it?"

"A mercenary who's known in our world as a ghost. He's difficult to track."

It's my mom who speaks next and stuns Enzo.

"Robert Simms."

I feel Enzo tense. His voice is a whisper, but it's as cutting as a steel blade.

"How do you know that name?"

"He's been around a long time. Calling him a ghost reminded me of a conversation I overheard my dad having with my grandfathers. It was a couple months before I found out I was pregnant with Chelle. I'd been chasing after her brothers and sister. My grandfathers wanted my dad to contact The Ghost. I guess that was his official name among them. Apparently, my dad knew the man personally. My maternal grandfather made it sound like that was unusual. I don't know if Dad and Simms were friends or what, but Dad said he would. I knew I was hearing things I shouldn't, so I walked away. It was the only time I ever heard my father talk about anything connected to the mob."

"That conversation stuck with you for you to remember

what they called him. How'd you know his real name if they called him The Ghost?"

"Because I asked my father. I didn't want anything to do with the mob within even a hair's breadth of my children. He said if I ever met or heard about a man named Robert Simms, I was to call him immediately and say, 'found it.' He would know I meant I'd found The Ghost — or rather, he'd found me."

I lean forward and rest my hand on the back of the seat between Mario's left shoulder and my mom.

"Did you make that call?"

"Yes."

My fingers dig into the seat as I wait for her to say more, but she's not forthcoming. This is not the time for her to clam up.

"Why, Mom?"

"I grew up with Killian Doyle *and* Donovan O'Rourke. Donovan was several years younger than us, but I knew him because his dad led the mob back then. Donovan approached me out of the blue about six months before he died. He knew my dad wouldn't talk to him, so he tried to corner me and pressure me to relay a message to Dad. I told him no. I didn't want to be involved, and I didn't want to get Dad involved. Donovan was *not* a reasonable man. He wouldn't have hurt you or your siblings or me, but he would've hurt your dad and mine. He never believed no is a complete sentence unless he was the one saying it. He gave me a phone number and address and told me we didn't have to play hide and seek anymore. At first, I had no idea what he meant, but the paper he gave me had R.S. written on it."

"What did Grandpa do?"

"I don't know, but the next time I ran into Donovan at a wedding, he wouldn't look me in the eye. When your grandpa came to stand next me, Donovan left the entire event. I haven't thought about this in years."

"Oh, my God. Was that at Kelly Collins's wedding?"

"Yes."

"They paired me up with Dillan O'Rourke because I was a bridesmaid, and he was a groomsman."

My dad scowls at me. He'd been watching Enzo the entire time, but now he focuses on me.

"And I told you more than once to stay away from him and his cousins. He called and asked you out the next day."

I keep myself from flinching. Enzo's going to think I kept that from him, but I just didn't think about it. It was just over ten years ago.

"And I said no. I knew you didn't approve and didn't want me anywhere near their family. If you and Mom hadn't been Kelly's godparents, we wouldn't have gone. I'm certain you didn't imagine Kelly would marry an O'Rourke when you stood up at her baptism. I haven't thought about that wedding in years. Not the ceremony, not the reception, not anyone I saw there. You basically cut ties with her parents after that because of who she married."

Enzo's voice is still unwavering when he chimes in.

"Who'd she marry?"

"Declan. He was Donovan's—"

"I knew Declan very well."

My brow furrows.

"You were friends with him?"

"I didn't say that. I said I knew him very well. He ran things for a few months after Donovan died. He made the same mistake his cousin did. He went after a Kutsenko wife."

I open my mouth, then snap it shut. I'm pretty sure this is one of those things Enzo won't tell me more about than that. He continues talking, but I know that part of the conversation is over.

"Declan put Kelly in the hospital twice before she left him. Donovan was about fifteen years older than me, and Declan was just under ten years older. I'd known them nearly my entire life. I boxed against Declan a few times, but he didn't fight fair. I made sure he knew our last match was my decision not his. That was around the time he put Kelly in the hospital a second time, and she left him."

It shocks me to discover how much Enzo knows about that family, but it shouldn't. Their lives are all embroiled in one another's.

"Boss."

Santo speaks up as we pull through a massive gate with a guard shack. I see the men with rifles. We're at Salvatore and Sylvia's.

"What the hell are they all doing here?"

Enzo mutters to himself, but I hear him. I look out the window and see a fleet of black SUVs parked in the driveway.

"Who?"

"Mrs. Russo, you're about to have a reunion with the O'Rourkes. I'm sure you'll recognize the Kutsenkos."

I strain to see, but no one is outside besides the guards.

"How do you know it's them?"

"There's enough light for me to see the hub caps. Believe it or not, we all use the same body shop to soup up our vehicles. The only way to tell whose vehicle is whose in a hurry is by the hub caps. The guy makes them custom."

In a hurry? Does he mean like during a shoot-out? Why would they all be leaving somewhere together in a hurry? It sounds like they can't stand each other even more than I believed. Enzo's tone is somewhere between mocking and humorous. Right now, I'm not quite sure which. I don't press it as he helps me out of the third row after Mario helps my mom out of the second row. He entwines his fingers with mine as we walk to the front door. He doesn't bother knocking, instead entering a code and pushing the door open. We hear voices, but they go silent the moment we step in.

Nicoletta shoves Carmine and Luca aside as she hurries toward us. Enzo lets go of me to hug his mom. He lifts her off her feet for a moment with his good arm, and I can tell he's as relieved to make it home and hug her as she is to hug him. When he sets her down with a wince, she releases him immediately and engulfs me in a hug, too. I know my mom is watching us, but I lean into it. It's comforting because it's accepting. Massimo's hugging Enzo, but he soon wraps me in a bear hug when Nicoletta steps away. When he lets go, I turn toward my parents.

"Mom, Dad, this is Nicoletta and Massimo, Enzo's parents. Mr. and Mrs. Mancinelli, these are my parents, Henry and Maeve."

Enzo's mom steps forward to shake hands, but she looks at me and whispers.

"You should call us Lettie and Massi by now."

As our parents greet each other, Enzo leans forward, so only I can hear.

"Only Papa, Auntie Lotta, and Uncle Dom ever called her that until Olivia married Luca. Pretty much everyone stopped calling my mom Auntie Lettie once we grew up. It's Auntie Nicoletta now. She likes you more than she likes me."

I feel his smile as his cheek brushes against mine. His hands rest on my waist just long enough to squeeze before he steps around me. Nicoletta — Lettie — makes the introductions, which is much easier for me since I still don't know people very well. My stomach tightens when my parents meet Salvatore.

It's clear my parents are sizing him up as much as he's

sizing up them. Sylvia intervenes and offers us something to eat and drink. Once she's brought coffee and cookies out, she and Lettie disappear. I hear other women's voices and realize the entire family gathered, but the women are out of sight since who knows what the hell is going to be said? Luca, Marco, Matteo, Carmine, and Gabriele say nothing after the introductions. All of them except Luca fade into the corners of the room, leaning against the walls. Are they guarding Salvatore and Luca? What do they think my parents are going to do?

It's on to introductions with the O'Rourkes and Kutsenkos, who'd hung back while my parents met the Mancinellis. My parents know Laura's in-laws from the wedding and a few other events, but they don't know them well enough to remember who's who. I haven't seen the O'Rourkes in a long time, but I remember them.

It's really more getting reacquainted than introductions, I suppose. When everyone takes a seat, it's interesting to see who gets a chair, and who stands behind someone. It's like a fucking mafia summit. No. The Mancinellis are the Mafia. The others are syndicates. I need to fucking remember that if I'm marrying a member of the *Cosa Nostra*.

Salvatore, Massimo, and Luca sit. Domenico stands behind Massimo. Maks, Aleks, Niko, and Bogdan take up two loveseats with Pasha and Misha standing behind one while Sergei and Anton stand behind the other. Only Dillan and Finn sit, while Sean, Shane, Seamus, and Cormac all stand. Enzo and I also sit on a loveseat while my parents have a sofa to themselves. Salvatore and Sylvia's living room truly is massive now that I see how many people can fit without it feeling crowded. This home is way more like a castle than a house.

I let my parents and Enzo do the talking as they tell everyone else what happened. This has been the longest fucking two days of my life. I ache everywhere now that I'm sitting down and know that I'm somewhere safe. I glance at a clock on the mantel and realize it's already the middle of the morning. The crash was hours ago, but it may as well have been weeks with all that's happened since.

"Do you want me to get something for your pain?"

Enzo's concerned expression makes me realize he's really nervous about how this conversation is going to end. He's worried about me and whether I'm physically okay. But he's also worried I'll be so emotionally damaged that I'll leave with my parents when they inevitably demand I go with them.

"Yes, please."

"Do you want to go to bed? I know you don't want to miss anything, but you look like you're about to drop."

"I can last, but I hope there's some Epsom salt here because I'd love to soak in a bath before we go to bed."

His eyebrows shoot up, and I can practically hear him asking, "we?"

"Some ibuprofen would be great now, but I already told you what I need later."

I try to keep my voice down, but my mom shoots me a look. It's the one I would get as a kid when I couldn't sit still somewhere I was supposed to be seen and not heard. I stopped paying attention a while ago, so I'm unprepared for Pasha to speak to me.

"None of us thought Simms would go after one of our wives' friends. Not that I'd ever wish anything on Sumiko's friends, but I'm the one he's angry at."

I've always liked Pasha — all of them really — but his expression matches how apologetic his voice is.

"We know that's just an excuse. I'm sure some of this is to retaliate by hurting Laura. But he's really trying to get revenge by drawing you into a fight. I'm just the bait."

Pasha nods, but then he glares at Finn. I follow his gaze, and Finn's expression is defiant. No one says anything, so I do.

"Finn, how's your family involved?"

"We've used Simms just like everyone else."

I wait for more, but nothing is forthcoming. I look up at Enzo, but he's just as tightlipped. My gaze sweeps the room, and I can see no one wants to get into any details. But I don't give a shit.

"Finn, tell me. Whatever you did to the Kutsenkos or the Mancinellis is what really pissed this psychopath off. I want to know how this is all connected."

Finn and Dillan exchange a look, but neither of them says anything. I look up at Enzo again. My expression is anything but loving. My fiancé concedes.

"The O'Rourkes thought they were smarter than they were. They tried to use my family as patsies while they went after the Kutsenkos. They used my family's history with the bratva as their cover. Pasha's wife figured it out, so the money stopped going to Simms. Pasha convinced Simms's son to go back to China."

I already knew half of that, but I'm still putting the pieces together.

"Back to the Wo Shing Wo, which is how I come in. He's pissed that investments he made that would connect him to the Wo Shing Wo, and I assume hopefully his son, didn't work out. He believes I ruined the deals."

I turn back to face Dillan and Finn, one eyebrow cocked. I don't know if I expect them to confirm, deny, or add to this. But I wait and stare. It's my dad who loses his patience first.

"Dillan, why are you here?"

"Because my family promised to always watch out for yours. It was a condition of Martin leaving. He agreed he'd take the fall if the feds ever came snooping, but in exchange, we had to protect all of you. The feds aren't involved, but your family's been threatened."

Besides my dad, there isn't a man in this room who doesn't look like he could be part of an NFL starting lineup. They're all huge. The bratva men are the biggest, but really not by much. Seeing them all together makes me realize just how big Enzo is. He's tall and broad shouldered, and I suppose that's why I have faith that he can hold up the weight of the world when I get scared. It's eye-opening to witness the level of danger my future husband deals with when he's around these men who would kill him if they weren't in a home with women and children.

My mom and dad exchange their own look before my mom responds to the pledge Dillan just shared.

"We appreciate knowing you've looked out for us. I don't want to know if you've had to do anything to protect us, but if you have, we thank you. But my dad left the mob to keep our family far from it. I want to honor that wish. I also know the Mancinellis are about to become more my family than the O'Rourkes have been in generations. I trust my daughter's safety to her future husband. Your help is no longer needed."

Did my mom just fucking fire the mob?

From the way Maks just snorted, and Salvatore smirks, I think she did. Short of saying she wishes them the best in their future endeavors, she dismissed them. Finn steeples his fingers as he leans forward, his forearms resting on his thighs.

"I wouldn't be so quick to have all your faith in them. Enrique Diaz just hired Simms to put a hit on a senior *Cosa Nostra* member. If you don't want your daughter caught in the crossfire again, you might not want to cut your ties with us just yet."

The entire room goes still except for the O'Rourkes, who believe it's their turn to smirk. Bogdan's leaning back in his seat, appearing far more casual than I know he is. It surprises me that he speaks up because only the family leaders have said anything besides Enzo. Then again, I know he, Aleks, and Niko lead alongside Maks, even if Maks makes the ultimate decisions.

"Just how senior? Should we be buying wreaths for Nicoletta or Carlotta to hang on their son's casket?"

My nails dig into the back of Enzo's hand that I'm holding. "*Stronzo.*"

Enzo mutters the word while he glares at Bogdan. I look up at him because I don't know what that means. He mouths *asshole*. I have to agree. That was a dick move for Bogdan to say that in front of my parents and me. This is getting way too deep into the inner politics of these rivals, and my parents shouldn't hear it as outsiders, and I shouldn't hear it as a woman. Prehistoric as fuck, but I'm more than happy to leave this to the men. But I'm terrified now that Enzo's the target.

Sean rolls his eyes as he crosses his arms. I remember he tended to be the quiet one, but when he spoke, people listened.

"He's not going after any of the don's family. He knows that would disrupt the balance we have right now. After losing two members of our family, we're the ones who should consider evening the score. But we're not. Peace is profitable, and Enrique knows that. It'd be all out war if he touched one of Salvatore's precious angels. But he's going for someone who matters. We don't want Michelle to be caught in the middle when this goes down. Her family and ours go all the way back to Ireland five generations ago. Consider this our wedding gift."

The O'Rourkes stand, and I assume that means the meeting is over. Dillan shakes Salvatore's hand, but he sneers at Maks. He offers me a smile and a courteous nod to my parents. Then they're gone. Once the door closes behind the mobsters, Maks and his family stand, and so do Enzo and I. He tries to stare down Enzo as he walks over to us. He gives me a hug, and I know he's doing it to be nice to me while antagonizing Enzo.

"Laura doesn't know the details, but she knows I'm here because something happened to you. Call her, please. She's worried."

"I will. Should I do it tonight?"

"If you could do it before I get home, that would be great."

"You live four streets over."

Maks cocks an eyebrow as if to say, "see." I nod before looking up at Enzo. Maks goes to say something to Salvatore and Massimo, and I pull out my phone.

"I don't want to just leave my parents here, but I also don't want Laura panicking. She'll come over here if she knows Maks saw me but didn't volunteer to bring her with him."

"Go in the kitchen."

I want him to come with me. My fear of being alone is irrational, but it hits me like a ton of bricks. I shift my weight from one foot to the other. Enzo looks over at Marco and tilts his head toward the kitchen before he leads me into the other room.

My call doesn't last long since Laura knows better than to ask what happened during the meeting, and I know I can't tell her. Maks will share whatever he believes his wife needs to know. But she and I both feel better after talking. We return to the living room, and we find Sylvia offering my parents one of the guest rooms since they obviously can't go back to our — their — home. My exhaustion wraps around me like a weighted blanket trying to smother me. I suddenly feel like I can barely stand up and keep my eyes open.

"Do you want me to run you that bath, *piccolina*?"

"I don't know if I can stay awake long enough."

"You can soak while I meet with my family. I'll wake you if you fall asleep."

"Meeting? Now?"

Enzo looks over my head, and I know the men are headed down the hallway to Salvatore's study.

"I may need to go out tonight."

I read the look in his eyes.

"And you don't know when you'll be back. Can I ask if this is about Simms or about the Diazes?"

Enzo is tightlipped. He just looks at me, and I know I won't get anything out of him. I sigh and nod. He presses a kiss to my lips then my forehead.

"I love you. I'll try not to be long. I won't leave without seeing you. Okay?"

"Okay. I love you, too."

I watch him walk down the hallway before I follow Sylvia and my parents upstairs. I don't want to talk to anyone. I just want to disappear. When I stop at Enzo's door, both of my parents look back in surprise. It's the room he uses when he's here, and I've been in it before. I just assumed it was the one I would use too. Sylvia's chin dips just enough for me to see. Mom and Dad want to know how I know which room to go to already.

"I'll see you in a bit."

I open the door, but Mom walks over to me and engulfs me in a hug that nearly crushes me. I feel her trembling, and know everything just caught up with her, too.

"I'm okay, Mom."

"Yeah, well, I'm not. I thought I was going to see my daughter die."

I sigh. My parents already lost one child. I have to be more empathetic to their fears. I know how they grieved after my brother died. I don't want to put them through that again.

"We're safer here than just about anywhere else in the

world. Get some rest. It's been a long morning already. We'll figure this out in a few hours. Love you."

"Love you."

I drag myself into the bathroom and discover a packet of Epsom salt on the side of the bathtub. I pour almost half of it in as I run the water. I strip out of my borrowed clothes and fold them. I'd be happy to never see them again, so I don't have reminders of today. I slip into the water that's a little too hot, but I suck it up. I'm careful to keep my bandaged hand out of the water. I've almost drifted off when I feel hands gently pressing me forward. Then I recognize Enzo's body as he slips into the tub behind me. He must have put on fresh waterproof bandages. I sigh and return to almost being asleep, especially when he rubs my shoulders.

"Daddy, do you have to go out tonight?"

"Yes."

That wakes me all the fucking way up. I twist to look at him, and he opens his arms to me. I shift to being on both knees, then we move, so I'm straddling his hips. I feel his cock rubbing against my clit, and immediately, I'd rather be fucking than talking about this.

But I need what I wrote in the car even more. Enzo knows it, maybe even needs it too, because he lifts my hip and guides me onto his cock. The moment he's all the way in, I curl up my legs, tuck my arms between us, and lean against his chest. It's like I'm trying to make myself as small as I can. He just holds me.

It's not until the water turns freezing that we abandon the bath. It had cooled by the time he joined me, but now it's uncomfortable. He carries me into the shower, and I marvel at his strength as he holds me with one arm as he adjusts the water temperature. He's using his injured shoulder too much, and his ribs aren't being spared either. It makes me wonder just what Carlotta gave him before we headed to my parents'. I know the injuries aren't nearly as serious as we feared, but still.

I reach for the shower gel and poof. I'm still one-handed since I'm trying to keep my bandage dry. He puts me down to help me, but then I'm in his arms with his cock in me a moment later. Once it's sudsy, I run it over his arms, back, and chest as he kisses my shoulders and neck. When I'm done, he holds me with one arm again and returns the favor. I've been doing Kegels since the moment he stood up, and now that we've also washed our hair, he backs me against the wall to thrust into me over and over.

"I don't know how long I'll be gone. This is going to have to tide us over. I'm going to come in you, *piccolina*. Then I'm going to dry you off and carry you to our bed. You're going to fall asleep with my cum inside your pussy. You're going to wake up with it smeared to your legs. You're going to remember that you're mine. When I get back, I'm going to fuck you so hard you can't remember I was ever away."

"When you get back, can we go to one of those clubs or do more at home?"

"You want more BDSM?"

"Yes. I like what we've done so far. But I want more pain and pleasure, and I want to submit more."

"Do you want to be a sub?"

"No. I don't think so. I just feel better when you remind me you're bigger than me and that you can control everything else around us. It quietens my brain."

"Whatever you need, little one. Now let me watch you come as I fuck you."

"Yes, Daddy."

He presses me against the wall, trapping me just the way I like. I do what I can to match his movements, but he's deciding how much of his dick I get and how fast or slow. He changes his pace over and over, so I can't predict, can't get used to it. It drives me wild, and I cover my mouth to smother my scream.

"Fuck. You're gorgeous every day, all day. But watching you come is exquisite."

"You say the nicest things."

I hold on as he thrusts two more times, then I know he's coming inside me. I haven't taken my birth control pills in how many days? I can't even count right now.

"Maybe today's the day we made a baby, *piccolina*."

"Would you really be all right with that?"

"I'd rather we were married first, but I know there's a good chance I will get or have already gotten you pregnant."

"Would it be totally fucked-up if we spent our wedding night at a club?"

I want to swallow the words the moment they come out.

"If that's what you want, then we do it. If you want us to order things to have at home, we can do that too."

He towels me dry and carries me into the bedroom, where he lays me down. He finally pulls out, and I groan in protest. He uses the towel to dry himself off as he speaks.

"Chellie, I want you and your parents to stay here until I get back. Would they be willing to be here for a few days? Can they take off work?"

"I don't know. I'm sure they're going to want to go to the house and deal with the insurance."

"The house is already repaired. I got the call from our construction team while I was in Uncle Sal's office."

"It's only been a few hours. How'd they do it?"

"They know what they're doing."

He says no more than that, and I have to accept it. I nod and sigh. This is a crash course in what part of our marriage will be. It's frustrating, but I can accept it. I think I'll get used to it rather than resent it because I know he tells me as much as he can. What he doesn't, he keeps to himself to protect the people he loves and the people who depend on him.

The shower sex left me wide awake, and I figured knowing he was leaving for an indefinite amount of time would keep me from sleeping. When I roll on my side as I watch him walk out in all black fatigue-looking clothes, I feel a little of his cum drip on my leg. I have part of him with me. I'm out like a light before he probably even leaves the house.

Chapter Twenty-Three

Lorenzo

The last three days have been an utter shitshow. We've been chasing our tails like a three-legged dog. The only bright side has been talking to Chellie. I fought with Luca and Marco about it, but I wouldn't give in. It meant I had to leave the garage where we handle shit no one can know about. I had to drive about ten miles away to make sure that when my GPS went back online, no one could easily connect me to the warehouse's location. When we go there, our phones get turned off five miles out and don't get turned back on until we're five miles away from there.

I was honest each time we hung up. I didn't know when I'd be able to talk to her again, but I had to make it work. I needed to hear her voice to keep from losing my ever-loving mind with how frustrating this is. But I also wanted her to know I'm thinking about her nonstop, and that I didn't abandon her to my family. Even though she doesn't say it, I can tell from her voice that she's having a hard time with it. She's trying to make me believe she's taking everything in stride, but I know she's scared for me, for her family, and for herself. I can't blame her. I feel exactly the same.

That's why I'm about to lose my fucking shit. We've worked over five guys who should have rolled on Enrique and given up what we needed. The phrase given up the ghost has never felt more apropos. I'm ready to admit defeat trying to find The Ghost. Motherfucking Simms. But I won't. I'm being pushed to my limits, but I won't quit because that means leaving Chellie vulnerable. That's not even remotely an acceptable option. But fuck, it's testing me.

As I stand in front of one of Pablo Diaz's top enforcers, I'm using all my restraint not to just unleash on him because he's here. We had him strung up for hours, naked and freezing. We have hooks that hang down from the garage doors. When we open them, it feels like our visitors' arms are going to be ripped off.

The metal chains make so much noise, no one can hear the men scream. Right now, this fuck face is strapped to a chair with his hand nailed to a table. Like with a nail gun to the back of his hand until it passed through his palm and into the table. I have a hammer, and I've already crushed his pinky and ring finger on his right hand.

"Give me something, Arturo. Where's Pablo hiding right now? How'd he get in touch with Simms? Who's the target?"

"I don't know. I swear. That's above my rank and pay grade."

I swing the hammer down on his middle finger, but I stop just before I make contact. The guy pisses himself. Good thing I'm standing off to the side. It's not the first time he's done that in the day-and-a-half we've had him here.

"You wanna try again?"

"I'm telling you the truth. I had no idea there was any hit

on someone in your organization. I haven't heard a damn thing. Pablo's not hiding. He's in Colombia with Alejandro. They have business down there."

Pablo is Enrique's oldest nephew and from his younger brother. He also happens to be the heir just like Luca is our uncle's heir. Alejandro is another nephew from one of Enrique's two sisters.

"How convenient."

"He's been there for like a month. I don't think he knows anything about you having a girl."

"She's more than a girl. She's my woman, and your family is fucking with mine. They hired a man to take out one of my family members. It's the same man who's targeting the woman I'm going to marry. What a coincidence."

"Seriously, *amigo*. Whoever told you this told you wrong. I'm going to die, so what would it matter if I told you the truth or a lie?"

"You're lying for Enrique's sake. You're loyal."

"I was. But I'm not feeling so loyal now. If my *jefe* could leave me here to die rather than negotiate with you, then I owe him *nada*."

Even if Enrique negotiated — which he hasn't — it wouldn't matter. Once someone comes here, they never leave alive. It's too big a risk. It sucks when we get it wrong like we might have with this guy. But this is how our life goes. You accept death long before it comes to you.

I turn away and head to the office. It has a two-way mirror so people in there can see out, but people out here on the floor can't see in. I grab a bottle of water and some paper towels to wipe my face and neck. I worked that guy over, and I'm sweating. I toss the used paper towel in a burn bin. No DNA gets left around in case somehow we get raided. I look at Uncle Salvatore and Uncle Domenico, who've been observing for the past hour. Uncle Domenico is like a second dad. He's Papa's best friend. He squeezes my shoulder as I walk past.

"He knows nothing. I know how frustrating that is. I know you're scared for Michelle, but she's safe while you deal with this."

"I know."

I sigh. He's right. She is safe. At least two men from my family go with her everywhere. She convinced me the morning after I left to let her go to work. I hate the idea that she's anywhere in public after being shot at, but she said it would be way more conspicuous if she just stopped showing up. Keeping her routine as normal as possible might keep Simms from thinking we know anything about him. I agreed partly because she might be right, but mainly because I feel horrible having her cooped up. So much of our relationship so far has been avoiding threats and keeping her locked away.

"I'm going to take a shower. He was the last one on the list. I'm going home to Chellie."

I strip down, not caring who sees me. Both men changed my diapers, and I apparently peed on both of them at least twice. I toss my clothes in the burn bin along with my empty water bottle. I drained it while turning on the shower. I step in and let the pinpricks of water beat down on me.

My injuries weren't nearly as bad as they seemed right after getting shot. Auntie Carlotta put stitches in my shoulder and ribs, but both bullets only grazed me. I thought one went into my ribs, but luckily, it didn't. I'm not a hundred percent back to normal because of those stitches. But I have a lot more mobility in my shoulder than I expected, and my ribs only ache rather than being cracked. I'd say I'm at ninety percent, give or take.

I breathe deeply as I bow my head, then tilt it back to let the water hit my face. I can't stay in here forever, even though I'd like to. I hurry to scrub my hair. While I'm scrubbing my body like a surgeon prepping to go into the OR, something comes to me.

"Motherfuckers!"

I rinse before turning off the water. As I wrap a towel around my waist, I lean out to see my two uncles.

"Those fuckers lied. The O'Rourkes. Enrique isn't doing shit to us, but they knew we'd go chasing down any lead. They fucking did this to distract us. They want to handle Simms themselves. They want to be the heroes. They want to prove that neither we nor the bratva can protect our women. They'd shame us while gloating."

I think back to when we all gathered at Uncle Salvatore's. Something clicks.

"This is Finn. He's the one doing this."

Uncle Salvatore's brow furrows.

"Why?"

"He wants Chellie. I saw the way he looked at her, but I didn't think much of it because I was concentrating on her. But now that I think back, he was definitely eyeing her, and not like someone he knew as a kid."

"That makes no sense. They haven't been around each other in years."

"Maybe they have, and Chellie never knew. If they promised Chellie's grandfather they'd watch over his family, then maybe he's been around Chellie more than we could guess. He wants to be the fucking hero."

Uncle Domenico shakes his head and frowns.

"That makes no sense. It was obvious how much Michelle loves you and that you return her feelings. There's no way she would leave you for him. He couldn't think that was possible."

"It would be if I got killed in the process of hunting down some Cartel member who doesn't exist. Enrique wouldn't order a hit on me, but we all know how possible it is to die during some meeting that gets fucked up. Then he'd swoop in and save her. Finn was the one who announced it."

I yank on fresh clothes and run my finger through my hair. I want to go straight home to Chellie, but I have another stop to make first. Uncle Salvatore's tone when he speaks is the one I hear when he's my don not my uncle.

"Enzo, don't do anything rash."

"I'm not going to. I'm thinking things through as you speak."

Chellie's my fiancée, so Uncle Salvatore will give me the lead on this. He'll let me do what I think is necessary. I drove here, so I back my car out of the bay where we park rather than torture. I watch the buildings I pass, and as soon as I know I'm safe to turn on my phone I do. I quickly glance at the names of missed texts and calls. None so important that I need to deal with them now. I hit my cousin's name on my speed dial.

"Hey."

"Carmine, I need you to locate Finn. I need to see him now."

"Why?"

"Don't ask."

"Well, now you know I'm not saying shit until you tell me."

I hear a door close, so I'm guessing Serafina's home since I'm positive he's in his home office at this time of day. He's probably going over construction invoices since he's our project manager on almost all sites. He enjoys going out there and working alongside the men, but he accepts that there are menial tasks that go along with it. The joys of being a structural engineer *and* the company owner's nephew.

"Car, I'll explain later. I really need to know this."

"Finn's the one who said the Diazes are coming for us. You've had no luck so far. Do you think Finn did that to distract us?"

"Yes."

"What's he want?"

"Chellie."

"Enzo, he wouldn't hurt her. That was Donovan's and Declan's thing. Dillan got stuck cleaning up their shit, but none of them are down with hurting women. We know that now."

"He doesn't plan to hurt he. He *wants* her. If this shit escalates, and I die at some meeting gone wrong, then he'll have the shoulder she can cry on. A blast from the past who comes out to save the day."

"Are you sure you don't have an overactive imagination?"

"I saw the way he looked at her at Uncle Sal's. I didn't like it, but I didn't give it much thought because there was more important shit going on. If his family's been watching hers for years, then who knows how much time he's spent getting to know her?"

"But she never got to know him. She wants you."

"And I don't doubt that. But who says that'll stop Finn?"

"Well, you're in luck. He's at McMillan's."

A boxing gym. Perfect. I head over there and grab the spare workout clothes I keep in my car. I wait for my chance and slip past the chick at the front desk, who's flirting with some guy who probably has a micro-penis after all the roids he's taking.

I head to the locker room and get changed. I walk onto the floor and look around. Finn's easy to spot. There are other big guys, but none with the deep russet hair most of the O'Rourkes have. I recognize his motorcycle helmet on a nearby bench, so I drop my stuff next to it.

I wait for when he takes a break from the speed bag he's using. I tap him on the shoulder. When he turns toward me, I drive my fist straight into his nose. Blood shoots everywhere. I hear people yell, but Finn waves them away.

"You want my fiancée? You'll have to kill me first. You. Not the Diazes. Not the Kutsenkos. Not Simms. You, moth-erfucker."

"The last time we fought, you lost and wound up with a broken jaw. Does your mommy have enough straws?"

That might be true, but I have a lot more riding on this fight than five grand.

"Bare knuckles, Finn."

"Fine. Step into the ring with me."

I'm good with that. It'll make it look like a fair fight. Neither of us is going to fight clean, but when people look back on it, they'll think it was all kosher while I beat his ass. We walk to separate sides, and both of us bound onto the raised platform with a smooth jump. We slip between the ropes, and there's no waiting for a bell. I'm confident I can do this after swinging a bat and tire iron at the guy we had in the garage. I'm sore, but I'm good.

We both go on the offensive. I let him land one to my left ribs—thank God not the side that has bandages he can't see — then one to my jaw. Let him think he's getting the better of me from the start. Arrogant prick. I'm watching him. I'm learning and remembering. After a fifth shot that lands against my kidney and almost drops me to my knees, I'm done observing and swinging punches not meant to do much.

My true offensive begins. I slam my fist into his face over and over. My hands fly fast, alternating sides and alternating landing my bare fist against his face and his ribs. I give him an uppercut that snaps his head back and drives him into the ropes. I plow my right fist into his gut as hard as I can.

"Ready to give up?"

"Nope."

"You're going to lose here, and you're going to lose any chance with her."

"If you're dead, there're all the chances in the world."

I motherfucking knew it.

"When she moves on, it won't be to you. There's no way she'd be with another guy like us."

Part of me wants to think she'd never get over me. But the other part wants her to be happy with whomever she's with. I just won't accept it being Finn Fucking O'Rourke. That oughta be his full name.

I grab his shirt and yank him back toward me before slamming my left fist into his cheek bone as hard as I can. I hear the bone break, and I watch his eyes roll back in his head. I let go and let him drop. I leave him where he slumps as people run forward. I jump down from the ring.

"Call his brothers or Dillan. I don't give a fuck."

There are mob guys in here. In fact, they're all mob guys. I know they recognized me the moment I walked in. But this was between me and one of their top members. They weren't going to step in. That said, I need to get the fuck out of here now before someone decides retribution is best served immediately.

I grab my stuff and head out to my car. I drive a block away before I pull over and look at myself in the mirror. Shit. I look barely better than how I left Finn. I need to go to my place and deal with the cuts and bruises before I see Chellie, or she'll lose her shit.

I haven't even put my keys down in my place when my phone rings. It's not our pattern, so I know it's not work. I pull it out and see the name on the screen. Dillan.

"I think I left your cousin's face prettier than I found it."

"Feck off."

For Christ's sake. That's how they prove they're Irish. They won't just say fuck. It's feck. Sounds like a kid too scared to cuss.

"He deserved it."

"How? By following through on a standing order to watch out for a woman he's been guarding for years?"

Years?

"He interfered because he's butt hurt that he'll never be with her. Any chance he ever had came and went. He regrets it and thinks he can get back something that was never his. Maybe waking up in the hospital with a crushed cheekbone, a dislocated jaw, and broken nose, and some fractured ribs will remind him to stay the fuck away from what's mine."

"You don't know shit for sure about anything Finn might or might not have done."

"*Fanculo.*" Fuck off.

See. I can say the fucking word in two fucking languages.

"Well, Enzo, while you had a hissy fit that we will pay you back for, you missed what happened to Simms."

I grip the kitchen counter I'm leaning against. I refuse to ask for anything from Dillan, so I remain silent. The seconds tick into a minute.

"Stop fucking pouting, Enzo. We can wait each other out all damn day and night."

He goes as silent as I do. I tap the mute icon and switch over to my texts. I click on the thread with Carmine.

ME

Did the orourkes do something to simms

I wait for something very different from what Dillan's waiting for on the other end of the line. I see the dancing dots and know Carmine's typing something.

CARMINE

Dillan sent a photo to Uncle Sal. Guess it's Simms but the guy's beaten so badly it's hard to tell who it is.

"Dillan, either tell me something or hang up. I'm bored."

He hasn't said a fucking word since I muted our call. I wait, but he still says nothing. I check to make sure the call didn't drop. When he remains silent, I go back to my text.

ME

Could it be a trick

CARMINE

No the guy's head is hanging forward. We all recognized the tattoo. It's some old Soviet one. Check your phone. I just sent you something.

I click on the photo he sent. I recognize one of the Triad leaders, Wing-hung, who's Simms's son's maternal grandfather. I also recognize a man lying on the tarmac with someone's boot about to land in his belly. I zoom in as far as I can, and I'm certain it's Robert Simms, looking like he wished he was dead. Next to the Chinese syndicate leader is a young man who's at most twenty-one. He's standing with his arms crossed, the hint of a dragon tattoo on his forearm. He's looking down at Simms, and even though his face is tiny in the photo, the disgust is obvious.

"I'm done waiting on you, Dillan. Speak now or I hang up."

"You don't know shit about what's happening, but you will know no one touches my cousin."

"Fuck off. I've beaten Finn's ass before, and I'll do it again if he doesn't leave my fiancée the fuck alone."

I hang up and go back to my texts with Carmine.

ME

Is the plan to kill him

CARMINE

Looks like it. I hope so.

> **ME**
> But we can't be sure

CARMINE
> Not yet at least. But enjoy the threat being gone

> **ME**
> I will I'm headed to mama and papa's to meet Chellie. I got a text saying that's where she's at.

CARMINE
> Marco and Matteo are with her today

> **ME**
> Thanks

I head into my bathroom and shower. I freshen up after going a round in the ring since I doubt Chellie would appreciate me stinking of sweat with blood on my face after not seeing me for three days. I grab some arnica and slather it on my face, ribs, and kidney. The hits I took were worse than the nicks the bullets gave me. Maybe the bruised face will keep everyone from saying I'm the pretty one in the family.

I'm scrolling texts when the elevator dings. I never let the doors open without looking around. The moment they slide apart to reveal my underground parking garage, I'm greeted with three guns trained on me.

"*Hola, Tres J's.* What the fuck do you want?"

I walk forward as though they don't have their guns cocked with their fingers on the trigger. If they shoot, it won't be to kill. The three brothers — Jorge, Javier, and Joaquin — could be triplets, but there's a year or two between each. They're still as inseparable as they were when they moved to America as teens. They saw some fucked-up shit growing up in Colombia.

They're fucking crazy. They can play nice and make people think they're civilized. But walking off an elevator to find them drawing on me shows they're anything but.

Javier takes a step toward me, so I ease my hand into my pocket.

"Uh-uh. Hands away from your knives. You went after our men for no reason."

"I had a damn good reason. Finn O'Rourke."

"What's that asshat have to do with anything?"

"He told us you had a hit out on one of our senior guys. We were investigating. Turns out Dillan and Finn wanted to handle something themselves and knew they couldn't without distracting us. It didn't last long, and I resolved it with them. They won't try making a fool of us again or go after something that isn't theirs."

"You mean Michelle Russo."

My gaze jumps to Joaquin as he says my fiancée's name. I want to demand they tell me everything they know about her.

"She's *muy bonita*." Very pretty.

Joaquin leers like Chellie is standing next to me. He even licks his lips. I keep telling myself not to take the bait. Instead, I walk to my car. I paid extra for the doors to unlock silently without the lights flashing. When I open it, I check to be sure the dome light goes on. It does.

"Give your *tío* my apologies for confusing his men with ones who matter. Move or I will drive over you."

I start my car and pull forward. They move, but they keep their guns raised until I'm out of sight. I glance back once before pulling onto the street. I look around, and I breathe a little easier. I survived to fight another day. I head to my parents', and traffic is actually on my side. I'm there faster than I expected.

"Chellie?"

I call out to her as I step into the foyer.

"Enzo!"

I look up to the second-floor landing and see her as she comes down the hall. She must have been in what I now consider our room when we're here. She races down the stairs and practically leaps down the last three and into my arms. I crush her against me, my ribs and chest silently screaming with pain. I need to give my body a fucking break. That ninety percent feels like about thirty right now. But all is right in the world again.

We both sigh as our lips meld together. I stroke hair back from her face, so I can palm her cheek and jaw. Her hand cups my neck, avoiding the bruises I know are forming on my face. Either she hasn't noticed, or she's too relieved to see me to care right now. We keep kissing until we accept we aren't alone. Before I put her down, she presses her lips near my ear.

"Do you really want to get married sooner rather than later?"

"Yes. Absolutely."

I don't bother whispering. She leans back and beams at me. But her brow furrows for a moment as she takes in the damage Finn did. She feathers her fingers over my cheeks near my ears, staying away from my cuts and bruises. I offer her a lopsided grin, hoping that eases her fears. She gives me a little nod then matches my smile.

"I might have gotten a little bored at work yesterday. I might have invited the girls and my sister to go wedding dress shopping with me. I might have bought one. They might have picked out gowns, too. Your mom might have told me you already own a tux and so does every man in your family. I might have convinced your priest to let us get married on Saturday without all the premarital classes. I might have promised we'd donate a rather substantial basket to their next silent auction."

"I might have been thinking about whisking you away to elope on Saturday. I might have been planning to book a honeymoon tonight. I might have been planning to call movers. I might have been hoping to have our wedding in the backyard here." I whisper the next part. "I might be stripping you naked the moment we get home. And I might be fucking you all night."

"Those last two can't be 'mights.'"

She looks earnestly at me as she shakes her head. Then she giggles and cups my cheeks loosely before diving in for another kiss. I pick her up, so I don't have to bend over. My fucking ribs aren't happy right now. We rest our foreheads together when I lean forward, after putting her back on her feet.

"Mama? Can Sera make a wedding cake by Saturday?"

"Saturday?"

I hear several voices mutter. Chellie and I look up at the entire family that's gathered in the foyer. They're all there, even Pia, Natalia, and Petra.

"Michelle, may we be flower girls?"

I have never seen Pia look bashful a day in her life, but I can tell how badly she wants my soon-to-be wife to say yes. Chellie leans forward and smiles.

"I suppose it's still a surprise if I tell you now. I already picked out dresses for you and your sister."

"Really?"

Both girls bounce on their toes, and it makes me think about daughters Chellie and I might have one day. I look at Luca, who's holding his infant daughter. I glance at Sera and Carmine, who I know are starting to try. When I look at Maria and Matteo, then Sinead and Gabriele, I get the sense both couples are waiting a little longer. But I doubt it'll be that far into the distance. Then I look at Marco. The last pillar standing after the mighty have fallen. He grins at me, and I can only imagine the bachelor party he's already hatching.

It's only after I've looked at my siblings and cousins that I realize Chellie's parents are standing off to the side with my parents and aunts and uncles. I slide my hand into Chellie's and lead her toward them. I don't know much of what they did for the past three days beyond staying with Uncle Salvatore and Aunt Sylvia at night. They still went to work, but Luca assigned them a detail with four men each. Chellie said it didn't seem to faze either of them. I guess they dealt with guards when they first got married because of their remaining ties to the mob.

"Welcome to our family, Lorenzo."

"Thank you, Mr.—"

"Henry. You're going to be my son-in-law in three days."

"Thank you, Henry."

"And I'm Maeve. I'm sorry that I was so quick to judge."

"Chellie's your daughter. I would have wondered why you didn't."

It's tentative, but Maeve opens her arms, and I step into her embrace. It's not like hugging my mom, but it's nice. It gets better a few seconds in as we both relax. I pull back, and Henry offers to shake my hand, then he tugs me in for a back slapping hug. When I step back, I see Chellie's standing between my parents.

This world we live in. It's as screwed-up as it gets. I've killed more men than I could remember to count. I'm a monster behind closed garage doors. I don't think twice about committing crimes that support my family and my people. But I'm also a lucky man to have a normal family when we're together and a woman I love more than life itself. Somehow, maybe that devo-tion to family is enough to redeem me, and that's why I have the happy home life that I do.

"Are you ready to go home?"

I reach out for Chellie's hand, but she shakes her head.

"Your mom and aunts cooked."

Fuck me.

"Great. I'm starving."

I'm not getting my soon-to-be bride alone for at least another three hours. Seven courses. That's what dinner means with guests. Chellie goes onto her toes and kisses me where my jaw meets my neck, just below my ear.

"Don't worry, Daddy. We're leaving early to have dessert. I hear we have some peaches and cream and an amazing cannolo at our place."

"We'll be right back. I need to ask Chellie something."

I drag her down the hallway to the half bathroom and push open the door, then lock it behind us.

"You shouldn't tease, *piccolina*."

"I wasn't, Daddy. I plan to suck the cream from the cannolo."

I growl and pounce. Our *conversation* makes us miss the first course, but neither of us cares. Being together is more important than anything else.

Epilogue

Chellie

"Liz, can you help me go to the bathroom? I'm like a scene from a rom com. I can't find the end of my gown to get it up high enough to pee."

My sister laughs at me as she helps me into the bathroom stall. Even with the gown bustled, it's hard to maneuver. It's bad enough Marco is stationed outside the restroom door. I need my sister to help me use the toilet like I'm four again. At least once we get the gown high enough, she backs out of the stall and leaves me alone.

"It really was a beautiful ceremony, Chellie."

"You're not upset that you and Laura were my matrons of honor?"

"You keep asking me that, and I've told you like twenty-hundred times, no. I'm not upset. I think it's awesome that she could attend. I worried she wouldn't be able to."

Only Laura and Maks attended the ceremony in Lettie and Massi's backyard. The one where Enzo and his brothers and sister used to play as kids. The one I hope our kids play in. But we're at one of the nicest hotels in Manhattan for the reception. The women already warned me the ceremony would be private. The reception is a chance for the who's who of polite society and the underworld to rub elbows. I remember from Laura's reception. Except Enzo isn't making the same mistakes as Maks. Enzo's been damn near perfect.

I flush the toilet, and Liz helps me out of the stall. We brush my dress down, so it settles back into place before I wash my hands. We look at each other in the mirror and grin just like we did as kids. Other than Laura, Liz's the only one I told about Enzo. I didn't tell her to keep secrets from Mom and Dad, but she understood why I wasn't ready to say anything. At least, not until I had to.

Things have been quiet this week. It's hard to believe it's actually been less than a week since men shot up my parents' home. It's surreal to think that. I saw Finn when he entered the reception, and it's clear someone beat the shit out of him. I'd guess it was my husband. Enzo says things are resolved, but he caveats it with a for now. I get the sense that the resolution was rather anticlimactic.

I'm fine with that because it means he came home in one piece. But it gives me the sense that this is the calm before the storm. It scares me to imagine what might be coming. But in the immortal words of Scarlet O'Hara, "I'll think about that tomorrow."

Liz opens the restroom door, and Marco pushes away from the door. Something flashes in his eyes that I can't interpret before he offers me his arm.

"Ladies, are we good?"

"Yes. Sorry to keep you waiting."

I notice him glance at Liz as he offers her his other arm.

"Waiting's not always so bad. They say good things come from it."

I don't have time to contemplate what he means because we return to the ballroom. Enzo's waiting near the dance floor, and he wraps his arms around me. We move together for our first dance, and it's like we're floating.

"Are you happy, *piccolina?*"

"Beyond words, Daddy."

"We're cutting the cake after this, then we're leaving."

A shiver skids along my spine. When we talked about it more, neither of us loved the idea of other people seeing us together when we go to a BDSM club together. We'd go incognito, but I don't like the idea of women getting turned on by watching my husband of a few hours. Enzo nearly lost his mind when I pointed that out, and he realized men would do the same.

Even if we weren't exhibitionists, we'd want the privacy of our home to take our time. So we did some ordering the night he came back from that place he won't name. Things have been arriving ever since. He won't let me into the spare bedroom in what's now our penthouse. He's even gone so far as to change the doorknob so that it locks. He's been assembling shit at odd hours, which only heightens my anticipation. He knows that too.

"Cut small pieces then, Daddy."

Enzo twirls me around the floor until the music ends. We end up compromising, so I can have the father-daughter dance, and Enzo can have the mother-son dance. Then it's quick slices of cake — neither of us would ever smash it in the other's face — then Marco and Liz are helping us to sneak out. As Marco agrees to escort Liz back inside, I'm still not sure what to make of the expression he had when my sister and I came out of the restroom. But I don't think about it for long. We make out on the ride home, but my dress makes it difficult to do anything more in the limo. But the second we're in our bedroom, all bets are off.

"Why, Mrs. Mancinelli, you aren't wearing any panties."

Enzo's hand glides up my inner thighs.

"Mr. Mancinelli told me he'd burn any I ever tried to wear again."

"This husband of yours sounds like an ogre."

"He redeems himself. The things that man can do with his tongue."

I giggle as Enzo launches an attack, licking and nipping at my throat. My handsome husband. The man I met again by chance. The man I love and trust more than anyone or anything in the world.

"*Piccolina mia*, the things I'm going to do to you tonight."

Marco Mancinelli is — was — the most confirmed bachelor in the family. But his brother's new sister-in-law is making him doubt that pledge. But old and new enemies lurk just beyond reach. Can he protect Elizabeth Russo and convince her to trust this rising *Cosa Nostra* star? The final installment of *The Mancinelli Brotherhood, Mafia Star*, is coming soon.

Thank you for reading Mafia Redeemer

Sabine Barclay, a nom de plume also writing Historical Romance as Celeste Barclay, lives near the Southern California coast with her husband and sons. Growing up in the Midwest, Celeste enjoyed spending as much time in and on the water as she could. Now she lives near the beach. She's an avid swimmer, a hopeful future surfer, and a former rower. She loves writing romances that will make your toes curl and your granny blush.

Subscribe to Sabine's bimonthly newsletter to receive exclusive insider perks.

www.sabinebarclay.com

Join the fun and get exclusive insider giveaways, sneak peeks, and new release announcements in
Sabine Barclay's Facebook Dubious Dames Group

Do you also enjoy steamy Historical Romance? Discover Sabine's books written as Celeste Barclay.

The Mancinelli Brotherhood

Luca

This asshole is pissing me off. We've been going around in circles for five minutes, and the longer we stand out here, the greater the likelihood someone will spot us. I have a sixth sense about these things. It's why I'm still alive at the ripe old age of thirty-one.

"Espinoza, enough already. Either sell to us or don't, but we set the price. Your tequila is good, but it isn't nectar from the gods."

I'm watching Carlos Espinoza, some lackey for the Mexican Culiacán Cartel, try to maneuver me into paying more than the agreed upon price. I know it's so he can skim off the top.

"It's as close as you're going to get. You've upped the order, so the price per case goes up."

My uncle, Salvatore Mancinelli, is the New York don. He negotiated this deal, and I warned him it was a bad idea. But what do I know as his underboss and heir? I'm not backing down.

"Haven't you ever heard of a bulk discount? The more I order the better the price should be. No one else around here is buying from you. You know we're your only choice in three out of five boroughs. You aren't going to the Bronx because you won't get more than pennies there. You aren't going to Queens because you don't want to run into the Colombians. You aren't going to Manhattan because then you face the bratva along with us. And what are you going to do in Staten Island? Sell to us anyway? We control Staten Island and Brooklyn when it comes to liquor stores, so take the money and go."

"Luca, there are plenty of liquor stores in Brooklyn that aren't owned by Italians. I'll go there."

We aren't friends. He's patronizing me by using my first name. Fuck him and the horse he rode in on. I have other solutions for this shit.

"And I'll just take what I want from them for free. That's not a half bad idea. The deal's over. Take your shit with the worm in it and go."

"Motherfucking racist. Not all tequila has a worm in it."

"You're selling Mezcal. It's known for the fucking worm. I wouldn't start calling me names, you *penche hijo de puta*." Fucking son of a bitch.

He has twenty-five crates of stolen tequila that he's trying to offload because he knows he can't sell it at his own liquor store.

"What did you call me?"

Carlos takes what he thinks is a menacing step forward, and his two bodyguards do the same. Not smart. Neither of my two bodyguards nor I react, but the three men in each of my cars open their doors. They won't do more than that. It's just a reminder that the Culiacán can try, but the *Cosa Nostra* still run New York City.

"This is the third and final time I say this. Sell or leave."

Every head turns toward the liquor store's back door as it opens. A gorgeous blonde steps out, and I wish I had the time to appreciate her beauty, but she's about to die. Carlos and his men draw their guns and pivot toward her. My men pull their weapons too, but we keep them pointed at the Mexicans. The woman stands like a deer in the headlights for a second before ducking behind the industrial garbage dumpster like a frightened rabbit. Three shots hit the metal almost at the same moment. That's all it takes for my men and me. The two bodyguards standing with me aim for a guard each, and I set my sights on Carlos. We squeeze our triggers, and the men fall.

Screeching tires tell me Carlos's driver takes off. I hear more gunshots as at least one soldier in my cars tries to shoot the escaping vehicle. Glass shatters, but the sedan keeps going. I hear more tires squeal as one of my SUVs takes off and chases the guy. I holster my gun and wave my men to do the same.

I inch forward toward the trash can, but I see the shadow shift. The woman bolts from the other side. She's still the frightened rabbit, but I'm the fox pursuing her. She's fast, I'll give her that. But she has to be at least a foot shorter than me. My legs are a lot longer and cover a lot more ground with each stride.

She weaves among the cars, most likely believing it's harder to hit a moving object. She isn't wrong, but I have no intention of shooting her. I push myself harder and pounce as she darts out and tries to cross the last stretch of parking lot to reach a better lit area near a bus stop. I lunge.

"Stop running, *piccolina*. I won't hurt you."

I wrap my arms around her and pull her back against my chest, but I'm quick to spin her around and put space between us as I grasp her arms. Of course, she fights me.

"If I wanted you dead, I would have shot at you, too."

"It doesn't mean you won't kill me after."

She's breathless as she continues to struggle. I almost let go to take a step back, insulted at what she implied. But I can't blame her. If I were a woman, I'd be terrified of the same thing.

"I'm not going to rape you. I'm going to talk to you."

"Talk? You are not a man who talks if you just killed a guy."

"To keep him and his men from killing you. I told you, if I wanted you dead, I would have shot at you too. And I wouldn't have missed."

She stops struggling against me, but her eyes continue to dart from one place to another, trying to find somewhere to flee. I know I can keep her in place with only one hand, so I release her left arm. I still have a firm hold on her right one, but I haven't held it nearly as tightly as I could.

"I'm Luca. I know you figured out you interrupted something you shouldn't have. Did that man know who you are?"

"Yes."

"What about his driver? Would he know you?"

"Yes."

"Do you have a name?"

"Yes."

"*Piccolina*, we won't get very far if yes is all you can say. Are you willing to answer me with more than one word?"

"No."

I knew that was coming, and I grin. I can't help it. I wasn't wrong about her being gorgeous, but I doubt she wants to know that's what I think. At least, not if I want her to know I won't assault her.

"Fine. I have more than twenty questions I can ask that you can answer with one word. Do you work at the store?"

"Sometimes."

Ah, an improvement.

"Did Carlos know you were still working?"

"No."

"Do you have a car, or do you take the subway or bus?"

She raises her chin and remains silent. Smart but counterproductive.

"The subway or the bus will get you killed. You're too easy to find and follow. Do you have a car?"

"Yes."

"Can you stay with someone instead of going home?"

She refuses to answer.

"If that man knew you and you sometimes work in the store, then he knew where you live. If he found that out, so will someone in his cartel."

"I know. Let me go. The longer I stand here, the more likely someone is to come back for me."

"No one will touch you while I'm here."

"Arrogant. If he shot at me, he would have shot at you."

"And he would have died, anyway. What's your name?"

"Jane."

"Look, I know you won't get in one of my cars and let me drive you somewhere. In most cases, I would say that's a smart move. But you did nothing wrong tonight except for leave work at the wrong time. I know that, and you know that. But the Culiacán won't see it that way, *piccolina*."

She freezes for no more than five seconds before she trembles so much that I can see it. I don't know what drives me next, but it's the same instinct that's made me call her little girl three times. I pull her to my chest and tuck her head against it. I stroke her hair down to her shoulders, rubbing my hand up and down her back. This is the most inopportune moment to notice she isn't wearing a bra. I will my body not to react.

"What does that mean?"

Her voice is barely more than a whisper, but I know what she's asking.

"It means little girl."

"I should be insulted, but the way you say it…"

"It has nothing to do with your height. I know you're not a child."

God, do I know she's not. She feels amazing. Her tits are soft as they press against me, and I can see she has the most delectable ass. I'd love nothing more than to cup it and squeeze until she goes up on her toes and begs for me to wrap her legs around my waist and fuck her. For fuck's sake. Stop, you disgusting asshole. That is not what you need to be thinking about.

"Why didn't you shoot me? Whatever you were talking about, if it was with a Cartel member, then it wasn't completely legal. Carlos didn't want me alive to talk about seeing you together. Why are you letting me live?"

"I told you. You did nothing wrong but try to leave work. He should have checked the building before starting the meeting. That was on him. The only thing I take issue with is you leaving by yourself and walking into a dimly lit parking lot. I suspect you do that often, and that's too dangerous. Jane Doe, I don't hurt women."

Mafia Sinner

Mafia Beauty

Mafia Angel

Mafia Redeemer

Mafia Star

The Ivankov Brotherhood

Bratva Darling

BOOK ONE SNEAK PEEK

LAURA

As I sit across from the four Kutsenko brothers, I press my lips together to keep from drooling. No four men should be so strikingly handsome. Not all from the same family, anyway. I fight a valiant battle against letting my gaze drift toward the eldest, Maksim, whose ice-blue eyes bore into me. After years of negotiating billion-dollar investment contracts while facing countless ruthless businessmen, I've learned to keep my expression studiously blank. But it's a true struggle today. Instead, I focus my attention on the squirrelly lawyer sitting across the conference table. While he's disingenuous with each comment, he's a good negotiator. But I'm better. How cliché am I?

While I feel Maksim watching me, I focus on Dmitry Yakovitch as he continues to argue the merits of the venture capitalist company I represent, RK Capital Group, merging with Kutsenko Partners. What he means is the merits of Kutsenko Partners acquiring RK Capital Group, then stripping it and making it another money-laundering shell corporation. While most people in New York have little awareness of the Russian mafia, I do. The Kutsenko brothers' names appear on no titles or deeds anywhere in New York City, but it wasn't difficult to determine which shell companies likely belong to them. Their assumption that I'm unfamiliar with them is proving beneficial to me as they continue to whisper amongst themselves in Russian. I think they may even believe they're convincing me that they don't speak much English.

The senior partners of RK Capital Group know who I'm negotiating with, though they may not know I'm aware of these Russians' more nefarious operations. They've given me the go-ahead to agree to a merger with an eventual acquisition, but only for the right price. A price to the tune of twenty billion dollars. Considering an investment firm like Goldman Sachs is worth nearly one-hundred-and-twenty billion dollars, my clients' asking price appears reasonable.

"Mr. Yakovitch, I shall stop you now." I raise my left hand, pen caught between my index and middle fingers. When I have his attention, I lean back in my chair and casually twirl the pen over my index finger and thumb. "Fifty billion is my clients' asking price. You know that. Your clients know that. RK doesn't oppose the merger. What they oppose is the insulting offer you've made. It's nearly noon, and I'm hungry, Mr. Yakovitch. I have a delicious ham sandwich waiting for me. I even have three chocolate chip cookies waiting for me. If we aren't going to make any progress, I shall let you go, so I can move onto my eagerly anticipated lunch."

I cant my head just enough for me to appear as though my gaze rests solely on the opposing attorney's face, but I can see each Kutsenko brothers' reaction. My face battles yet again against showing my emotions as I fight not to smirk. Their muted but surprised expressions confirm what I already know.

"Please tell your clients to make a reasonable counteroffer, or I will conclude this meeting and enjoy my ham sandwich and cookies."

Dmitry glares at me before turning to Maksim and his three brothers. In rapid Russian, he doesn't interpret my suggestion. Oh no. There's no need for that. I can't catch every word because his voice is too low. But I catch something along the lines of "The bitch refuses to budge. What now? A fucking ham sandwich. More like a stick up her ass."

Maksim swivels his chair to look at his brothers. In Russian, he says, "Fifty billion is ridiculous. She's not so stupid or naïve not to know that. My guess is they'll settle for twenty billion. We offer fifteen."

"That's barely better than what we already offered," Aleksei, the second-oldest brother, argues. "She'll be eating the fucking sandwich and dipping her cookies in milk before we walk out the door. We need the buildings."

"We offer twenty, Maks," Bogdan, the youngest, insists.

As I watch the brothers discuss, their voices barely lowered, I pull my lunch sack from the black leather satchel by my feet and set it beside my laptop. It's a ridiculously pink floral bag with an embroidered monogram, the L and D overlapping. It's an empty prop, but they don't know that. I watch as five sets of eyes narrow. I offer a smile that would appear innocent in any setting other than this meeting. It's patronizing, and I know it.

Bratva Sweetheart

Bratva Treasure

Bratva Beauty

Bratva Angel

Bratva Jewel

www.ingramcontent.com/pod-product-compliance
Lightning Source LLC
Chambersburg PA
CBHW020007120726
47903CB00004B/1178